VENGEANCE

A Legal Thriller

Deborah Hawkins

Published by Deborah Hawkins
ISBN: 978-0-9992180-3-7 (paperback)
ISBN: 978-0-9992180-4-4 (ebook)

"Revenge is an act of passion; vengeance of justice."

Samuel Johnson

Contents

PROLOGUE

Someone was trying to kill her. But Charlotte Estes had no idea who. Or why.

For months there had been footsteps behind her in the Metro at night. Yet when she'd glanced back, no one had been there. When the footsteps had stopped, there had been the car that had almost run her down in the crosswalk in front of her office at lunchtime. The witnesses had all said it looked deliberate. Detective Merrill of the D.C. police had warned her to be careful.

It was freezing outside when she closed the door of her townhouse on O Street at four o'clock, ready to do her favorite neighborhood run for the last time. The ink had been dry on the merger agreement with Goldstein, Miller for months. The Estes Law Firm's offices on K Street had long been emptied, and the firm's sixty-five attorneys had been disbursed throughout Goldstein, Miller's web of national and international offices. She, alone, had remained behind to oversee the final arrangements for the end of the criminal defense firm that she and Matt had built together. Now The Estes Firm and Matt were dead, and the bits and pieces of her life with her husband were boxed and ready for the moving van in the morning. She was headed back to San Diego where she had been born.

She began to run slowly to warm up, but also so that she could savor the quaint European atmosphere of her neighborhood for the last time. When she reached M Street, she passed the red brick townhouse, sandwiched between the antiques store and the Thai takeout joint, where she and Matt had started their firm in 1985. Her eyes misted over as she pictured her husband as he'd been in those days. Dark hair, gentle gray eyes. A trim five foot eight, with a ready smile, a generous disposition, and a keen intelligence. She had never imagined her life without him. Yet here she was, running from their shared past, looking for the comfort of oblivion a continent away.

When she reached Wisconsin, she turned left and headed for the path along the C & O Canal. The late afternoon light was thinning, and she knew for security reasons she shouldn't go far because sunset was imminent. But she wanted to say goodbye to one of her favorite places, a place where she and Matt had often run together in the days when she'd never imagined anyone or anything coming between them.

She increased her pace when she reached the canal path. Her father, the track coach, had taught her how to maximize her endurance. Obviously, she hadn't the speed or the mileage she'd had at UCLA all those years ago when her track scholarship had paid for her undergraduate degree. But if her father were still alive, he'd have been proud of the distance she still covered every week at age fifty-eight.

Overhead, the trees were bare and brown. It was hard to believe that in twenty-four hours she'd be in the lush, eternal sunshine of Southern California. She had mixed feelings about leaving her home of more than thirty years. But Matt had been gone since mid-November, and she wasn't making any progress with moving on with her life. Every street corner, every restaurant, every nook and cranny of their house on O Street was full of memories that haunted and tormented her because she could not understand why Matt, the one person she had trusted without question for over thirty years, had died in another woman's bed.

There had been no sign that anything was amiss in their marriage, she thought as she ran. Or had she been too quick to overlook the nights he'd stayed late at the office in the months leading up to his death?

The sunlight was dissipating rapidly. The D.C. detectives had warned her about what she was doing at that very minute. Another reason to leave town. Surely whichever disgruntled, but unidentified client had tried to run her down on K Street in early December wouldn't bother to follow her all the way to San Diego. Today was her anonymous assassin's last chance. Death threats came with the territory of criminal defense work. But actual attempts were rare. Charlotte turned back toward home, suddenly aware that she'd pushed the envelope farther than she'd intended. She quickened her pace yet again. And then she heard the crack of the rifle shot coming from the trees behind her.

THE LOST BOYS

CHAPTER ONE

Sunday, June 10, 2018, Rancho Santa Fe, California

Lucas Owens struggled to open his eyes. His cell phone was ringing. The faint light seeping through the custom mahogany plantation shutters in his master bedroom suite told him it was barely dawn. The phone's jarring demand for attention sounded ominous in the uncertain, yellow light. As he fumbled for it on his night table, he realized that his fifty-nine-year-old body was naked, and he had a twenty-something honey next to him. Who was she, and how had she gotten there?

As he punched the button to answer, he saw that it was five thirty a.m. and Andy was calling. Andy, who never woke before noon. *God, no!* he thought. *Who has he killed this time?*

"What is it, son?" he used the calm, bored tone that he used at work with his least favorite brokers, the ones who couldn't sell a piece of real estate if their lives depended on it. It was his way of communicating his belief in their incompetence.

"It's Nate, Dad!" Andy's breathless, high-pitched wail was straight out of middle school.

He's thirty-two. When will he stop being a baby?

"Calm down, son. What's wrong with Nate?"

"We can't find him!"

"Are you at the Cays?" Lucas had bought the white Mediterranean four-bedroom villa in the Coronado Cays ten years ago to use as a hideout from his wife. To cover his tracks, he had used the excuse that it came with a boat slip at the Coronado Cays Yacht Club for the yacht that he intended to buy to entertain potential clients and his staff at Owens Commercial Real Estate and Construction. Lucas smiled at the memory of skimming across San Diego Bay with a cargo of bikini-clad lookers, sipping cocktails and admiring his navigational abilities, among his other skills.

Ella had bought his story for a few years, but soon it became apparent that his real object had been to lead a separate life. She hated the Cays villa, and she hated all of his boats, but most especially she hated his latest and most expensive baby, a 2018 Cobalt A40 Coup. Unfortunately, Lucas had had little opportunity to test the chick-magnet properties of the yacht because Andy had taken over the villa, supposedly to study for the California Bar for the third time, but in truth to party and avoid his parents. Lucas had been forced back into the Rancho Santa Fe marital residence, and even seven thousand square feet and a separate casita were not enough to separate him from Ella Lawrence Owens, his wife and the mother of his only known child. He had given thanks when she'd announced this ten-day trip to London for the International Financial Services Conference.

"Yes, Dad. Where else would I be?"

Getting ready to go to work? Doing something productive with your life?

"When was the last time you saw Nate?"

"A little after one a.m. Kyle and Gavin and I decided to have a pre-bachelor party for him last night."

"Couldn't you wait for Vegas?" Lucas demanded. Nate's father, Brian McClellan, a high-priced criminal defense attorney, was paying for the party so that he could invite his old-guy friends, including Lucas. He had booked two suites at the Bellagio, and Lucas had added a group of expensive, exclusive call girls. He was looking forward to every minute of what was going to be an unforgettable Fourth of July weekend.

"It was just a spur of the moment decision. The four of us decided to meet at Il Fornaio for dinner."

Why hadn't Andy passed the bar like Gavin and gone to work at Warrick, Thompson? But Lucas knew the answer to that question. *Because Andy didn't have the grades or the LSAT's to get into a top-notch law school. And even with a degree from California Western, a respectable academic institution, he had flunked the bar twice.*

"Okay. Well I doubt you lost Nate at Il Fornaio."

"We—uh—took *The Escape* down to IB after dinner."

"You took the yacht to Imperial Beach?" Lucas was so angry that he sat up and put his feet on the floor. The honey stirred in her sleep and rolled toward the opposite side of the bed. Andy was absolutely forbidden to drive his $800,000 pride and joy.

"Well, to the California Yacht Marina in Chula Vista. We used a guest slip and took an Uber to the strip club. Sorry, Dad. I know. I'm not supposed to take *The Escape* out without you. But Gavin and Kyle had never been on the boat. I meant to take them on a quick turn around the bay just to give them a taste of what a smooth ride she has, but we decided to go to The Naked Lady instead."

A strip club. Lucas glanced over at his bed partner. Now he remembered why she was there. She wasn't a stripper, but she was a barfly that he'd picked up last night at the Blue Note in Solana Beach. *The apple didn't fall far from the tree.*

"And after that?"

"There were four dancers who hit on us pretty hard. Nate wasn't having a good time. He felt guilty about Kinsley, so he asked me to bring him back here."

Who names a girl Kinsley? Levi Wyatt, Brian McClellan's law partner. They had just made Nate a partner in their firm, and their children's marriage was supposed to cement the McClellan, Wyatt legal dynasty.

"Don't worry." Andy reacted to his father's disapproving silence. "I got *The Escape* back in one piece."

"So what happened after you got home?"

"We tied up at the Cays Yacht Club, and Nate and I sat on the boat for a while and drank beer. He's got cold feet about marrying Kinsley."

"Everybody has cold feet about getting married," Lucas said.

"Right. I told him that."

"Then what happened?"

"Kyle and Gavin came back with the girls from the club and some more people they'd picked up there. It was around one in the morning."

"How many people?"

"Um, twenty? Maybe thirty?"

"God, Andy! Did you know any of them?"

"Uh, one or two. Tina's brothers came with them."

Jose, Sebastian, and Luis Hernandez. All undereducated and underemployed. And all of them probably on drugs. Andy's drinking was out of control. The last thing Lucas needed was for him to add a meth or heroin addiction.

"I thought we'd agreed that you'd stay away from the Hernandez brothers. And I thought you'd broken up with Tina."

"She broke up with me. And I didn't invite them here. Gavin did."

"That doesn't make it okay."

"Dad, please. I have to find Nate."

"So why don't you know where he is?"

"Because I left him sitting on the boat when everyone arrived so I could let them in. He said he wanted to be alone to think about what he really wanted. I had a couple more beers, and then I went to bed and passed out."

"So how do you know he isn't in the house?"

"Because I woke up just now and came to the kitchen to get some Tylenol for the hangover. And I suddenly remembered that I never saw him come back to the house last night before I went to bed. He was so upset when I left him that I just wanted to make sure that he had come back and was okay. He was sharing the green guest room with Kyle, so I opened the door to check on him. Kyle was there, but Nate wasn't. And his car's still out front in the drive."

"Maybe he bunked in with Gavin."

"No, I looked."

"Did you check to see if he was sleeping on the boat?"

"That's it, Dad! You're brilliant."

"Then go back to bed and let me get some sleep."

Andy rang off, and Lucas heaved a sigh of relief. The light through the shutters was becoming more persistent. The sun would be fully up soon. The hands on his antique carriage clock were edging toward six a.m. He debated whether to start a pot of coffee and get ready to give the girl breakfast before driving her back to her car at the Blue Note. Too much trouble. He'd rather try to catch a few more winks and pack her off in an Uber when she woke up.

He had just closed his eyes when his phone began to ring again. Andy. This couldn't be good news.

"What's wrong, son?"

"Nate's not on the boat. I took the dingy over to check, and he's not there."

"Okay. Then he took an Uber home to get away from the party."

"I don't think so."

"Why?

"It's *The Escape*, Dad."

"*The Escape?*" Lucas' blood ran cold.

"It's been damaged."

"Damaged?" He shouted loudly enough to wake up the girl, who pulled up the sheet and frowned at him. "How? What in God's name have you done, Andy?"

"Dad, calm down. I swear it wasn't me. Nothing was wrong when I left Nate last night."

"*Tell me about the damage!*" Lucas thundered, and the girl pulled the sheet over her head.

"The front part. What do you call it?"

"The bow!"

"It's–it's crumpled."

"Oh, God! I'll be right there."

CHAPTER TWO

Sunday, June 10, 2018, The Coronado Cays

It took Lucas a little over an hour to reach 12 Green Turtle Road. The girl, whose name turned out to be Sunny, refused his offer to pay for an Uber and demanded a ride to her car. The delay was irritating, but he was afraid that she'd find a way to make trouble for him with Ella, so he gave in and swung by the Blue Note before making his way to the I-5 where he pushed his Mercedes S63 AMG through the sparse traffic as fast as he could without creating the risk of meeting a cop.

Once off the I-5, he had to slow as he drove down Orange Avenue, the main drag through the village of Coronado. At seven thirty on a Sunday morning, a handful of joggers were weaving their way through a smattering of early-bird tourists in search of breakfast. But as soon as he hit Silver Strand Boulevard, he was back at seventy miles an hour, fueled by his anxiety over the damage to *The Escape*.

After he turned into the entrance to the Cays, instead of turning left toward Green Turtle, he headed right on Coronado Cays Boulevard and then left onto Grande Caribe Causeway, toward the yacht club. He wanted to see the boat before he saw

Andy. He parked in the club's parking lot and almost ran toward slip AB-23. From the rear, *The Escape* was her breathtakingly beautiful self. He hoped against hope that Andy had still been drunk this morning and completely wrong about damage to the bow.

But he had to know for sure, so he walked past the two adjoining slips until he came to the third one to the right of *The Escape*, which fortunately was empty. He positioned himself so he could see the front of the boat. And to his horror, Andy had been right. The graceful V of the bow indeed looked like crumpled paper. And there was a huge gash that spread from the center of the V, across the starboard side of the boat. He felt sick.

He walked slowly back to the parking lot and got into his Mercedes. Not even the smooth purr of its finely tuned engine could lessen his grief. It was obvious what had happened, he told himself, as he retraced his route to Cays Boulevard and turned onto Green Turtle Road. Nate had taken *The Escape* out after Andy had left him and then vanished rather than own up to the damage he'd done. Lucas would make sure that Brian McClellan paid through the nose for the repairs even if it meant withdrawal of the coveted invitation to the bachelor party in Vegas. Nate McClellan was a low-life coward.

Lucas parked behind the blue, silver, and black BMWs in the drive, evidence that Gavin, Kyle, and the now-hated Nate were still with Andy. He hurried up the walk and opened the front door. The house had been trashed. Beer cans, bits of food, napkins, and soggy paper plates were everywhere.

But the damage to the carpet and upholstery were the least

of his worries. He heard voices coming from the kitchen, so he crossed the living room to find Andy, Kyle, and Gavin, all wearing T-shirts and shorts, sitting at the small breakfast table, drinking coffee. The three of them, along with Nate, had been inseparable since they met in the first grade at the exclusive Francis Parker School.

A wave of envy smothered Lucas as he stood in the doorway to the kitchen. Gavin and Kyle were thirty-two years old, fit, intelligent, and single. They were both blond. Gavin had blue eyes; Kyle's were hazel. Gavin had a high forehead and a round, open face that made him seem friendly even when he wasn't smiling. Kyle's face was long and square, and his at-rest expression was always serious. They were just a couple of years away from partnership at Warrick, Thompson. Gavin Neal was a tough, savvy civil litigator, and Kyle Jamison was a transactional attorney, the son of the founder of Jamison Biotech, one of Warrick's leading clients. They exuded professional confidence and achievement. Andy, on the other hand, looked like he was floundering. He had been overweight since he was a small child. He craved sweets and potato chips and preferred to sit in front of the television, playing video games instead of sports. Now, as a grown man, he lacked not only the discipline to study for the bar, but also the discipline to work out regularly. Instead of being toned and fit like Gavin and Kyle, he had rolls of fat around his middle, saggy arms, and chubby cheeks that made him look like a chipmunk.

Andy jumped up and hurried over to his father and tried to give him a hug. "Thanks for coming!"

But Lucas recoiled from his touch. "I went to see the boat."

"I'm sorry, Dad."

"I've only had it for three months."

"Nate must have taken it out again after I left."

"Where were the keys?"

"I must have left them in the ignition. I was tired, it was late—"

"And you'd been drinking!" Lucas cut him off angrily. "It's obvious he went for a joyride, had a wreck, and has run off to hide somewhere."

Andy's cell rang and he answered it, turning away slightly from his father's wrath and covering one ear so that he could hear the caller better. He was frowning as he talked.

"He's probably gone to tell his dad," Gavin said mildly.

"That's the most likely possibility," Lucas agreed, soothed by Gavin's levelheaded tone. "Brian is going to have to pay for the damage."

"And he will," Andy chimed in after he ended his call. "That was Kinsley. Nate isn't with her. So he probably went to his parents' house. And I'm sure he's sorry. He was really upset last night. That has to be the explanation for why this happened. He's got experience with boats. His dad has a Sea Ray Sundancer 350."

For the first time since Andy had told him there was damage to his beloved yacht, Lucas felt himself begin to calm down. Andy was right. Brian would step up to the plate for Nate's mistake. And the kid was under a lot of pressure to marry the girl of his father's dynastic dreams. It hadn't been exactly the same for Lucas, but he'd realized when it was too late to back out that marrying Ella Lawrence for her money was going to be a lifetime of pure misery. And he'd been right.

"I'll call Brian," Lucas said. "In the meantime, the living room is wall-to-wall trash."

"We will take care of it," Gavin promised. "We didn't mean for things to get out of hand. Kyle and I will pay for a cleaning service to come in and do the carpet and the upholstery."

"And the drapes," Lucas added. "Someone had a food fight in there."

* * *

After he'd dispatched the three well-educated young professionals like naughty teenagers to do their chores, Lucas dialed Brian McClellan.

"Hi, Lucas," Brian's deep baritone was so loud that Lucas turned the volume down on his iPhone.

"I'm at the Cays," Lucas began. "The boys had a party here for Nate last night, but he apparently left without saying goodbye. Is he with you?"

"No. I haven't seen him since Monday when he asked me to come with him for his final tux fitting."

Lucas' anxiety began to climb again. "Well, Andy left him aboard *The Escape* last night after he tried to talk Nate out of his pre-wedding jitters. Not that Andy knows much about those. Anyway, this morning, there's a huge gash on the starboard bow that's going to be very expensive to repair. And Nate's nowhere to be found."

"So you're thinking he's responsible?"

"Yes, I do," Lucas said.

"Well of course I'll pay if Nate's to blame," Brian began, "but

I doubt he'd run from facing the responsibility of the accident. You and Ella and Andy are like family.

Nate would just come tell you and apologize. And unless he was very, very drunk, I'd bet on his competence with that boat. He's had mine out in all kinds of weather and even storms, and he's never put a scratch on it."

"Well, I'm more worried now than I was before I called you," Lucas said.

"Could he be with Kinsley?"

"Could be, yes. Is he, no. Andy talked to her."

"What about your surveillance cameras?" Brian asked. "What do they show?"

"Haven't had a chance to play them back. I'll take a quick look when I hang up."

"And I think one of us should call the police," Brian added.

"Right. At this point, I agree. I'll call them," Lucas promised.

"Should I come over there?" Brian asked. "I know more about how to handle cops than you do."

"I don't think I need your help—yet."

CHAPTER THREE

Sunday, June 10, 2018, The Coronado Cays

Lucas hung up and dialed the Coronado Police Department. A bored female voice promised officers would arrive within thirty minutes. He could hear the sound of glass bottles clinking in the garbage bags as Andy, Gavin, and Kyle tackled the trash in the living room. He walked down the hall to the bedroom that had been set up as an office, turned on the computer, and tapped into the surveillance app. But before he could pull up the videos from the house and the boat, his cell began to ring. Ella. If he didn't answer, she'd just keep calling until he did.

"Good morning, sweetheart."

"It's not morning here. It's four thirty in the afternoon."

"Sorry. I wasn't thinking." She always made Lucas feel inadequate.

"I was calling to let you know that I'm coming home on Tuesday instead of Wednesday."

Damn!

"I see. How nice." He'd counted on being without her for a full ten days. Her decision to revoke his freedom two days early was devastating. There was no way that she could have known about Sunny. Unless she had surveillance cameras in their bedroom. *Oh, God. I'll check for them when I get home. I wouldn't put it past her.*

"I'll be in at five in the afternoon. I was thinking you could pick me up, and we could have dinner at Mille Fleurs on the way home."

"Sorry, I have to be in Orange County all day on Tuesday. I'm inspecting that apartment complex we're building. I'm meeting with the investors afterward for dinner in Beverly Hills. I think it's going to be a late night. I won't be back until Wednesday midday."

"Oh." The tone of her voice said she was pouting. Lucas could picture her perfect little Cupid's bow mouth covered in her signature bright-red lipstick pulled into a tight circle of disapproval. She was doubtless wearing one of her designer sack dresses most likely in black or navy, accented with an Hermès scarf. Ella was short, barely five feet. She'd been on the heavy side when they met in college, but the thirty pounds that she'd retained after her pregnancy with Andy had completely destroyed any semblance of a figure. Although she had the money to buy any piece of clothing she wanted to wear, her choices were limited to dresses that would cover the extra pounds around her middle. She'd ordered Lucas into couples' counseling almost thirty years ago when she'd first discovered he was unfaithful. When asked what would improve their marriage, he'd suggested that she lose weight. She'd been so furious that she'd stormed out of the session and begun an affair of her own.

Since then, she'd had affairs as regularly as he had. While her figure was not appealing, her money and power were. And she had large, intense dark eyes that, when fixed on a potential lover, made him feel like the most important being in her world. It was also a talent that had brought her great success as a financial advisor at her father's firm, Lawrence Securities and Investments. She knew that she had power over the objects of her desire, and she wielded that power possessively. Lucas had hoped for years that she'd fixate on one of her many lovers and decide to cut him loose from the life of slavery that he'd unwittingly entered into thirty-three years ago when he became her husband. But no luck. To his eternal disappointment, he remained her most prized possession.

"I'll see you when I get back from Orange County on Wednesday," he said to placate her.

"We'll have dinner at Mille Fleurs on Wednesday night, then," she decreed.

"Of course. Listen, Ella. There's something else you should know about. Andy, Gavin, and Kyle decided to warm up with a pre-bachelor party for Nate last night here at the Cays."

"You're at the Cays?" She spoke sharply. "You're not thinking of moving back down there, are you?"

"No, of course not. But Andy called me this morning because Nate's disappeared."

"Disappeared? But how could that happen?"

"We don't know. We think he took *The Escape* out last night after talking to Andy about his wedding. He's got cold feet."

"Well, who wouldn't have cold feet? Kinsley Wyatt comes with some pretty profound baggage. She's been a brat since the minute she drew her first breath."

Kinsley's self-centeredness was one of the few subjects he and his wife agreed on.

"Then let's just be happy that Andy didn't get involved with her," Lucas soothed. "Listen, *The Escape*'s been damaged. We think Nate is responsible. Looks like he ran to avoid owning up to an accident with the boat."

"That's ridiculous!" Ella scoffed. "He would know that insurance would cover anything that happened to that monstrosity of yours."

"Well, I'm waiting on the police to arrive."

"The police?"

"Brian thought I should call them and report Nate missing."

"God, Lucas. How stupid can you be? The last time Andy wrecked something and the police got involved, it cost us four million dollars."

"That was different, Ella. There's no indication that Andy's responsible for this."

"Really? Have you looked at the surveillance tapes from the boat and the navigation log?"

"No, I haven't had time."

"Well, you'd better erase them."

"But the tapes and the log will back up Andy's story. He says he didn't see Nate again after he left him on the boat when he opened the house for Gavin and that crew he brought back from the strip club."

"Strip club?"

"I told you, Ella. Pre-bachelor party. They had dinner at Il Fornaio and took the boat down to IB to The Naked Lady."

"Andy is supposed to be studying for the bar."

"Don't tell me what I already know."

"We agreed that he could live at the Cays—alone—only if he stayed out of trouble and didn't drink and party."

"That's true," Lucas agreed. "But Nate's wedding is a big deal for Andy and for all of those boys. Nate's the first one to get married. Anyway, I don't have any indication that Andy violated our agreement other than taking the boat out after dinner. He wasn't supposed to do that. But he wasn't the one who wrecked it, and he didn't know that Gavin was going to bring the party back to the house. Andy said he let them in, had a couple of beers, and went to bed."

"And you believe him? How stupid can you be, Lucas? Andy never tells us the truth. You'd better erase those tapes. And that navigation log. God knows where he actually went in the boat."

"I want to see them first, Ella."

"You know our son!" she snapped. "You don't need to see them!"

"I think we owe it to Andy to give him the benefit of the doubt."

"And I don't care what you think!" she shot back, which sadly was the theme of their marriage, he reflected helplessly. "I'll erase them. And I'm coming back immediately, and you're going to cancel that trip to Orange County. Andy's made another expensive mess that we will have to clean up."

And as soon as she hung up, she used her phone to do exactly as she'd promised. Just as she finished, the doorbell rang. Lucas heard the front door opening, and then he heard Andy say, "Yes, Officer. My father made the call. I'll go get him."

CHAPTER FOUR

Sunday, June 10, 2018, The Coronado Cays

Gavin was talking to two uniformed officers when Lucas entered the living room. Lucas watched Gavin take his business card out of his wallet and hand it to the older, tough-looking, skeptical one, whose name tag proclaimed that he was Officer D. Brooks.

The round-faced blond, who had the physique of a surfer and probably was one and whose name tag said he was Officer R. Perkins, looked up as Lucas entered. "Are you the homeowner?"

"Yes. Lucas Owens. And this is my son, Andy." Lucas held out a hand for the officer to shake, but he ignored it and wrote something on the notepad he was holding. Lucas saw Andy shift his weight from one foot to the other nervously as they stood facing the officers.

"Rick, you take a statement from the son," Officer Brooks directed his companion. "I'll take the dad, here."

Officer Perkins motioned for Andy to follow him deeper into the living room. Lucas wished he could prevent a one-on-one between the officer and his son. Andy had been to law school, but that didn't mean he would remember to hold his tongue in a police interview. In fact, he had zero legal skills, which was why he kept flunking the bar.

"Were you here last night for this party?" Officer Brooks' tone was not friendly.

"No. I live in Rancho Santa Fe. Andy called me early this morning when he realized Nate was missing."

"And Nate is?"

"Nate McClellan. Andy, Nate, Kyle, and Gavin have been friends since preschool. Nate's getting married in August, and they decided to have a warm-up bachelor party for him last night. The main party is in Vegas on the Fourth of July weekend."

Lucas could tell the coveted Vegas gathering meant nothing to the officer.

"So you don't know when anyone last saw Nate?"

"Andy said he left him on the boat around one a.m. to let the others into the house."

"The boat?"

"My boat. Over at the yacht club."

"The one that's been damaged?"

"Right."

"Show it to me."

It was only a mile from the house at Green Turtle to the Cays Yacht Club, but the ride in the back of the patrol car with Andy seemed to last forever, and it ratcheted up Lucas' anxiety several notches. *They're going to see the surveillance cameras and ask for the video. Ella has made us all look so guilty. God, I hope they find Nate soon. And I hope he's okay.*

Lucas led them up the wooden walkway just past *The Escape* so that they could view the bow. The gash looked sharper and more vicious in the midmorning sun.

"Wow!" Officer Brooks sounded somewhat human as he looked at the damage. "What does one of these babies cost?"

Lucas shifted uncomfortably from one foot to the other. He remembered the first time he'd seen a display of this kind of wealth when Ella had invited him to meet her family when they were in college. He had grown up as an Air Force brat, moving from base to base, as his father advanced to full-bird colonel. His parents had managed to retire comfortably to an avocado farm in Fallbrook, but only because they were wise money managers. After seeing the Lawrence mansion with the pool and the tennis court and the stables up close and personal, Lucas had decided to woo and win Ella Lawrence. But since she had already targeted him as the man she wanted, putting an engagement ring on her finger had required little effort.

Before Lucas was forced to reveal the price of a Cobalt A40, Officer Brooks said, "I want to take a look around on board."

Lucas obediently led the way back to *The Escape*, but when he reached the gangway, Officer Brooks stepped in front of him and said sharply, "You two wait here while we look."

Lucas felt helpless as he watched the two officers board his yacht. Andy, who was standing beside him, said softly, "I'm sorry, Dad."

He wanted to scream in frustration, but he managed to control himself. He said flatly, "Your mother and I trusted you not to get into any more trouble."

"It was just a boat ride, Dad. I had no idea Nate would disappear."

"You were told about *The Escape*, Andy. It's not yours."

"I—I understand, Dad."

Lucas looked at his son's dark eyes, the replica of his own. He could see that he was hurting. Andy's ability to be sorry for his recklessness made Lucas soften a little.

But the sight of the officers returning from their search hardened his heart again.

"There's no sign of him," Officer Brooks said as he and Officer Perkins stepped off the boat, onto the wooden dock. "We did find this, though. Do either of you recognize it?"

Officer Perkins held up a cell phone in a black leather case.

"That looks like Nate's phone," Andy said.

Officer Perkins flipped open the front cover, and as he did, he hit the home button. The screen came to life, and Lucas could see a message. Officer Perkins held the phone out for Andy to see the text. "Is this 'Tina' someone your friend knows?"

Lucas could see the shock on Andy's face as he read the words. After he finished, he stepped away and covered his face with his hands and said nothing.

"Do you know if this 'Tina' person was a friend of the missing guy?" Officer Perkins asked Lucas, thrusting the phone at him. Lucas read,

"Family is everything and yours would never understand. And I don't think you want to destroy your relationship with Andy. But I will meet you for breakfast in the morning to talk. Love, Tina."

Lucas looked over at Andy. He had taken his hand away from his face, but he had begun to cry silently. Lucas said, "Tina is my son's former girlfriend."

"Did you know your friend was seeing your ex?" Officer Brooks demanded.

Still crying and unable to speak, Andy shook his head.

At that moment, Officer Brooks' shoulder microphone squawked, and he frowned. He said, "Rick, stay here with these two while I find out what this is all about."

The younger officer nodded and motioned for Lucas and Andy to move some distance away from Brooks so they couldn't hear the message from dispatch.

Officer Perkins kept his eyes on Lucas and Andy and said nothing. His silence and the discovery of the phone and its message made Lucas even more uncomfortable.

After what seemed like an hour, but could only have been minutes, Officer Brooks walked back over to them and said, "They've found your missing friend."

"Thank God!" Lucas felt his knees go weak with relief. "Where is he?"

"His body washed up on the beach in front of the Hotel Del. A couple of tourists actually saw the waves bring it on shore. Seeing that freaked them out, and they had to call paramedics for one of them."

"But—how can you be sure it's Nate?" Lucas' mouth was so dry that he had trouble speaking. *Please, God,* he prayed. *Please don't let this be true.*

"Young man, about thirty-two years old. Sandy hair, five eight," Officer Brooks said as he turned to Andy. "And didn't you say he was wearing jeans and a Dodgers T-shirt?"

Andy nodded as fresh tears rolled down his face.

"Well, we've found him," the officer said. "And obviously he wasn't alone on your yacht last night."

"Obviously." *Stay calm,* Lucas told himself. *Never talk to the police.* Brian McClellan had warned him a hundred times. Still, he had nothing to hide. Right? *What about the surveillance tapes Ella erased? Had the officers seen the cameras at the house and on The Escape?*

"He was alone when I left him," Andy finally managed to say quietly.

"What were the two of you talking about?" Officer Brooks demanded.

"He had pre-wedding jitters. I was trying to make him see it would all be okay."

"Did those jitters have something to do with this girl?" Officer Brooks asked.

"If they did, Nate didn't mention her."

"Are you sure?" The officer frowned.

"Positive," Andy said. But Officer Brooks looked unconvinced.

"When was the wedding date?" he demanded.

Not was. Is, Lucas thought. *This can't be true. Nate's going to marry Kinsley as scheduled. This is some kind of nightmare, and I'm going to wake up.*

"August fourth," Lucas said.

But Officer Brooks wasn't finished with Andy. "So you were the only one with him from the time the two of you left the strip club until you say you left him here at one a.m."

"Well, yes. But—"

"How do I know that you brought this guy back from the club?"

Lucas did not like the officer's tone, and he decided to let him know. "Are you saying Andy threw Nate overboard on the way back from The Naked Lady?" Lucas' voice rose in anger, and he took a step closer to Officer Brooks only to have Officer Perkins place himself in his path.

"I'm saying there's a dead guy on the beach, and the last person with him was your son," Officer Brooks barked, gesturing toward Andy.

"No, that's not true," Lucas insisted. "Andy left him on the boat when Gavin came back with the others. There were twenty to thirty people at my house last night, and they all had access to the dingy that's tied up at our boat slip. Any one of them could have rowed across to see Nate or walked around Grand Caribe to get to the boat. It's only a mile walk to the yacht club from my house."

Officer Brooks shrugged as another police car pulled up right beside them, and two officers got out. One was tall. One was short. They were wearing the same uniform as Officers Brooks and Perkins.

"Put these two in the car and take them back to the house," Officer Brooks told the tall one. "Rick and I will stay here and watch the boat until the search warrant arrives." He paused and turned to Lucas. "Unless you want to give us your consent to search your house and your boat."

Lucas' mouth was so dry that he couldn't speak at first. *Never talk to the police. How many times had Brian said this to him? But this was Brian's son. Surely if there were clues here, Brian would want the police to search. But Andy was his son. And the last time—*

He stopped himself in midthought. "I believe my attorney would tell me not to give consent."

Officer Perkins, still holding Nate's phone, adopted the role of good cop. His tone was reasonable and friendly. "Since you're sure your son is innocent, a consent to search would help him with the district attorney."

"I—really—without talking to my attorney, I can't."

Officer Brooks shrugged. "Well, then, we'll get a warrant."

CHAPTER FIVE

Sunday, June 10, 2018, The Coronado Cays

There were two police cars in front of the villa when the tall officer, whose name plate said P. Matthews, parked the black-and-white and instructed Lucas and Andy to go inside the house. All the neighbors were outside to witness Lucas' walk of shame. Although the living room was full of cops, he was relieved when the front door closed behind him and Andy. Gavin and Kyle had been forced to stop cleaning up. They were now sitting on the sofa under the watchful eye of the officers.

Officer Matthews motioned for Lucas and Andy to take the chairs opposite Gavin and Kyle. Lucas was seething, but he knew he shouldn't lash out at the police.

"Nate's dead." He told Gavin and Kyle, speaking softly so that the officers would not overhear their conversation.

"We know," Gavin said, also very softly. "The cops told us. They asked for a number to contact the family so that they could ID him. And they said they'd have a search warrant within an hour."

"How much trash did you take out before they showed up?" Lucas asked.

"Only three bags, and they're all in your trash cans. Why are you asking?"

"On the way back from the yacht club, the tall cop's partner accused me of destroying evidence because I instructed you to clean up," Lucas explained.

"That's ridiculous," Kyle said.

"It is," Lucas agreed. "I'm going to go call Hugh and tell him we need an attorney here as quickly as possible."

He got up and turned toward the hallway, but one of the police officers gestured for him to go back into the living room. "Stay where you are," he commanded as he laid his hand on his gun.

"But I need to speak with my attorney. In private. My office is just down the hall."

"Well, leave the door open!"

But Lucas went inside and quietly closed it anyway. He dialed Hugh Mahoney, who lived in an ocean-front mansion named Crown Manor near the Hotel Del Coronado. *Please, God, let him be in town.*

A minute later Hugh answered. *At least one thing is going my way.*

When Lucas finished the story of Nate's disappearance, Hugh said, "Yeah, Andy's going to need representation. You'll probably need someone, too. But we'll sort that out later. Erin's here. The two of us will come over and hold your hand while the cops are searching. That's about all we can do for now."

* * *

After they got their search warrant, the police made Lucas sit on the curb in handcuffs with Andy, Gavin, and Kyle. Hugh objected, but Officer Brooks laughed in his face and snapped the cuffs on Lucas. The sun was climbing toward noon, and it beat down on the four of them as they sat helpless under the scrutiny of the neighborhood like bugs under a magnifying glass. Anger choked Lucas. Andy had been in trouble for most of his thirty-two years, but he'd never done anything that humiliated his father as much as having to sit on the curb in front of his own house in handcuffs under the gaze of his neighbors.

Hugh and Erin had counseled all four of them to remain silent during the search. Hugh went into the house to watch the officers tear the place apart. Erin went down to the boat to monitor what they were doing to *The Escape.* Lucas envied Hugh when it came to Erin. She was a year younger than Andy, but unlike his son, she knew how to set professional goals and achieve them. She was smart, beautiful, and an accomplished attorney like her father. She had left Craig, Lewis, and Weller in New York to work with Hugh at the Andrews-Cooper Innocence Project, which her father had founded after corrupt President Hal Edwards had tried to destroy his career. Lucas envied Hugh the purpose that the Innocence Project had restored to his life. Before Hugh had met Kathryn Andrews and founded the Project, he'd been living the same empty life that Lucas was currently living. Hugh had been a middle-aged high roller, sleeping with party girls and young associates in his firm, all of whom were willing to overlook his looks and his age to get close to his money and his power. But the suit to vindicate the death of Kathryn's husband, Public Defender Tom Andrews, had changed Hugh's life. Sitting on the curb, sweating in the advancing morning sun, Lucas wished something or someone would change his. And he wished his son had been able and willing to follow him into his business the way Erin had joined Hugh in his efforts to save the innocent from wrongful conviction. Lucas didn't understand Andy. He and Ella had spent a small fortune to educate him and buy him anything he wanted. Why, then, wasn't he happy? Why was his only goal in life the timing of his next drink?

But Tina had changed him. The thought irritated Lucas more than the sun which was making the jacket of his tracksuit unbearably uncomfortable. He couldn't take it off because of the handcuffs. *Andy settled down and started studying for the bar after he met Tina. No*, he told himself. *That was a lie. Andy had been putting on an act to impress her, but it was an act that wouldn't have lasted. Ella ruined Andy's life when she bought off Tina. No*, he wanted to scream. *No! No! No! Tina took the money. Tina didn't love their son.*

"Here!" Officer Brooks towered over Lucas, glowering at him. He was thrusting a clipboard in his face. "Sign this."

Lucas stood up slowly and took the clipboard in both hands, still restrained by the handcuffs. The print on the form swam in front of his eyes. He heard Officer Brooks say, "We're going to impound the boat at the Marine Group Boat Works across the bay in Chula Vista. The Harbor Police are here to tow it."

Lucas stared at the form on the clipboard and realized he couldn't stop the police from taking possession of *The Escape.*

Hugh came out of the house and planted himself between Officer Brooks and Lucas. In chinos and a knit collared shirt, he looked more like a golfer than a lawyer. But Hugh Mahoney was one of the best, regardless of his attire. He said, "He can't sign anything in those handcuffs."

Brooks shrugged. "Department policy."

"Why do I have to sign this since you have a search warrant?" Lucas asked as he held up the clipboard with both bound hands.

"It relieves us of liability for damage to the vessel during towing."

"He's certainly not going to sign that!" Hugh barked and shoved the clipboard back in Brooks' face.

"Suit yourself," he sneered. "I'll need your cell phone, too," he said to Lucas. "Which pocket is it in?"

Lucas panicked. *If they get my phone, they'll see Ella's call. Will they know she erased the surveillance videos?*

"He doesn't have to give it to you," Hugh replied, waving the search warrant in the face of the increasingly irritated officer. "My client's cell phone is not within the scope of this warrant. He wasn't even here when Nathan McClellan disappeared."

Brooks sneered again but went back into the house.

"I'll call Erin and tell her to video the yacht being towed," Hugh said. He put his hand on Lucas' shoulder. "How are you holding up?"

"It's too hot."

"I'll say something to them."

A few minutes later, Officer Brooks grudgingly moved them to the porch where there was some shade. But it seemed like hours before the search was over. Lucas sat helplessly on Ella's wicker settee, wondering if he'd ever see his beloved *Escape* again. He watched as a tow truck removed Nate's blue BMW from the driveway. A procession of officers carried box after box after box to the police van parked in front of the house. His heart sank when he saw his computers in some of the boxes. Could they figure out that Ella had erased those surveillance tapes? Finally, after swabbing everyone for DNA, producing a lab technician to draw Andy's blood, and removing the handcuffs, the hoard of official locusts got back into their vehicles and drove away. Lucas rushed into the living room and poured himself a tumbler of scotch.

"Hey, slow down," Hugh advised when he came out of the kitchen and found Lucas on the couch with Andy, Kyle, and Gavin.

"Sorry, but I need this," Lucas said as he gulped the scotch.

"I'll make some coffee," Kyle offered and headed for the kitchen. Lucas felt guilty about the example he was setting but not guilty enough to put down his drink.

A few minutes later, he heard the front door open and close. Erin appeared in the living room and accepted a cup of coffee from Kyle, who methodically offered one to everyone else. She showed Lucas the video of the boat being towed. He shivered as he watched his pride and joy being taken into police custody. Andy refused coffee and went to the kitchen to fetch a beer. Kyle and Gavin remained on the sofa, uneasily sipping their coffee.

"What's going to happen now?" Lucas asked Hugh and Erin when Andy returned.

"Well, clearly they're looking for probable cause to arrest Andy," Hugh said.

"But Nate was alive when I left him."

"What time was that?" Erin asked. She was sitting in the armchair next to the one Hugh occupied. Her light-blue blazer gave authority to her jeans and white shirt outfit. She had taken a small notepad out of her purse and was holding a pen, poised to take notes. From time to time she pushed unruly strands of her shoulder-length caramel hair off her heart-shaped face as she waited for Andy to respond.

She's beautiful, Lucas thought, *and rich. But she'd never consider a screwup like Andy.*

"Around one o'clock."

"What about you two?" Hugh turned to Gavin and Kyle. "Did you see Nate come back to the house after you brought the party back from Imperial Beach?"

They both shook their heads. *They're going to distance themselves from Andy as soon as they get a chance,* Lucas thought. *They know that being accused of being an accessory to murder could hurt their careers. It would destroy their chances of making partner.*

Gavin said, "But there were a lot of people in this room. And I was drinking a lot, and I wasn't looking for Nate. I just assumed he was around here somewhere in the crowd."

"Same with me," Kyle chimed in. "I knew he had come back with Andy, but I had no reason to be looking for him."

"What about Andy? Did the two of you see him leave the party after he returned with Nate?" Erin asked.

"I saw him in here with a beer in his hand," Gavin said. "But I wasn't watching him all night, either."

"He spent a lot of time talking to one of the strippers," Kyle said. "She was sitting on the end of the couch, and Andy was standing beside her, drinking beer and flirting with her. Eventually, he sat down in front of her and put his head in her lap."

"Do you remember doing that?" Lucas asked his son.

"Sorry, no."

"So you were in a blackout at some point," Erin suggested.

"I didn't think so," Andy said, "but I don't remember the conversation that Kyle is talking about. I do remember leaving Nate on the boat to let everyone else in the house."

"Does anyone know the name of the woman Andy was talking to?" Erin asked.

Kyle frowned. "I talked to her, too, while we were still at the club. She only gave me her stripper name, Crystal Diamond."

As Erin wrote that on her notepad, Hugh glanced at his watch and placed his mug on the table next to his chair and stood up. "Erin and I have a court appearance tomorrow for an Innocence Project client. We set aside this afternoon to prepare. We'd better get going."

Lucas followed Hugh and Erin outside and accompanied them to Hugh's silver Mercedes, which was parked across the street from the villa. "Thanks for coming," he said as Hugh unlocked the driver's side and prepared to get in.

"Erin and I were glad to do it. You've been a client for a long time. And a friend. I'm going to talk to Charlotte Estes about representing Andy. She's the new name on the letterhead."

"Is she the one who replaced Mckenzie Fitzgerald?" Lucas asked.

Hugh nodded. "We merged with her boutique criminal defense firm in the early part of this year. Just after Mckenzie went back east to work for Craig, Lewis."

Lucas saw a shadow cross Hugh's face. *He had wanted McKenzie to stay for personal reasons. I wished I cared enough about someone to miss her if she left me, but I can't wait to get rid of girls like Sunny fast enough. And then, there's Ella. If only someone would get her off my back.*

As Hugh started to get into his car, Lucas put his hand on Hugh's arm. "Before you go, I have a question. Do you really think they're going to arrest Andy?"

"I think we need to be prepared for that," Hugh said. He patted Lucas on the shoulder. "I can't say don't worry, but I can say take it one day at a time."

"Okay. I'll try."

Lucas watched the big Mercedes make a U-turn and head back down Green Turtle Road. *What if the cops are right, and Andy never brought Nate back from the party at the strip club?*

CHAPTER SIX

Monday, June 11, 2018, Offices of Goldstein, Miller, Mahoney, and Estes, Emerald Shapery Center

Charlotte Estes had slipped out at lunchtime for a short run along the Embarcadero. Thank God the attempts on her life hadn't followed her to California. Detective Merrill of the District of Columbia Metropolitan Police, who hadn't yet been able to identify the shooter at the canal, had counseled her to be careful. But after six months of caution, she was certain that the threat was gone. And she was making progress in shaping a new life for herself, although she still dwelled too often on the puzzle of Matt's unfaithfulness.

She had showered in the firm's gym on the twenty-seventh floor and had just sat down at her desk to pick at the salad her secretary had fetched for her, when someone knocked on her office door. Hugh Mahoney opened it a crack and asked, "Got a few minutes?"

"Of course," she told him.

He came in and sat down in one of the two leather chairs in front of her massive mahogany desk, almost the same size as the one in his office in the penthouse, one floor up, a testament to her status as a name partner on the firm's letterhead. Charlotte planted her plastic fork in the greens in their transparent box and prepared to give Hugh her full attention.

"Something's come up that I'm hoping you'll agree to take on for the firm. Lucas Owens is one of our biggest clients. Millions in billing annually. And his wife is the President of Lawrence Securities and Investments, another client whose work is worth millions to us."

Charlotte frowned. *Should I tell him I know Lucas? And that I don't like him? I'd rather not rake all that up.* "The Owens account is all about real estate and construction defect litigation," she said instead. "The Lawrence work is Securities and Exchange Commission work. Neither is my expertise, as you know."

"But I'm coming to you because this isn't the usual Owens/Lawrence matter. Andy Owens has been involved in a boating accident that killed one of his friends, Nate McClellan, son of Brian, one of the founders of McClellan and Wyatt."

"I know Brian and Levi by reputation," Charlotte said.

"Lucas called me yesterday because the police were going to search the boat and the residence at the Cays that were involved in the death. Erin and I went over there and spent a good part of the day. It's likely Andy's going to be charged with something."

"I take it he was driving the boat when Nate was killed?"

"It's not clear right now. But that's law enforcement's position. And it's pretty obvious that he was under the influence."

Charlotte looked at the tiny streets below and asked the Universe what ghastly cosmic accident had brought Lucas

43

Owens and his baggage to her door just when she was beginning to emerge from her past.

She said carefully, "I'm afraid I'm not the right attorney for this, Hugh. My sympathies are with Brian McClellan. He's lost his son. I've just lost my husband, as you know."

Hugh's dark eyes were sympathetic, but he didn't budge. He said slowly, "Of course, I understand. I feel for Brian, too. But Lucas and Ella are going to lose their son—their only child—without someone like you to help Andy. The lawyers at the Estes Firm are among the most highly rated criminal defense attorneys in the country. That's why I wanted all of you, and most particularly you, to be a part of Goldstein, Miller."

Matt had warned her about this. The downside to Hugh's merger offer was there'd be pressure to take clients they would normally have turned down. She'd known when she agreed to the merger that Lucas and Ella were important to the firm, but only on the corporate side. She'd never expected to have to deal with them personally.

"I appreciate your kind words, Hugh," she said carefully. "But I knew Lucas Owens in college, and I didn't have a very high opinion of him. I didn't know Ella as well, but what I did know was not favorable."

Hugh looked surprised. "Really? But that was a long time ago. I've been close to both of them for more than twenty years. Andy's only a year older than Erin. They went to the same school from first grade through high school. And, of course, the Owens/Lawrence accounts have been crucial to the firm's bottom line for over twenty years. They are expecting Goldstein, Miller to help them, and their loyalty to the firm entitles them to the best representation we can give their son."

She felt the screws tightening. And she had the definite impression that even if she told Hugh everything that she'd learned about Lucas when they'd been students at UCLA, it wouldn't have mattered in the slightest. As she knew only too well, an excellent lawyer is, above all, an accomplished pragmatist. Her relationship with Hugh and her new firm had to run smoothly.

"Of course, I understand. I'll see what I can do to help Andy."

Hugh beamed at her. "Thank you, Charlotte. It means a lot to me personally and to the firm to have you on Andy's case. I'm going to give you Sean Donovan as co-counsel. He's been a partner for a couple of years. Smart guy. He'll be valuable to you. He knows all the players in the local criminal defense bar, and he can take a lot of the burden of defending Andy off your shoulders."

And he was one of the partners who opposed the merger with my firm.

"Thanks, Hugh. I'll look forward to working with Sean."

Hugh stood up, signaling he'd gotten what he wanted. But he paused before heading for the door. "By the way, tell me about the twins. How are Ian and Hayden doing in D.C. without you?"

Charlotte smiled. "Like me, they miss our old firm."

"Are they happy working in our D.C. office?"

"They are. But I hope they'll eventually follow me out here."

"Did you decide to buy that place in La Jolla that you've been renting?"

"Not yet. I've got a lease until December. Plenty of time to look around for the house of my dreams with an ocean view, although this one is pretty close."

Hugh smiled. "I'm anxious for you to find a permanent place, so you won't go back east with the twins."

He really means that. His genuine friendship took some of the sting out of being asked to take on Lucas' son and Sean Donovan. In response, Charlotte smiled, got up, and walked Hugh to the door where she accepted the hug that he gave her before he vanished down the long corridor of the twenty-ninth floor. She went back to her desk and closed the lid on the tasteless salad. She watched a helicopter inbound to North Island. As it circled in preparation for landing, she asked the Universe why it had put the offspring of Lucas Owens and Ella Lawrence squarely in her path when she wanted nothing more than to put the past, all of the past, behind her.

CHAPTER SEVEN

Monday, June 11, 2018, The Metropolitan, 165 Sixth Avenue, San Diego

Sean Donovan had had, without any doubt, one of the worst days in his forty-three years. He poured himself a double scotch and stared out at the view from his penthouse on the twenty-fourth floor of The Metropolitan, the glass tower that also housed the Omni Hotel on its lower floors. He gritted his teeth in frustration and tossed back some scotch. He could see the San Diego Convention Center and the downtown Hilton, and Coronado Island across the bay, all shining like rubies, diamonds, and emeralds in the dark.

He had arrived at his two-million-dollar home at eight p.m., looking forward to the soothing comfort of his girlfriend of six months only to find Lisa packed and waiting for an Uber.

"I'm leaving."

"What?"

"I'm leaving you."

"But, Lisa—"

"There is no 'but, Lisa.' I've had enough. I'm leaving. You're never here. This is not a relationship."

"But I—"

"Don't insult me by saying you love me. You don't. You love your job at Goldstein, Miller. You do not love me."

He had stood in the front hallway as she'd proceeded to place the key that he'd given her on the table and walk through the door without looking back. It was a moment of déjà vu. In 2012, the year he'd made partner, his wife of eight years had done exactly the same thing. His girlfriend's exit was a disappointment because he'd gotten used to having her waiting for him when he came back from a long day at the firm. But he'd get over her. On the other hand, he had never gotten over the loss of Sherrie.

He'd wanted to run after his wife screaming, "No, wait. You don't understand!" But he knew all too well that she did understand. He was married to his job, not her.

They'd met in 2003 when Sean had still been an Assistant U.S. Attorney in the San Diego office. Sherrie had been the date of one of his colleagues at an office party. They had been married a year later in 2004.

As he polished off his scotch and poured more and then resumed his study of the Convention Center below and Coronado Island, he told himself that if he'd stayed in the U.S. Attorney's Office, Sherrie would never have left him. It was the long grind to partnership at Goldstein, Miller that had cemented the rift in their relationship. He'd bought this castle-in-the-air for her to make up for his sixteen-hour days and his travel and all the weekends that he'd had to leave her alone. But a two-million-dollar view of San Diego Bay and Petco Park plus unlimited maid and room service from the Omni Hotel had not made up for his absence. And for their failure to have a child. He'd known during the last six months of their marriage that she was seeing a younger man. And having the time of her life. He was honest enough to realize that life with him had been endless days and nights of waiting for him to return from the office. He didn't begrudge her the chance to start over with someone who had time for her. He'd offered her the expensive condo in the divorce settlement to assuage some of his guilt over the end of their marriage. But she'd turned it down and taken her share of the cash instead.

Sean turned away from the window and studied himself in the mirror in the gilded frame that hung over the drinks tray. Had his looks also influenced Lisa's exit? Probably. Sometimes he looked older than his forty-three years, he decided as he sipped his scotch, and this was one of those nights. On a good day, when he was well-rested, his high, square forehead balanced his similarly square jaw, and the combination made him look powerful and confident. But tonight, the creases in his otherwise attractive forehead stood out deeply and his smile wrinkles, which had begun as dimples that were visible only when he smiled, were deeply etched. His deep-set blue eyes, which seemed to be always smiling because they turned up slightly at the corners, looked washed out and hollow. His brownish-blond hair was curling behind his ears and needed cutting. And he was deeply aware that five eight was not a commanding height. Some people didn't think a few inches mattered. But he did. If only he could claim six feet.

He sat down on the white linen sofa that Sherrie and the interior designer had decided was perfect for the living room.

He finished his scotch and reminded himself not to drink any more. Tomorrow was Tuesday, and he'd gotten the unhappy news this afternoon that he was going to have to face The Dragon Lady in the morning. Best not to face her with a hangover.

Hugh Mahoney had appeared in his office at four thirty.

"Sean! So glad to find you here. I need to talk to you."

He watched apprehensively as Hugh took the chair in front of his desk. He had the distinct impression that bad news was on the way. And it was.

"I've got a very important assignment for you," Hugh began. "Something that will make up for Intech."

Sean winced. "I don't need to be reminded that my reputation took a big hit over that loss."

Sean knew it shouldn't have happened. He'd done everything right in preparing to defend the software startup over Securities and Exchange Commission violations. He had lived and breathed that case for two years, and he'd been certain when they went to trial that the company had presented an accurate picture of its earnings to its shareholders in its Securities and Exchange Commission disclosure documents. But after a two-month trial, a jury had decided that Intech had intentionally misled them. The damage award in the millions had shut down the company. Sean knew very well it was the kind of loss that could end his career at Goldstein, Miller. He'd been waiting uneasily ever since to find out if Hugh would allow him a chance at redemption or would show him the door. Apparently, it was going to be redemption, but the look on Hugh's face said that Sean wasn't going to like the terms.

"I'm making you co-counsel with Charlotte Estes on the Andy Owens' case."

"Andy Owens? Lucas' kid?"

"He's not exactly a kid. He's thirty-two. He may be charged with something in the death of Brian McClellan's son."

"Nate's dead?"

"I'm afraid so. Did you know him?"

"Of him. I'm still friends with some of my colleagues in the U.S. Attorney's Office. They've mentioned him as a good defense attorney. He wasn't very old."

"Same age as Andy. Engaged to Levi Wyatt's daughter, Kinsley. Andy and his friends had a pre-bachelor party for him at the Owens' place in the Coronado Cays on Saturday night. Nate's body washed ashore near the Hotel Del yesterday morning."

Sean shook his head. "That's sad news. But I don't see why Charlotte Estes needs any help from me. When you proposed the merger, you portrayed her, her husband, and her firm as defense attorneys with superpowers, far above anything the rest of us could ever hope to possess."

"I know that you and all of our white-collar-crime partners opposed the Estes merger. None of you spared any words about why we didn't need the Estes lawyers at Goldstein, Miller."

"And we didn't. Our group is small, but we were doing a good job."

"And as I said when I presented the merger to the partnership, business expansion in the current legal market is crucial to business development."

Sean shrugged. "I concede that I was on the losing side in

the partnership vote. But since Mrs. Estes is the best of the best, she doesn't need me."

"Charlotte. She's your partner, and her name is Charlotte. And she does need you.

Her husband died last November. She went ahead with the merger to get away from the memories in D.C. She's tough, but she's been through a lot. And the firm has a lot riding on a good outcome for Andy."

"I'm not a shrink, Hugh."

"I didn't say you were. But you're experienced in the local bar, and you know the most reliable local experts. And this case is probably going to need good expert witnesses."

"So I work my ass off, and Charlotte Estes gets the credit."

"No!" Hugh spoke sharply. 'I said that you're going to be co-lead counsel, not second chair."

"What do you think the kid's going to be charged with?"

"Most likely boating under the influence and leaving the scene of an accident. Possibly involuntary manslaughter. I'm betting you can negotiate a plea that will give him no prison time and put him on probation for a couple of years because you know the lay of the land in the District Attorney's Office. Charlotte, for all her experience, doesn't know the players over there. If you can get Andy out of this without prison time, that would more than wipe out the Intech blot on your career. You know how important the Owens/Lawrence account is.

"Look, Sean, I like you and I know that Intech was just a bad break. I want to keep you at Goldstein, Miller. I'm giving you a way to show the firm just how valuable you are to us."

"Thanks, Hugh." Sean smiled. He had no doubt that Hugh

meant what he'd said. He was no longer the ruthless legal machine that he had once been. He had developed compassion, and Sean realized that he was now the beneficiary of that compassion. If only saving his career didn't mean working with The Dragon Lady.

Sean put down his empty glass and turned off the lights in the penthouse. Maybe he should think about selling this place and finding something so small that there would be no temptation to find another girlfriend. Or another wife.

CHAPTER EIGHT

Tuesday, June 12, 2018, Offices of Goldstein, Miller, Mahoney, and Estes, Emerald Shapery Center

The Dragon Lady had sent him an email asking him to meet her in her office at eight thirty the next morning. She suggested they become acquainted before interviewing Andy and his parents at nine. Although technically Sean was her equal as co-counsel in the case, he knew very well that she, as a named partner of the firm, outranked him. So he had no choice but to obey her summons, as irritating as it was.

But when he arrived at the Dragon's door at the appointed time, her secretary informed him that she had gone for a run and he was to wait in her office. He didn't like the idea of sitting around waiting for anyone unless the time was billable. And he doubted that the Owens/Lawrence fortune was willing to pay him to wait while the Dragon finished her run. But he did have a trace of a hangover from last night's bout with the scotch bottle, and hangovers made him passive. So he slumped in one of her client chairs and read a copy of the police report that she had left on her desk.

So far the cops didn't have much. Everyone agreed that Nate

McClellan and Andy Owens had left the strip club ahead of the rest of the partiers. And everyone agreed that no one but Andy saw Nate after they returned to the Cays. There was some speculation that a text message was evidence of a love triangle involving Andy, Nate, and a woman named Tina Hernandez. But Sean could see that the officer who wrote the report had no evidence that Andy knew about Tina and Nate before the officer illegally searched Nate's iPhone. So the police theory that Andy dumped Nate overboard because he was jealous had no traction. And the illegal search of the iPhone was something they could work with, thank God.

The door swung open and a warm and charming female voice proclaimed, "Oh, there you are. I thought I had time for a quick mile to the Embarcadero and back before our meeting. Sorry, I was wrong."

Sean turned to find a very attractive woman in a simple green dress advancing toward him with her hand extended for a handshake. She was glowing from her run, and her hazel eyes were smiling at him. Her chin-length brownish-blond hair was slightly damp, and Sean realized she'd just stepped out of the firm's shower and into her work clothes. Her biography said she was fifty-eight, but she looked closer to mid-forties like himself. She was about five five and had a runner's lean build. If she hadn't been who she was, he would have liked her. Even been attracted to her. But he was determined to resist her obvious charm.

"Sean Donovan," he said and shook her hand, focusing on how much he wished she were back on K Street.

"Well, you know who I am, of course," she smiled as she

released his hand and sat down at her massive desk. "*The* Charlotte Estes, head of the invading hordes of white-collar-crime defense attorneys from D.C."

Her candor caught him off guard. "I—"

"Oh, that's okay. You don't have to pretend." She gave him a smile as penetrating as a ray of sunshine shining through a cloud on a rainy day. "I know that you and all your white-collar partners voted against the merger. I'd have done the same thing if I'd been in your position. We won't take over your clients, I promise."

But Sean knew better, and he steeled himself against her attempt at empathy. He still didn't want her at Goldstein, Miller, and he still didn't want to work with her. "I had a chance to read the police report while I was waiting for you."

"Oh, good. So you're up to speed."

"More or less. This report is nothing but a lot of speculation. But we won't know for sure what they might have on him until we talk to the client. It's five to nine." He made it sound like the reproach that it was meant to be.

She glanced at the ornate silver clock on her desk. For the first time her mask of pleasantry broke, and she looked annoyed by his subtle reminder that keeping a client waiting was bad manners. But she gave him another smile, although this one seemed slightly forced. "We'd better get going then."

* * *

Sean followed Charlotte down the hall to the small conference room overlooking San Diego Bay. He noticed that she was careful to enter the room with him, not ahead of him. He appreciated the gesture of equality, but that didn't lessen his antipathy at having to work with her.

Hugh was sitting at the head of the table with Andy across from him, flanked by a parent on either side. Everyone stood for introductions. After handshakes all around, Charlotte sat down on Hugh's right and Sean took the seat next to her.

While Hugh outlined his observations during the police search on Sunday, Sean studied his new client and his parents. Andy was about five foot five and on the heavy side. Sean doubted he could have buttoned his navy suit coat, and the buttons of his starched white shirt showed some strain. His dark hair was trimmed neatly above his ears. His dark-brown eyes were fixed on his hands, which had open wounds on the knuckles. As they listened to Hugh, Andy's eyes met Sean's briefly and then darted away to study the view as if he were afraid he'd given away a secret. He had his father's large dark eyes. Although Ella had brown eyes, too, hers were penetrating like lasers. Andy and Lucas' were expressive and gentle. Both father and son looked acutely apprehensive at that moment.

Sean figured that Lucas had a personal trainer. His navy suit fit perfectly except for a tiny hint of a bulge above his expensive leather belt. He was taller than his son, about five eight. His dark hair was peppered with gray. Even on the verge of sixty, he was still handsome. Lucas had placed one arm around the back of Andy's chair protectively, and Sean saw emotion come and go in his face as Hugh talked about the death of Nate McClellan. He'd given Charlotte a long look during the introductions. Obviously, he had an eye for attractive women.

Ella Lawrence's intense eyes seemed to look right through

Sean for several seconds when they were introduced. When she looked away, Sean wondered if her gaze had left burn marks on his cheeks. She was wearing a dark-blue dress that looked like a sack made out of expensive wool with long sleeves. She had draped a blue-and-white silk scarf around her shoulders to soften the severity of her outfit. She was wearing a string of pearls that Sean assumed were real and very expensive.

When Hugh reached the end of his summary, Ella said impatiently, "They don't have any evidence that Andy was responsible for Nate's death. Can't we sue them for searching our house and for tearing apart *The Escape*?"

She was as arrogant as her expensive clothes suggested she would be. Sean was relieved when Hugh diplomatically opened the way for a private interview with Andy.

"No, Ella. I wish we could, but that's not possible under the circumstances. Charlotte and Sean need to have a confidential interview with Andy. My secretary has coffee waiting for us upstairs."

Lucas and Ella looked unhappy about being banished, but Andy looked relieved as the door closed behind them.

Charlotte turned to Sean and asked, "Do you want to start with your questions for Andy?"

He could see that she was going out of her way to be collegial. But he was not impressed. "I'll let you take the lead," he said without trying to keep the resentment out of his voice.

"Let's start from the beginning," Charlotte suggested as she turned to Andy with a smile. "What happened that night? Why were you on the boat with Nate?"

"It's just like I told my parents and the police. Gavin and

Kyle and Nate and I got together for dinner. Afterward, we decided to go to the strip club as a pre-bachelor party for Nate."

"And he was getting married when?"

"August fourth. His father was throwing a huge party for him in Vegas over the July Fourth weekend. But that one included the guys my father's age. We just wanted to do something among ourselves that night."

"I take it you are close to your parents?" Charlotte smiled encouragingly again.

Andy looked uncomfortable. "I'm not sure what 'close' means."

"Tell us about Nate and Gavin and Kyle," she suggested. "I gather you guys have been together for a long time."

"Preschool through high school at Francis Parker. They're my brothers because I don't have any of my own."

A hint of bitterness there, Sean thought.

"So private school?" Charlotte continued. "Where did you go to college?"

"I went to Berkeley."

"And when did you graduate?"

"I flunked out in the middle of my freshman year." He looked away, obviously embarrassed.

"Was that it for you and college?"

"No, I graduated from San Diego State with a major in business."

"And what did you do after that?"

"Gavin and Kyle and Nate all went to law school. So I did, too."

"So you have a law degree?"

"Yes. From California Western."

"And have you passed the bar?"

"No. I tried twice after I graduated." He looked embarrassed again.

"So what happened after you didn't pass the second time?"

"My mother sent me to New York to work for a friend of hers."

"What's the friend's name?"

"Sam Wentworth. He owns Wentworth Investment Securities. They do the same kind of work my mother's firm does. Asset management and stock trading for clients."

"I've heard of Wentworth Investment," Charlotte said. "What was your job there?"

"Market research. And supposedly I was studying to be a financial planner. That was my mother's idea," he added.

"I gather you weren't putting much effort into those studies."

"Oh, I was doing the homework. I just didn't care about getting the certification. I wanted to be a lawyer."

"How long did you work for Wentworth Investment?"

"Not quite three years."

"What brought you back to San Diego?"

"I—I just didn't like my job."

No eye contact and he's squirming in his chair. There's more to that part of the story than he's telling us, Sean thought.

"So where have you worked since?" Charlotte smiled again. Sean grudgingly admitted to himself that she was good at building rapport with their client.

"I, uh, well, I haven't exactly worked. I made a deal with my parents. If they'd let me live at the house in the Cays rent-free, I'd study for the bar again."

"So that's what you've been doing since New York?"

"Right. I'm signed up for the July exam."

"Okay. Well, unfortunately, you're going to have to put that off for now. Tell us about Tina Hernandez. Did you go to school with her, too?"

"It's hard to talk about Tina." Andy looked out the window. Sean could see that he was ready for the interview to end.

Charlotte poured a glass of water from the pitcher in the center of the table and handed it to Andy with a reassuring smile. "Try," she advised.

Sean watched him sip the water, knowing Charlotte had defeated his reticence. "She's working on her Ph.D. in genetics in the Biology Department at UCSD. I met her last June, about this time."

"How did you meet?"

"She was waiting tables at Il Fornaio in Coronado on weekends to pick up some extra money during the summer. During the school year, she teaches undergraduate biology courses. Year-round she works in the genetics lab at the Salk Institute as part of her Ph.D. program."

"How did your parents feel about Tina?"

"My mother didn't like her. Her family runs a moving company in Chula Vista. She's the first to go to college."

"And your father?"

Andy shrugged. "He follows my mother's opinion, regardless."

"When did things end between you two?"

"Two months ago. She had a break from school in mid-

March, so I planned a trip to New York. She'd never been there. I bought a ring, and I was going to propose on a carriage ride in Central Park."

"And did you?"

"No. We were supposed to leave for New York the Friday after her classes ended. Instead, she told me on Monday she didn't want to see me anymore."

"Do you know why she broke it off?" Charlotte's hazel eyes were sympathetic. More rapport building, Sean noted.

"She didn't give me an explanation. It was just out of the blue. She'd been really excited about the trip to New York."

Suddenly, Andy's eyes filled with tears. Sean pushed the tissue box on the table toward him. He remembered how much he still missed his wife.

"I'm sorry this is hard for you," Charlotte said sympathetically.

Andy nodded as he finished wiping his eyes.

"And have you seen her since your breakup?" Charlotte continued.

"No, I've tried to, but no success."

"Tell me about trying to see her."

"Well, I went to her lab at Salk once, but I couldn't get past the receptionist. Then I went to Il Fornaio once in late May, hoping that she'd be working that night. She was, but she asked the manager to kick me out. And he did."

"So she wasn't working there when you and Nate and your friends had dinner last Saturday?"

"No. She quit the night she asked the manager to kick me out."

"How did you know that?"

"Because I'm still friends with her brothers."

"And they were at your party for Nate last weekend?"

"Yes, but it wasn't planned. We happened to run into them at the strip club in Imperial Beach. Gavin and Kyle asked them back to the house after Nate and I left."

"So what did you know about Nate's relationship with Tina?" Sean watched Charlotte put down her pen so she could study Andy intently as she waited for his answer.

"Nothing until Sunday when the cop showed me that message from her on Nate's phone."

"Nate didn't tell you that he was seeing her when the two of you were alone on the boat coming back from the strip club?"

"No. I asked him to take the wheel because his father owns a yacht, and Nate's had a lot more experience with a boat that size than I've had. And I knew I'd had a lot to drink, and I wasn't supposed to be driving the boat in the first place without my dad on board. After we moored at the dock, he wanted to stay and have another beer. I could tell he was upset and needed to talk. So we sat there and drank another beer, and he told me that he didn't want to marry Kinsley because he was in love with someone else."

"Did he tell you who the someone else was?"

"No."

"Did you ask him?"

"No. I figured he'd tell me when he was ready. I didn't have any reason to think it was Tina. Look, you have to understand. Nate and I had been together for almost our entire lives. He was my brother in every way except for shared parents. He was trying to talk himself into going ahead with his wedding. And if he went ahead with it and married Kinsley, there was no point in telling me that he'd been involved with Tina except to hurt me. And he wouldn't have wanted to do that." Andy's voice broke again, and Charlotte saw him wipe another tear with a tissue.

"So you two sat and talked about Nate's doubts about his wedding, and then you left to let the others in?"

"Right," Andy agreed.

"Why didn't he just tell his father that he wanted to call it off?"

"He felt as if he couldn't. Nate was always under a lot of pressure to do what his father wanted. After college, he didn't really want to go to law school, but he didn't have the courage to say no. After law school, he didn't want to work for his father, but he couldn't find a way to say no to that either. And then that night on the boat after we came back from the strip club, he was telling me that he didn't want to marry Kinsley, and this time he didn't think he could go through with what his father wanted."

"And you think Nate never got off the boat after everyone came back?" Sean asked.

"I don't know. I drank some more after I went inside. My memory after I left Nate is pretty hazy."

"What about your memory when you were with Nate?"

"I'm very clear about that."

"Who else was there that night besides Kyle and Gavin?"

"Just a bunch of people we met at the strip club. Gavin brought them back to keep the party going. I couldn't tell you the names of any of them except for Tina's brothers."

"What are their names?"

"Jose, Sebastian, and Luis. They all work for the family moving business."

"They knew Nate, didn't they?"

"They met Nate when Tina and I were dating because I had several parties at the Cays and invited them."

"Do you think they knew that Nate was seeing Tina?"

"I think they would have told me if they'd known."

"Why do you think so?"

"Because they were on my side in the breakup. They knew I was going to propose, and they thought Tina was nuts to turn me down."

"And you're sure that you didn't drive the boat again after taking everyone down to the strip club?"

"Yes. Nate brought us back."

"And you were in the house all night after you came back from the club?"

"That's what I remember. But I was drinking more after I came back."

"How long did it take the two of you to get back to the Cays Yacht club after you decided to leave the strip club?"

"Not long. We took an Uber to the California Yacht Marina where we'd left the boat. I used my dad's yacht club pass for one of their guest slips. Once we were underway, it was a quick trip back to the Cays Yacht Club. It's a straight shot across the inlet."

"So maybe twenty minutes?"

"If that. More like fifteen after we actually got going."

"Did anyone see you at the marina?"

"Yeah. The guard on duty checked out my guest pass and told us which slip we could use. Heavyset guy, but I didn't pay any attention to his name."

"Was he wearing a uniform?"

"Yes. He also signed the form that I filled out to use the slip. You might find him that way."

"Exactly how many trips did you make in your father's boat that night?"

"One from Coronado to Imperial Beach to the club and the return trip."

"So two total?"

"Yes."

"And you went straight back to Coronado from Imperial Beach? No joyrides around the bay first?"

"That's right."

Charlotte looked over at Sean and smiled. *Still trying to be charming, and I still don't like you.*

She said, "Those are all my questions for now. Do you have any?"

"Yes," he said. "Just one. What happened to your hands?"

CHAPTER NINE

Tuesday, June 26, 2018, Offices of Goldstein, Miller, Mahoney, and Estes, Emerald Shapery Center

Charlotte sipped a latte at nine on Tuesday while she waited for Kyle Jamison. Sean didn't believe Andy's story that he'd injured his hands sparring with Kyle at the gym on the morning of June ninth. He was convinced that Andy and Nate had had some sort of fight over the girl and that Andy's friends were lying for him.

But Charlotte had other, more pressing considerations on her mind. Someone was watching her house, and she had no idea who it was. A week ago, on the day they'd interviewed Andy, she'd come home from work at five-thirty and changed into her running clothes. When she'd gone outside for her pre-run warmup, she'd noticed a white Nissan Sentra parked in front of the first house on the Caminito Azur cul-de-sac with its motor running. She'd assumed it was an Uber summoned by her neighbor. And, indeed, the car had been gone when she'd returned from her run.

But around nine o'clock, as she'd been closing the curtains in her upstairs bedroom, she'd seen the car again. It had changed positions and was now parked in front of the house directly across the street from her. Its motor was off as if it intended to be there for a while. The windows were tinted. Charlotte's heart began to race.

She went into her darkened bathroom and peered through the shutters so that she wouldn't be seen. But apparently she'd revealed her presence when she closed her bedroom curtains. The car's engine had come to life, and it was now heading out of the cul-de-sac, its lights still off. Charlotte strained to get a license number, but the light from the streetlight wasn't strong enough, and the car was too far away. She thought of calling 9-1-1, but she had nothing to report now that the car had vanished.

When it didn't return on Wednesday and on Thursday, she'd reassured herself that the occupants had been casing her neighborhood for a robbery but had realized that all the houses had security systems and most of them had wives and housekeepers and nannies tending to small children during the day. But the car was back on Friday and Saturday. It took up the position across from her house around ten o'clock on both nights. On Friday, it left when it saw her closing her bedroom curtains around eleven. But on Saturday, it didn't budge when she turned the lights out at midnight.

She had sat at the bathroom window, gripping her cell phone for almost an hour, waiting for it to leave. She'd grown more concerned by the minute when it didn't. She could hear Matt telling her to call the police. She rehearsed over and over what she should say to them. She had no proof this car was connected to the incident at the canal. She couldn't say her life was in danger. And she tried to believe that it wasn't. Her house had a full security system that would alert the police the minute anyone tried to open a window or a door. She was safe, she kept telling herself. She was safe.

But at one fifteen she couldn't stand the tension any longer. She called 9-1-1, and the dispatcher told her she was fortunate because there was a patrol car in the area. As soon as the black-and-white turned into the cul-de-sac, the Sentra's lights and engine came to life. It shot past the patrol car. The officers chased it, lights on, siren blaring, but when they came back twenty minutes later, they informed Charlotte that it had managed to elude them in the twisted tangle of streets and alleys on Mount Soledad. And although they'd been able to pick up the car's license number, in the end that had been no help because the plates were stolen.

Now in the bright sunlight of Tuesday morning, she told herself to stop worrying. The car hadn't been back after the officers chased it away. She had nothing to connect it to the incident at the canal. She was a continent away from whoever fired the rifle that day, and the D.C. police had assured her they thought it was a crazy with a gun who had decided to take a potshot at a runner.

Nine fifteen. Kyle was late. Someone knocked on her door, and she assumed it was Angela, her secretary, bringing Kyle in from reception, but it was Sean Donovan, armed with a large mug of coffee and an attitude. Charlotte had invited him to her meeting with Kyle, but she hadn't expected him to appear.

"Come in and sit down. Kyle isn't here yet."

Sean plopped himself into one of the chairs in front of her desk and found a place to park his mug beside her desk lamp.

"That's not why I came to see you, but since I'm here, I'll stay for the meeting. In the meantime, I've got some bad news. I got a call last night from Axel Saldana about Andy Owens."

"Who's Axel Saldana?" She sipped her latte slowly.

"He's the Number Two in the District Attorney's Office. Bart Stephenson made him his Senior Assistant after the Jeff Ryder debacle."

"The Jeff Ryder debacle?"

"Oh, that's right. You're not up on the local news. Noah Hendricks, the former Senior Assistant, tried to frame Jeff for several murders only to be caught out at Jeff's preliminary hearing as the one behind the killings. Noah and his bad cop partner, Tony Lopez, were working for the Menendez Cartel. They set Jeff up as a fall guy."

"Lucky Jeff, then. But why was Axel calling you and not me?"

"Because he knows me, not you. He's been opposing counsel in a number of cases that I've handled. You may be famous in D.C., but you're not famous here."

"Yet." She gave him her most brilliant smile, but his face never changed. *He's hard to charm. He would be easier to work with if I could.* "So what did your friend Axel tell you?"

"He's charging Andy with first-degree murder."

Charlotte frowned. "That sounds excessive. If your theory is right that they fought over the girl, it would be voluntary manslaughter. Did he give you any clue about why he's charging premeditated murder?"

"Not really. He said I'd have the autopsy report by the end of the day."

"*We'd* have the autopsy report," she corrected him.

Sean shrugged, picked up his mug, and took a long sip of coffee. "Whatever you say. You're the name on the letterhead."

She bit her lip to avoid lashing out at his rudeness. She took a deep breath and pasted on a smile that she hoped didn't look fake and said, "I'd rather we not look at our relationship that way. Matt and I liked to work together, and I miss that. I'm happy for the opportunity to get to know you and to work with you. After all, we're partners no matter whose name is on the firm's stationary."

To avoid answering, he picked up his mug again and drank some more coffee. A second knock on her door signaled that Kyle had finally arrived.

* * *

"Yes, we had a sparring match that morning," he said after introductions. He was tall and thin, with serious hazel eyes set in a long, square face. His jeans and navy blazer made him look credible and friendly, Charlotte thought.

"Andy was still hurting over Tina," Kyle went on, "and I wanted to do something to take his mind off of her. So I suggested that we meet at my firm's gym that Friday for a workout. We put on some gloves and went a couple of rounds."

"He says that he didn't tape his hands properly and that's why his knuckles were injured," Charlotte explained.

Kyle shrugged. "I didn't see his hands afterward. I don't know."

"What about that night when you met for dinner?" Sean asked. "Did you notice any injuries then?"

"Honestly, I don't remember looking at Andy's hands. Nate's wedding was coming up, and we all knew our chances to hang out together were about to, if not come to an end, be fewer and farther between. So we decided to get together for dinner and then afterward, we took the party down to the strip club. We were all drinking quite a bit."

"Did Nate say anything to you about cold feet?" Charlotte asked.

"No."

"What about Andy's drinking that night?" Sean asked. "Did you see how much he had to drink?"

"No, but Andy has problems with alcohol. He was in rehab after that accident in New York three years ago."

"What accident?" Charlotte asked.

"He was driving back to the city after a Christmas party in the Hamptons. He was on the wrong side of the road when he hit an oncoming car."

"What was he convicted of?" she asked, dreading the answer.

"Not much. His parents managed some sort of deal with the state's attorney. I don't know too much about it except they paid millions to the family of the man he killed, and they sent him to rehab in Arizona for almost a year."

"But he never stopped drinking?" Sean asked.

"Only when he was with Tina. He got serious about studying for the bar when he was with her."

"What can you tell us about Andy and Tina?" Charlotte asked. "Did Andy know that she was seeing Nate?"

"I have no idea." Kyle frowned. "Gavin knows more about Tina and Andy than I do. Gavin met Tina's entire family. I've only had contact with her older brothers, the ones who work in the family's moving business. She must be finished with her Ph.D. by now. She was almost finished when she met Andy."

"And Andy said she worked at the Salk Institute?" Charlotte asked.

"When she was a grad student at UC San Diego. If she's finished her degree, I have no idea where she is now. Again, Gavin knows more about Tina than I do."

* * *

"Did he convince you that Andy hurt himself in the gym that morning?" Sean asked after Kyle left.

"I'd say more the other way around. Did he convince *you*? You're the one who didn't believe Andy when you asked him about his hands." Charlotte wished she hadn't let his sarcasm goad her into sounding testy. She'd let him see that his hostile attitude was annoying her. She was relieved when someone knocked on her door. Sean's secretary had brought copies of the autopsy report and the complaint that the District Attorney had filed against Andy.

They were silent as they read. One count of first-degree murder, one count of assault with a deadly weapon, and one count of boating under the influence.

"So what do you think?" Sean asked when he finished reading.

"I think they don't have very much evidence that Andy killed Nate," Charlotte said. "Dr. Tavoularis' report says that the body showed abrasions and cuts consistent with being beaten with fists and with a club or bat. But the police never recovered a weapon."

"Axel will claim Andy threw it overboard with Nate's body."

"Pure speculation."

"Right. But juries often buy prosecutorial speculation. As you know."

"Still, we have Kyle as a witness."

Sean's shrug annoyed her, but she didn't react.

"Tavoularis concludes that Nate was dead when he went into the water," Sean said. "That conclusion does not help an accident defense."

"Which is the defense that you think we should use."

"It's the only one we have," Sean insisted. "And it fits the facts. Andy was in a blackout; he ran the boat into something, and the impact threw Nate overboard. Andy was too drunk to realize what he'd done until he got back home, and by then it was too late to save Nate. So he made up the crazy story about pre-wedding jitters and leaving Nate on the boat alone. It all fits, especially now that we know about his drinking problem and about what happened in New York."

"It fits except for Tavoularis' conclusion that Nate didn't drown. If he'd accidentally been thrown off the boat, there'd be evidence of drowning."

"And I'm not convinced that Tavoularis is right. His report states that bloody froth was present in Nate's airway. That's evidence of drowning. I'm sure we can find an expert who'll testify to that based on this report."

"But what if Andy is telling the truth when he says that when he left the boat, Nate was alive?" Charlotte frowned.

"That can only be true if the navigation data shows that the boat went out again after Andy went back to the party."

"Your friend Axel will have to turn that over in discovery," Charlotte said.

"I wouldn't call him my friend, but he did offer to let us surrender Andy voluntarily."

"I think we should accept his offer."

"So who's going to call our client and the parents and break the bad news?"

"I will."

* * *

Thirty minutes later, Charlotte sat in the waiting room on the fortieth floor of The Owens Tower, at the end of Broadway, with a view of San Diego and San Diego Bay that rivaled her view from the offices of Goldstein, Miller at the Emerald Shapery Center. She'd sat in silence for a few minutes after Sean had left her office, wondering if she'd been wise to take on the responsibility of dealing directly with Lucas and Ella. Charlotte had been able to see even in the brief meeting with Hugh, Andy, and his parents, that Ella still harbored animosity toward her. Shouldn't more than thirty years have been enough to quell Ella's resentment? After all, in the end, Ella had gotten her prize: Lucas had broken off his engagement to Charlotte, dazzled by the life of wealth that Ella had dangled under his nose. And that disappointment had led Charlotte to Matt. And eventually to the torment of wondering why he had died in another woman's bed.

The difficult people that came with this case made her wish that she hadn't been forced to accept it. Once again, she remembered Matt's warning that there were downsides to being part of Goldstein, Miller. Not only did she have a hostile co-counsel, she had an irresponsible client backed by a pair of arrogant parents, one of whom harbored a ridiculous grudge toward her. But she was a parent, herself. Although Ian and Hayden had never put a foot wrong in any major way, she could empathize with what Ella and Lucas were facing—the possible loss of their only child. However, walking into Ella's deep freeze of resentment didn't seem like a good idea. Lucas should be the first to hear that his son was in life-threatening trouble. Above all, she felt that professionalism dictated delivery of news like this in person. So she picked up her phone and informed Lucas' secretary that she would be there within thirty minutes.

Now, as she waited in his reception area, she had to admit that her former fiancé's success was impressive. He'd parleyed his marriage into the Lawrence's wealth, which had been built on financial management, into a real estate empire. *How like Lucas to fly his own flag. And yet Andy had said, "He follows my mother's opinion, regardless."*

The door to the inner sanctum swung open, and Lucas appeared. His expressive eyes said he was glad to see her. Charlotte remembered the mixture of love, regret, and ambition in them the day he'd ended their engagement because Ella Lawrence wanted him.

His face, although weathered, was still round and boyish, like his son's. His hair, although flecked with gray, was full and still mostly dark. His Air Force colonel father had impressed upon him the value of staying in shape. Their love of running had been the beginning of their relationship in high school. Her father had been their track coach. She knew he was fifty-nine because he was a year her senior. But he could pass for ten years younger, she thought. He was wearing dark pants and a white shirt without a tie. His face was drawn and worried.

He knows I've come with bad news.

She followed him down a maze of corridors to an office that occupied the entire corner of the building. He motioned for her to sit on one of three sofas in the corner set up as a living room. He sat down on the one across from her.

"Coffee?"

"No, thank you. I just finished mine at the office."

He filled his own mug and took a sip before he asked, "I gather you've come about Andy. And it's bad news."

"I'm afraid so. The District Attorney is charging him with first-degree murder."

He looked as if he'd received an actual blow. He stared out the window at San Diego Bay shining in the midmorning sun. Charlotte watched him as he processed his disappointment.

Finally, his eyes met hers, dark and full of pain. He said, "Can you get him off?"

The question was so blunt that it startled her. "I have no idea. Sean and I have been over the autopsy report. The coroner thinks Andy beat Nate to death on the boat and then dumped his body into the water."

Lucas shook his head. "That doesn't make any sense. All the boys have always been close, but Andy and Nate were the closest. He loved Nate."

"But what about Nate's involvement with Andy's ex-girlfriend?"

"Andy was more upset about the end of that relationship

than I've ever seen him. I will admit that."

"And he'd been drinking a lot that night," Charlotte reminded him. "Sean and I just finished talking to Kyle Jamison. He told us about Andy's drunk driving accident."

Lucas sighed and sipped some coffee. He seemed to be considering what to say.

"Ella and I were hoping no one would bring that up."

"He has a conviction in New York, doesn't he?"

"Yes. Reckless driving."

"Not driving under the influence?"

"We made a deal with the prosecutor that involved sending Andy to rehab to avoid that."

"Well, it will come up. The District Attorney who's prosecuting Andy will find it in the criminal conviction database."

Lucas looked disappointed. "I suppose I knew that, but I hoped maybe there was a way it wouldn't be found. What does it do to his chances?"

"Of acquittal? It certainly doesn't help."

"I don't want him to go to prison," Lucas said. "Couldn't we cut a deal to put him back in rehab the way we did before?"

"Not this time."

Lucas sighed again and looked out at the bay. With his eyes still far away, he said as if partly to himself, "He's got a good heart, but he's not very grown up."

Charlotte thought of Ian and Hayden who were two years younger than Andy and attorneys with clients of their own. Sadly, Lucas seemed to be right. "Has he ever had a job besides the one he told us about at Wentworth Investment?"

"Not really. He spent some summers in high school and

college working here or at Ella's place working as an intern." Lucas' eyes came back to hers, and he gave her a rueful smile. "Since Gavin, Kyle, and Nate became lawyers, Andy's been obsessed with being one, too. He just doesn't have the smarts to pass the bar."

"Aren't you being rather hard on him? Are you sure it's a matter of intelligence? The California bar exam is one of the toughest in the nation."

"I wish that were the problem. But Andy's never been much of a scholar. We tried everything. Tutors, attention-deficit medications, psychologists. I am afraid the truth is my son is fundamentally lazy in addition to being not very bright. What happens now that he's been charged?"

"Sean has worked out a deal with Axel Saldana, the Senior Assistant D.A. who's going to prosecute Andy, to allow him to surrender voluntarily at four this afternoon. Sean and I will go with him. There'll likely be press. We'll deal with that."

"Ella and I should go, too. As a show of support."

"If you'd like."

"When will we get to hear the evidence they think they have against him?"

"At the preliminary hearing. He has a right to one within ten days after he enters his not guilty plea."

"Ella and I will bring him to your office at three o'clock if that's a good time."

"It's fine. Thank you for making my job and Sean's easier." She started to get up, but Lucas put out his hand.

"Wait! I wanted to thank you for coming in person to tell me the bad news. I'm grateful that you were willing to take on

Andy's case after…well, everything. I'm sorry about your husband. Hugh told me."

"Matt and I had a very happy marriage." *Or did we?*

"I guess you could see yesterday how my decisions have turned out. "

"You wanted an empire. You created one." *You won't get any sympathy from me.*

"How are your parents? Your dad was such an inspiring teacher. I thought you'd go on with your plan to be a track coach, too."

"You asked me to return your ring because I was going to be a teacher, and I'd always be poor."

"Ouch!"

Charlotte shrugged. "I should be grateful to you. I'm not a track coach, and I'm not poor."

"Well, I apologize for that. I was younger than Andy then. Just not quite as self-centered and reckless. And please convey my apology to your parents."

"My father passed away three years ago. My mother is still living in their house in Allied Gardens. One of the reasons Matt and I accepted Hugh's offer to join Goldstein, Miller was to be closer to her. I'm afraid I didn't come to catch up on the past, Lucas."

"No, of course not." His tone said he knew he deserved her reprimand. "I'm sorry for bringing it up. I just wanted to apologize and clear the air."

"Consider it cleared."

* * *

"I didn't kill Nate," Andy said that afternoon just after three o'clock. He was sitting in one of the two chairs in front of Charlotte's desk. Sean had the other. His parents were in the reception area with Hugh. "I told you that the last time I was here."

"I understand," Charlotte said, "but you're being charged."

"My mother told me." Charlotte could see the anger in his dark eyes. His jaw was set stubbornly.

"Reporters will be waiting at the jail to take your picture," she cautioned. "I know you're upset, but try not to show that to the press."

He remained silent and sullen.

"There'll be a bail hearing on Thursday," Sean said. "Your parents obviously can afford to get you out, so you won't be in jail long."

Andy shrugged and said nothing.

"We'll be leaving soon," Charlotte warned him, "and we won't have another chance for a private meeting for a few days at least. You know what you tell us is always confidential. Kyle said you had a lot to drink that night. And your father told us that Tina was very special to you. Sean and I have heard a lot of stories, and we'd understand if you were drunk and lost it when you found out about Nate and Tina."

Andy shot her a look of pure venom. "Except I didn't 'lose it,' and I wasn't drunk when I was on the boat with Nate, and I didn't know he'd been seeing Tina."

Charlotte studied him carefully. "You're sure."

"Of course I'm sure." Andy bit off each word.

"When we start looking at the evidence, we're not going to

81

find anything that contradicts what you've just told us?" Sean asked carefully.

"No, you're not. Nate and I came back early from the club. He drove the boat. We had a beer or two after we tied up at the Cays. And he was very much alive when I went to open up for the rest of the party. That's the whole story. There's nothing more."

"All right, then." Charlotte gave him her warmest, most charming and reassuring smile. But it had the same effect on him as it did on her co-counsel. Andy still looked sullen and angry.

CHAPTER TEN

Thursday, June 28, 2018, Department 10, Courtroom of the Honorable Marshall S. Carter, San Diego County Courthouse, 330 West Broadway

"I'm sorry, Mrs. Estes, did I understand you to say that your client refuses to surrender his passport?" Judge Marshall S. Carter's kind blue eyes studied Charlotte as she stood at the podium to make Andy's bail request. Andy had been arraigned and had pled not guilty. They had reached the bail portion of the hearing, the portion that Sean had refused to handle because Ella's position was so unreasonable.

Charlotte felt as if she were sweating drops of blood. She could feel Ella Lawrence's cold brown eyes staring holes through her back as she argued, illogically, that Andy wasn't a flight risk and shouldn't have to surrender his passport. Ella had created an uncomfortable scene at the firm that morning when Charlotte and Sean had tried to explain that the court would require Andy to surrender his passport as a condition of being granted bail.

"Absolutely not!" Ella insisted.

"Then he'll have to stay in custody," Charlotte said.

"Oh, this is ridiculous! Hugh, she's incompetent. My son needs another attorney!"

Lucas frowned. "We should listen to the attorneys," he said. "They're the professionals." Ella shot him a look of pure contempt, and he slumped slightly in his chair. Charlotte wondered what it must have been like for Andy to grow up in the toxic atmosphere of their marriage.

Charlotte gritted her teeth while Hugh explained the bail process, but Ella refused to hand over the passport. So Charlotte had no choice but to make an argument that, frankly, she was ashamed of.

"So let me be sure that I understand your position, Mrs. Estes," Judge Carter said. "You're saying that surrendering your client's passport isn't necessary because there is no possibility that he's a flight risk? Even though his parents, who are responsible for posting bond, could afford to lose his bail money if he absconded?"

"I wouldn't agree that 'afford' is the correct word, Your Honor. I'm very sure that Andy's parents don't want to lose five million dollars."

"Unless he surrenders his passport, he stays in jail."

* * *

That afternoon, Charlotte left her office a little after three, determined to run off a week of tension that had culminated in harsh words from Ella after Judge Carter denied bail for Andy. By four, she was in her running clothes and headed out for a long run through her neighborhood. She wished she didn't have to deal with Ella's hostility, she reflected as she ran. At that moment, she profoundly regretted her decision to go through with the merger after Matt's death, and she wished she was running her usual route through Georgetown, free of everything to do with Lucas and Ella and free of Sean Donovan and his professional rivalry.

But, she reminded herself, she'd had compelling reasons to leave her old life behind, not the least of which had been that mysterious gunshot at the canal. She reassured herself that the Sentra in her new neighborhood had had nothing to do with that. The appearance of the police appeared to have ended the surveillance of her house. Her world was safe and secure now, she concluded, as she turned the corner of the last leg of her run onto her own street, Caminito Azur.

Suddenly, fear gripped her. A black Mercedes was parked in front of the beige stucco, red-roofed, Italian-style villa that for now she called home, and she could see a man standing by the car, waiting. She stopped running and tried to identify him. She was terrified and not thinking clearly. He was about Sean's height. Had he followed her home to talk about the case? But he didn't know where she lived.

She hadn't taken her cell phone with her. Best to run to a neighbor's house and call 9-1-1. She tried to remember which houses were always occupied in daylight hours. But she didn't have much time because the man was walking toward her.

Just as she was about to turn and run, she realized it was Lucas.

"I hope you don't mind," he called as he approached.

Relief followed by annoyance flooded through her. "Actually, I do." She spoke more sharply than she'd intended.

"I needed a break from work, and I left the office early. How did you find my house?"

At least he has the decency to look ashamed.

"I convinced your secretary you wouldn't mind since we are old friends."

Ah, yes. You charmed my twenty-something assistant. Made her think there was something in it for her. The rich, unhappily married middle-aged male. I'm going to have to have a very stern talk with her on Monday morning.

"This is now a professional relationship, Lucas."

"I'm sorry." He looked hurt. "It's just hard to think of you as a complete stranger. I felt like part of your family once. Your father—"

"You hurt my father and my mother and me. But that was a long time ago. We all went our separate ways. I've made it clear to you that I'm Andy's attorney because Hugh asked me to represent him. That decision has nothing to do with the past. You know these things. You shouldn't have had to come here on a Friday afternoon to hear them from me again."

"I see. Of course, I'm sorry." He sounded sincere. He was wearing a black Ralph Lauren tracksuit. In his middle-aged face, deeply lined and now furrowed in disappointment, she could see the ghost of the boy she'd wanted to spend her life with.

He turned and opened the driver's door of the Mercedes and prepared to get in, his shoulders hunched in defeat.

But he's an important client of the firm, and he could lose his son. I lost Matt. I know how loss feels. And I suppose Hugh would be unhappy if I didn't give him a few minutes.

She relented. "Since you're here. We can talk, but not long.

I have plans for dinner tonight." *That's a lie, but he'll never know.*

"Thank you." She saw relief and genuine gratitude in his eyes.

He followed her through the front door and down the hallway to the kitchen. She opened the refrigerator and took out a bottle of water, her drink of choice after a run. "Want one?"

"Thanks."

She handed him the water and then picked up a small towel from the laundry room to dab at the sweat on her neck and face. She left the towel draped across her shoulders as she led the way to the sunroom that opened off the kitchen. She liked this room, furnished in white wicker sofas and chairs with bright red-and-green tropical print cushions and tubs of potted palms in strategic corners. The floor-length windows overlooked the turquoise pool, and the impeccably green backyard was accented with red bougainvillea vines along the boundary fences. She'd had a small desk put in one corner so that she could work here whenever she wanted to bask in the sun. She gestured for him to take a seat on the sofa. She took the chair opposite.

He sat down on the edge of the cushion, as if acknowledging his uncertain welcome. "I wanted to apologize for Ella," he began.

Charlotte shrugged. "I understand she's upset."

"It's more than that. She always has to be in control."

"Well, her control is going to leave Andy in jail indefinitely."

"Can you try for bail again? I've brought his passport." Lucas reached into the pocket of his jacket and took out the dark blue book and handed it to Charlotte, who eyed him skeptically.

"Did Ella agree to turn it over?"

"No, but I want Andy out of jail."

"We can bring it up again with Judge Carter if Andy is bound over for trial at the prelim."

"And he will be, won't he?" Lucas looked afraid of her answer.

"I'm afraid so."

He shook his head. "If only rehab had helped."

"Kyle told Sean and me that he stopped drinking when he was with Tina."

"That's right. She was good for him. It's the only time I've ever seen him with any sense of purpose or direction. But it turns out that her real interest was Nate."

"You'll have to tell Ella that you gave me Andy's passport, so she won't make a scene in court."

Lucas gave her the ghost of a smile. "There'll be hell to pay."

Charlotte started to let that go, but she couldn't resist observing, "I don't understand, Lucas. You're head of a multimillion-dollar real estate empire. Doesn't that give you the right to make decisions, too? Especially about your son?"

His gaze shifted from Charlotte's face to the pool and the backyard. He still looked troubled, but he remained silent. Instead of answering her question, he turned to the irrelevant, apparently for comfort. "This is a lovely place."

"Yes, it is. My lease runs out in December. Maybe I'll decide to buy it."

"It's not yours?"

"Not yet. I tried to put as many personal decisions on hold as I could after—" Her voice broke, and she was annoyed that she'd shown any emotion in front of him.

His eyes focused on her face again, this time soft and sympathetic. For a moment she saw the boy he'd been before he met Ella, but she brushed the thought aside.

He said, "If you need any help finding a place, I'll personally provide it."

"Thanks. Hugh has someone at the firm who does relocations for us."

"Of course." He looked disappointed.

There was that annoying hint again that he wanted their relationship to be something more. Now she was sorry that she'd relented and agreed to talk to him. She stood up to signal it was time for him to leave. "Thank you for bringing Andy's passport. I have to get ready for dinner now."

He stood, too, but didn't head for the door. "Just one more minute. I need to answer your question about why Ella's in charge."

"That's not really necessary."

"I think it is. Since you're representing Andy, you should know the truth about his parents." He paused for a moment. What he was about to confess was obviously painful. "When Ella and I were first married and I started my real estate business, neither she nor her father would lend me a dime. I had to go to the banks, hat in hand like everyone else, to get working capital. In our personal life, she put me on an allowance. It was humiliating.

"Then my business became profitable. For a lot of years, I was the high earner. She hated me for that, but I had a say in everything. But then, in 2008 real estate took a downturn, as you probably know. I've been working ever since to bring the business back. But Ella's now in the driver's seat financially. And she never lets me forget it. Just like when we were first married."

"I see." *I'm sorry that I opened the door to personal confessions. Better to change the subject.*

"Does Ella really think she can get Andy out of the country?"

"Yes. She has a lot of international connections."

"That would be the stupidest of all possible moves. He'd be found and extradited. And being hauled back after running would foreclose any meaningful defense. Sean and I would never be able to convince a jury that he killed Nate accidentally."

"Well, you have his passport now, so that's not a risk."

He turned toward the hallway, and Charlotte was relieved that he was going at last.

When they reached the front door, he opened it but then turned to her and said, "Would you ever consider having dinner with me? Catch up on old times? Clear the air?"

"There's nothing to catch up on," Charlotte told him. "And we cleared the air at the meeting in your office when I told you Andy was going to be charged."

"But it all feels so awkward," he protested. "I've missed you, Charlie."

Charlotte stiffened. "I'm sorry, Lucas. That was my father's nickname for me. No one uses that now."

"I apologize."

"I'm an attorney, Lucas, not a therapist. Whatever is troubling you, I can't help."

"Look, the long weekend is coming up for the Fourth of July. Couldn't we meet for dinner just once? There's so much more I'd like to tell you."

"I'm going to D.C. tomorrow to visit my children. I'll be away most of next week."

"Children?"

"I have two. They're attorneys in our Washington office."

Lucas gave her a rueful smile. "And my only child can't even pass the bar."

CHAPTER ELEVEN

Wednesday night, July 4, 2018, San Diego County Jail

Jail reminded Andy of the pricey rehab clinic that his parents had sent him to three years ago. Rules governed every waking minute and every bodily function. Jail guards, like orderlies, watched him constantly. The food was lousy. And, of course, there was nothing to drink. And he wished there was.

This was his eighth day in jail. He didn't know what he would do if he had to go to prison. County jail was miserable, but everything he'd heard about state prison certified it as hell on earth. He'd much rather die than go there.

A sudden boom told him that the fireworks over San Diego Bay had started. He was supposed to be in a penthouse suite at the Bellagio in Vegas right now. And Nate was supposed to be alive, and his father was supposed to be luxuriating in the abundance of female gorgeousness that he had hired for the long weekend.

Andy shook his head as he sat on his bunk, thinking about his father's excitement over his plans for Nate's bachelor party. Andy didn't share his father's enthusiasm for getting laid. Since he was in middle school, he had been aware that his father was constantly on the hunt for bed partners, and this obsession drove his mother to overeat and to indulge in affairs of her own. For months, Lucas had talked about looking forward to the opportunities for sex with women his son's age at Nate's party. Andy wasn't glad that his friend was dead, but he took a perverse satisfaction in knowing that his father was bitterly disappointed that the orgy in Vegas was off.

Nate. Andy stared up at the tiny window and wished he could see the moon. Or even a star. The night was so dark in jail. He bet it was even darker in state prison.

He struggled to remember his last conversation with Nate. He remembered tying up the boat and getting back on board to find Nate lounging on the seats in the rear, his long legs stretched out, a beer in his hand.

Andy had gotten his own Corona out of the refrigerator and taken the seat opposite his friend.

"Thanks for coming back with me, man," Nate said and took a swig of his beer.

"I was ready to go, too," Andy agreed.

"I wish I had the guts to tell my father how I really feel."

"About Kinsley?"

"About everything."

"Why don't you just do it, then?"

"For the same reason you drink instead of telling your parents what you really feel and want."

"Ouch! I thought this was about you and your pre-wedding nerves."

"Ask a stupid question, get a stupid answer. You know as well as I do what my father would do if I told him I hate law and I don't want to marry Kinsley. The same thing your parents are going to do if you don't pass the bar this time around."

"You mean, throw me out on the street?"

"Precisely."

Andy sipped his beer and shrugged. "I don't know. Maybe life as a homeless person would be easier than having to deal with my parents. Maybe my subconscious knows that I don't want to see my parents anymore."

"Why didn't you just stay in New York?"

"I couldn't after the accident. They were going to charge me with manslaughter if I didn't cooperate with my parents' plan to send me to that clinic in Arizona."

"That's an idea," Nate said. "I could get drunker than I already am and smash my car tonight, and then my parents would have to send me to rehab. And I couldn't marry Kinsley."

"What about 'stand by your man'?"

"Trust me, she'd give the ring back in a heartbeat if I went AWOL and crashed my car."

"But you might hurt someone else. Like I did."

Nate considered this for a moment. Then he said, "I'd make sure I hit a tree or a pole or an inanimate something."

"Marrying Kinsley can't be as bad as that," Andy said. "She's tall and blond and just plain hot. The sex has got to be great."

"But I'm not in love with her," Nate said. "That's the problem."

"So? You'll probably fall in love with her later. I mean, she's gorgeous."

"She's an entitled brat, Andy. Everyone knows. How do I fall in love with that?"

"You never know. You'll have the money to give her everything she wants. It will be all right."

"No, it won't be all right."

Andy remembered how unhappy Nate looked as he said it. Andy watched him polish off his beer and reach into the nearby mini fridge for another.

He opened the new beer, took a long drink, and stared at the bottle for a minute as if trying to make up his mind about something. Then his blue eyes met Andy's, and Andy could see the conflict in them. He said, "It won't be all right because there's someone else. Someone I really do love. Someone who's nothing like Kinsley."

Andy put his nearly empty beer down and sat in silence as he tried to absorb the consequences of Nate's defection from the girl who represented the dynastic choice of both her father and his. Finally, he said, "I still think you have to tell not only your father but Kinsley as well. It's not fair to marry her if you're in love with someone else."

"And you speak from experience," Nate retorted sarcastically.

"I do. My parents."

"That's bullshit."

"No, it isn't. My father was in love with someone else, but he married my mother for her money. And they've both been miserable."

"And you know this how?"

"God, Nate! I've lived with them for thirty-two years. They've been having the same fights and hurling the same insults at each other since I was old enough to understand and remember. The only reason I'm even alive is so that my mother could strengthen her hold over my father. She didn't want kids. They interfered with her career. And after me, she refused to have any more. You should tell Kinsley that there's someone else."

"But that's the thing. I tried."

"And?"

"And she just brushed it off. She said that neither of us really has a choice, and she wants to make her parents happy. I was good-looking and good in bed, and I had money. That was enough for her."

"What about the one you're in love with. What did she say?"

"She said it was impossible, and she wouldn't see me anymore. But I don't want to accept that, Andy. I've never been able to bring myself to fight my parents for what I really wanted. This time, I want to fight."

Andy's phone had buzzed at that moment, and he'd looked down and read the text message. He said, "Gavin and Kyle are at the front door with a bunch of people from The Naked Lady. They brought the party back to the house. I've got to go let them in."

Nate smiled and saluted him with his beer. "I'm going to hang out here for a while."

Andy heard the fireworks finale sputter and fizzle out. *God, what I'd give for enough alcohol to make me pass out right now,* he thought as he lay down on his bunk and wished he could go to sleep. But his mind kept racing. Had Nate said anything else to him as he'd walked away? Something about Tina? He struggled to remember. But it wouldn't come into focus, like so many of his alcohol-blurred memories.

CHAPTER TWELVE

Monday, July 9, 2018, Department 10, Courtroom of the Honorable Marshall S. Carter, San Diego County Courthouse, 330 West Broadway

"Good morning." Judge Marshall S. Carter's kind brown eyes surveyed his courtroom where everyone had obeyed the bailiff's direction to stand. "This is the preliminary hearing for Andrew Lawrence Owens, Case No. SD421389."

Sean glanced quickly at Andy, who was wearing his best suit and standing between himself and Charlotte at the defense table. He was so nervous that the top of his shirt collar was damp with perspiration. His parents were sitting in the first row of public seats behind the defense table. "Try not to look so scared," he whispered to Andy. He himself was nervous but determined not to show it. If he could stop the D.A.'s attempt to bind Andy over on the murder charge, it would save his career at the firm.

"If the attorneys would please state their names for the record? We'll start with the prosecution."

"Axel Saldana, Senior District Attorney."

He's started working out, Sean thought. *He used to be twenty pounds heavier. Must have a new girlfriend. Maybe his second chair? No, wait. She's wearing a wedding ring. I didn't realize Axel was close to my height. He always seemed under six feet. I guess that's because he was on the heavy side.*

"Kaitlyn Green, Deputy District Attorney." *I have a weakness for blondes in red suits. Thank God, she's married. No more girlfriends.*

"Thank you," Judge Carter gave the two prosecutors an especially warm smile. *I don't like this,* Sean thought. He had already warned Charlotte about Judge Carter. Good-looking, late forties, salt-and-pepper hair, a former Senior Deputy District Attorney and unabashedly pro-prosecution. Sean was taking the lead today because he had experience with him.

That had been her idea. "You're going to have better rapport with this judge because you've been in front of him before."

He hadn't expected her to offer him first chair for the preliminary hearing. Her offer was probably a ploy, so she could grab the lead at trial.

"And for the defense?" Judge Carter turned his portly body slightly in the direction of the defense table and gazed down at Andy, who still looked terrified. Sean saw him squirm under the judge's scrutiny. *Not a good idea, kid. He's the one who can decide you didn't do it.*

"Sean Donovan, Goldstein, Miller, for the defendant."

"Charlotte Estes, Goldstein, Miller, for the defendant."

"Thank you," Judge Carter said, "are there any preliminary matters to dispose of before Mr. Saldana calls his first witness?"

"No, Your Honor," Axel said.

"No, Your Honor," Sean agreed.

"Then proceed, Mr. Saldana."

"The prosecution calls Dr. Gus Tavoularis."

Sean watched the familiar figure of "Dr. Gus" amble toward the witness stand. He was in his sixties, slightly bent, with a full head of gray hair, and horn-rimmed glasses with thick lenses. Everyone in San Diego County knew Dr. Gus. He'd been in the coroner's office for almost twenty years. Axel quickly established Dr. Gus' credentials and then launched into case-specific questions.

"Now, Dr. Tavoularis, did you conduct the autopsy of Nathan McClellan?

"I did."

"On what date?"

"Monday, June 11."

"And are these the diagrams you prepared during that autopsy?"

"Yes."

"Can you describe your findings depicted in these drawings, People's Exhibits 1, 2, and 3?"

"I can. There was evidence that he was involved in a fistfight prior to his death. I found abrasions on his hands, particularly on his knuckles."

"And what else did you find?" Axel prompted.

"I found abrasions on both shins and his knees, suggesting he'd been dragged along a hard surface."

"A hard surface such as the deck of a boat?"

"That's right."

"And on this diagram, you've marked an area on the back of his head." Axel handed Dr. Gus a piece of paper. "This is People's Exhibit 4."

"There are several lacerations, eight to ten inches long, in this area. He was beaten with a hard object."

"And what was the cause of death?"

"The cause of death was blunt force trauma."

"But what about drowning? How do you know that wasn't the cause of death?"

"Because I found a buildup of fluid in the tissue that lines the lungs."

"And why are those findings significant?"

"Because they support a finding that he was no longer breathing when his body went into the water."

"So your conclusion is that Nate was beaten to death on the boat and his body thrown overboard?"

"That is correct."

"No further questions," Axel said and sat down.

"Any questions from the defense?" Judge Carter looked at Sean, who stood up.

"Yes, Your Honor."

Sean took Axel's place at the podium.

"Dr. Tavoularis," he began, "does your autopsy report state a time of death?"

"I—no. I couldn't make that determination."

"So you can't say if Nate McClellan died before or after one a.m. on the night of June 9, correct?"

"Correct."

"Now you testified that you found abrasions on his body. And you testified that these were inflicted before he died, correct?"

"Correct."

"If you were unable to determine the time of Nate's death, how were you able to determine when these abrasions were inflicted?"

"There were indications that they were sustained before death."

"And those indications were?"

"I–I would have to review my report. But at this moment, I recall discoloration that indicated blood pooling in those areas, meaning that he was alive when he received those injuries."

"But what about the effects of being in the water? Doesn't your report state that the body was found around eight forty-five on Sunday, June 10?"

"That's right."

"So Nate's body was in the water for up to eight hours, wasn't it?"

"Yes."

"And skin changes when it is submerged for several hours, does it not?"

"So-called 'washerwoman skin.' Correct."

"Meaning the skin shrivels and begins to decompose?"

"Yes."

"So how would you be able to determine if blood pooled in these areas, based upon the appearance of the skin?"

"I–I would have to review my report. But that was my conclusion. Those injuries were sustained before Nate McClellan died."

Bullshit, Sean thought.

"Now, Dr. Tavoularis, how can you be sure that the blows to the back of Nate's head were inflicted by a weapon? Couldn't the injury have happened as the body drifted in the ocean currents?"

"I don't think that's true."

"Why?"

"Because he had defensive injuries on his hands."

"What kind of defensive injuries?"

"Abrasions, scrapes."

"But aren't these equally consistent with offensive injuries or with the body coming into contact with debris in the water?"

"I… Well… I guess…maybe."

"And you don't know if Nate started a fight with someone or if he reacted to an attack, do you?"

"I—"

"How about the so-called murder weapon? Have you recovered the instrument that you say killed Nate McClellan?"

"Uh…I haven't personally recovered it."

"What about the officers investigating Nate's death? Have they recovered it?"

"I, uh, don't believe so."

"Moving to another area of your report, Dr. Tavoularis, you have concluded that Nate McClellan was not alive when he went into the water, yet your report states that you found bloody froth in his airway. Doesn't that finding show that he was alive and breathing when he went into the water? Couldn't he have accidentally fallen overboard when the boat hit something?"

"Could he? Possibly. Did he? I don't think so."

"But isn't bloody froth in the airway a sign that drowning was the cause of death?"

"Not always. The pleural fluid accumulation was a more significant finding."

"Aren't the injuries that you've attributed to a blunt force attack often caused by trauma to a body when it has been submerged for period of time?"

"I—would have to say occasionally."

"One final question, Dr. Tavoularis. Even assuming that you can tell the difference between blunt force trauma injuries and postmortem injuries, you have no evidence that my client, Andy Owens, was the person who attacked Nate McClellan, do you?"

"I personally don't but—"

"That will be all, Dr. Tavoularis. Thank you."

And Sean sat down. *They don't have a case.*

"Please call your next witness," Judge Carter said.

"The prosecution calls Officer Jason Farrell of the Coronado Police Department."

Officer Farrell in full uniform took the oath and sat down on the witness stand.

"Good morning, Officer. Are you familiar with the defendant?" Axel began.

"I am. I was one of the officers who responded to the Owens Villa on the morning of June 10."

"And did you have an opportunity to examine the defendant for cuts and abrasions that morning?"

"I did."

Axel clicked on his computer and pictures of Andy's hands appeared on the overhead screen. "Do you recognize these photos, Officer Farrell?"

"I do. I took them to document the injuries that I noted on the defendant's hands and forearms. Here we see the backs of his hands."

"Anything that is particularly significant about these injuries?"

"There are abrasions on his knuckles that, in my experience, are consistent with being in a fistfight."

Axel clicked again. "And what do we see here?"

"That's a bruise on his right palm."

"And is that also consistent with a fistfight?"

"Yes."

"And do you know if the defendant is right-handed?"

"Yes. I watched him sign his booking forms."

Axel clicked again. "And what is this?"

"This is the other side of his hands. Again, there are signs of healing cuts and abrasions consistent with using fists."

"No further questions." Axel smiled at Judge Carter and sat down.

Sean got up and made his way to the podium without waiting to be asked.

"Officer Farrell, did you interview any witnesses who had seen Andy Owens in a fistfight with Nate McClellan?"

"I—well, no."

"So your only evidence of the origin of these injuries is your own speculation?"

"I—well—"

"Thank you. No more questions." Sean watched with satisfaction as the officer slunk off the witness stand.

Officer Brooks, also in uniform, took Officer Farrell's place.

After establishing Brooks' training and credentials, Axel asked, "Did you take possession of Nate McClellan's cell phone on the morning of June 10, 2018?"

"I did not, personally. My trainee officer, Rick Perkins, did.

But I was present when it was found."

"And where did the two of you find it?"

"On the deck of the yacht that belongs to Lucas Owens. It was in the rear of the boat."

"And did you discover anything of significance upon your initial examination of the victim's phone?"

"My trainee officer noticed a text message on the lock screen."

Axel clicked on his computer and Tina's text message appeared on the overhead screen.

"Is this the message you observed?"

"Yes."

"Would you read it for the record?"

"*Family is everything and yours would never understand. And I don't think you want to destroy your relationship with Andy. But I will meet you for breakfast in the morning to talk. Love, Tina.*"

"And were you able to identify the 'Tina' in that message?"

"Yes. She's Andy Owens' former girlfriend."

"What time did the victim's phone receive this message?"

"At ten twenty-nine p.m. on June 9."

"Thank you, Officer Brooks."

Judge Carter looked at Sean. "Questions from the defense?"

"Thank you, Your Honor." Sean rose and went to the podium that Axel had just vacated.

"Good morning, Officer Brooks. Did you take a statement from Andy Owens on the morning of June 10?"

"I did."

"And what did Andy tell you about the last time he saw Nate McClellan?"

"He said that he left him on the yacht just after one a.m."

"So Andy told you Nate was very much alive when he left?"

"That's correct."

"Now as far as this text message goes, do you have any evidence that Andy Owens was aware of this message from Tina Hernandez before your trainee officer showed it to him on the morning of June 10?"

"I personally do not."

"Thank you, Officer. No more questions." And Sean sat down.

Undeterred by Sean's small victory, Axel rose and announced, "The prosecution calls Juan Aguilar to the stand."

Who is that? He looks like a pimp, Sean thought, as a thin, forty-something man in a shiny gray suit, white shirt, and skinny black tie took the oath and was seated on the witness stand. He had a full head of black hair that was slicked back into a ponytail.

"Please state your name for the record," Axel began the litany.

"Juan Carlos Aguilar."

"And how are you employed, Mr. Aguilar?"

"I own a nightclub in Imperial Beach."

"And would that club be called The Naked Lady?"

"Yes."

"And did I ask you to produce a certain business record for me from the night of June 9-10 involving the defendant, Andy Owens?"

"Yes."

Axel clicked on his computer and a video appeared on the overhead screen.

"And did I also ask you to bring some of the surveillance video from the club to the hearing today?"

"Yes."

Axel clicked and the surveillance tape came to life. Sean watched as Andy and Nate paused by the back door before exiting the club. The two of them appeared to be bent over something in Nate's hand.

The surveillance tape lasted less than a minute. Axel turned off his laptop and turned back to Mr. Aguilar.

"Was that the tape you furnished me?"

"Yes."

"And the timestamp on the tape says ten thirty-five p.m. Is that accurate?"

"Yes."

"Thank you, Mr. Aguilar. No further questions."

"Mr. Donovan?" Judge Carter looked at Sean.

Sean was on his feet quickly. "Mr. Aguilar, can you identify the object in Mr. McClellan's hand?"

"No."

"Could it be the tab for the evening's round of drinks?"

"It could be."

"Did you bring that business record to court today?"

"No. I was only asked to bring the surveillance tape."

"No further questions." *He hasn't said anything that hurts Andy.*

"Anything further from the prosecution, Mr. Saldana?" Judge Carter asked.

"No, Your Honor. That concludes the prosecution's case."

"For the defense, Mr. Donovan?"

"Yes, Your Honor. We call Kyle Jamison."

He had fought bitterly with Charlotte over calling Kyle. They didn't have to present witnesses, and Sean thought Axel's case was so weak without any evidence of an actual murder weapon that putting on Kyle's questionable explanation for the injuries to Andy's hands would hurt them. He'd persuaded her to let the whole Kyle-sparring routine go. But she'd summoned him to court anyway for backup. And her reaction to the surveillance tape had been a big note scrawled on her legal pad that said, "We have to put Kyle on." And he'd scrawled back, "You do it then."

Now, as he watched Kyle recite the story of sparring with Andy at the Warrick, Thompson gym under Charlotte's questioning, he knew this evidence was going to obscure the weaknesses in Axel's case. They should have saved Kyle for trial. His story was worthless on a prosecution judge like Carter. And Sean didn't believe it either.

Axel had only one question for Kyle on cross-examination. "And did you see injuries on Andy Owens' hands after your sparring match?"

"No."

"Thank you," Judge Carter said after Axel sat down. "If there's nothing further from the defense, I'll hear arguments of counsel. You can begin, Mr. Saldana."

"It's pretty simple," Axel said. "Nate McClellan left the party at the Imperial Beach strip club with the defendant at 10:30. The defendant has admitted as much in his police statement. The surveillance tape shows them together and shows the moment when the defendant learned that his ex-girlfriend was involved with Nate. The two proceeded to the defendant's father's yacht, where the defendant beat Nate to death and then disposed of the body."

"Mr. Donovan?" Judge Carter turned to Sean.

"Thank you, Your Honor. The state has offered nothing but speculation. There's no murder weapon, and there's no evidence that Andy Owens attacked his friend. The state hasn't produced any evidence that the injuries found on the body of Nate McClellan were sustained before he died, and we know the body was in a powerful surf for several hours before it was found. The state's murder charge is built on pure speculation."

As Sean sat down, he noticed that Judge Carter had put on his reading glasses and was studying his notes. *That's good. At least he's considering our evidence.*

But after a minute or two, the judge looked up and announced, "The testimony of the coroner and the condition of the defendant's hands is sufficient to demonstrate that a crime has been committed. And the text message is evidence of motive. The defendant is held to answer."

"Your Honor, there is one more thing."

"Yes, Mrs. Estes?"

"My client is prepared to surrender his passport."

Judge Carter motioned for the bailiff to take Andy's passport from Charlotte.

"Very well. Bail is set at five million dollars. Anything else?"

"No, Your Honor."

"Then these proceedings are adjourned."

LIAR, LIAR

CHAPTER THIRTEEN

"I don't know how many times I have to tell you. I didn't kill Nate."

Charlotte studied her client's face carefully. His dark eyes were puffy and tired at eleven o'clock in the morning. He'd thrown a dark-blue blazer over his T-shirt and jeans for their meeting. He fiddled nervously with his coffee mug. Lucas and Ella had taken him back to their house in Rancho Santa Fe to live. No more partying at the Cays villa while he was out on bail.

She and Sean had decided to meet with him in Charlotte's office instead of in the formal conference room. They were hoping that the more relaxed atmosphere created by sitting on the small sofas with the expansive view of the bay and the city below would persuade him to open up and tell them the truth.

"Nate and I left the club a little after ten thirty. He drove the boat back to the Cays. We drank some beer. We talked. I went to open the door for the others. He never mentioned Tina or a text message. That's the whole story. I can't tell you a different one because there isn't a different one." His hostile tone said he was out of patience with them.

"What about your hands?" Sean asked.

"Just what Kyle said. I hurt them at the gym. My fault for not doing a decent job taping them."

"And you're sure you never took the boat to the side of the island where Nate's body was found?"

"Absolutely positive."

"Do you have any idea when your ex-girlfriend began to see Nate?" Charlotte asked.

"None."

"Could she have been dating him while the two of you were together?"

"I don't see how she would have had time for that. But anything is possible."

"But you had no idea they were involved?" Sean asked.

"Not until the cop showed me Nate's phone."

"And you're sure you weren't driving the boat back from the club that night?" Charlotte asked.

"Positive."

"What did Nate hit on the way back from the club?"

"Nothing."

"Then when was the bow damaged?" Sean asked.

"I have no idea."

* * *

"We didn't get anywhere with him," Sean said after they had turned Andy over to the custody of his father. Charlotte had felt uncomfortable as Lucas' gaze lingered on her while the four of them stood by the elevators, waiting for a car to take Lucas and

Andy away from the lofty offices of Goldstein, Miller. Fortunately, if Sean noticed he'd said nothing about it.

"He's still scared to tell us the truth," Charlotte said as they reentered her office and sat down on the couches. Sean seemed in a friendlier mood than usual. Maybe being stumped by their client made him more collegial, but it didn't help in figuring out a defense.

"If we can't get a plea deal out of Axel, we'll be going to trial with a client who's a liar and who looks like a privileged idiot."

"That sounds so harsh," Charlotte cautioned.

"It's meant to. I detest clients who are obvious liars, and juries do, too."

"Maybe he'll open up to us later," Charlotte suggested.

"I hope he does before it's too late for us to help him. And speaking of helping him, Russell Blake has finished a preliminary analysis of the boat's navigation data. He invited us to his office tomorrow to see what he's come up with so far."

Charlotte smiled. "Let's hope we get some good news."

* * *

Tuesday, July 17, 2018, Offices of Blake & Associates Forensics, San Diego

The next morning, Charlotte accepted Sean's offer to drive them to Russell Blake's office in a nondescript, squat concrete and glass office building in Kearney Mesa, one of San Diego's least attractive commercial neighborhoods. Blake & Associates was doing well enough to have half of the top floor of the eight-story building. The receptionist showed them to a comfortable conference room set up with a large screen on one wall and a laptop, open and ready to go.

"Russ will be with you in a few minutes," the receptionist said. "The coffee in the pot is freshly brewed. The croissants are plain and chocolate."

Without being asked, Sean proceeded to pour coffee for them both. "Cream, sugar?"

"Cream." She smiled.

Sean handed her the coffee and offered her a croissant from the tray. But she shook her head.

"Okay. But I have a weakness for the chocolate ones." He smiled as he helped himself.

He sounds nearly human. I hope this lasts.

The conference room door swung open, and a lanky man with a boyish face appeared. His curriculum vitae said that Russell Blake was thirty-five, an MIT-trained software engineer who had worked for Microsoft before setting up his own digital forensics consulting firm. His only concession to the formalness of their meeting was to throw a well-tailored navy sport coat over his jeans and black T-shirt.

"Good morning, I'm Russ." He crossed the room to the side of the conference table where Sean had taken the seat next to Charlotte.

"Charlotte Estes." She stood and smiled and returned his handshake.

"Sean Donovan. I was the one who spoke with you last week about setting up this meeting." Sean, too, stood to shake hands.

"Well, let's sit down, and we'll talk about the work we've done and what we've found so far." Russ smiled as he took the seat at the end of the table. "First, as you know, we are still waiting for cell phone records and for access to the computer hard drives that the police took from the Owens villa. I've received copies, but I want to examine the originals."

He had dark hair and friendly light-blue eyes. *He'd make a great defense witness,* Charlotte reflected. Aloud she said, "Do you have any results to show us yet?"

"Well, as far as the surveillance videos, my news is disappointing. I've discovered that the yacht club security cameras weren't directed at *The Escape.* So they're worthless for our purposes. I haven't had time to look at the private tapes from the Owens' residence and from the cameras that they had on and around the boat. But the one item that my team has processed is very interesting."

Russ picked up a remote control that dimmed the lights and then brought up a map on the overhead screen that showed the Coronado Cays, Imperial Beach, the California Yacht Marina, and San Diego Bay. A tiny red dot glowed at the Coronado Cays Yacht Club.

"Now this is an animation of data from the navigation equipment on *The Escape.* I should mention that someone tried to erase this information."

"Are you sure?" Charlotte asked.

"Positive."

"So that would have been Andy," Sean said, "because he was the last one to operate the boat."

Russ shrugged. "Could have been. But it could have been his father. Lucas Owens' phone has an app that accesses this data. At any rate, this is what we know so far."

He clicked and the red dot came to life. "At eight p.m. *The Escape* traveled across the bay to the California Yacht Marina. It's a short trip, fifteen, twenty minutes max. The yacht stayed at the marina until ten forty-five. Then it left the marina, but it didn't head straight back to the Cays, its point of origin."

Charlotte frowned. "Are you sure? Andy told us that he went straight back to the Cays."

Russ shook his head. "The navigation data doesn't back that up. *The Escape* traveled north in San Diego Bay, heading toward the Coronado Bridge. It cruised around the bay for about a half hour. You can see how it circled around on the animation."

The red dot traveled north, then turned south before it reached the bridge and looped around several times.

Russ went on. "Then it headed north again toward the bridge, this time at close to the boat's top speed, around forty miles an hour. It passed under the bridge and turned left at the end of Coronado Island and headed into the Pacific. It slowed and stayed along the coast of the island, stopping again when it was almost even with the North Island Naval Air Station. Then it turned and headed back around the island, back into San Diego Bay. When it reached the Coronado Bridge on the return trip, it paused briefly. That was at twelve fifteen. Then it took off going pretty fast again. It reached the Cays at twelve thirty-two a.m."

"Can you tell when the bow was damaged?" Sean asked.

"Logically it would show up as a pause in the boat's movement. Since there's a pause near the bridge on that return trip, I'm guessing it happened there. Probably hit a buoy that marks the channel under the bridge."

"But what about the body being found on the other side of the island? If Nate fell in at this point, his body would have washed up on the Barrio Logan side of the bay."

"Unless the tide carried it around to the other side," Russ said. "Tides aren't my field of expertise."

"So if the yacht reached the Cays at twelve thirty-two, it had been there for about a half hour when Gavin and Kyle showed up," Charlotte said.

"According to the navigation log," Russ agreed.

"So Andy was either sitting on the boat alone during that half hour, or he was talking to Nate," Sean said.

Charlotte stared at the red dot for a minute. Then she asked, "Is there any possibility that what Andy told his father about going straight back to the Cays from the marina in Chula Vista is true?"

"None."

"And the prosecution has this evidence?" Sean asked.

"They were the ones who sent us the data."

"So it looks like Andy killed Nate during that pause by the bridge and then went to the ocean side to dispose of the body," Charlotte said.

"That's what I'm thinking," Russ agreed. "He should have gone into deeper water if he didn't want the body to be recovered."

"I think we knew he was lying," Charlotte said, "but we were still hoping that he wasn't."

"Sorry to have to give you bad news right off the bat," Russ said, "We'll keep looking. Maybe something better will turn up."

"That doesn't seem likely," Charlotte said. "This navigation log is pretty damning evidence of guilt."

* * *

"I've got more bad news," Sean said that afternoon at five thirty as he stood at the door of Charlotte's office. "Do you want to hear it here or go downstairs to the Westin bar for a drink?"

"Is it really that bad?" Charlotte asked.

"Right on par with what we already know: our client is a shameless liar."

"Come in and sit down, then," Charlotte invited. "Let's get it over with."

"I'd have preferred to do this over a double scotch. You run instead of drink, right?" he asked as he settled himself in the chair in front of her desk.

"Not always. How much worse could this get?"

"Try Andy's fingerprints, and only Andy's fingerprints, were on the boat's wheel and navigation equipment."

"Oh, God. Not even a single print from Nate?"

Sean shook his head. "Nary a one."

Charlotte stared down at the miniature world on the street below.

"You're very quiet," he observed.

"I'm processing."

"Processing what?"

"My disappointment. You know what it's like at the beginning of a case when you can still allow yourself to think your client might not be guilty? And then you find out he's just as guilty as the DA says he is."

"Well, I'm in deep shit because my continuing to be a partner in this firm hangs on winning this case. And we are not going to win."

"Surely Hugh wouldn't remove you from the partnership."

"Indeed, he has said as much in so many words."

"But that's not fair. We don't make the facts. We just have to deal with whatever the client creates."

"And Mr. Andy Owens has created a sure loser."

Charlotte studied the tiny world below for a few more seconds. Then she said, "I'm not too happy about a bad outcome for my first major case at the firm."

Sean grinned, but it was the friendly grin of two people who shared a burden, not his old disdainful look. "We'll be famous for losing the Lawrence/Owens account."

"Don't remind me."

"I think we should confront Andy with the fingerprint report."

"And the navigation data," Charlotte added. "Some clients will never admit that they've lied. Looks like he's going to be one of those."

"In the meantime, let's go get that drink," Sean said. "And try to think of some incredibly clever way to pull this one out of the fire."

CHAPTER FOURTEEN

Thursday, July 19, 2018, Offices of Goldstein, Miller, Mahoney, and Estes, Emerald Shapery Center

"Why did you lie to us?" Charlotte demanded at two p.m. on Thursday afternoon. "Didn't you realize the yacht's navigation system was going to give you away?"

Andy, who was again sitting on one of the sofas in Charlotte's office, looked apprehensive. He'd lost a little weight in jail, and he looked thinner in his navy suit and maroon tie.

"I thought I'd turned the tracking device off," he said.

"Turned it off?" Sean frowned.

"You can turn it off. Didn't your expert tell you that?"

"No. He said you tried to erase it," Charlotte said.

"No, I didn't. That's ridiculous. I never tried to erase it because I thought I'd turned it off."

"Well, it was on," Charlotte insisted. "You lied about going straight back to the Cays from Imperial Beach."

Andy sighed. "Okay, okay. I lied. After we left the club, Nate wanted to ride around the bay."

"So you looped around several times," Sean prompted.

"Okay, I admit it, we did."

"Why did you do that?"

"Because Nate was upset. He wanted time to calm down before we went back to the Cays."

"Are you sure you weren't looking for a place to whack him over the head and throw him overboard because he'd stolen your girlfriend?" Sean asked.

Andy frowned and banged his fist on the table. "I didn't kill Nate," he said through clenched teeth.

"Who was at the wheel when you had the accident?" Charlotte asked mildly.

"We didn't have an accident."

"But the boat returned to the Cays damaged," Charlotte reminded him.

"That happened after I got off the boat."

"Andy, it would be better if you stopped lying to us," Sean said. "We know Nate wasn't driving the boat that night. His fingerprints were not found on any of the operational equipment."

Andy's face went from surprise to resignation. "All right," he agreed. "I admit I lied about that, too."

"Why?" Charlotte asked.

"Because I'm not supposed to touch my father's boat or my father's car unless he's present. But I can handle *The Escape*. I lied to keep him off my back. And despite what he thinks, I didn't wreck it."

"So who did?" Sean demanded.

"Whoever killed Nate."

"But Andy," Charlotte said, "there's no navigation data that shows the boat left the dock again after twelve thirty."

He shrugged. "So whoever went out again with Nate after I

left knew how to turn off the tracking. And killed him."

Charlotte shook her head. "Sorry, but that story doesn't hold up." She opened her laptop and pulled up the navigation animation that Russell Blake had shown them. "Watch this. You'll see not only the loops you made in the bay, but you'll also see *The Escape* go around to the Pacific side of Coronado Island. The boat stopped long enough to offload a body not far from where Nate was found."

"I don't have to see it," Andy said. "I admit we went around to the Pacific side. But I didn't kill Nate. He was on board with me when we decided to go back to the Cays, and he was on board when I left to open the house for the others."

Exasperated, Charlotte closed her computer. "Andy, Sean and I can't help you if you keep on lying to us."

"I'm not lying. At least, not now. I admit I was trying to keep my father from finding out what Nate and I actually did that night."

"Why did you go over to the Pacific side of Coronado?"

Andy shrugged again. "Tired of circles in the bay. Nate wanted to see the Navy base at night. We cooked up this fantasy about leaving our parents behind and changing our names and joining the Navy and learning to fly helicopters. But we couldn't see much of the base from that side of the island, and I was getting nervous about being on the ocean after dark in my father's beloved boat—in case anything did happen—so we went back."

"So it's just a coincidence that you were in the exact spot at midnight where the currents would move anything tossed overboard toward the beach where Nate's body was found?" Charlotte asked.

"I realize how it sounds, but yes, it is."

"Let's try this another way," Sean suggested. "Let's play the navigation animation again."

"You can play it a hundred times," Andy said sullenly, "and my story isn't going to change. I wasn't lying when I said I didn't kill Nate."

Charlotte opened her laptop and hit play again. When the tiny red dot paused by the bridge, Sean reached over and stopped the video.

"What about here?" he asked. "Isn't this the spot where you had the collision? And Nate fell off and you were too drunk to realize what happened, so you kept on going? And then when you got back and Nate was gone, you made up that wedding jitters story as a cover-up? Don't be afraid to tell us the truth, Andy. We're on your side. We can argue that Nate's death was an accident. This tape will back that up. Don't you see? You likely won't do any prison time if you just tell the truth."

Through gritted teeth Andy said, "I am telling the truth. I wasn't blacked out when I was on the boat, and I didn't wreck it. And I didn't kill Nate! When are the two of you going to start listening to me?"

* * *

"That went well," Sean said after they had ushered Andy to the elevators and resumed their seats on the couches in Charlotte's office.

"Sarcasm isn't going to help."

Sean smiled. "You're right. For a kid who comes on with the IQ and mental age of a middle schooler, he's a tough nut to crack.

If only he'd agreed that he blacked out and wrecked the boat."

"Do you think the prosecution's expert is going to see what Russell saw: someone tried to erase the navigation log and failed?"

"Of course. And they're going to point their fingers straight at Andy, who probably did it. They'll request an 'Attempt to Hide or Destroy Evidence' Instruction, suggesting he knew he was guilty."

"Then that means we have to find out if Lucas erased it."

"True," Sean agreed. "Are you up for confronting him this afternoon?"

"We might as well."

* * *

"One Owens down and one to go," Sean said as they waited for Lucas in Charlotte's office at four thirty that afternoon. "And this one is late."

"Punctuality has never been one of Lucas' virtues."

"You knew him from before, right?"

"In college."

"How about truth? Is he any good at the truth?"

She shook her head. "Andy is the classic illustration of the apple doesn't fall far from the tree."

The door to her office stirred, and her secretary opened it to admit Lucas. Judging from the smiles on their faces, he was still trying to woo her favor with his middle-aged rich-male charm. Clearly some additional administrative discipline would be in order on Monday morning.

"Apologies for being late. You said you needed to see me, Charlie."

"Charlotte."

"Sorry, Charlotte. Old habits die hard." Lucas looked up at her and smiled as he arranged his suit jacket on the back of his chair before he sat down.

"Well, let's keep that one buried." She gave him a tight smile and a look that said she knew the use of her old nickname had been deliberate.

"Charlotte and I met with our digital forensics expert on Tuesday," Sean began.

"Any good news?" Lucas smiled expansively as he reached for the coffee pot in the center of the table and poured himself a cup.

"Quite the opposite," Charlotte informed him. "Andy's been lying to us from the beginning. And maybe you, too."

"Me?"

Charlotte opened her laptop and pulled up the animation. "Our expert compiled this from the yacht's navigation equipment. You can see that Andy and Nate had quite a cruise around the bay and then went into the Pacific before heading back to the Cays."

"Damn!" Lucas stared at the screen as he took a sip of coffee. His smile was gone.

"Russell says someone tried to erase this data," Charlotte said. "Someone with a navigation app on his phone. Someone like you."

"Me?"

"Russell says your phone has the app," Sean said.

"I, uh, yes, but... I didn't try to erase anything."

"Well, Andy said he didn't erase it because he thought he'd turned the tracking feature off."

"I don't see what difference it makes who tried to delete it." He sounded defensive.

"It makes a big difference," Charlotte informed him. "If you tried to erase it, you can be charged as an accessory after the fact. If the DA can show it was Andy, he can get a jury instruction that says Andy knew he was guilty because he tried to destroy evidence."

Lucas put his coffee mug on the table and contemplated it for a few seconds.

"It would be better for you to tell us the truth," Charlotte advised. "Lying hampers our ability to defend Andy."

"And he's done nothing but lie to us so far," Sean added.

Lucas' gaze shifted from his cup to the city below where Lilliputian figures ambled along the sidewalks and miniature cars moved along the tiny streets. He was lost in thought for several more seconds before he spoke without looking at either Charlotte or Sean. "Ella erased it."

"And how do I know if this is the truth?" Charlotte asked.

His sad dark eyes met hers. "You don't know unless you believe me."

"But you told us that Ella was in London on the Sunday Nate went missing," Charlotte reminded him.

"She was. She called not long after I got to the villa. When I told her what was going on, she tried to erase the navigation log and the surveillance tapes. I told her not to, but she never listens. Apparently, she didn't succeed with the log. What about the tapes? Were they erased?"

"As far as the navigation log goes, she didn't succeed," Sean said. "Russell doesn't know about the surveillance tapes. He's still looking at them."

"Of course." Lucas picked up his coffee mug and took a sip. "Maybe I should be sorry she didn't succeed in erasing the log."

"There's more bad news," Charlotte said.

"Couldn't it wait?" Lucas asked. "I'm not sure how much more I can deal with right now."

"I'm afraid we have to tell you," Sean said. "The fingerprint evidence has come back. Nate's prints weren't on any of the boat's controls. Just Andy's."

"I'm not surprised. I never believed Nate was driving that night." Suddenly there were tears in Lucas' eyes. Charlotte was shocked by his show of genuine emotion. Sean picked up the tissue box on the shelf behind him and put it in front of Lucas, who took a tissue and wiped his eyes.

"I'm sorry," he said. "I loved Nate like a son, too. I haven't wanted to admit that Andy is responsible for his death. What happened in New York was hard, but at least we didn't know the young man. This is so much worse. I feel so responsible, but I don't know what else his mother and I could have done.

"Andy has never wanted to listen to us. The more we tried to make him understand that we were trying to protect him, the more he did exactly what we told him not to. Drinking and driving *The Escape* without permission is just one in a long line of examples. He's always flouted us at every turn."

"What else has he done?" Sean asked.

"Did he tell you he flunked out of Berkeley in his freshman year?"

"He did." Sean nodded. "Partying and drinking. Not going to class."

"It cost Ella and I a building to get him a degree at San Diego

State. An addition to the computer lab at the business school."

"But he went to law school after that," Charlotte said.

"Ella and I wanted him to come into one of our businesses. Andy was drinking heavily by the time he graduated from State. We didn't think he could make it through law school. And we told him that. But he wouldn't listen. Gavin and Kyle had gone to law school, and Andy was determined to keep up with them."

"But he did graduate," Charlotte repeated.

"Yes, but he flunked the first time he took the bar in 2011. And then he tried again in 2012 and flunked again. That's when Ella decided to send him to New York to work for a friend of hers."

"Andy said his name was Sam Wentworth," Charlotte prompted.

"Right. He and Ella know each other from financial circles. We're all close friends. Sam knew the trouble we'd always had with Andy. He was drinking a lot after the two bar exam attempts. He was unhappy because he wasn't able to keep up with Gavin and Kyle and Nate. They'd long ago passed the bar and gone to work."

"Andy said you sent him to a rehab clinic in Arizona after the accident," Charlotte said. "What did he do after the clinic?"

"Ella and I brought him back to Rancho Santa Fe. He wanted to live in the guesthouse where he'd live during college and law school, but we couldn't risk allowing him to be alone. So we made him live in the main house with us. That lasted less than a month. He moved into the villa at the Cays and announced that he was going to study for the bar yet again. Neither Ella nor I wanted him there. I use the villa to entertain high-end clients. Lots of parties and drinking and so forth. It wasn't a good place for Andy."

"So what did you do?" Sean asked.

"Well, short of getting him arrested for trespass, Ella and I couldn't budge him out of the villa. It was about that time he met Tina, and even though Ella didn't like her, I have to admit she was a good influence on Andy. He quit drinking and partying, and he got serious about studying for the bar."

"But Tina broke up with him," Charlotte said.

"And Andy fell apart again."

Lucas' voice broke. The tears were back in his eyes. He tried to speak, but emotion choked him. Finally, he managed to say, "Look, please, save my boy."

CHAPTER FIFTEEN

Thursday, July 19, 2018, Offices of Goldstein, Miller, Mahoney, and Estes, Emerald Shapery Center

"I need a drink," Sean said to Charlotte as the elevator doors closed behind Lucas, who had departed, still teary-eyed. "What about you?"

"I need a run."

"It's five thirty. What if we go over to my place at The Metropolitan and order dinner from the hotel's room service and talk about a way not to lose this case."

But Charlotte shook her head. "I need a run. It's the only thing that's going to clear my head and make me feel better. I wasn't expecting that kind of emotion from him."

"Nor was I. I guess you know about Lucas' reputation in town."

"No, I don't."

"He's a tough, take-no-prisoners negotiator who drives a hard, hard bargain. And he can't keep his pants zipped. Although, I guess the wife's looks and attitude have something to do with that."

Charlotte shrugged. "No idea."

"What was he like in college?"

"It's been too long for me to remember," she lied. "Tell you what, come over to my house at seven. That'll give me time for a run. I brought Matt's wine cellar with me when I came west. He loved good wine. He left some great bottles. Or you can come earlier if you want to run with me. My father always said running together is the foundation of teamwork."

"And your father was a track coach?"

"Right."

"I could never keep up with you. It's been too long."

"Well, come at seven then. I'll open a bottle of Matt's best cabernet and throw some steaks on the grill. And we'll eat and talk about our options. That is, if we have any options."

* * *

Charlotte chose the short route through her neighborhood to make sure she had time for a quick shower before dinner. She wasn't surprised to hear Sean's take on Lucas' reputation. It was obvious that his moves with her twenty-something secretary were second nature to him. But his tears this afternoon had been real. Maybe something of the Lucas she had known had survived. But she doubted it.

Sean arrived promptly at seven, wearing jeans and a red T-shirt with the Bulldog Brewery logo. She ushered him into the kitchen and handed him a bottle of Napa Cabernet and a corkscrew and smiled.

"Here. Teamwork. This is your job. The glasses are on the shelf in the cabinet to the left of the sink."

He returned her smile and proceeded to open the wine while

she lit the gas grill on the stove and took salad and steak out of the fridge.

"I take it you've now forgiven me for the merger," Charlotte said as she put the meat on the flame. The fat sizzled, and the smell of grilling beef filled the kitchen.

"What makes you think that?" He grinned.

"You haven't said anything snarky about it lately."

"I've been too busy worrying about the two of us going down together on the Lawrence/Owens ship."

He poured the wine and handed her a glass. "And I've decided I like you because you eat something besides lettuce and green smoothies, and you like a good glass of wine. Now and again. I was beginning to worry that you weren't human."

Charlotte laughed and then paused.

"What's wrong?" he asked.

"Nothing. I just realized that I don't laugh often, anymore."

"Because of your husband?"

"Yes. I used to laugh all the time." She sipped her wine thoughtfully and studied the progress of their steaks. After a few seconds she said, "I suppose it's time to begin laughing again. Matt would say that."

"I looked forward to meeting him when the merger was first suggested."

"But not me?" Her smile and her tone said she was teasing.

"Actually, I wanted to meet both of you, and then send you right back to D.C."

Charlotte laughed. "At least I always know where I stand with you."

"Hey, if you can figure out a way to pull this Owens case out of the fire, I will gladly write down every negative word I said about the merger and eat them one by one. In your presence."

Charlotte threw back her head and laughed. "Deal. And I'll pick one of Matt's best bottles to go with it."

When their simple meal was ready, she led the way to the dining room, and they settled in the dark mahogany Queen Anne chairs that had looked so right in the Georgetown house but seemed far too formal in this new one overlooking the sea.

"So you know about me," she began. "And Matt and Hayden and Ian."

"I know you and Matt. I don't know about Hayden and Ian."

"My daughter and my son. Twins. They're thirty, and they elected to stay in D.C. in the Goldstein, Miller office there."

"That must be hard for you."

"I miss them," Charlotte smiled. "But their clients are all in D.C. And they grew up there. I understand why they didn't want to come here and start over."

"Do you mind if I mention noticing that Lucas has a thing for you?"

"You mean that bit by the elevator when he came to get Andy the first time we met with him after the prelim?"

"Yeah. He was like a junior high kid in the presence of his greatest crush."

Charlotte smiled. "You do have a colorful way with words."

"So what's the real story? Not just the 'I-knew-him-in college' kiss-off version."

"Lucas and I go back to high school. My father was our track coach. We went on to college together. We were engaged in our senior year. And then Ella and her millions came along."

"So you enjoy letting him know now that you have zero regrets about how things turned out?"

"Enjoy isn't the right word. Lucas is trying to step over the professional line, and that makes me uncomfortable. Matt was a far better husband and father, and I was lucky Ella and her red Mercedes turned his head."

Sean refilled their glasses. "I'm glad you suggested this. I feel as if I'm finally getting to know you. So Ella had a red Mercedes in college?"

"Yeah, one of those little sports car things with only two seats. I'd see Lucas driving her around in it all over Westwood."

"UCLA?"

"Right. Track scholarship."

"I should have known." He smiled.

"Okay, now it's my turn," Charlotte said. "Your firm bio says Princeton undergrad, Harvard law. You clerked for Judge Francis on the Ninth Circuit. Why'd you leave San Francisco for San Diego?"

"Tired of the rain, fog, and cold. I grew up here in University City. My father was a career federal prosecutor. I got a job as an Assistant U.S. Attorney, following in his footsteps."

"Why'd you leave the U.S. Attorney's Office?"

Sean smiled ruefully. "Greedy. The lure of Big Law Money was too much for me. I lost my wife because of it."

"I'm sorry."

"I am too. She left six years ago, when I made partner. I thought I was on top of the world when Hugh told me I'd been voted in, and then a month later I lost the person I loved most in the world."

"What was she like?"

"Adorable. She was blond, petite, funny, and a non-lawyer and therefore utterly captivating. Most of all, she could make me laugh, something I've often had trouble doing."

"You do seem to focus mostly on the serious side of things," Charlotte agreed.

"Sherrie said that. Many times. The last time was when she left me for a younger man who had time for her."

"Children?"

"No. That was another reason she left. I was always at work. You know the grind of making partner at the firm."

"I suppose I do, but Matt and I had a different kind of grind. Building your own firm is like building any business. Seven days a week. Not many holidays or vacations."

"But you were lucky because your marriage stayed together."

"Yes, I was."

"And you had your twins."

"We raised them in the office. Their toys were scattered in our conference room. Sometimes we held them on our laps when we talked to clients if the babysitters had to leave early."

"Another advantage of running your own shop. Why did you give it up? I assume Hugh made you an offer that you couldn't refuse?"

"I wouldn't say that. Matt and I refused it at first. But my father passed away three years ago, and my mother is living alone now in their house in Allied Gardens. And Matt and I were tired of practicing law and running the business. We wanted to see what letting someone else handle the business side was like."

"And what it's like?"

"I'm not sure. And that's not fair. It's my turn to ask the questions. Come on. Let's clear the table and go sit in the sunroom where it's more comfortable and talk about the Owens problem."

* * *

"This is my favorite room in the house," Charlotte said. Sean was seated on the sofa where Lucas had sat. She took the same chair opposite. Sean had poured the last of the wine into their glasses.

"I can see why. You must have a nice view of the ocean and La Jolla Shores in daylight."

"That's right, I do. So how are we going to defend Andy Owens?"

"I think we can get the charges dropped if we can keep out that text message," Sean said. "The trainee officer needed a warrant to access that message. And he didn't have one."

"I was thinking that, too. We should move to suppress the text as the product of an illegal search."

"And that will keep out not only the text but the navigation log, too, because the police wrote their request for the warrant citing that illegally obtained text as the basis for their search."

"You're smiling. That's a good sign that we've got a good idea," Charlotte said.

"I'm sorry I was a jerk in the beginning. You're right about teamwork."

"My father was right about teamwork."

"So we're in agreement then? We'll bring a motion to suppress the search of Andy's phone and the boat and the house?"

"If we win, they have no motive for murder because they can't use that text," Charlotte said.

"And if we win, we'll save my career at the firm."

"And the Lawrence/Owens account."

* * *

After Sean left around ten thirty, Charlotte made herself a cup of tea and sat down in the sunroom to read for a bit before going to bed. But the wine had made her sleepy and she drifted off as she sat on the couch.

A noise woke her. It sounded like someone climbing over the fence in the backyard. At first, she thought she'd just had a bad dream. But then she heard it again, as if a second person had landed on the ground inside her fenced-in yard. She quickly switched off the lights and crouched by the open drapes, trying to see who or what was outside.

Her heart was pounding so hard that she felt as if her whole body was shaking. She willed herself to breathe deeply as she gazed at the dark yard though the glass doors. She wished she'd remembered to turn on the outside lights as she usually did at night. But she'd been absorbed in cooking dinner, and she'd forgotten.

Suddenly, she saw them. Two dark hooded shapes creeping out of the cover of the bougainvillea vines, around the corner of the pool, and toward her house. Her cell phone was upstairs in her bedroom. She was afraid the intruders would see her if she crossed the room toward the hall. She held her breath, praying that she'd remembered to arm the security system after Sean left.

The two figures crept toward the back door and then

vanished from sight. A few seconds later the alarm triggered a banshee wail throughout the house. Charlotte could see the lights in the upstairs of the house behind her go on. Thank God, the neighbors had heard it. There'd be more than one 9-1-1 call.

Less than a minute later, Charlotte saw the two dark forms run toward the back fence and climb over. Gone! Thank God! She rushed upstairs, grabbed her phone, and punched in 9-1-1.

"Two units are on the way," the dispatcher said.

CHAPTER SIXTEEN

Friday, July 20, 2018, 4280 Caminito Azur, La Jolla, California

The previous occupant of the house had been an art collector, the detective told Charlotte at two a.m. The two black-and-whites had arrived first and secured the backyard. Then the officers had summoned the CSI Unit to look for physical evidence of the intruders. A half hour later, the detective had arrived in jeans, a T-shirt, and a leather jacket. By then, Charlotte had been so sleepy that all she had wanted was to go to bed. Instead, she had listened as the detective reassured her that everything was going to be okay. At that point, fatigue replaced anxiety.

But she woke at ten on Friday morning, still frightened. She lay still for a long time, watching the bars of sunlight that the blinds created on the ceiling. She reflected on her need to believe the earnest young detective who had insisted that the cars watching the house and the intruders in the garden were after the former owner's Picassos and Monets, not her. She had wanted to believe his reassurances so much that she hadn't told him about the footsteps in the Metro or the car in the crosswalk or the shots at the canal.

Now, in the reassuring sunlight, she told herself that the detective had been right. The intruders had been burglars and not very accomplished ones at that since they hadn't anticipated the house's security system.

She got up and made a strong cup of coffee. In the daylight, she could see the damage to the bougainvillea plants. The reality of the broken plants and trampled flowers momentarily brought back the terror of seeing those two black figures creeping toward the house.

She thought of going outside to inspect the damage close up, but she went upstairs instead and called the gardener to ask him to come by that afternoon. Then she called her office to say that she would be late. A thought had occurred to her about the suppression motion that she and Sean had been so enthusiastic about last night. They'd assumed that excluding the phone search would eliminate the evidence of Tina Hernandez's involvement with Nate. But what if Tina herself could say that Andy knew about her relationship with Nate even before that phone message? What if their brilliant solution was not so brilliant after all?

Charlotte put on what she hoped was a professional, yet friendly light blue dress and matching jacket. Then she got into her silver Mercedes and headed north on Torrey Pines Road to the Salk Institute, hoping Tina Hernandez would be willing to talk to her.

* * *

Friday, July 20, 2018, The Salk Institute, La Jolla

At eleven forty-five, Charlotte arrived at the Salk Institute, a perfectly symmetrical canyon of what appeared to be raw concrete pillars perched on a bluff overlooking the Pacific. The "pillars" were actually four stories of office buildings and laboratories that rose majestically above a travertine plaza bisected by a trough cut into the stone. The trough, which was filled with water, was called "the channel of life," and as Charlotte approached from the street side of the Salk campus, it appeared to vanish over the edge of the bluff into the Pacific.

The route to the South East Building where the visitor desk was housed was through the plaza, down the corridor formed by the North and South Buildings. These two wings of the institute had been constructed to look like modern Stonehenge giants, and Charlotte felt small and insignificant as she passed by. The architectural message of the enormous buildings said that the lifesaving research the Institute conducted here was much larger than any single human being.

At the visitor's desk, a pleasant twenty-something blonde in a light green dress welcomed her with a smile.

"I'm Charlotte Estes," she explained as she presented her business card. "I'm an attorney with Goldstein, Miller. I'm here on behalf of a client to see Tina Hernandez."

"So Dr. Hernandez is expecting you?" The blonde continued to smile pleasantly.

"Yes." Charlotte lied, sensing that any equivocation would cause the blonde to send her away empty-handed.

The receptionist punched a button and a security guard, who

looked intimidating in his uniform, appeared.

"Steve, Ms. Estes is an attorney and is here to see Dr. Hernandez. Would you escort her to the genetics lab?"

Charlotte's heart began to race as she followed the broad-shouldered guard back outside and across the plaza once more.

They walked toward the northwest corner and into the North Building. The Molecular and Cell Biology Lab on the second floor was a maze of hallways lined with shelves of gadgets, beakers, and busy workers. Charlotte's escort paused in front of a glass window where two men and a woman in white lab coats were standing next to a microscope, engaged in earnest discussion.

"If you'll give me your business card, I'll tell Dr. Hernandez that you're here," the guard said.

Even in a white lab coat with her hair wrapped in a tight bun, Tina Hernandez was breathtaking. Her large almond-shaped brown eyes were beautifully complimented by her perfect olive complexion. The jeans and T-shirt that she wore under her lab coat revealed her supple, athletic figure. She had the grace of a dancer, Charlotte noted, as she stretched out her hand to take the card from the security guard's hand. Twelve jurors would take one look at her and believe with all their hearts that a spoiled rich kid could be driven to jealousy and murder over the loss of such a beautiful and obviously talented woman.

She smiled at the guard, but her smile faded when she read the card. She looked up at Charlotte, standing on the other side of the glass. Her dark eyes were curious but hostile. Her gaze shifted back to the security guard as she shook her head and handed Charlotte's card back to him. She turned her back ever so slightly to the window and resumed her discussion with her colleagues. Her message was clear even before the guard rejoined Charlotte in the hall.

"Dr. Hernandez says that she's very busy this morning and doesn't have time to speak with you."

"Would you tell her I'm here to help Andy Owens?" Charlotte hoped Andy's name would change her mind.

The guard looked dubious, but he went back into the lab and spoke to Tina Hernandez once more. This time, she kept her back to Charlotte and shook her head emphatically as the guard conveyed Charlotte's second message. When the guard held out Charlotte's card again, Tina pushed it away.

Charlotte's heart sank. She thanked the guard for trying a second time and asked him to point the way back to the parking lot as they left the North Building. As she drove toward the office, she wondered what had happened between Andy and Tina to engender so much hostility. Andy had described a sudden breakup without any obvious reason. But, as Charlotte knew all too well at this point, Andy was a world-class liar. She and Sean would have to hope that they'd win their suppression motion, and that it would turn out to be the brilliant solution to this case that they desperately needed.

WINNERS AND LOSERS

CHAPTER SEVENTEEN

Tuesday, July 31, 2018, Department 23, Courtroom of the Honorable Regina S. Gibson,
San Diego County Courthouse, 330 West Broadway

Andy tried not to squirm as he sat next to Sean and Charlotte at ten a.m. in Department 23, waiting for Judge Gibson. He wasn't comfortable because he'd lost weight and his clothes didn't fit. His suit pants and coat were too big, and his belt chafed whenever he moved. His attorneys were convinced that this suppression motion would be a knockout blow to the state's case against him. But Andy knew that Charlotte and Sean were bringing this motion because they thought he was guilty. And that made him angry.

He cast a sideways glance at the prosecution's table. Axel Saldana, taut and toned, his dark hair shaved so that he was nearly bald, looked like a tiger licking his lips as he contemplated his prey at the defense table. Beside Axel, his overly serious assistant, Kaitlyn Green, was scribbling on a legal pad. From time to time, she brushed Axel's arm, gave him a grave smile, and forced him to read what she was writing. She didn't look like a lawyer, Andy reflected. She looked like she belonged to the pack of rich girls who were the daughters of his mother's society friends. They put on expensive suits after college and became overly serious about their careers because they felt they had something to prove. His mother loved the ones who worked for her.

No matter how dumb and dishonest you think she is, he reminded himself, *she's passed the bar. And you haven't.*

"All rise."

The door behind the bench stirred, and Judge Gibson swept into the courtroom. She was tall and thin, with short gray hair and wire-rimmed glasses. Her robes billowed as she entered, making her look like a ship in full sail as she crossed the short distance to the bench. Her complexion was weathered as if she'd spent a lot of time outdoors. Andy guessed that the woman who held his fate in her hands had been some sort of serious athlete like Charlotte at some point in her life. Maybe she'd bond with Charlotte because of it.

"Good morning." The judge's severe countenance broke into a warm smile. "This is People versus Andrew Lawrence Owens, Case No. SD421389, and we're here on the defendant's motion to suppress evidence. Would the attorneys state their appearances for the record?"

Andy watched Charlotte and Sean rise and announce that they represented him after Axel and Kaitlyn Green proudly stated their allegiance to "The People." He wondered if the mythical "People" would be more willing to believe that he didn't kill his best friend than their fierce legal representatives. Or even his own parents, who sat behind the defense table in black-and-white outfits, looking as friendly as the couple in American Gothic.

Being the defendant in a murder trial was a lonely proposition he had discovered. Not one single person in this courtroom believed that he was innocent. His assertions that Nate had been very much alive when he left him fell on uniformly deaf ears. Andy felt as if his mouth was open in one long wail of innocence, but no sound was coming out. He had been lonely all his life. But this was a new and more isolating loneliness than anything he had ever known.

"Since this is the defendant's motion, I'll hear from the defense first." Judge Gibson smiled warmly again. She reminded Andy of a schoolteacher welcoming new students to her classroom.

He watched Charlotte rise and take her place behind the podium. Sean's eyes were following her, too. He had a thing for her. Andy had noticed it in their meetings. But Charlotte was oblivious. Andy thought it was because she was solidly focused on her own life and because she was still grieving for her husband.

She looked very trim and professional in her navy suit and white blouse. She smiled at Judge Gibson. "Good morning, Your Honor."

First rule of oral argument, Andy remembered from his Legal Research and Writing Class. *Establish rapport with the judge.*

"The evidence taken in the search of the Owens' premises, including the search of the Owens' boat, must be suppressed," Charlotte began, "because the officers failed to obtain a warrant to search Nate McClellan's phone."

Riley v. California. Andy had read that case when he studied for the bar. Now his freedom depended upon Judge Gibson's willingness to apply its holding to him. Four years ago, the

United States Supreme Court had decided that the police must have a warrant to search a cell phone. Before that, phones were routinely searched without a warrant as part of an arrest.

"The information from the illegal search of the phone was included in the affidavit presented to the magistrate to obtain the warrant," Charlotte continued. "As a result, the approval for the search was obtained in violation of the Fourth Amendment. And all of the evidence found during the search must be suppressed."

The navigation data, Andy thought. *That stupid navigation data that they all think makes me so guilty. And that message from Tina that supposedly means I wanted Nate dead. God, why won't anyone listen to me? I didn't kill him.*

"Thank you, Mrs. Estes," Judge Gibson continued to smile although Andy sensed she was about to come in for the kill shot. "I have read your motion, of course, and I understand your arguments for suppression. But what I would like for you to do is address the subject of your client's standing to bring the motion at all. This wasn't his phone. It belonged to the victim. I don't understand why you think you have any standing to challenge the search of someone else's phone."

Andy winced at the term "victim" and then hoped the judge hadn't noticed. Sean had cautioned him repeatedly about showing emotion in court. But it was hard not to react. The autopsy photos of Nate's bloated, dissected body haunted him day and night. How could they believe he would have done that to Nate?

"Of course, Your Honor," Charlotte continued to smile. "I'd be happy to address the question of standing."

Andy admired her unshakeable poise. *Would I ever have been that good if I'd passed the bar? No, of course not.*

"Nate's cell phone contained messages from my client, both written and oral in the form of voicemail. Andy has a privacy interest in all of that material."

"But what about the message that you're saying was found in violation of the Fourth Amendment? Wasn't that in plain sight on the lock screen of his phone?"

"No, Your Honor. The message from Tina Hernandez was not visible until Officer Perkins pressed the home screen button. And he wasn't entitled to press that button without a valid warrant."

"Hmmm. Interesting," Judge Gibson mused. "Anything else?"

"Not unless there is something else the court wishes me to address."

"No, I understand your position. I'll give you a few minutes for rebuttal after I've heard from Mr. Saldana."

"Thank you, Your Honor." Charlotte resumed her seat next to Sean at the defense table. Andy saw him whisper in her ear, and she smiled.

Andy stomach fluttered as the prosecutor sprang to the podium. He was smooth and sleek and supremely confident. Andy had once interviewed for an internship in the prosecutor's office and had been told "we never lose."

"Good morning, Your Honor," Axel, too, began with his most charming smile. "This wasn't an illegal search. It—"

"I don't understand how it wasn't an illegal search," Judge Gibson frowned. Andy's stomach began to relax. *There's hope after all.*

"I have an iPhone like Nate McClellan's," the judge continued. "When the screen is locked, nothing is visible, including recent messages. The only way to see a recent message is to push the home button. And to do that, as the Supreme Court said in *Riley,* your officers needed a warrant."

"But, Your Honor, Officer Perkins stated in his affidavit that pushing the button was an accident. He was opening the phone case to show it to the defendant and his father, and his finger slipped."

"I haven't read anything from the Supreme Court about an "accident" exception to the Fourth Amendment," Judge Gibson said.

"We're relying on the 'good faith' exception," Axel replied.

"I don't see how your officer could have any 'good faith.' The *Riley* case made it clear that he needed a warrant to view any information on that phone."

Andy's heart began to beat faster. The tide was turning their way. Out of the corner of his eye, he looked at Sean and Charlotte. But their faces were inscrutable.

"Your Honor, we strongly disagree that Officer Perkins was not acting in good faith. But there's a more fundamental problem with the defense motion."

"And that would be?" Judge Gibson raised her eyebrows.

"Standing, Your Honor. As you said to Mrs. Estes, this was not the defendant's phone."

"But what about the defendant's communications on that phone?" Judge Gibson frowned.

"Those weren't viewed until after the police obtained the warrant," Axel insisted. "The text message that was viewed without a warrant didn't come from the defendant."

"But it mentions the defendant," Judge Gibson said. "Doesn't he have a privacy interest because of that?"

"I…I…I don't see how." Axel's confidence was wilting like a flower in too much sunlight.

"Is there anything else, Mr. Saldana?"

"I—No. Just that it was a fully legal search."

"Based on what?"

"The good faith exception."

"I see. Thank you, Mr. Saldana. I'll hear from Mrs. Estes, again, for no more than five minutes."

Charlotte went back to the podium. "Clearly this was an illegal search, Your Honor. If you read the affidavit, it mentions the text message as the basis for probable cause to issue the warrant on pages one, two, and three."

"Is that the only basis for probable cause, Mrs. Estes?"

"Yes, Your Honor."

"I see. Anything else?"

"No, Your Honor." And Charlotte resumed her seat.

They were going to win. Andy's heart beat faster at the prospect of a victory that could end his ordeal. Charlotte and Sean had said that without the navigation evidence and Tina's text, the state had no case against him. Andy tightened every muscle in his body in anticipation of the judge's ruling.

"I'm going to order a short recess," Judge Gibson said, "so that I can retire to chambers and read the affidavit again before I rule."

Upon the "all rise" command, Andy scrambled to his feet with everyone else and watched Judge Gibson billow out of the courtroom.

As soon as the door to the judge's chambers closed, Andy's father leaned toward Charlotte at counsel table and whispered, "Great job." Andy noticed that his father was smiling, but his mother looked annoyed and angry.

"Thank you." Charlotte gave Lucas a tight half-smile that said 'I don't care what you think' and turned her back to him so that she was facing the front of the courtroom.

Ouch! Andy thought. *She really hates him. And my mother really hates her. Even after all these years.*

"It looks good for us," Sean whispered to Andy and Charlotte.

But she shook her head. "Hush. Matt would have said that's like talking about pitching a no-hitter in the top of the ninth."

"She bought our argument on standing, though," Sean insisted.

"Maybe." Charlotte was as taut as wire, Andy noticed. *I don't see why she's so worried. Judge Gibson gave the prosecutor the hard time that he deserved.*

Ten more minutes ticked by on the courtroom clock before the bailiff announced that Judge Gibson was ready to rule. They all stood as Her Honor swept out of chambers and resumed her seat on the bench. She beamed her benign smile at all of them.

"I've had time to read the affidavit again," she said. "And I agree with the defense that Officer Perkins' search of Nate McClellan's cell phone violated the rule of *Riley v. California*. Officer Perkins should have had a warrant to view that text message on Nate's phone."

We've won! Andy struggled not to show the relief that poured through every cell in his body. But next to him, Sean and Charlotte remained impassive. *What's wrong with them? We've won!*

"But although I find a violation of the Fourth Amendment, I don't find the search to be invalid," Judge Gibson continued.

How is that possible? Andy struggled to remember his constitutional law class.

"Relying on the doctrine of severance," Judge Gibson explained, "I find that when the invalid portion of the affidavit—the portion that talks about the text message from Miss Hernandez—is severed from the rest of the warrant, the remainder of the affidavit states probable cause for the search."

"But, Your Honor," Charlotte spoke up. "The remainder of the affidavit just says that Nate McClellan was found dead a couple of hours after he was reported missing."

"But it also says, Mrs. Estes, that Mr. McClellan was last seen alive boarding a boat that was under the control of your client."

"But that's not enough to show probable cause that a crime was committed," Charlotte replied. "Nate's death could have been the result of an accident."

"I disagree, Mrs. Estes. I'm finding that the remaining portion supports probable cause to believe that your client murdered Mr. McClellan. If you disagree, you can take it up with the court of appeal. The proceedings are adjourned."

* * *

Tuesday, July 31, 2018, Offices of Goldstein, Miller, Mahoney, and Estes, Emerald Shapery Center

"She's wrong," Sean said as they sat in Charlotte's office drinking coffee and licking their wounds.

"I know." She sighed.

"I thought she was going to rule for us after your argument."

"Thanks." She smiled and took a sip of coffee.

"Without that message from Tina," Sean said, "what's left of that affidavit is just an invalid general warrant. It says, 'Nate disappeared so we have to search Andy Owens' house, yacht, and cell phone."

Charlotte agreed. "Her Honor is wrong. But we can't do anything about that right now. The appellate lawyer will have to take that up with the court of appeal. We're going to have to figure out a way to defend Andy."

Sean nodded. "I'll call Joe Cerna and see if he'll review the autopsy report for us. I've worked with him before. Let's hope he agrees with me that Nate drowned, so we can go with accident. The kid drove drunk on their joyride, hit something with the boat on the way home, and Nate went overboard."

"Except Andy will deny it."

"We won't put him on the stand."

CHAPTER EIGHTEEN

Tuesday, July 31, 2018, Rancho Santa Fe, California

Andy wished he could say it was good to be home. But it wasn't. His parents had stuffed him into the back of his father's Mercedes just the way they had after rehab and driven him back to the Mansion of Doom. Being more or less locked up in his childhood room was only a reminder of how far he had not come. At least he had hidden several stashes of vodka in his chest of drawers. He hated drinking without ice and proper glasses, but his bathroom tumbler would have to do for now because he needed something to dull the pain of having to listen to his parents quarreling down the hall in the master suite. It was always the same with them. They both shouted, and his mother threw things. She tried to remember to grab the unbreakable knickknacks, but in the heat of her anger, she often smashed china and glassware.

"That woman is incompetent!" Andy heard his mother's outrage clearly through his closed door and theirs. "You heard her in court today. And she lost!"

"That's ridiculous," Lucas shouted back. "She did a brilliant job. The judge was prejudiced against Andy. You could see that in the way she looked at him."

"You're the one who's prejudiced because you're still in love with Charlie Patrick!" His mother's accusation was accompanied by the sound of glass breaking and a door being slammed.

Less than a minute later, there was a knock on Andy's door. He was relieved to find his father, and not his mother, when he opened it.

"I came to see how you're doing," Lucas said.

Andy didn't want company, but he knew he had to let his father in. Lucas immediately eyed the glass on the table by the sofa in the living room portion of Andy's suite.

"That's not water, is it?"

"No, Dad. I don't want to talk right now."

Lucas crossed the room and picked up the glass and went into the adjoining bath and poured it out. Andy sat down on the sofa and waited for him to come back. He had plenty more put away. His life would be easier if he didn't argue about his drinking with his father.

Lucas put the empty glass on the table in front of the sofa and sat down next to Andy. "You've got to lay off," he said.

"I know." Andy shrugged. "It's just hard, right now. I need something. It's only vodka anyway."

"Tell you what, now that you're home, we'll have a few beers together."

"You mean I have to ask permission, and you'll dole them out."

"I mean we'll have some father-son time."

"Isn't it kind of late for that?"

Lucas' face told Andy that his shot had hit the mark. Lucas

was silent for a few seconds. Then he said, "Look, I know I've done a lot of things wrong. And what's happened in many ways is my fault, too."

"I didn't kill Nate, Dad." Andy looked directly at his father, who turned his head. "Don't look away from me!" Andy raised his voice in frustration. "I'm not lying. I didn't kill Nate."

"But you do lie," Lucas said.

"Not all the time."

"But how do I know when you're lying and when you're not?"

"I'm not lying now. Besides, as far as lying goes, it's not as if I didn't learn from the master."

Andy could see his second shot had hit home even harder than his first. Lucas looked down at the empty glass on the table. Finally, he said, "I've never killed anyone and lied about it."

"And neither have I!" Andy shouted. "Why won't anyone listen to me?"

"Because the evidence says you're lying."

"Then you don't have all the evidence!"

"Look, your mother tried to protect you. We thought she'd erased that navigation data."

"Dad, I didn't kill Nate. That was just a joyride around the bay because he was so upset. Do you think I was lying when I called you and said we couldn't find him? Do you think I knew all along he was dead?"

Andy could see that his father was thinking over his response carefully. After a few seconds, he asked, "Do you want my honest answer?"

"I don't need your answer. But you're wrong!" Andy's tears

of grief and rage overflowed. He wiped his eyes with the back of his hands, but his tears kept flowing. He didn't care. Without enough alcohol to dull his emotions, he had no weapon against them.

Lucas moved closer and put his arm around Andy's shoulders. Andy instinctively recoiled from his father's touch, but if Lucas noticed, he didn't react. "Look, son. We'll get through this somehow. Your mother and I have decided that you need something to do. I'm going to put you in the Commercial Real Estate Division. You'll be a Vice President. You'll oversee the new executive office park in Carmel Valley. Construction on the main building is just about complete, and we're looking for tenants. And two other buildings in that complex are going to be completed soon."

"I don't want to work in commercial real estate."

"What do you want to do, then?"

"I want to keep my promise to Tina. I want to be an attorney. I want to protect the people you screw over every day!" Andy spat out the last words through his tears.

Lucas let go of Andy's shoulders and stood up. He looked down at his son, and Andy could feel his father's contempt pouring over him like water. Lucas said patronizingly, "It's time to grow up, son. You're no good at law. You're going to have to settle for what you can do, not what you want to do. It's time for you to start pulling your weight in the family business. Tomorrow morning, I'm taking you down to your new office."

"I won't go."

"Yes, you will. You'll go in with me every morning, and you'll come home with me every night."

"Ha! That won't last long," Andy suddenly wiped his eyes and stood up and confronted his father triumphantly. "The first time you decide to shack up with one of your assistants, I'll be on my own."

"I—"

"Who's lying now?"

CHAPTER NINETEEN

Wednesday, August 22, 2018, The Owens Tower, San Diego

At one o'clock, Andy sat in his office in The Owens Tower and contemplated San Diego Bay spread at his feet. The sunlight was dancing off the blue waves like a million shattered crystals. Here and there a few sailboats were skimming along, powered by the gusty winds. Several flocks of tourists ambled along the sidewalks, taking in the sights.

He had just signed a medium-sized law firm to a three-year lease in his father's new building. The last three weeks had taught him that renting commercial space in the Carmel Valley area was ridiculously easy because his father had authorized a price per square foot that was considerably below market. Potential tenants snapped up the chance to rent in a brand-new building at a bargain price. Of course, Andy knew his father's tactics only too well. No lease would be allowed for a term longer than three years because Lucas always hit every tenant with a hefty increase at the end of the lease. That was as long as his father would permit an under-market lease, and his strategy almost always worked. Most of the tenants would opt for paying the increase rather than incurring the expense of a move.

Andy looked around his well-appointed office with its light mahogany desk and pristine white sofas and chairs. It certainly beat a jail cell, but he had no illusions about what this place was: a fancier version of that cell. His father's threat to drive him to and from work had lasted only two days, just as Andy had predicted. And, just as Andy had foreseen, Lucas' oversight had been overturned by his interest in a new and highly attractive broker. But Andy was forced to share Lucas' secretary, a dour, middle-aged woman named Jeanne. Ella had chosen her to keep track of her husband, which made her equally useful for reporting Andy's movements.

Still, he reflected as he studied the bay, he was better off than in jail. And he had the opportunity to look for evidence that would prove he didn't kill Nate. His father had given him an office next to his, presumably all the better to police Andy's comings and goings. But with his door open, Andy could hear bits and pieces of his father's phone calls. And he'd overheard one that had set his blood boiling. On his speakerphone, his father had promised Sean Donovan to write a check for fifteen thousand dollars to pay for an expert witness whom Sean thought would testify that Nate's cause of death was drowning which meant that he'd fallen overboard accidentally. Andy had wanted to storm into his father's office and demand a new legal team, one that would believe him when he said he didn't kill his best friend.

But Andy had come to realize that the odds against being believed were squarely stacked against him. Everyone thought he was a dumb, screwed-up, rich boy. The accident in New York proved it, along with his repeated bar exam failures. And while

Andy realized that his life so far had amply supported the
conclusion that he was a failure at being an adult, he knew that
he'd been on the road to better things when Tina had been in
his life.

He would never forget the first time he'd seen her in Il
Fornaio. She moved with the grace of a dancer although later he
would learn she had never studied dance. Instead, she had been
a star goalie in women's soccer in high school and college.

She was tall, around five nine. Her long dark hair, which had
been pulled back into a ponytail for work, accented her wide-set
dark eyes. She had a round face and a generous mouth. Her
smile was warm and genuine, and her eyes, too, projected
warmth and kindness. Andy's lonely soul, parched for love,
understanding, and a purpose in life, immediately fell in love
with Valentina Kiara Hernandez.

He'd been eating alone that night, and he flirted with her,
praying that she'd return his interest. Her poise and grace and
intelligent banter made him sense that her achievements far
exceeded his. Asking for her phone number had felt cheap and
wrong. But he had desperately wanted her to open a door for
him into friendship if nothing else.

He'd asked if he could come back when her shift ended and
take a walk with her on the little beach behind the restaurant.
To his joy and amazement, she'd agreed. So at midnight, they'd
walked under the stars and talked, and he'd lost his heart.

Her beautiful, fierce determination to be part of the cure for
cancer inspired him.

"My grandmother and my two aunts died of breast cancer,"
she'd told him on that first starlit walk. "At first, I wanted to be

a doctor. But then I saw I could do more by earning my Ph.D. and becoming a researcher."

Visiting her in her lab at the Salk Institute had been his first opportunity to meet people who weren't obsessed with wealth. His parents and their friends were all about amassing millions. Here were highly intelligent people whose lives were dedicated to saving others.

Until he met Tina, his life had been driven by the winds of his parents' demands. But after he'd spent time with her and her colleagues, he began to think for the first time about finding a purpose for his own life. He suddenly wanted to devote himself to doing something for others, too. He realized that when he eventually inherited his parents' fortune, he could make substantial donations for medical research. The thought pleased him, but it wasn't enough, and he didn't want to wait to contribute to the greater good. And then, through his friendship with Tina's family, he discovered what he wanted to do.

He spoke Spanish, of course, because all his nannies had been from Mexico. Tina's entire family was bilingual, but they spoke Spanish among themselves. He'd loved speaking Spanish with them and feeling that he was part of her large family. To his surprise, they hadn't held his wealth against him. He'd grown close to all of Tina's brothers and sisters, but he'd been especially close to eight-year-old Marco whose ambition was to play professional soccer when he grew up. Marco constantly begged Tina and her brothers to do practice drills and play pick-up games with him in the backyard during his parents' weekly Sunday afternoon barbecues. Andy was thrilled when they invited him to join even though he didn't possess the innate athletic skill of Tina and her brothers.

The one glitch in his relationship with Tina's family had been the story of the Hernandezes' eviction from an Owens apartment building. It had happened long ago, when Tina was a baby and when her father and uncle had been struggling to get their moving business off the ground. They'd been short of cash as they'd waited on clients to pay them. A few more days, and they would have had the money to stay in their apartment. But the Owens management team was not sympathetic.

Andy had been well accepted by the family before anyone told him that very old story. It didn't change his relationship with Tina or the Hernandezes. Instead, it inspired him. He knew that his father's organization did not have a stellar reputation when it came to its low-income properties. Andy loved the thought of representing low-income tenants against them, sticking it to his parents for their heartlessness.

Suddenly, passing the bar actually meant something to him. It wasn't just one more thing he had to do to keep up with Gavin, Nate, and Kyle and to show his parents that he was an adult. He decided to buckle down and put his all into trying to pass. He made that promise to himself and to Tina. And then, not long after that, she walked away for good without any explanation.

Suddenly Andy's world was shattered again. The Hernandez clan had been his only experience of belonging to people who loved each other. Losing that and losing Tina had left him wondering how he could go on. His only comfort had been clinging to what relationship he had left with her brothers.

Now, as he sat boiling about his father's agreement to pay an expert to contribute to the story that he killed Nate accidentally, Andy realized that no one was trying to find out what had really happened that night. And no one was trying to prove that he was innocent. So he would have to do it himself. But how?

He decided that unraveling the mystery of that message from Tina on Nate's phone had to be the starting point for vindicating himself and for getting justice for Nate. But it was too risky to show up at Tina's lab and demand an interview because she'd undoubtedly refuse to see him. Instead of north to La Jolla, he needed to go south to Hernandez Moving in Chula Vista to see if Luis, Jose, and Sebastian would help him.

His intercom buzzed and Jeanne the Terrible announced that she was leaving for the day. A dentist appointment. That probably meant his father was lurking in his office, but it could also mean that his parents had resumed their usual preoccupation with their own lives and were getting careless about monitoring him. He decided to take a chance that it was the latter.

He waited until he was sure that Jeanne was safely out of the building and then made his way to the parking garage and to the company's Toyota Camry that his father had allowed him to drive. Andy's own BMW had been impounded to be searched for evidence. He was grateful for the Camry because his parents' original plan had been to force him to rely on them for transportation.

He exited the dark hole of the garage and made his way to the I-5 South. At four o'clock, traffic was picking up, but rush hour was not yet underway. Surely Luis, Jose, and Sebastian would help him, he told himself.

When he pulled into the parking lot on J Street in Chula Vista, he saw Luis climbing down from the cab of one of the three moving trucks parked on the lot. Andy put the Camry in one of the automobile spaces next to the brick building that housed the office, got out, and headed across the asphalt toward Luis. No one else was in sight.

But Luis didn't seem to notice Andy moving rapidly in his direction. When his feet touched the ground, instead of waiting for Andy to reach him, he turned away toward the rear of the truck.

Andy had a sinking feeling that Luis had seen him but was pretending he hadn't. "Luis!" he called out as he drew closer.

Tina's brother turned and studied Andy as he approached. When he was near enough for a bear hug, the usual greeting he received from Tina's brothers, Luis' arms remained at his sides.

"Hey, man," Andy said, "how are you?"

"Busy. Just got back from a job. Got to go to the office now and do the paperwork." There was no warmth in his voice.

Andy tried to fight back his disappointment. Luis was the oldest Hernandez sibling and the only one of Tina's brothers who was married. He had two sons, one eighteen, the other sixteen. He had been forced to drop out of high school in his senior year because his girlfriend, now his wife, had become pregnant with their oldest son. He was fiercely proud of Tina for her educational achievements, and he was determined to send both of his sons to college. Although Luis was only thirty-six, he looked much older. Years of working seven days a week, plus the physical toll that heavy lifting exacted, had aged him. And as his father and uncle grew older, more responsibility for the business fell on his shoulders. He was now the de facto manager of Hernandez Moving.

"I need to talk to you and Jose and Sebastian about that night at The Naked Lady."

Luis frowned. "Jose and Sebastian are on a job. They won't be back until after eight tonight."

"Well, then I need to talk to you."

"I don't know, man. I've got a lot of paperwork to do. And I don't really want to talk about that night. My old lady wasn't happy with me for going to a strip joint."

Andy felt his heart crumple like a piece of discarded paper. He was no longer welcome in the only place on earth where being welcome mattered to him.

"Please, Luis. I wouldn't ask if it wasn't important."

"Well, okay. Come into the office. But only for a few minutes."

Andy followed him to the square brick building next to the parking spaces for automobiles. Luis pushed open the front door and walked across the small reception area to a large office at the back of the building. He picked up a light-blue checked cotton shirt that had been hanging on the chair behind the desk and put it on over his white T-shirt that was tucked into his jeans. He sat down at the desk and reached into a small refrigerator behind him and pulled out a beer. There were stacks of paper all over the big desk, and Andy remembered that Tina had worked here, filing for her father, when she was in high school. He wished she were here now, and he wished she would talk to him.

"Want one?"

"No, thanks. I've got to keep my mind on business," Andy said.

Luis popped the top off the Corona with an opener that he took out of the desk and took several long swigs before he put the bottle down and said, "You should know there have already been people here asking questions about that night."

"Who?"

"Cops, mostly. And a private investigator from those lawyers who are representing you. They're all asking the same question."

"Which is?"

"How much did you drink that night."

"What did you tell them?"

"That I had no idea. You know the drill, man. Nobody talks to the cops. Or to fancy attorneys."

"Thanks for keeping quiet."

"That don't mean Jose and Sebastian minded their tongues."

"What did they say?"

"No idea. They wouldn't talk to all three of us at once."

"Then I need to find out what Jose and Sebastian told them."

Luis looked grave as he sipped his beer. Finally, he said, "They aren't going to talk to you."

Andy felt as if he'd been sucker punched. "But why not?"

"I don't think I should go into that."

"Luis, please. My life's at stake. Everyone's convinced I killed my best friend. And I didn't."

"But you've killed someone before," Luis said quietly.

"Who told you that?"

"That PI your attorneys sent."

"I— Okay, I have. But it was an accident."

"You never told us."

"I told Tina. It's not something I like to talk about."

"That PI said you were so drunk you were in a blackout. I blacked out at my wedding. There're videos of me dancing on the tables. I don't remember any of it."

"Well, I wasn't in a blackout at The Naked Lady. Or when I came back on the boat with Nate."

Luis shrugged. "You were drinking a lot that night."

"Listen, there's something else I have to know. Was Tina dating Nate?"

"I can't talk to you about Tina no more. She don't like it."

"But you and Jose and Sebastian were my friends, too. You thought she was crazy to dump me back in March."

"Maybe. I don't know. You're a nice guy, Andy, but Tina can do better."

"She sent Nate a text message not long before he died. Do you know what that was all about? Here, let me read it to you."

Luis held up his hand. "I already heard it from the cops who were here earlier. They're asking about Tina and Nate, too."

"Do you know anything?"

"Yes, but I didn't tell the cops. Or that PI."

"Would you tell me?"

Luis drank some more beer and stared at the piles of paper in front of him. Finally, he said, "If I do, will you leave? And not come back?"

"I'll leave. I might have to come back. I've got to find the truth, Luis. I don't want to go to prison for the rest of my life, and I didn't kill Nate."

"Jose and Sebastian will be really upset with me if I tell you about Tina and Nate."

"Why?"

Luis finished his beer and threw the bottle in his trash can. "Because they got arrested for possession, and Tina went to Nate for help."

"What? That's impossible. None of you are involved in drugs."

"Right," Luis agreed. "But we're a working-class Latino family in the barrio. An undercover cop planted cocaine on Jose and Sebastian one night when they were partying at Club Red in Chula Vista. They both have tattoos, and the cop took them for gang members."

"When did all this happen?"

"April. Not long after Tina broke up with you. Dad and I didn't know what to do. We talked to a bunch of lawyers who we could afford, but we didn't trust none of them. They said Jose and Sebastian had to take a plea even though they were innocent. That didn't make no sense to us. Tina knew Nate did criminal law because she'd met him through you. We didn't figure we could afford him, but she went to him to get the name of someone honest for Jose and Sebastian."

"And he took their case?"

"Right. He was really nice," Luis said. "Like you."

"Thanks. What happened to Jose and Sebastian? Are they on probation?"

"No. Somehow, and we never knew how, he got all the charges dropped."

"Did you know if that was when Tina started dating him?"

"I have no idea. She never brought him around the family the way she brought you. That message the cops showed me was the first I knew of anything other than they were friends."

Luis shifted uneasily in his chair, and Andy realized he'd more than overstayed his welcome. He stood up. "Thanks, man. I better get going."

Luis stood, too, and to Andy's surprise he came around the desk and gave him a bear hug. "Good luck, *amigo.*"

CHAPTER TWENTY

Thursday, August 30, 2018, Rancho Santa Fe, California

For more than a week, Andy's conversation with Luis haunted him. Even in his inexperienced law-student world, he knew that once criminal charges were filed, they stuck. Innocent people pled guilty all the time to avoid a jury trial which was highly likely to send them to prison. Nate had complained more than once that he hated telling innocent clients to take a deal. So how had he pulled off the miracle of getting Tina's brothers completely out from under the drug charges that had been filed against them? Andy didn't believe undercover cops gave up that easily.

Even worse for Andy, he realized that Jose and Sebastian had needed a lawyer's help, but Tina had turned to Nate, not to him. Would it have been different if Andy had actually passed the bar? He couldn't bear to think about it. But he strongly suspected the answer was no.

The diamond ring he'd bought for Tina was in a box at the back of the drawer in his chest where he kept his vodka stash. He looked at the black velvet box whenever he took out a new bottle to numb his feelings. At least rehab had taught him to recognize why he drank. He'd been lonely all his life. Drinking was preferable to loneliness.

But during the week after he'd talked to Luis, the vodka had become less attractive. At night, instead of brooding over the ring that Tina had never seen, Andy had considered what his next move should be. He still needed to unravel the riddle of the message on Nate's phone. That meant he needed to understand the relationship between Nate and Tina's brothers. So he needed to see Nate's file. That meant he needed to talk to Nate's father. That is, if Brian McClellan would talk to him.

On Thursday night his parents were not at home to Andy's great relief. He had correctly predicted that their commitment to their social lives would quickly outweigh any plans they had made to oversee him. Their absence made it easy for him to slip out of the Mansion of Doom and drive the half mile to the McClellan's. He arrived at eight fifteen and parked in the gravel circle in front of the enormous house where he had spent so many happy times.

He walked up to the front door and rang the bell. He knew he was taking a big chance. All he could do was hope it would pay off.

A housekeeper, wearing a gray uniform identical to the one his parents' housekeeper wore, answered the door.

"*Bienvenido,*" she said, "I will inform Señor McClellan that you have come to see him."

Andy waited nervously in the marble hall where he had always been assured of his welcome in the past. He studied his watch to calm himself. Five minutes went by before the housekeeper appeared.

"Señor is in the study," she said, "and he will see you. This way."

Andy followed her through the familiar halls. He had no need of a guide. He'd been this way a thousand times. But he'd been family then. And now he was something else entirely.

Brian McClellan was sitting in an oversized armchair next to an unlit fireplace. Nate and his father had always been on the thin side, but Brian had lost so much weight since his son's death that he looked frail. Although he was seventy-four, he had always appeared to be at least ten years younger. Until now. The lines in his face were deep and obvious. He had fathered four daughters before his longed-for son was born. Andy fully realized the depth of his grief, and it took all of his courage to face it.

"What do you want?" he demanded when Andy entered the room.

"Mr. McClellan, I need to talk with you."

"Can't Hugh Mahoney afford investigators anymore?"

"There's one assigned to my case. But he's got the story wrong."

"How's that?"

"I didn't kill Nate."

"Of course you did."

"No. I—"

"I know you think you didn't do it," Brian said, "but you did. You were in a blackout the way you were the night that man in New York died."

"No, I wasn't. I didn't drink that much. I swear Nate was fine when I left him."

"He was dead when you left him. The DA showed me that navigation data."

"Nate wanted to go on a ride around the bay. And then he wanted to go over to the ocean side of Coronado. He was upset. He needed to talk."

Brian studied him for several seconds before he said, "What did he want to talk about?"

Andy was relieved that he was going to let him stay even if only for a short time. "Is it all right if I sit down?"

Brian nodded toward the sofa opposite his chair, and Andy took a seat, grateful for even grudging hospitality.

"He wanted to talk about his wedding. He didn't want to go through with it."

"That's what the cops said you told them."

"I didn't lie to them."

"Did he tell you that he wanted to marry that Tina woman?"

"No, he never mentioned Tina. And please don't talk about her disrespectfully. When she broke up with me, she was about to complete her Ph.D. in Genetics at UCSD. She's part of a team at the Salk Institute researching a cure for breast cancer."

Brian looked surprised. "I had no idea."

"You thought the same thing my parents did. That she was a low-life, barrio freeloader."

"That's rather harsh."

"It's something my parents said repeatedly when I was dating her."

Andy saw sympathy in Brian's face when he mentioned his parents. Brian went on in a gentler tone. "Look, son, I know those two haven't been there for you. You've spent a lot of holidays in this house because Ella and Lucas were traveling without you. And now you're facing the fight of your life, and they're nowhere to be found. I know what you're going through.

I've been a criminal defense attorney for over forty years. I've gone out on my own many times to look for evidence in a case where I just didn't think my client was guilty. It's a lonely journey even when you are not the accused."

His genuine sympathy brought tears to Andy's eyes. He struggled to hold them back, but they overflowed. He swiped at them awkwardly with the back of his hand.

"Sorry," he mumbled. "That's the first kind thing anyone's said to me in a long time."

"Well, I wish there was more that I could say. But, honestly, Andy, you're in denial, and you're on a fool's errand."

"Why won't anyone believe me? I didn't kill Nate."

"Because there's no other reasonable explanation," Brian said. "The only defense your attorneys can use is accident. I don't have to tell you that the navigation data puts you at the exact the spot where Nate's body most likely went into the ocean. And there is no doubt that you and Nate left that strip club together, and he was never seen again."

Andy struggled not to let his tears get the best of him again. "I loved Nate. He was my brother. You know that. You know how much he meant to me."

Brian was silent for a few moments as if considering what to say. Andy prayed he wouldn't say that he believed him capable of killing someone whom he had loved so much.

Finally, Brian said slowly, "I know you loved Nate. I know he loved you. But I don't see any other explanation for his death except your drinking. It's New York all over again. You were operating the boat in a blackout. Nate went over and you didn't stop to help him."

"Do you really think I wouldn't have noticed that?"

"I've seen you that drunk, Andy."

He stared at Brian for several seconds, awash in the horror of his heavy drinking past. A thought began to nag him like a stone that had been in his shoe for hours but whose presence had only just crossed his threshold of pain. *What if he's right? What if I did kill Nate, and I don't remember? I don't remember the car crash in New York. Oh, God, please don't let this be true. But what if it is? What if Charlotte Estes and Sean Donovan are right after all?*

"I remember everything," he insisted. "Nate was on the boat when I left."

Andy could see that his resistance to Brian's version of events had irritated him. He wanted Andy to leave. He said coldly, "Did you have a specific question that you came to ask me?"

"Yes," Andy agreed, glad to be back on topic. "I found out how Nate became involved with Tina. It was after she broke up with me. He represented two of her brothers on drug possession charges. I think the key to finding out who killed Nate is related to that case."

"I remember," Brian said. "The Hernandez family couldn't afford a decent lawyer, and Nate asked permission to take the case without being paid. He said they were friends of yours."

"That was right."

"I didn't have any involvement in the matter, so there's very little I can tell you other than that."

"I heard Nate got all the charges dropped."

"Right. He did. It was a big win."

"But do you know how that happened? Luis, the older brother who wasn't arrested, said that an undercover cop planted the drugs in order to make an arrest."

But Brian shook his head. "No idea. Nate told me not long after he agreed to represent your friends that it was over, and all the charges had been dropped."

"Could I see that file? Maybe there's a clue in it somewhere that explains why the DA was willing to give up so easily."

"And you think that's important to proving you didn't kill Nate?"

"I'm on a fishing expedition. I can't tell you for sure if it helps me, but I need to find out."

"Well, I can't give you access to the file. It's full of attorney-client privileged information."

"If Sebastian and Jose say I can see it, will you let me?"

Brian sighed. "If they say 'yes,' I will."

CHAPTER TWENTY-ONE

Friday, August 31, 2018, Rancho Santa Fe

His mother was the only one in the dining room the next morning. His father apparently had scored with the blond broker. His parents required him to show up for breakfast. It was one of their less onerous requirements.

"You were in bed when I came home last night," his mother said with satisfaction. She stopped reading emails on her phone and smiled at Andy across the table. "The coffee has just been brewed."

Andy poured himself a cup from the pot on the buffet, added cream but no sugar, and sat down at the table on his mother's right.

"Aren't you going to eat anything?"

Her plate contained a hard-boiled egg and a piece of whole wheat toast. That was a sure sign that she had her eye on some young guy, probably around his age. She dieted whenever a new prospect appeared. Her diets never did much good because they never lasted more than a week or ten days.

"I'll grab something on my way downtown. I'm not hungry yet."

"Your father says you're doing very well at the office."

Andy shrugged.

"Don't you care that we're pleased with how you're doing?"

"I went to see Brian last night."

"What? Are you out of your mind?"

"Possibly. He was very nice."

"To your face, maybe. Why in the world did you go to see him?"

"To tell him I didn't kill Nate."

"And did he believe you?"

"Of course not. And you don't, either. But I didn't."

Ella got up from the table and grabbed her phone impatiently. "I'm not the right person to talk to about innocence, Andy. Not after New York. Better you talk to Charlie Patrick and her sidekick about that."

"Charlie Patrick?"

"Oh, I forgot. That was her name in college. Charlotte Estes. Your father's eternal flame."

"I don't think sarcasm is appropriate, Mother."

"Don't lecture me. I've got to get to the office now. I'll call Jeanne in an hour to make sure you're where you're supposed to be. Don't go back to the McClellans'."

"I wasn't planning on it."

"Good." She gave him a peck on the cheek. "We'll have dinner tonight at Mille Fleurs. I'll have my secretary make a reservation and instruct your father to join us."

So what was that like, Andy wondered. *Being commanded to appear for your wife's dinner plans while in bed with your new mistress.* He never intended to find out.

"Fine, Mother. What time?"

"Let's meet at seven thirty. We can have drinks before dinner."

"Very well." Andy nodded as he knew he was meant to do.

* * *

He stopped at McDonald's on his way downtown and ordered two Egg McMuffins, the comfort food of his childhood. The hot, greasy combination of egg, cheese, and toasted bread was the perfect foil for the smooth Jamaican Blue Mountain coffee that filled his travel mug. His mother would drink nothing else when it came to coffee.

Jeanne glowered at him when he passed her desk on his way to his office.

"Your father's already here."

And what you don't know is he never came home last night.

"Hope your dentist appointment went well."

But she only grimaced and went back to reading emails on her computer. Although she had gray hair that she didn't bother to color, she had a smooth, unlined face. Andy guessed she was only about mid-forties, but she dressed in drab, black dresses and suits without style and with no personality. She often did not bother to substitute dress shoes for her walking sneakers while in the office. He wondered if she'd been mad at the world since birth or if some terrible life event had turned her into the sour gateway dragon of a human that his mother prized and that he now had to confront daily.

Andy hung his suit coat on the rack in the corner of his office and settled himself at his desk with the remainder of his coffee and his feast. A lease contract for another floor of the office building was staring up at him, waiting for his signature. Another law firm could hardly wait to be extorted for rent three years hence.

"Hi, son. Looks like you bypassed breakfast at home." Andy looked up to see Lucas standing in his doorway.

"As did you." Andy smiled as his dagger hit home.

His father was in his shirt sleeves, smelling of fresh shaving cream and soap. Andy knew very well that he'd just showered and put on clean clothes in his private bathroom.

"Your mother called. She said you went to see Brian last night. That wasn't a smart move, son."

"I've already heard that lecture from her."

"Andy, I know you aren't in the habit of listening to either of us, but your life depends on not screwing up. Again."

He started to repeat his mantra, *I didn't screw up. I didn't kill Nate.* But he knew his denials were becoming stale, and they weren't convincing anyone.

"I understand, Dad. Now, if you'll excuse me, I've got a contract to review."

He felt his father's dark eyes boring angry holes in him, but he didn't give him the satisfaction of looking up. Defeated by Andy's refusal to fight, Lucas went back to his own office.

Andy waited until he heard his father leave for a board meeting. Then he closed his door and called Hernandez Moving. Luis answered.

"Yeah, Sebastian and Jose are in the office. I'll put them on speakerphone."

Overjoyed by his luck in reaching both Hernandez brothers at once, Andy asked their permission to view Nate's file.

"Look, we're sorry for your troubles, man," Sebastian said.

"But we don't want to go back and think about that time," Jose finished. "We were terrified that we were going to prison."

"But can't you see? That's exactly how I feel right now. I've got a hunch there's something in your file that will help me prove I'm innocent."

"I don't see how," Sebastian said.

"Me, either," Jose agreed.

"Sorry," Luis came on the line, "they refused permission, Andy. That's the end of it."

"But I—I really need to see that file. My life probably depends on what's inside."

"That's not possible," Sebastian said. "The file is about us, not you."

"Could you at least tell me the name of the undercover cop who planted the stuff on you?"

"No way," Jose said. "We don't even know it."

"But how could you not know?"

"Because we were paying attention to the guns on the belts of the six guys he called to arrest us, and wondering if they were going to shoot us before we even saw the inside of a jail."

"Oh, God!"

"Give it up, Andy. We don't want anyone to look at our file. We just want to forget that it ever happened."

* * *

Andy ended the call and stared at the bright-blue summer sky and the white sailboats on the equally bright-blue water of San Diego Bay. He thought about the day last summer when he'd

187

rented a boat and taken Tina sailing. It had been her first time; the wind had been strong, and she'd said that it felt like flying. He had thought, wrongly of course, that they were on their way to a lifetime of firsts together. He reminded himself that bitterness over her sudden departure would get him nothing.

But for the moment, she was the person he most needed to see because she was the only person left who could help him prove there had been no love triangle. If she was willing to do that, he'd have no need to unlock the mystery of her brothers' arrest. He could drive to her lab and take his chances that she'd see him, but if he seemed to be forcing a meeting, he would hurt his cause.

He decided calling and asking for an appointment was his best bet.

"I'll transfer you to Dr. Hernandez's secretary," the receptionist said after Andy identified himself and his errand.

In the silence, Andy thought with satisfaction that Tina had completed her Ph.D. since the last time they'd spoken. He liked the ring of "Dr." in front of her name.

"Dr. Hernandez's office," the second friendly voice announced.

But luck was not on his side. Tina's schedule for Friday was full, and she was leaving for a conference in New York at six that evening.

Andy smiled ruefully as he hung up. So she'd see New York for the first time, but without him. He stared at his cell phone with all the concentration that he had formerly directed to the view from his window. After several long minutes, he decided to throw his Hail Mary pass.

He still had her number. Maybe she hadn't blocked his texts.

> Could we meet at a place of your choice for just a few minutes? Nate's dad told me that you went to Nate to help your brothers. I know your personal life is off limits to me now. But I honestly didn't know about you and Nate. I'm looking for evidence to help me prove that I'm innocent. I thought if I could read Nate's file on your brothers, I could figure out what was going on without having to bother you. But Jose and Sebastian won't let me see Nate's file on their case. Will you help me?

He hit send and waited. He sighed and tried to focus on the contract on his desk, but his mind kept wandering back to the problem. He told himself that Brian McClellan would eventually relent and let him see that file. But probably not until after he had been convicted of murder. The day passed, but Tina never responded. At six, Andy stood at his window and watched the planes taking off from Lindbergh Field and wondered which one was Tina's. Well, he had his answer. She wasn't going to help.

At seven, he packed his briefcase with leases that he was supposed to review overnight. He felt empty and let down by Tina's silence. All day long, he had hoped against hope that she'd help him. She probably believed that he'd killed Nate in a fit of jealous rage. He wished she'd given him the chance to explain that he'd known nothing about her relationship with Nate until the young cop opened Nate's phone on Sunday morning. Even if she wouldn't tell him anything that would help him prove he was innocent, he still wished for the opportunity to tell her in person that he was.

He needed to shake his depression. He decided to walk down to P & J's Brewery and Tasting Room in the Gaslamp. It wasn't alcohol he wanted. It was companionship. He just wanted to sit on a barstool in the big crowded room and be with people who weren't his parents in a place that wasn't Mille Fleurs, the pricey French restaurant in Rancho Santa Fe that his mother adored. He was on bail, and he wasn't supposed to be in a place like P & J's, but he'd rather risk going back to jail than going back to the Mansion of Doom and dulling his pain by getting drunk alone on vodka shots in his bathroom tumbler.

* * *

He sat on a stool at the bar where he could see the door. He assumed the cops weren't following him, but in case they were, he hoped for a chance to duck out the back. He ordered coffee because he didn't want a drink at that moment and because if he was caught at the bar, maybe the fact he was drinking coffee would soften the blow of being in violation of the terms of his bail.

In the low light, the dark-paneled room was welcoming and even comforting. Andy felt as if he could sit on the stool all night without being noticed. The patrons were mostly twenty- and thirty-year-olds, nicely dressed in suits or in business-casual jeans and blazers.

By eight o'clock, the bartender expressed his unhappiness that Andy was occupying one of his stools and not drinking. So Andy ordered a burger for himself and sent a round of Cosmopolitans to the five very attractive young women at a table across from him. They all smiled and toasted him from afar when the bartender explained their good fortune.

As he chowed down on his burger, now armed with an iced tea because alcohol still didn't appeal to him, his phone buzzed and his heart skipped a beat. Tina had answered him after all! But when he pulled his phone out and opened it, the message was a threat from his mother to send a car for him because he hadn't shown up for dinner.

He thought of texting back some lie such as he was working or had gone out with friends. But it wasn't worth the effort. So he turned off his phone and put it back in his pocket.

He finished his burger, sent another round to the ladies, and asked the bartender for a decaf for himself. Just as he began to sip the rich, hot warmth of the coffee, the heavy wooden front doors of the tasting room burst open and a fresh wave of young professionals swarmed in. A tall, thin blond waif with a pixy cut that enhanced her large, deep-set blue eyes caught his attention. His stomach lurched. Kinsley Wyatt had just walked in. Alone apparently. And she was staring at him and heading his way. He saw at once that his escape plans had never been the least bit realistic.

"What are you doing here?" she demanded, halting in front of him as he sat on his barstool.

"I could ask you the same thing."

She shrugged. "I didn't kill anyone. Why aren't you in jail?"

"Out on bail. Working for my father."

"Well, don't you have a curfew or something?"

"It's only nine o'clock."

"You don't seriously expect anyone to believe that's coffee in that cup."

"You can taste it if you want to." Andy held out his mug.

"No, thanks."

The bartender was now hovering expectantly, so Kinsley ordered a glass of white wine. The patron next to Andy suddenly got up and headed for the door, apparently unwilling to listen to their acrimonious banter.

Kinsley pulled up the skirt of her short, tight black dress just enough to allow herself to perch on the vacant stool. She let her long legs dangle as she sipped her wine and studied the crowd. Andy envied her air of supreme confidence.

"How've you been?" he asked in a more conciliatory tone. At least she was company, and he had come to P & J's for company.

She shrugged. "How do you think I've been? Working a lot helps."

"The interior design business is good, then." She had wanted to make him feel awkward, and he did.

"For now. I've got two new commissions in La Jolla and an office building in Carmel Valley."

"Probably close to the place I'm handling for my father."

"Well, you know who to call if you need design services."

Andy wondered what it would be like to work with the notoriously spoiled Kinsley. But then, he, too, had a reputation for being spoiled, he reminded himself, so he was not in a position to judge anyone.

"He called me that night," Kinsley suddenly volunteered, her eyes fixed on the crowded room.

"Who?"

"Nate. He called me. Said he wanted to talk."

"What time?" Andy tried to keep the sharp note of desperation out of his voice.

"I'm not sure. He said the four of you were at some strip club. He told me you were taking him back to your father's place at the Cays. He wanted me to meet him there in a half hour. I told him no way."

"That must have been around ten thirty," Andy said. "That's when we left the club."

Kinsley sipped her wine and shrugged. "Whatever."

"Have you told anyone else that Nate called you?"

"No, of course not. No one's asked me." Her lovely blue eyes studied him carefully for a minute. Then she asked, "Why is this so important, Andy? It doesn't change anything."

"It's important because the cops are saying I beat Nate to death and dumped him overboard because he wanted to marry Tina. When he called you, did he say he wanted to talk about his doubts about the wedding?"

"Of course not. That's ridiculous!" She threw back her head and laughed.

"I wish it were funny, but it isn't."

"Oh, sorry, then." She couldn't stop laughing. "Don't be ridiculous, Andy. Nate didn't have any doubts."

"Nate told me that night that he did."

"God, Andy. Now I know there's something more than coffee in that cup. Of course Nate never said he had doubts about getting married. You know better than anyone that we've been together since we were little. We've always known we'd be getting married."

"But Nate told me that night that he'd told you that he had

193

doubts, and you'd brushed them off."

"Oh, Andy, Andy. That never happened. You were drunk and you were hallucinating."

"But I wasn't!"

Kinsley shrugged again. "Whatever. I can only tell you that Nate never said a word to me about any doubts."

"But what about Tina's text message?"

"Oh, that girl has a greatly inflated opinion of herself. Nate was never interested in her."

"Would you tell my attorneys that?"

"God, no, Andy! It's New York all over again. You're not safe to be with. We all know you were drunk and you wrecked the boat and killed him."

The door to the tasting room swung open, and a tall dark-haired man wearing a T-shirt, jeans, and a dark blazer entered. He looked around until he saw Kinsley and waved. She waved back and slid off the stool.

"Who's that?" Andy asked.

"A client. I'm decorating his house in La Jolla. He wanted to talk about his must-haves for the project. Got to go. Good luck trying to get yourself off."

BLINDSIDED

CHAPTER TWENTY-TWO

Wednesday, September 5, 2018, Office of Dr. Joseph M. Cerna, Ximed Building, La Jolla, California

Dr. Cerna had an impressive view of San Diego that stretched all the way to the Pacific, Charlotte reflected at one in the afternoon as she and Sean waited to see the expert witness they had hired to critique Gus Tavoularis' autopsy report. This was the first day when she hadn't felt jet-lagged after her trip to see Ian and Hayden over the Labor Day weekend.

The early autumn afternoon sunlight was hard and sharp, and the tall white buildings in the distance seem to have edges that would cut your finger if you touched them. That was how the world felt to Charlotte at that moment. Hard and sharp and full of things to be avoided. Someone had been following her in D.C. during her Labor Day visit. She'd turned around a hundred times to try to catch a glimpse of who was tailing her. But no luck. She'd hoped that the watching had ended when she'd boarded the plane at Dulles. But she couldn't be sure. The knowledge that her life was constantly in danger was wearing on her nerves.

Dr. Cerna himself came to the waiting room to greet them.

Mid-fifties. Short and bald with scholarly wire-rimmed glasses. He was wearing a conservative tweed sport coat over his white shirt and navy tie and dark-gray slacks.

He escorted them to his conference room, which had the same breathtaking view of San Diego as the reception area. Charlotte took the seat next to Sean who positioned himself next to Dr. Cerna. Dr. Cerna sat at the head of the table, facing the screen at the end of the room.

"I've been over all of the autopsy photographs and Dr. Tavoularis' report," he said.

"And can you say that the bloody froth in his airway means that Nate was alive when he fell off the boat?" Sean asked.

"No, I can't," Dr. Cerna said. "I can't give an opinion as to how he came to be in the water, but it's not likely that he fell in."

"I was hoping there would be evidence that when the boat collided with whatever our client hit, Nate was hurled overboard," Sean explained.

"I'm afraid I didn't find evidence of that," Dr. Cerna said.

"So you agree with Dr. Tavoularis that blunt force trauma was the cause of death?" Sean frowned as he asked his question, indicating his disapproval of the answer in advance.

"No, I don't agree with him," Dr. Cerna said. "The cause of death was a gunshot wound to the head."

"What?" The word came out before Charlotte had time to stop herself. She sat up straighter and leaned toward Dr. Cerna. "Are you sure you've got the right case? No one has ever mentioned a gun. Or found one for that matter."

Dr. Cerna, who had worked with Sean before, eyed

Charlotte with disdain. He said condescendingly, "I'm certain I have the correct file. And I can show you the bullet path in the young man's skull."

He doesn't have to be rude to me, Charlotte thought.

With a touch of a button, Dr. Cerna dimmed the lights and closed the shades in the conference room. The screen came to life with a picture of an X-ray of a skull.

"The bullet entered the left temple," Dr. Cerna began, using a laser pointer to illustrate his finding. "It traveled left to right and downward before exiting the back of his skull." Dr. Cerna clicked and another picture from the autopsy appeared on the screen showing what might have been a hole in the back of Nate's head.

"Are you sure that's a bullet hole?" Sean asked. "The body was in the water for quite a few hours. And there was a lot of surf that night and into the following day."

"You're saying this is evidence of surf damage and not a bullet wound?" Dr. Cerna arched one eyebrow skeptically.

"That's possible, isn't it?" Sean asked.

"Possible? Maybe. But in this case, no. Nate McClellan died from a gunshot wound to the head. I'd say probably from a nine-millimeter bullet. Tavoularis was careless when he overlooked the actual cause of death."

* * *

"Where does this leave us?" Charlotte asked as soon as she and Sean were in the elevator on their way to the lobby.

Sean shook his head. "Honestly, I don't know. I never expected anything like this."

"We should get another expert's opinion," Charlotte said.

"So we go shopping for what we want to hear, that Nate drowned?"

"There's nothing wrong with asking someone else to look at the autopsy report."

"And you have someone in mind?" He sounded combative.

"Larry Walsh. He's in D.C. Matt and I worked with him a lot. He has an international reputation as a pathologist."

"That's fine," Sean said, "but this legal community is not receptive to outsiders."

Since he had returned to his original competitive attitude, she did nothing to hide her irritation. "So I've noticed."

They walked the rest of the way to Charlotte's car in silence and got in. The silence grew as she navigated out of the parking lot and across the surface streets to the I-5 South.

Finally, Sean said in a more conciliatory tone, "If Dr. Cerna turns out to be right, we've got a much bigger problem on our hands. No accident defense."

"That was my first thought, too. But Dr. Tavoularis hasn't said that a gunshot wound was the cause of death."

"True," Sean agreed. "And Axel doesn't have any reason to send Dr. Gus back to look at his autopsy findings again."

"I know I'm resisting believing Dr. Cerna's opinion," Charlotte admitted as the glass towers of downtown came into view. "But I don't see Andy Owens with a gun."

"I don't, either. And his hands were bruised, which doesn't suggest he used a gun. Unless you buy Kyle's story."

"I could see him getting angry about the ex and taking a swing at Nate. Maybe even hitting him with something. But a gun? I question that."

"There's one way we might find out if Cerna could be right. Instead of going back to the office, we could go down to the villa and see if we find anything."

"But the police have already searched."

"But they weren't looking for a gun."

* * *

They reached the Owens villa on Green Turtle a little after four p.m. Charlotte parked in the drive and looked over at Sean.

"Now what? We've come to search a house without a key. Or the permission of the owner."

Sean grinned. "Fortunately, we are not the cops, so the Fourth Amendment does not apply to us. We're just ordinary trespassers. I think the back window by the kitchen is vulnerable. Come on."

It took only a few minutes for Sean to remove the screen from the back window, open it, and reach around and unlock the kitchen door. By entering through the unlocked door, they were able to avoid triggering the alarm. Sean found the master switch that controlled the security cameras and turned them off.

"When they discover the gap on the surveillance video, they'll think it was a power outage."

The house was full of pictures, Charlotte noticed as she went from room to room. Not family pictures as she would have expected. They were images of Lucas on the boat, mostly with women. Sean's appraisal of Andy's father seemed accurate. Not only could he not keep his pants zipped, but he liked to brag about it.

They looked for over an hour and found nothing. Then

Charlotte opened the utility closet in the kitchen and noticed that a panel in the back had come loose. She jiggled it slightly, and it fell out in her hand. Behind it was a Glock 26.

"Oh, God, a baby Glock, nine-millimeter," Sean groaned when she called him to take a look at what she'd found.

"We can't jump to conclusions," she said. "We have no idea if this is connected to Nate's death. If Andy had used a gun, he'd have thrown it overboard with the body."

"I don't think he's that smart. Particularly because we've found this hidden in the kitchen. A gun hidden in the house that the kid came back to plus Dr. Cerna's opinion gives us a pretty good idea that it is connected."

"But we don't think Dr. Cerna's right," Charlotte insisted.

"We hope he's not. But this gun makes his theory look more convincing. What are we going to do with this thing?"

"The ethics rules say if it's evidence of a crime, we have to turn it over to the prosecution."

"God, no, Charlotte! We can't do that. We don't actually know this is the murder weapon. It hasn't been tested for fingerprints or ballistics or DNA, and the cops aren't claiming a gun was used to murder Nate."

"But what are the chances that it's not? We just heard Dr. Cerna say that there's a through and through wound from a nine-millimeter bullet in Nate's head. Our bar cards won't be in danger if we turn it over to Axel now and recuse ourselves from representing Andy."

"And lose the Lawrence/Owens account? No way. My career at the firm would be over, and even though they'd probably let you stay, they'd take your name off the letterhead."

Matt's words about the consequences of accepting the merger offer came back to haunt Charlotte once again. She studied the gun for several seconds. Finally, she said, "Maybe you're right. We don't know what this means, if anything. We need to get Dr. Walsh on board to see what he thinks."

"We should take it back to the firm and put it in the safe," Sean said.

But Charlotte shook her head. "No, we shouldn't touch it. We should put this panel back and hope it never becomes important."

"I don't think leaving it here is a good idea," Sean insisted.

"But we have to leave it here. If we take it back to the firm and if it does become important later, then we'd have to turn it over to Axel and recuse ourselves. There wouldn't be anything else we could do under the ethics rules. We're better off just leaving it here."

"And saying nothing."

"And saying nothing," she agreed.

CHAPTER TWENTY-THREE

Wednesday, September 5, 2018, Offices of Goldstein, Miller,
Mahoney, and Estes, Emerald Shapery Center

Charlotte was a tense knot of nerves, so she went for a short run
down to the Embarcadero and back before leaving for home.
The traffic to La Jolla was congested at six thirty, and she wished
that she'd gone on a longer run and had waited until later to
leave the office.

She had hoped that running would take her mind off the
small black gun at the back of the closet. She still wasn't sure if
keeping quiet about it met the requirements of the ethics rules.
Lawyers liked to sit around in seminars and argue about what to
do if they came into possession of evidence of a crime. But in
real life, by the time an attorney-client relationship existed,
clients had destroyed their trail of guilt or the cops had already
discovered it. So coming into possession of evidence of a crime
was rare.

As she inched forward through the traffic, she considered
Sean's point that they didn't know for sure that the little gun
was a murder weapon. She'd have felt more comfortable with
that position if Dr. Cerna hadn't sprung his bombshell on them.

But, of course, if he hadn't announced a gunshot wound as the cause of death, they wouldn't have been at the Cays in the first place.

Sean did have a point about the effect disclosure would have on their careers, not only at the firm but in the community, too. There'd be no way to keep it out of the papers. Plus, Charlotte didn't want to be known as the criminal defense attorney who'd betrayed her client to the police. No, she told herself as she moved forward slowly on the I-5 North. Leaving the gun where they had found it and keeping quiet had been the right thing to do.

It took a full hour to inch her way home. She changed into gray yoga pants and a matching T-shirt and called her mother. She was feeling better and did not need Charlotte to drive her to the doctor in the morning. She briefly considered calling Hayden or Ian or both of them to ask their opinion about the gun. But it was past ten o'clock in D.C., and her children were early risers because they ran before going to work. Besides, the decision had been made. Soliciting more opinions wouldn't change what she and Sean had decided to do.

Charlotte still felt restless, and she briefly contemplated another short run. But her knees were telling her what a bad idea that was. She finally decided it was a night for some Merlot from Matt's wine collection. She had just finished pouring herself a glass when the doorbell rang.

She went to the front door, glass in hand, and looked out through the security window. A beefy man in a brown suit whose arrogant face she knew all too well was standing on her front porch. Her practiced eye could see the bulge of the shoulder holster under his coat. She froze, afraid that he knew she was just inside the door, inches from where he stood. She held her breath and waited for him to go away.

But he didn't. Instead, he rang the bell again and knocked aggressively. "Mrs. Estes! It's Detective Merrill from the D.C. Metropolitan Police. I need to talk to you about your husband."

She turned and tiptoed across the hall and up the stairs to her bedroom where, thankfully, the blinds were closed and no lights were on. She sat in the dark and sipped her wine and shook with grief and anger. How dare this man destroy the peace she'd created for herself a continent away from the nightmare of Matt's death?

She peeked through the blinds and saw a gray Toyota Corolla in the drive. As long as it was there, she'd know the detective was lurking downstairs, trying to get inside. Would he be sleazy enough to call the San Diego police and make up some excuse to break in? The thought sent shivers down her spine. She felt trapped.

Visions of the night of Matt's death began to spin in her head despite her best efforts to put her thoughts somewhere else. There'd been the phone call in the wee hours of that cold November night just days before Thanksgiving.

"Mrs. Estes, I'm Detective Merrill. Is your husband Matthew William Estes, date of birth July 3, 1960?"

"Yes."

"Then I've got bad news for you. He's dead, and I need you to identify his body. A patrol car is on the way to pick you up."

"But where is he? How did it happen?"

"He was at the Four Seasons. He had a heart attack."

Charlotte scrambled out of her pajamas and into jeans, boots, and a heavy sweater while her mind whirled. Her clock said that it was two a.m. So what had Matt been doing at the hotel not far from their house in the wee hours of the morning? When she'd left the office earlier, he'd said he was staying behind to work. So how had he wound up at the Four Seasons? He hadn't mentioned dinner with anyone.

What she remembered best on the ten-minute ride to the hotel in the black-and-white was Detective Merrill's bulk in the front passenger seat and the strong scent of his cheap floral aftershave. The odor made her head hurt.

The entrance to the hotel was jammed with police cars with flashing overhead lights that transformed the tranquil darkness of the night into a macabre carnival of reds and blues. The flags of the United States and District of Columbia, which flew over the hotel's marquee, were being battered by the sharp wind and spitting snow.

As Charlotte waited impatiently for the officers to make a path for her through the milling throng of police and press, she told herself it had to be a mistake. *Matt wasn't dead. Matt wasn't dead.* She repeated that mantra over and over as she crossed the lobby with Detective Merrill by her side. They rode the elevator to the top floor and walked down a hall to a set of double doors labeled "The Presidential Suite."

The detective pushed open both doors and motioned for her to follow him through. She stepped into a beautifully appointed living room full of sofas and chairs swathed in gold linen. There were fresh flowers on the coffee table. Clothes were strewn on the sofa and the floor. A woman's red dress. A pair of black heels.

Expensive, Charlotte noticed. Manolo Blahnik or more likely Louboutin. Bra, panties. All lace. La Perla. And there was Matt's gray suit coat draped over the arm of the sofa. His pants and shoes were next to the red dress. His white shirt and tie were on the floor a little farther on. His white T-shirt and boxer shorts were right at the entrance to the bedroom. The story was outlined on the furniture and on the floor and was easy to read. But Charlotte didn't want to read it.

The door from the living room to the bedroom opened, and Charlotte could see a police officer talking to a tall, thin blond woman wearing a thick white terry bathrobe. Early forties, probably. Strikingly beautiful. She moved her head from side to side as she talked. She seemed to be speaking quickly and earnestly as if trying to convince her listener to believe her.

Charlotte winced when Detective Merrill tapped her arm and nodded toward the bedroom. She didn't want to see what else was in there. But the detective gave her a little shove in that direction that left her no choice.

Inside, she could see the lump in the middle of the king-size bed that a sheet was covering. A white terry robe identical to the one the woman was wearing lay discarded at the foot of the massive bed. *He took it off and placed it there before he got into bed with her. Who is she? A prostitute?*

Charlotte felt a pair of blue eyes boring into her. She looked over and met the gaze of the woman in the robe. The woman studied her face for a few seconds before lifting her chin in a tiny gesture of contempt and then shifting her focus back to the questions coming from the policeman. Absently, the woman reached up and released the tangles of her long hair from the sparkling clip that had pinned it up on her head.

Rhinestones? Diamonds? From Matt? Was he embezzling from the firm to buy this woman jewels? God, I don't want to know.

"If you'll come this way, Mrs. Estes. I know how hard this is for you. But we need a positive identification."

Charlotte moved closer to the bed and stood transfixed as the man in dark-blue scrubs pulled back the sheet with one hand wearing a blue latex glove. Tears sprang into her eyes at the sight of her husband's face. He looked peaceful as if he were sleeping. She had to resist the urge to touch him and tell him to wake up. He was naked under the sheet. She could see the circles where the EKG sensors had been.

Detective Merrill's piggy little eyes were burning holes in her face. He appeared to be taking sadistic pleasure in her misery and grief. She nodded affirmatively and said quietly, "That's Matt."

"Thank you, Mrs. Estes." Detective Merrill smiled as the man in scrubs dropped the sheet back in place. "I'll need to take a brief statement from you."

"From me? But I have no idea how this happened."

"Still, I need to ask you some questions. Let's go into the living room and talk for a few minutes."

Never talk to the police. Never talk to the police. Her mind chanted every defense attorney's mantra as she followed the detective into the living room and sat down on one of the sofas. Detective Merrill took a chair opposite her.

"When was the last time you saw your husband?"

"Around six this evening, maybe a little after."

"Where were you?"

"At the office. I was ready to go home. He said that he was staying on to work a little longer."

"Do you know what he stayed to work on?"

"No, I don't. But before we go any further, I want to know the name of that woman in Matt's room."

"Don't you know her? Her name is Rosemary Spencer. She's British. She says your husband was representing her on conspiracy charges."

"I've never heard of her. I don't think we represent her. She looks like a high-priced call girl to me."

"We're checking that out, too. Did your husband frequent escort services?"

"Not to my knowledge. But then, I'm the wife, so I'd be the last to know, wouldn't I?" She gave the detective a tight-lipped smile.

"She says she's employed as a lobbyist by James and Mitchell Communications and that she lobbies for Light Source Ventures. Ever hear of it?"

"James and Mitchell, yes. They're one of the biggest lobbying firms in Washington. Light Source Ventures, no." Charlotte kept her voice flat and unemotional. "And I'm sure neither James and Mitchell nor Light Source Ventures are clients of our firm."

"So you know the name of every client your husband represents?"

"I—well, not every one. But certainly I know that James and Mitchell is represented by Warrick, Thompson. Who is she supposed to have conspired with?"

"We're going to have to take her downtown to get to the

bottom of that story. Did you husband have a heart condition, Mrs. Estes?"

"No. He and I are avid runners. We did marathons together."

"I see. Well, these things happen even to healthy people. That's all the questions for now. Do you need a ride home?"

I don't want to get back into a police car. "No, I need to call my son."

The detective continued to sit beside her as she dialed Ian's number and told him the unbelievable news. *The least you could do is have the decency to let me tell my son in private that his father is dead.*

She ended the call and stood up.

"Where are you going?" Detective Merrill demanded.

"Downstairs to wait for Ian."

"No, there'll be press down there. We don't want to compromise the investigation."

But I don't want to be close to you. And I have to make some private calls to arrange for a funeral home to take charge of my husband's body. And I have to call my daughter.

She opened her mouth to object, but at that moment the front doors of the living room swung wide to admit two more blue-uniformed EMTs who pushed a wheeled stretcher toward the bedroom.

"What's that for?" she demanded.

"We're taking your husband's body downtown for an autopsy," Detective Merrill said.

"No! No, you're not!" Charlotte's voice rose a little more hysterically with each word. The thought of Matt's body being dissected on an autopsy table was unbearable. "My son and daughter and I will make the arrangements for him."

"I'm afraid we have to do an autopsy first, Mrs. Estes. You husband died under suspicious circumstances."

"But you just said he had a heart attack!"

"That's what we think based upon what Ms. Spencer has said. But obviously we won't know without a complete autopsy and a toxicology screen."

"I won't give consent to that."

"We don't need your consent," the detective said.

"I'm going downstairs to wait for my son." Charlotte started toward the door, but the detective stepped into her path.

"I'd prefer you wait here."

"But I've answered all your questions."

"I might have more." His tone was menacing. *Does he think I'm a suspect?*

Suddenly she was shaking with fear and rage. She sat down on the sofa because her legs were wobbly. She was careful to keep her back to the bedroom so she wouldn't see them taking Matt's body out on the stretcher. But that didn't keep her from seeing two officers escorting Rosemary Spencer out, still in her white robe but now in handcuffs. *They suspect her. They suspect me. This is crazy.* Charlotte closed her eyes to keep from seeing any more and tried to keep her mind empty.

But she heard sheets rustle when the EMTs moved Matt's body from the bed to the stretcher. A few seconds later she heard the wheels of the stretcher sliding across the bedroom carpet and then across the living room to the front door. She squeezed her eyes shut and prayed that Ian would hurry. A few minutes later, she felt arms around her. It was her son. She opened her eyes and looked into his, gray and steady. Matt's eyes. She began to sob.

"It's all right, Mother. I'm here, and Hayden is on her way to the house. Let's go home."

CHAPTER TWENTY-FOUR

Thursday, September 6, 2018, Offices of Goldstein, Miller, Mahoney, and Estes, Emerald Shapery Center

Charlotte had realized when she refused to answer the door last night that Detective Merrill was bound to show up at her office eventually. When her secretary announced his presence at ten the next morning, she knew she would have to bow to the inevitable.

He lowered his bulk into the chair opposite her desk and eyed her coldly. The smell of his aftershave brought back the ride in the police car on that cold November night. She steeled herself to deal with him.

"You wouldn't answer the door last night."

"I have no idea what you're talking about. Why are you here? Matt's death was very traumatic for me and my children. Please leave us alone."

"Unfortunately, we were wrong about your husband's death. Your husband did not die of a heart attack. He was murdered."

"But the autopsy that you insisted on against my wishes stated clearly that he died of a heart attack, apparently brought on by his sexual activities with Ms. Spencer."

"Well, the coroner was wrong," the detective said. "Your husband was poisoned by a drug that stopped his heart."

Charlotte frowned. "But the toxicology report showed only alcohol in Matt's system."

"The drug we found is very uncommon. It's made overseas. We don't routinely test for it."

"Then what made you go back now and open all this up again? Don't you realize how hard this is for me and my children?"

"I do, and I'm sorry. But you had to know. If you recall, you were the target of a bullet just before you left D.C."

I'm not going to bring up the things that have happened at the house.

But it was too late. He'd already been told. "And I understand there have been some suspicious activities at your residence since you came here."

"The San Diego police have already explained that it has nothing to do with me."

"Well, that's an explanation that they've realized is outdated now. You're in danger. You've got to take that seriously."

"But I don't understand this theory that Matt was poisoned by some mysterious drug."

"It's called Nerine. A British laboratory worked on it as a treatment for cardiac disorders in the mid-sixties. The trials revealed that there were no really safe doses, so it was scrapped. I'd never heard of it until Scotland Yard informed us that this Rosemary Spencer had been involved in London in a death similar to your husband's in June. It's hard to trace unless you know what you're looking for."

"A death similar to my husband's?"

"We received a surveillance videotape from Scotland Yard that shows Spencer with a British lawyer at the Four Seasons in London. They met at the bar, and then they were joined by another man. The three of them had a drink together, and then Spencer left. The two men proceeded to a table in the dining room where the victim became ill. Scotland Yard was suspicious because Spencer was involved and the facts were similar to your husband's death, although not identical."

Charlotte held up her hand. "I don't want to hear anymore. It's too painful."

"I understand. But I should tell you that the tissue samples from your husband's autopsy tested positive for this drug. And we are in the process of recovering the hotel's security tapes from the night of his death."

"I see. Have you spoken with either of my children?"

"No. Do you want to inform them, or shall I meet with them when I get back to my office?"

"That won't be necessary. This is a family matter."

* * *

Charlotte had just put the phone down after a three-way call with Ian and Hayden when someone knocked on her office door.

"Charlotte, it's Sean. Do you have a minute?"

I want to send him away, but he'll find out. Detective Merrill said it would be in the papers back east in the morning. It won't take long for the news to reach San Diego. I have to practice telling people. I may as well begin with Sean.

"Come in."

He smiled as he entered and closed the door behind him. "I came to ask what Larry Walsh said about reviewing— What's happened?" He stopped before he got to the chairs in front of her desk. His eyes were full of concern.

"The detective who called me to ID Matt the night he died barged into my office about an hour ago to tell me that Matt's death was a homicide." Tears choked her when she got to the last word, and she swiped at them ineffectually. *I wouldn't have let him in if I'd known I was going to break down.*

"Oh, God! Charlotte!" He hurried around her desk and pulled her to her feet and gave her a hug that she found unexpectedly comforting.

"I'm going to be okay," she said, when he let her go. "It's just the shock of the news."

"You had no idea I take it?"

"None. The coroner was very certain that Matt had a heart attack—" Her voice broke. After a few seconds, she managed to go on. "Brought on by sexual activity with the woman who was with him at the time."

"There was a woman with him?"

"Right. It'll be in the papers tomorrow. Her name is Rosemary Spencer. Matt was representing her. They had dinner at the Four Seasons in Georgetown that night and then went upstairs to her room."

She motioned for him to follow her over to the sofas in the corner of her office. She sat down and took a tissue out of the box on the coffee table and wiped her eyes. Sean took the seat next to her.

"What do you know about Spencer?"

"To be honest, not much. I haven't wanted to dig into it very deeply because it hurts. What I've been able to make myself face is that she is British, and she was working as a lobbyist for James and Mitchell, one of Washington's oldest and most respected lobbying firms. But she was new to the job and got herself in trouble."

"What kind of trouble?"

"She offered expense-paid vacations to some Congressmen, hoping to sway them to support offering defense contracts for security software to the company she represented, Light Source. It's a tech startup headquartered in San Francisco. They hired James and Mitchell to get them in on the action, but Miss Spencer wasn't acquainted with the lobbying laws. One of the Congressmen reported her to the U.S. Attorney, who then began to circle around Spencer and her firm. Warrick, Thompson has long represented James and Mitchell, so they were conflicted out of representing their employee. That's why they referred her to Matt."

"How did you find this out?"

"I couldn't bring myself to read Matt's files after he died. I was afraid there'd be personal messages back and forth, and I didn't want to read the details of my dead husband's love affair. So I called the attorney in Warrick's D.C. office who was handling the James and Mitchell end of things. And he told me the basics."

"Did he tell you what charges the U.S. Attorney was looking at against the firm and the Spencer woman?"

"Bribery and conspiracy to bribe."

"Anyone else?"

"Well, Light Source, of course."

"Did your husband ever set up a proffer session for his client with the U.S. Attorney?"

"If he did, I don't know about it. It would make sense that he would have been trying to do that, to keep her out of prison."

"That was my first thought," Sean said. "And if he was talking to the U.S. Attorney about a proffer session, that means his client had already told him all the dirt she had on her co-conspirators."

"So she killed Matt after she told him all her secrets?" Charlotte frowned.

"It's possible. If she changed her mind about snitching on her co-conspirators. Where is she now?"

"No one knows. She was involved with a death similar to Matt's in the London Four Seasons in June. Detective Merrill told me she left the country before Scotland Yard discovered it was a homicide. She used a drug that isn't routinely tested for in tox screens. When Scotland Yard alerted Detective Merrill to the similarities in the two deaths, he had them analyze Matt's autopsy samples again. Everyone's looking for her, but she's disappeared."

"Did you do any work on her case?"

"No. The night Matt died, I didn't even know she was his client. She looked like she'd come from a high-priced escort service."

"So she's seen you? She knows who you are?"

"Yes. She was still in the room at the hotel when the police brought me there to identify Matt."

"Have you given any thought to the fact that your life is probably in danger? She's killed two people to protect her secrets, and she probably thinks you've read your husband's file and know them, too."

Charlotte studied the tissue box for a few seconds before she took a deep breath and said, "Actually, there have been some things that have happened since Matt died."

"What kinds of things?" he asked sharply.

"Someone took a shot at me when I was running on the canal path in Georgetown right before my move."

"What about since you've been out here?"

"Someone has been watching my house. And there was an attempted break-in on the night you came over for dinner, after you left."

"So I would say Rosemary Spencer is not alone in whatever illegal activity she's up to. She and her friends believe that you know the things that got your husband killed."

"But I don't."

"Then you'd better find out what they are because that's the only way you're going to find out who's trying to kill you."

"It all sounds so real when you say it out loud."

"It is real."

"But I don't want it to be!" Charlotte couldn't keep the anger and frustration out of her voice any longer. "I've been tormented almost every day since Matt died, wondering if there were cracks in our marriage that I didn't see."

"Well, now you know there weren't." He spoke gently.

"That's something, at least," she agreed. "But knowing he was murdered hurts just as much if not more. I wasn't there to say goodbye and tell him how much I loved him."

"I know."

His quiet sympathy made her tear up again. He took her hand and gave it a gentle squeeze. With the other hand, she took another tissue from the box and wiped her eyes.

"I'm sorry," she said.

He released her hand and smiled again. "There's no need. But there are some practical things you need to consider. How is the security system at your house? You saw how easy it was for us to get through the one at the Cays."

"It worked the night of the attempted break-in. And the police have responded quickly to my calls. I'm not worried."

"Well, I am," Sean said. "And you shouldn't go running alone anymore."

"I was afraid you'd say that. You should buy a pair of running shoes then."

"And I was afraid you'd say that." He smiled again.

Are we finally becoming friends? Matt would be pleased. He would have liked Sean.

"And there's something else," Sean went on. "You need to get your husband's file on Spencer and her activities out of your house. And then you need to read it. Actually, it would be a good idea for you to give it to me for safekeeping, and both of us should read it."

"Safety in numbers?" She smiled.

"Well, I was a U.S. Attorney, if you recall. I've conducted proffer sessions. And I might even know the attorney back in D.C. who was working on Spencer's case. And besides my professional expertise, I bring my pure self-interest to the table."

"Self-interest? How?"

"Because it's going to be more trouble to try to kill two lawyers who know Rosemary Spencer's secrets than one. I need to reduce their odds of getting to you because I need you alive to share the blame for losing the Lawrence/Owens business for the firm if we can't keep Andy Owens out of prison."

BEING INNOCENT

CHAPTER TWENTY-FIVE

Wednesday, September 12, 2018, Offices of Russell Blake, Kearny Mesa

Andy had been brooding for almost two weeks about the way Kinsley and everyone else for that matter had rejected his protestations of innocence. He still had a valid Lexis ID, so he researched ineffective assistance of counsel. He wanted to find case law that said prissy Charlotte Estes and cynical Sean Donovan had to actually listen to him and look for evidence to support his claim of innocence.

The search for legal authority to wave under his snooty defense team's noses had given purpose to his nights since Kinsley had scoffed at him at P & J's. Even his parents' prolonged shrieking fights and his mother's propensity to smash vulnerable objets d'art had not deterred him from all-night Boolean searches to find case law that said defense attorneys must listen to their clients when they say they are not guilty.

But although Andy was the first to admit he was no legal scholar, he could see that the appellate opinions were stacked against him. Defense attorneys could pretty much ignore the protestations of their hapless clients with the blessing of the courts of appeal because, at least at the appellate level, the presumption of innocence was a myth. Over the course of many nights of legal researching, it became abundantly clear that not only had Andy's life as an irresponsible party boy and his various academic failings left him screwed, the law was equally willing to screw him and deem him guilty from the get-go. So, he concluded, he, Andy Owens, twice-failed bar examinee, ranked 205 out of 250 in his law school class, was going to have to figure out a way to save his ass. And prove his worth to a skeptical world.

After ruminating for nearly two weeks, Andy had come up with a plan to find the evidence that no one else was willing to look for. There were two keys to the Nate-Tina story. One was the file on her brothers that, so far, none of them would agree to let him see. Two, was the navigation data from *The Escape*. The trip numbers should show either the trip where Nate had been killed after Andy left the boat, or should show that the record of the second trip had been erased. Russell Blake held the key, and Andy needed to get access to Russell Blake.

He decided that the fastest way to get Blake's contact information was to imitate his old man's technique: bribe Charlotte's attractive, twenty-something secretary. To that end, he stole a robin's egg blue Tiffany's box from his mother's closet and filled it with a pair of cubic zirconia earrings that his mother had segregated in her jewelry box for items that were beneath her but suitable for gifting the staff at Christmas. Andy would gladly have heisted a pair of her diamond studs for the occasion, but there was greater risk in being caught.

His offering did the trick because now it was Wednesday

morning, and he was walking brazenly into Blake's office without an appointment to confront him. He'd come dressed in his second-best navy suit and maroon tie, hoping the air of professionalism would offset his reputation as an irresponsible loser that undoubtedly had preceded him.

The receptionist, who was far more attractive than Charlotte's gatekeeper, smiled.

"Do you have an appointment?"

"No." He wished he'd had the foresight to put another pair of fake diamond studs into another magical blue box sitting empty in his mother's closet.

"I'm afraid Mr. Blake is only available by appointment."

"I'm pretty sure he'll see me. I'm Andy Owens. My mother is Ella Lawrence, and my father is Lucas Owens. My attorneys at Goldstein, Miller met with him earlier, in my absence." He emphasized the last three words slightly.

The secretary looked intimidated as she was meant to. "I— I'll see if he is willing to see you."

A few minutes later, a tall thin man close to Andy's own age appeared. He was wearing jeans and a black T-shirt with the Microsoft logo on the front. Andy felt overdressed in his suit and tie.

Russell Blake walked over to Andy and shook his hand. He looked friendly and not the least bit disturbed by the unscheduled interruption. "Hi, Andy. I'm Russell. I understand you want to talk to me."

"Sorry to barge in without an appointment. But it's important."

"Of course. Come on back to my office. Would you like something to drink? Water? Coffee?"

"No, thanks. I appreciate your giving me a few minutes." He sincerely did, and he hoped his gratitude showed. He was self-conscious in the presence of the kind of person he wished he had grown up to be: self-confident, self-reliant, and successful.

Andy followed Russell along a narrow corridor toward the end of the hall. He could see Russell's employees at their computers through the open doorways. He wished he was the owner of his own business and not dependent upon his parents. If only he had managed to pass the bar.

When they reached his office, Russell motioned for Andy to enter first and to take a seat at the small conference table in the corner. Russell sat down next to him and used a remote control to lower a screen on the wall behind his desk.

"I can show you what we were able to recover from the navigation log on your father's boat."

"That's okay. The attorneys have already shown it to me. That's actually the reason that I came to see you."

"Okay." Russell looked intrigued. "Tell me more."

"Well, Sean and Charlotte say that the navigation log proves that I killed Nate."

"Well, that conclusion is going a bit too far," Russell said. "The data does show your father's boat traveling to a point where a body could have been dumped, given where it was found. But the data doesn't establish who was on the boat."

"Right. The thing is, I lied at first and said Nate and I never went that far. I thought I'd turned the navigation recording off because I didn't want my father to know Nate and I had gone for a joyride on his precious boat. But apparently I didn't turn it off because you found the log from that trip. So I had to admit to the attorneys that Nate and I went out alone on the way back from the strip club. But I didn't kill Nate. He was alive when I left him. There's got to be more navigation data that shows the trip the actual killer made to dump his body."

"There isn't any more data," Russell said. Andy thought he noted a trace of sympathy in his voice.

"But there has to be," Andy insisted. "Nate went out again with someone who killed him."

"All I can tell you is that I haven't found any evidence of that. As I told your attorneys, someone tried to erase the data that I did find."

"My parents did that. Or at least, my father blames my mother. She probably blames him."

"Was she the one who erased the surveillance tapes, too?" Russell asked.

Andy's stomach tightened. "Are you telling me those don't exist, either?"

"Your parents did a job on those, too, I'm afraid."

"Oh, God!" Andy sat back in his chair and closed his eyes for a minute, trying to steady himself. When he opened them, Russell was watching him sympathetically.

"Are you sure you don't want some water, at least?" he asked.

"Yeah, I'd like that. I just need a minute to get my bearings. From what you're telling me, my parents destroyed the evidence that I need to prove I'm innocent."

Russell poured some water into a glass from the pitcher on his desk and handed it to Andy who took several sips as he tried to regain his composure.

"Can't you recover any of what's been lost?" Andy asked. "I

still think there's more navigation data there. Unless, unlike me, the killer knew how to turn it off."

"Your attorneys haven't asked us to try to recover anything. Our contract is just to analyze what's been provided. Recovery is expensive. And we probably won't be successful."

"I want you to try, anyway. I'll pay you myself."

Russell frowned. "But it's almost certain to be a waste of money."

"But it's my only shot at proving I'm innocent. I've got the money to pay you. As you probably know." He hated playing the entitled rich kid card, but he had no choice.

Russell studied him for a few seconds, and Andy felt as if he was sizing him up, trying to decide if he was worthy of help.

"I'll beg if that will persuade you," he offered.

Russell smiled. "No, no. I didn't mean to make you feel that way. I just don't like taking anyone's money if I don't think I can help."

"Look, I'm desperate. No one believes me when I say I didn't kill my best friend. And my attorneys aren't doing anything to help me prove that I'm innocent. And I have to admit that I haven't led a life that says I should be believed. So I've got to do what I can to help myself. I'm alone in this, even though it doesn't look that way. Please try for me."

"Okay. I'll send you an invoice. We'll get started as soon as you've paid the deposit."

* * *

Andy pushed the Camry hard on the trip to his office, staying just enough under the speed limit to avoid any entanglements with the cops. More police in his life was the last thing he needed. He was seething, and he was determined to have it out with his father.

Jeanne barely nodded as he went into his own office and hung up his suit jacket. But when he came out and walked toward Lucas' door, which was closed, she intervened.

"He doesn't want to be disturbed right now."

"I don't care!" Andy snarled as he put his hand on the knob and tried to open the door. But it was locked.

"I told you. He doesn't want to be disturbed." Jeanne turned back to her computer as if the matter was settled. Andy had that futile feeling that always came over him when confronted by the fact that he was merely an inconvenience in his parents' lives.

But he was no longer willing to accept that treatment from them. "Tell him I'm out here, and I have to see him."

Jeanne kept her eyes on her computer screen. "You'll have to come back later."

Andy remained where he was. "Tell him to open the door, or I'll call security to open it for me."

Jeanne finally looked up at him, incredulous. "You wouldn't!"

"Watch me."

Reluctantly, she picked up her phone and activated the intercom. "Andy's out here. He says he has to see you immediately."

After a long pause, Andy heard the lock click, and his father opened the door. His face was red, his tie was off, and his shirt had been misbuttoned. Andy wondered which unfortunate object of his father's lust was adjusting her clothes in the executive bathroom before escaping through the back door.

"What's the emergency, son?" Lucas demanded.

Andy walked in and took command of the situation by closing the door. "You and my mother erased the evidence I need to prove I didn't kill Nate!"

"I didn't erase anything, and I told your mother not to. Besides, the attorneys have informed me that she didn't succeed, anyway," Lucas said as he tucked his shirt back into his pants and rematched the buttons and buttonholes. "The navigation log shows you're guilty."

He walked back to his desk and heaved himself into his high-back leather chair as if he were exhausted and bored. Andy could see that his righteous anger didn't impress his father. And he felt even more futile.

"There's got to be more data," Andy said. "Mother erased the data from the trip when Nate was killed. And she erased the surveillance tapes that showed who got on the boat with him after I left."

Andy felt himself flush under his father's pitying gaze. He knew what was coming: lots of parental shaming.

"Andy, it's time for you to grow up and start accepting responsibility. Denial and more crazy stories aren't going to help you at this point. You were drunk that night. You don't really remember what happened. Your mother was trying to help you. She didn't want the police to see you coming back and getting off the boat without Nate."

"I do remember getting off the boat that night. And Nate was still alive."

"So you keep saying." Lucas waved his hands dismissively.

"Why won't anyone believe me!" He knew his face must be

red. He hadn't meant to lose his cool. But he had.

"Don't shout, Andy. And you know the answer to that question. Now go to your office and get to work and stop trying to play lawyer. It's Goldstein, Miller's job to defend you. You've got far better attorneys over there than you could ever be."

Andy wanted to make a biting return about his father's morning activities. But that would only feed Lucas' image of him as volatile and immature, an image he dearly wished he had not justified by losing his temper. Instead, he said evenly, "I've asked Russell Blake to recover that data."

"Fine." Lucas shrugged. "But I hope you realize that I'm not wasting money on a search for evidence that never existed. And the salary you're receiving here won't cover that kind of expense."

"I've got that money that Grandpa Lawrence left. It's mine. I can do what I want."

"Well, throw it away if you like."

* * *

He went back to his office and tried yoga breathing to calm down. Tina had advocated meditation and had taught him some simple yoga poses that made him look like a contorted teddy bear. Oddly enough, the rage coursing through his veins didn't inspire him to wish for a drink. There was an unopened vodka bottle in the bottom drawer of his desk. But he didn't want any of it. Instead, he turned on his computer and scanned his email. Russell Blake's invoice was there as promised. He transferred the money from his savings account to cover the first installment and felt better.

He tried to read a lease contract, but the urgency of his situation predominated his thoughts. He considered approaching Jose and Luis again. But in his heart, he knew Tina was the only person who could talk them into allowing him to see Nate's file. And only if she was willing to help him. And so far, the answer had been no.

But he was desperate. So he picked up the phone and called the Salk Institute.

"I'm sorry, but Dr. Hernandez is no longer with us," the friendly voice informed him.

Andy remembered the conference in New York. She must have found a new job. Probably on the East Coast. But that made no sense. She would never leave her family.

"Do you know where I could reach her now?" Andy asked, trying to keep the tension out of his voice.

"No idea. She did not leave any contact information."

Andy put down the phone and saw that his hands were shaking. Researching at Salk was Tina's dream job. She'd devoted her whole life to getting a place there and being part of the breast cancer team. Something terrible had happened. He was afraid to know. Yet he had to.

Luis answered. "Hernandez Moving."

"Luis, it's Andy."

"What do you want, Andy? We're busy this morning." Luis' voice was uncharacteristically hostile.

"I'm sorry to bother you. And I'm always glad when you're busy—"

"Cut the shit, Andy. It's not that kind of busy. People from your father's Foundation are here to repossess the trucks."

"*What?*"

"They've terminated the leases on the new equipment."

"But those are six-year terms. I helped set them up with the Owens Small Business Foundation."

"Yeah, but your lawyers don't think so. Look, Andy. I don't have time for your problems anymore. This is going to shut us down all together. No trucks. No moving company."

Andy was horrified, but he had to press on and find Tina. "I called Salk because I need to talk to Tina. They said she's not there."

"She's not. They let her go."

"What? But that's not possible."

"It's as possible as four of our five trucks being towed out of the lot right now."

"Has she left town?"

"She's helping Aunt Esmeralda."

"But how?"

"How do you think? She's cleaning houses! This is all your fault, Andy. Now please, for God's sake, leave us alone!"

Luis slammed the phone down.

Andy's hands were trembling even more now. His head was spinning. He got up and opened his office door. Across the way he could see that his father's door was closed again. He started toward Lucas' office anyway.

"Haven't you had enough of him yet?" Jeanne asked without looking up from her computer.

"I have to talk to him again."

"I wouldn't if I were you. He's in there with Bert."

Bert Campbell, his mother's Chief Financial Officer, and his godfather. "What's he doing with Bert?"

"I have no idea," Jeanne said. "But he's raised his voice five or six times now. Whatever is going on in there, your father is not happy."

"Well, I'm not happy, either. I have to talk to him."

Jeanne shrugged. "I've warned you. I can't do anymore."

Andy knocked on the door. His father's angry voice replied, "Who's there?"

"Andy. I need to talk to you."

"We've already talked. There's nothing more to say."

"Why is the Small Business Foundation repossessing the trucks that Tina's family leased from it?"

The door suddenly opened, and Bert was standing there. He was the same age as his parents, tall and still handsome in the square-jawed way of the actors on his nanny's favorite soap operas. His dark eyes were calm and friendly. Behind him, his father's were blazing with rage. He was wearing a gray suit that made him seem professional, but friendly.

"Hi, Andy," Bert smiled. "This might not be the best time. I've had to give your father some bad news."

Andy wanted to ask what bad news from his mother's business was relevant to his father's, but the Hernandez problem was more urgent.

"Sorry, but it can't wait. You should stay. You are one of the trustees of the Small Business Foundation."

Bert motioned for Andy to take a seat in front of his father's desk, and Bert took the other chair.

"You've been snooping around the Hernandezes I gather," his father said dryly.

"I called Luis. The Foundation has revoked their leases on

the new moving trucks. There's no possible reason for that. I set up six-year lease-to-buy agreements for all the trucks." He'd been proud of being able to help Tina's family business with the foundation his father had created to aid small businesses.

"Well, I'll call over at Goldstein, Miller and tell the team that manages the Foundation to see what's going on," his father said.

"But that will take too long!"

"Andy, calm down." His father used the tone he'd use with a five-year-old.

"No, it will. They move slowly on Foundation matters. And besides, they're the ones who authorized taking the trucks. The Foundation people are there right now, towing them away. The company has contracts to move people. Without those trucks, they'll go under in a heartbeat. They don't have the time or the money for prolonged legal proceedings."

"Like I said," Lucas repeated slowly and insultingly, "I'll have the attorneys deal with it. I'm sure there's a good reason to take back the trucks. The Hernandez clan plays fast and loose with the rules."

"That's absolutely not true!" Andy reminded himself to keep his voice down.

"Well, calling the attorneys is all that I can do."

"I'll go back to my office right now," Bert offered, "and find out what's going on." His tone was conciliatory. He smiled reassuringly at Andy.

"You've got to stop them from towing the trucks!"

"I'll do my very best." Bert smiled again. "And I'll call you within the hour."

CHAPTER TWENTY-SIX

Thursday, September 13, 2018, Rancho Santa Fe

But, of course, Bert never called. His promise had been a kiss-off to get Andy out of his father's face, the kind of slight-of-hand trick that parents play on toddlers by distracting them with a favorite toy. Andy called his godfather's cell phone ten times that night, asking for news about the trucks. But there was only silence. Another reminder of just how unimportant Andy was in his parents' world.

Oddly, because his stress and misery levels had risen to all-time highs, he still didn't want a drink. The half-empty vodka bottles in his chest of drawers had no allure.

He sat up into the wee hours trying to think of something he could do to get the equipment back to the Hernandez family. He blamed himself because he'd encouraged them to let the Owens Small Business Foundation help them replace their aged moving vans, but he'd had no reason to think the Foundation would double-cross them.

In the morning, he discovered that neither of his parents had come home overnight. Only one place had been set for him in the dining room when he went down for breakfast at seven thirty. Relieved that he had neither parent to deal with, he filled his travel mug with Jamaican Blue Mountain coffee and headed for his office via the nearby McDonald's to pick up his two Egg McMuffins.

From her desk outside his office and his father's, Jeanne saw him get off the elevator, breakfast in hand.

"Your father has scheduled a meeting for you at ten," she announced, looking up from her computer only briefly as Andy passed by her desk on his way to his office.

"With someone from the Foundation?" His spirits rose at the thought of being able to right yesterday's wrongs.

"No." Jeanne shook her head. "Peter wants an accounting on his building."

Andy's heart sank. Peter H. Whittier was one of the major investors in the Carmel Valley Office Building complex that he was in charge of. Peter was seventy-five, enormously wealthy, but without much to do in retirement except count his money and demand reports on how his investments were doing.

On most days Andy wouldn't have minded a meeting with him even though they were always long and tedious because he asked way too many picky questions about things that really didn't matter to the success of the property. Andy felt compassion for the lonely old man who was a widower and whose two sons and his grandchildren lived on the East Coast. He treated Andy like a favorite grandson, and Andy usually had plenty of time to cater to his whims.

But today was different. He'd decided in the wee hours that he would have to find Tina and beg her to tell him the whole story of what was going on. The sooner he could get to the bottom of why so much misfortune had suddenly descended upon the Hernandez family, the sooner he could find a way to do something about it. And he still needed Jose and Sebastian's consent to see Nate's file. This wasn't a good day for a meeting with Peter.

After he finished his Egg McMuffins, he called Hernandez Moving, hoping against hope that Luis would answer and report the trucks had been returned. But a recording announced that the business was closed for the day because of a family emergency. Andy's heart sank.

At nine, Jeanne appeared with a thick manila envelope. "This is for you. From accounting. For your meeting with Peter. The latest numbers on the building."

"Is my father going to meet with Peter, too?"

"No. He's up in Orange County. It'll be just the two of you."

"Thanks, Jeanne. Which conference room are we meeting in?"

"The small one on this floor. The usual spot."

"Thanks." Andy gave her a smile.

She surveyed him thoughtfully for a moment but didn't return the friendly gesture.

Instead, she turned and went out of his office. Andy wondered if she'd been instructed by his parents never to smile at him. Andy proceeded to open his email, hoping there were no fires to put out since he was going to be occupied with Peter all morning. Bert had emailed him.

"Sorry not to get back to you yesterday. The attorneys at Goldstein, Miller looked into the Hernandez

situation. They've missed three months of payments
on the lease-purchase, so the Foundation had to
repossess. Warnings were sent per the contract terms.
Sorry I don't have better news."

Andy felt a moment of pure gut-wrenching rage. He knew
that Tina's mother kept the books meticulously. There was no
way she would have let those payments fall behind. He hoped
Peter could be placated quickly for once.

He was so preoccupied with the Hernandez trucks that he
forgot to pick up his copy of the Commercial Division's
Financial Statement as he headed to his meeting. He noticed he
didn't have the balance sheet as he reached the door of the
conference room. His father's office was slightly closer, so he
hurried back down the hall and picked up the financial
statement on his desk.

"What's going on?" Jeanne demanded as Andy walked by her
desk, headed for the copy machine. "Where are you going your
father's paperwork?"

"Back in two seconds," Andy promised. "I just need a copy
for my meeting with Peter."

"Where's your own copy?" Jeanne yelled as he ran toward
the copier at the end of the hall.

"Left it on my desk. Dad's was closer. Will put it back in
under a minute."

"That statement was prepared for your father!" Jeanne yelled
after him. "You aren't supposed to have it!"

"Well, then, pretend I don't," Andy advised when he
returned from the copy machine. He hurried into his father's

office and dropped the financial report on Lucas' desk in the exact spot where he'd found it. Then he went back outside and planted a kiss on Jeanne's indignant cheek and headed back down to the conference room to meet with Peter Whittier.

* * *

Luck was with him. Peter was happy within the hour and ready to leave. Andy rode down with him in the elevator and made sure his car and driver were out front, waiting for him. The old man's grateful smile as Andy closed the car door and waved goodbye warmed his aching heart.

By eleven thirty, he was in the Camry headed south on the I-5 to Chula Vista. He thanked the Universe that his parents were unavailable to monitor his activities, and Jeanne had taken an early lunch break, allowing him to escape from his gilded prison undetected.

Tina's mother's sister, Esmeralda Ruiz Ramirez, had begun her career with the job most readily available to young Hispanic women with children and little education, cleaning houses. But like all the Ruiz women, she was bright and ambitious. Now at fifty-five, she operated her own cleaning service, sending teams of cleaners to residences and businesses throughout San Diego. Tina's married sisters worked for Aunt Esmeralda as had Tina herself during her summer breaks during high school and college.

Esmeralda's offices were in another slightly seedy strip mall, about five blocks from Hernandez Moving. Andy drove by the moving company, still hoping that the trucks had been returned. But the parking lot was empty and the "Closed" sign was on the office door.

Andy approached Ramirez Cleaning and Janitorial Services half afraid of being tossed out immediately. Esmeralda had liked him in the days when he'd been a regular guest at family dinners and part of Marco's soccer threesome, but she had every reason to send him packing now.

She was alone at the service desk when Andy entered. She'd been beautiful, like Tina, when young. But hard work had left deep lines in her face, and age had put extra pounds around her middle. The buttons of her dark green dress strained a little over the bodice. Her dark hair, which she had wound into a loose bun, was streaked with gray. She was wearing a small silver cross on a thin chain and a pair of large silver earrings that looked like lace. She had changed so much in middle-age that her current face bore little resemblance to the face of the young woman with her crews displayed in pictures behind her desk.

"Andy." She looked at him with her dark, honest eyes. "I thought you'd come."

"Sorry to intrude. Luis hung up on me yesterday. I don't know what's happened at the Foundation. They shouldn't have taken the trucks. I want to fix it, but no one is listening to me."

"I know." Esmeralda came around the counter and gave him a hug. The unexpected touch and her sympathy brought tears to Andy's eyes.

"I'm sorry," he said when she let him go.

"It's okay." She handed him a tissue from the box on the counter. "No one in that family of yours listens to you. I know."

"And I'm in trouble. Do you know that, too?"

"I do. I'm so sorry."

"I'm trying to find out what really happened to Nate. Do

you know anything about his relationship with Tina?"

"Not really. And I couldn't talk to you about it if I knew. All I do know is she went to him when Jose and Sebastian were arrested. And it all turned out better than any of us thought it would."

"Why isn't Tina at Salk? Luis said that she's working for you. What could have happened to make her leave? A Ph.D. geneticist cleaning houses doesn't make any sense."

Esmeralda looked troubled. "I know, and I want to help you, Andy, but I can't betray Tina's confidences."

"I'm sorry. I wasn't trying to put you in the middle. It's just that suddenly everything's gone nuts, and I don't know why. I can't get Nate back, but maybe I can get the trucks back. And find out who killed Nate and why."

"And you think Tina has information that would help you?"

"I do. I texted her a few weeks ago. She was still at Salk then."

"This all happened very suddenly."

"Is there any way that I could talk to her? Just for a minute?"

Esmeralda turned slowly and went back to her place behind the counter and sat down. She began to write something on a piece of paper. When she finished, she handed it to Andy. "Here's the address of the house in La Jolla where she's working today. She didn't want to be on a crew. She wanted to work alone. I can't promise she'll talk to you, but I can give you a chance to ask her if she will."

Andy's eyes filled with tears again, and she came back out front and gave him another hug.

"Good luck," she said when she let him go. "I'll say a rosary for all of us. And light a candle."

CHAPTER TWENTY-SEVEN

Thursday, September 13, 2018, La Jolla Farms, La Jolla, California

He drove north to La Jolla with his heart beating fast and his stomach in a tight knot. He hadn't seen Tina since she'd canceled their New York trip in March. He hoped she'd wouldn't slam the door in his face.

The address Esmeralda had given him was in La Jolla Farms, a community of estate-sized homes sitting above Black's Beach and just south of the Torrey Pines Golf Course. Andy found the three-story, Italian-style villa easily and parked in the circular drive where a small van bearing Esmeralda's logo was also parked.

The massive, carved mahogany double doors were meant to intimidate. Andy rang the bell and waited under their shadow. No answer. He tried twice more without success. His heart sank. Had she looked through the security peephole and decided to ignore him?

He noticed a sidewalk that led to the back of the house. Luck was with him because the massive wrought iron gate was ajar. He followed the pavement to the backyard where the view of the beach and ocean took his breath away.

The back of the house was all glass except for a pair of French doors that, miraculously, were open. Andy walked over and peered inside.

Tina was absorbed in mopping the floor of the enormous kitchen. Andy could see at once that she was unaware that anyone else was there. He stood for a moment taking in the sight of her and trying to keep the tears out of his eyes.

She was wearing jeans and a sleeveless white T-shirt. Her beautiful, well-defined arms moved the mop rhythmically over the red tile floor. Her dark hair was pulled up into a tight ponytail. She looked thoughtful as she swished water across the floor. When she paused to dip the mop in the bucket, she looked up. Her eyes were suddenly guarded.

"I—I know you don't want to see me," Andy began, "but I know about the trucks. And I know Nate tried to help your brothers. I need to know the whole story because I didn't kill Nate, and I feel as if all of this is somehow connected."

"Who told you how to find me?"

"Esmeralda."

Her aunt's name seemed to sway her. She leaned the mop against the marble island in the center of the kitchen and walked toward him, motioning for him to follow her.

She took a seat at a table in the corner of the yard covered by a large red patio umbrella. Andy sat next to her. They were facing the magnificent ocean view.

Tina said, with her eyes on the Pacific, "I'll give you a few minutes, but only a few. I have to finish here before the family comes back."

"Okay." Andy knew better than to press his luck.

"What do you want to know?" she asked sharply as she turned toward him abruptly and studied his face carefully with her beautiful dark eyes.

What's she looking for?

"Why are you here cleaning houses?"

She looked away toward the ocean again. Now her eyes were angry. "Because I was put on administrative leave at the Institute. They accused me of embezzling research funds."

"Tina! No! That's impossible!"

"That's what I said." Her tone was bitter. "Until I opened my personal account and saw the money there."

"What? But how?"

She shook her head, and Andy could see there were now tears in her eyes. He wanted to comfort her but knew touching was forbidden.

"Someone hacked my accounts and moved the money. Then tipped off one of the trustees, who alerted the department. Robert was the one who was able to detect the hack."

"Thank God for Robert!" Andy said. Robert Corry was an assistant professor in the computer science department at UCSD. He and Tina had dated as undergrads, then drifted apart in grad school. But they remained friends. Andy had met him several times.

"But why aren't you back at Salk, then?"

"Because I'm not going back!" Her dark, angry eyes met Andy's. "I've worked there for almost five years. They know me. They know my integrity. And yet they let one of your mother's friends undermine my reputation. If it hadn't been for Robert, my research career would now be over."

"I understand," Andy said. "I wish I could believe that couldn't be true, but I know you're right. Which one of my mother's friends is responsible?"

"Well, Salk won't say, but I know it's Harriet Baker."

"True. She's tight with my mother. But I never told you that."

"Your mother told me."

Andy felt as if a bullet had hit his heart. If he'd had any hope that Tina would eventually forgive him for whatever had gone wrong, her tone said that her anger and disgust were uncompromising.

"My mother?"

She sighed. "I never intended to tell you all of this, but I suppose you've got a right to know. Your mother found out about the trip to New York, and she thought we might become engaged. She arrived at my lab one afternoon and offered me two million dollars to break it off with you."

"What?"

"I showed her the door. Or to be more accurate, I had the security people show her the door. As she was being escorted off the premises, she was reminding everyone within hearing distance that she was a very close friend of Harriet Baker, and she'd have me fired. When the Institute informed me that one of the trustees had received the tip about my bank accounts, I knew exactly who was responsible."

"So my mother fought back through Harriet? But why did she wait so long?" Andy asked.

"Because Nate's dead, and I can't afford an attorney to sue her and her friend for defamation."

"So you and Nate—there was something going on between you two?"

"Not like it says in the news stories," Tina said. "In April, Jose and Sebastian were at Club Red, blowing off some steam one night. All of a sudden, a guy in jeans and six cops had guns pointed at them, accusing them of dealing cocaine. When they were searched, they found baggies in their pockets."

"But no one in your family is involved in drugs!"

"Right. But who's going to believe two young Latino men in a run-down night club in Chula Vista? Anyway, after they were arrested and after my father and Luis discovered we couldn't afford a lawyer who wasn't a crook, I went to Nate for help."

"Luis said he got the charges completely dismissed. That's nearly impossible, as you probably know."

"Yes, I do know."

"Did he tell you how he managed to get the DA to walk away completely?"

"No, he said his information was confidential, and it would be better if it stayed that way."

"Did you keep on seeing him after that?"

Tina looked away at the ocean. She was silent for a minute as if thinking about what to say. Finally, she said, "I was in an awkward position. He'd helped my brothers and me. And never charged us a dime. And he and I had gotten to know each other. I was worried about Jose and Sebastian, and I did talk to him a lot and met him for coffee fairly often because he was so reassuring. I could see why he was your friend.

"But, of course, he was engaged, and I didn't want to interfere with that. And, honestly, after dating you and seeing what wealthy families can do to families like mine, I didn't want to be involved with anyone else from your world. When I

249

realized that Nate was questioning his engagement, I did try to cut it off. But, again, he'd been kind to my family, and I didn't think I could ignore him completely. If we had met for breakfast that morning, I would have told him that he should go ahead with his wedding because there could never be anything serious between us."

"So there's no chance for me?" Andy asked.

"Afraid not." She gave him a friendly pat on the hand.

Andy smiled ruefully. "I can't blame you."

"The prosecutor in your case keeps calling me," Tina said.

"I'm not surprised."

"I've told him I won't talk to him."

"He can call you as a witness and make you testify."

"I know. But if he does, he won't hear what he wants. I'd better get back to work now."

Sadness that his time with her was over flooded Andy. But he knew he'd have to deal with the feeling later. "Thanks for seeing me. But please tell me you aren't going to go on cleaning houses for Esmeralda forever."

"No," she smiled. "It's just a break to think things over. I'm considering applying to medical school after all. When I saw how influential donors could cause people I trusted to turn on me without even investigating the charges, I began to rethink my commitment to research. I could set up a clinic in the neighborhood where I grew up."

She stood up, and Andy followed suit. Her beauty and kindness overwhelmed him, and he had to fight back tears again. She noticed and put her hand on his arm.

"I know you didn't do this. I wish there was more I could do to help. I knew they'd twist what I had to say if I talked to them. So I've stayed quiet."

"Would you talk to my attorneys?"

She considered the question for a moment. "I suppose so. One of them came to the Institute one day. A woman. I wouldn't talk to her because I wanted to stay out of everything."

"But you'd see her now?"

"I suppose. Give her Esmeralda's number. She can reach me through her."

"And there's one more thing. I need to see the file on Jose and Sebastian."

"You think you can find out how Nate got the charges dismissed?"

"I think the reason is in there. And I think it might explain who killed him and why."

"I'll see what I can do with the brothers to get them to agree. They can be stubborn."

"Not with you," Andy said, and she smiled again as they turned back toward the house.

At the door of the kitchen, Andy held out his hand, not for a handshake, but for a clasp in the name of friendship. "Thanks, Tina. I wish when I met you, I'd been clear of my parents. Or that I'd been someone else entirely."

She gave his hand a friendly squeeze. "I know you didn't kill Nate, Andy."

The treacherous tears were back and stinging his eyes. "And you're the only person in the world who believes that."

He turned, hoping that she hadn't seen the return of his tears, and took the path back to the front of the house. He got in the Camry and headed out of the drive. Now he wanted a drink. He wanted to drink and drink and drink until he was oblivious to the pain in his heart and his soul.

But he knew he wouldn't have one. He was all he had between himself and prison. He had to stay sober, and he had to keep looking for the truth.

CHAPTER TWENTY-EIGHT

Friday, September 14, 2018, Offices of Goldstein, Miller, Emerald Shapery Center

The next morning, the reception from Charlotte and Sean was decidedly frosty.

Andy had called and begged to meet with them. At ten o'clock, they sat facing him on one of the two sofas in Charlotte's office. He sat alone on the other. He'd been excited to tell them about his meeting with Tina yesterday, but clearly they weren't the least bit happy about it. Both faces staring at him looked bored, skeptical, and hostile.

"Tina? For God's sake, Andy, where?" Charlotte frowned.

"At an estate in La Jolla. She's cleaning houses for her aunt."

"She's left the Salk Institute?" Charlotte asked.

"She's decided to apply to medical school."

"Andy, you can't be interviewing witnesses," Sean said sternly.

"But why not?"

"Because you're the defendant. That opens you up to charges of witness tampering."

"But I wouldn't do that. And Tina wouldn't lie for me."

"Girlfriends, even ex-girlfriends, will lie for someone they care about," Charlotte insisted.

"Tina will tell you, if you go to see her, that she's telling the truth. She and Nate were friends, but nothing else. And there's nothing left between us. Because of my parents." He realized that he had spoken bitterly without meaning to.

"I'm afraid it doesn't add up, Andy," Charlotte said. "She sent him a message that night offering to meet him for breakfast so that he could persuade her to overcome her scruples about accepting a marriage proposal."

"No!" Andy tried to control his temper and his voice. "That's not what her message meant. She was going to tell him to go on with his wedding. If you talk to her, you'll see."

"Calm down," Sean advised. "We've got a better defense than he-said, she-said, anyway."

"You mean accident?" Andy frowned.

"Right," Sean smiled reassuringly. "We've made progress on finding evidence to support that defense."

"Except there is no evidence that I killed Nate accidentally or otherwise because I didn't!"

But Sean ignored him. "Charlotte has found an expert witness who agrees with me that Nate was alive when he went into the water. He doesn't buy Dr. Tavoularis' theory about a beating. The body was damaged by being in strong currents for several hours. And we think we've found the buoy that you hit near the bridge as you were going back to the Cays. We are pretty sure the paint scrapings from the marker are going to match the paint on *The Escape*. And our tides expert has informed us that he can testify that the currents were particularly strong that night, so that explains the damage to Nate's body and how it reached the beach at the Del after your accident."

Andy was so angry that his stomach was churning. "The pair of you have got to be the worst defense attorneys on earth! How are you going to get around the fact that Nate and I sat on the boat and talked for a half hour before the others came back?"

"You just think that happened," Charlotte said. "You don't actually remember it because you were blacked out. Our minds create 'filler' memories when we have memory gaps. I know you believe that you talked to Nate after you got back to the Cays, but that's just a defense mechanism that your brain is using to help you handle the trauma of what happened."

Andy wanted to say that he didn't know she was a psychologist, too. But he reined in his sarcasm and said instead, "So using this defense, I'll be convicted of at least murder two, probably murder one."

"No, no," Charlotte insisted. "Involuntary manslaughter. Four years tops."

"But I didn't kill Nate."

"No, you don't *remember* killing Nate."

* * *

Andy walked the eight blocks to his office in the Owens Tower, seething and wishing for a drink to take the edge off his anger.

Not at ten thirty in the morning. And not when the world is upside down.

He took a deep breath as he rode the elevator up to the fortieth floor and reminded himself that self-control was everything in the presence of his father. Who was probably in his office that morning.

And he was right. He could see Lucas in his shirt sleeves at his desk, engrossed in reading reports as he crossed the open space to his own office. Jeanne gave him a grudging smile which made him wonder what that was all about. Had the kiss on the cheek finally melted her? Not likely.

He closed his door and took off his own suit coat and hung it on a hook on the back of the door. He sat down at his desk, closed his eyes, and made a stab at Tina's yoga breathing. He felt his heart begin to slow, and the anger that was paralyzing his brain began to subside.

Someone knocked. *Not now. Please, not now. I can't deal with anyone right now.*

"Andy!" his father called, then opened the door.

Damn! Andy opened his eyes.

"Please wait to be invited in, Dad!"

"What are you doing in here, son? Praying?"

Without waiting for an answer, Lucas came in and sat down in front of Andy's desk.

"Bert looked into those trucks. The Hernandez clan hasn't been making their payments. Sorry, son. Your mother and I tried to tell you about trying to help people like that. Did you know your ex has been kicked out at Salk for stealing?"

"She wasn't stealing. Mother set her up."

"Oh, Andy. Don't!" Lucas laughed derisively. "Is that why you were out of the office yesterday afternoon?"

"Who told you I wasn't here?"

"Jeanne. And don't lie to me and say you were visiting the

office buildings because I checked with on-site management, and you weren't in Carmel Valley yesterday."

So that's why Jeanne smiled at me this morning!

"I went to see Tina's aunt to find out if the trucks were back. No one else in the family would speak to me." *He doesn't need to know that I saw Tina.*

"I've already told you to stop playing attorney and to leave your defense to the professionals. And I'm not paying you to work on Owens Small Business Foundation matters. The attorneys for the Foundation have looked into the problem with the Hernandez lease, and that's the end of the matter as far as we are concerned. You're employed in the Commercial Real Estate Division, and you've got plenty to do. Is that clear?"

"Yes, it's clear. Did Jeanne tell you that I spent the morning with Peter, and that he was happy when he left?"

"He left me a message to thank me for the meeting," Lucas said grudgingly. "But that doesn't give you a blank check to leave the office all afternoon on an unrelated matter. And you missed breakfast with us this morning."

"I didn't know the two of you were at the house." *I'm entitled to get in a dig of my own.*

Lucas compressed his lips as if holding back his own retort. He said, "Your mother has a reservation at Mille Fleurs tonight at seven thirty. Don't stand her up again."

Lucas got up and walked to the door. Andy was relieved that he was leaving. But he couldn't resist one last barb.

"And what about you?" he asked. "Are you going to stand her up?"

Lucas threw him an angry look over his shoulder and slammed the door behind him.

* * *

He sat at his desk for a long time, his mind whirling. He wished he could get on an airplane and fly as far away as possible and change his name and never look back. He knew Tina had meant it when she'd said there was no possibility of anything with her again. And without that hope, he had nothing to tie him to San Diego. He was good at real estate. He could get a license in another state. Or even take the bar exam in a state that had a decent pass rate and set up his own practice in some storefront somewhere.

But in his current situation, flight was impossible. It would only bring jail time and more accusations of guilt. He wished he could call Tina and see if she had made any progress with Jose and Sebastian. But he knew that he shouldn't.

His thoughts turned to his meeting with Charlotte and Sean. They wouldn't even consider the possibility that he was innocent. And his parents had hired them and would never have agreed to let him fire them, as much as he wanted to. He wished there were someone he could go to for help.

Suddenly, he thought back to that first morning at the villa when his father had summoned Hugh Mahoney. Erin had come with her father. She was cast in the same mold as Tina, except she'd had no barrio to climb out of through hard work and determination. Like Tina, Erin was beautiful. She had a heart-shaped face, high cheekbones, and caramel hair that fell in luscious waves to her shoulders. She had her father's height which had contributed to her quiet authority that morning in the midst of the chaos the police had created at the villa. And she had her father's expressive brown eyes which told Andy that she, like Tina, had compassion for people in trouble, rich or poor. And like Tina, she was an accomplished professional in her own right, beholden to no one.

She'd left Craig, Lewis, and Weller in New York to join Hugh in the Andrews-Cooper Innocence Project. Of all people, she'd be the one who might listen when he said he was innocent. His aching heart warmed when Erin answered his call and invited him to come to her office at three that afternoon.

* * *

"How are you holding up, Andy?" Erin gave him a bright, sympathetic smile when she met him at the elevator in Goldstein, Miller's pale gray and blue marble lobby.

"That's what I've come to talk to you about," he said as they walked down the long hall to her office.

Even though she was Hugh Mahoney's daughter, she had the same mid-size office that all mid-level associates in the firm were assigned. And it was furnished like all of the others, impressive mahogany desk and two simple client chairs. Her window did afford a partial view of San Diego Bay. But only partial.

He immediately felt at ease because she took one of the two chairs in front of her desk and motioned for him to take the other. The gesture of not putting the massive desk between them reassured him that she was willing to listen.

"Tell me what's going on," she invited.

As he talked about everything that had happened since he had last seen her at the Cays, his eyes filled with tears over and over again, especially when he talked about Nate and about his recent visit to Tina. Without taking her lovely eyes off his face, she reached over and took a tissue out of the box on her desk and handed it to him.

He swiped at his eyes and went on with his story. He wished he had her cool, but sympathetic poise. He knew people called him babyish behind his back. And it was, in part, because his emotions were so close to the surface.

He was waiting for the moment in the narrative when he'd lose her sympathy, the moment when she'd withdraw because he was criticizing the work of partners in her father's firm. But her expression remained kind and sympathetic throughout his story.

When he finished, she said, "One of the things I've learned since Dad and I started our Innocence Project is that defense attorneys often don't listen to their clients. In the criminal defense world, few clients are actually innocent. So there's a bias."

Andy gave her a little smile. "That makes me feel a tiny bit better. You're saying it's not all personal."

"Not always," Erin said. "And I know that Charlotte is going through a lot because she's lost her husband. In some ways, it's not an ideal time for her to be representing someone in your position. And my father has put Sean Donovan under the gun because Sean's lost several trials in a row. And one was a particularly big loss for a client named InTech. He needs to win your case to keep his partnership. That's at least one reason why they're being conservative with your defense."

"But I'll go to prison," Andy said. "And I'll be a convicted felon forever."

"You might not go to prison, depending on what they convict you of. Maybe probation. But the convicted felon part is, of course, true. I see why an accident defense isn't right for you."

"They won't even consider talking to Tina."

"Unfortunately, they've got a point there. Juries often believe girlfriends and family members are lying to save a loved one."

"So a statement from Tina wouldn't help me?"

"I wouldn't go that far," Erin said. "It just wouldn't help as much as, say, those surveillance videos."

"Which are probably lost forever."

She gave him another sympathetic smile. He felt like a wilted plant coming back to life in the warmth of her acceptance. For the first time, he didn't feel as if his past unworthiness was being held against him.

"Have you thought about getting surveillance tapes from the other boat slips around your father's? There are millions of dollars' worth of boats at the Cays Yacht Club. Those owners are not leaving them unmonitored."

"The ones from the club's cameras didn't cover *The Escape*."

"I'm not talking about those. I'm talking about the ones the boat owners themselves undoubtedly have."

Her thought gave Andy a glimmer of hope. But it was quickly dashed when he remembered this morning's prohibition on further evidence gathering. "You're right. But it would be a risk for me to try to contact the owners. Charlotte and Sean were upset because I'd been to see Tina. Still, I'm the only person on my side. I'll take the risk. How do I go about finding out who owns the boats near Dad's?"

"I'll do it," Erin said. "I'll get the names from the club, and I'll contact the owners."

Andy was stunned. "You will? You'll help me?"

She gave him her warm smile again, the one that made him feel like a person instead of an inconvenience. "We started the Innocence Project to help people who've been wrongly convicted. So far, we haven't had the chance to intervene before the wrongful conviction. But here's a chance. Helping you is perfectly consistent with the goals of the project. And besides," she added, "I can see that you could use a friend."

"Thank you." He hoped she wouldn't see that his eyes had misted over again. "I wasn't expecting this."

"I left New York to make a difference as an attorney instead of being all about the money," Erin said. "Here's an opportunity."

"I can never thank you enough," Andy said.

CLOSING IN

CHAPTER TWENTY-NINE

Saturday, October 6, 2018, 4280 Caminito Azur, La Jolla, California

Charlotte had lived with the news of Matt's murder for a month. Thirty days of trouble sleeping. Thirty days of crying sporadically. Thirty days of knowing she should read his file on Rosemary Spencer along with thirty days of paralysis instead of action.

Ian had told her to turn the file over to the police after she found it and let Detective Merrill deal with the contents. Her son believed that the privilege that had attached to Rosemary Spencer's confidences had evaporated because they were evidence of a crime.

But, in fact, none of them knew what was in the file. Some statements might yet be protected by privilege. And Charlotte had a defense attorney's distrust of the police, a distrust that Matt had shared. Handing his unread notes to the arrogant Detective Merrill didn't feel right.

Although the past month had been a roller coaster of emotions, at least the Owens case had been largely dormant. She and Sean had their experts on board. They had lined up evidence to support their accident defense if they needed it. But the best news was that Axel Saldana had approached them about the possibility of working out a plea deal to avoid trial. Sean had smiled at her after their meeting with Saldana and said, "He and Dr. Gus haven't changed their beating theory, and Axel knows that without a murder weapon, his case is largely speculation."

Charlotte didn't remind Sean that the murder weapon was likely in the broom closet at the Cays. That was another thing she didn't want to think about.

She preferred to believe that there was a good chance that the Owens matter would be settled soon, and she'd be free of the career pressure that came with it. Granted it would be hard to sell Andy on taking a plea deal that would probably include at least two years of prison time, but a deal was his only hope of avoiding a murder conviction. And if he took a deal, she and Sean wouldn't have to listen to any more of his childish protestations of innocence.

So on the one-month anniversary of Detective Merrill's horrible news, Charlotte drove home from work at six, determined to get over her reluctance to find Matt's file and read it. It began to rain as soon as she turned into her drive. The light sprinkles quickly became a heavy, steady downpour that lasted all night. The sound of the rain on the roof was company for her in the wee, sleepless hours as she tried to steel herself to the task of going through Matt's files in the morning.

Sean had offered to help, and she'd seriously considered accepting his offer. But in the end, she'd felt that if Matt had left a clue for her about the danger he was in, that message had been intended for her alone. So after a short run and a light breakfast, she went upstairs to the spare bedroom that she used as an office to begin her search.

She'd had the boxes of Matt's files retrieved from storage a month ago when the necessity of looking for the Spencer file had become evident. They were just the ones he'd been working on at the time of his death. The others had been archived digitally and were housed on the Goldstein, Miller servers.

Last year, it had been hard to go through his things, his clothes, his shoes, his books, all the everyday objects that reminded Charlotte of their life together. Now her tears came back as she searched the records of his work for his clients. Several times that morning, she thought of giving up and of calling Sean to come and find the file and post it to Detective Merrill unread.

But she plowed on. After a couple of hours of searching, she found it. "Rosemary Spencer, Matter No. 487382."

She went into the kitchen and made herself a cup of tea. She noticed that the rain had begun again. She felt as dreary and sad as the wet, gray day. When her tea was ready, she carried the file into the sunroom and sat down in one of the comfortable chairs. She opened it to page one and began to read the story that she had never expected to have such a tragic ending.

His first meeting with Rosemary Spencer had been in July 2017. Matt's spidery scrawl had noted the referral from her lobbying firm, James and Mitchell. Her assigned client was Light Source Ventures. Matt's notes documented her confession that she had offered expensive vacations to two Congressmen, one from California, the other from Washington State, in exchange for their efforts to assist Light Source in selling cybersecurity software to the U.S. government. One of the

Congressman had reported the bribe to the Department of Justice.

Matt's notes showed meetings with the U.S. Attorney in charge of the case in July, August, and September. In September, he had documented the possibility of an offer to drop the charges if Rosemary Spencer would provide information about Light Source to the government. A proffer session to determine the value of her information had been set for October and then rescheduled for November. But the proffer never took place because Matt died a week before it was scheduled. Charlotte wrote down the name and telephone number of the U.S. Attorney who had handled the Spencer case.

Charlotte felt confident that Matt had documented the information that Rosemary Spencer had been willing to offer in the proffer session. But there were no notes in the file. That made little sense because Matt had always kept meticulously accurate records. She went back to the boxes and spent the rest of the afternoon looking for the proffer notes but without success.

That night, after taking her mother to dinner, she put on her pajamas and tried to relax in bed with Netflix. But her lack of success in finding anything to explain Matt's death haunted her.

She got up, found her laptop, and searched for Light Source Ventures. But the search yielded little information. They had offices in New York and San Francisco, both devoted to software development. The company had been founded by three software engineers. It was publicly traded, but its most recent SEC filings didn't tell Charlotte much more than it seemed to be paying healthy dividends to its shareholders. There were no red flags that suggested the kind of illegal activity that the U.S. Attorney would have been interested in.

* * *

Monday, October 8, 2018, Offices of Goldstein, Miller, Emerald Shapery Center

On Monday, she phoned David Hays, the partner at Warrick, Thompson in D.C., who had represented James and Mitchell. Hays told her that Matt had mentioned the possibility of a proffer session but had assured him that Rosemary Spencer's information did not implicate her employer. Nothing more had been said beyond that. And Hays was certain that no one at James and Mitchell knew anything about illegal activities by Light Source.

She tried to contact the U.S. Attorney who'd worked with Matt, but he was no longer with the Department of Justice.

"You look disappointed," Sean observed from her doorway.

"I am. Come in, and I'll tell you all about it."

Charlotte finished the litany of her unsuccessful search by pulling up Light Source's website on her computer. The landing page had a picture of the three founders.

"I know two of those guys," Sean said.

"What? Are you sure?"

"Absolutely. Wish I didn't know them."

"Who are they?"

"The two on the right were the Chief Operating Officer and the Chief Financial Officer of InTech, the company that earned me my black eye with the firm."

"You mean that big trial you lost?"

"Right. Those two characters are Tim Daily and Martin Bernstein. They convinced me that their SEC disclosure documents about InTech's financial health were accurate. That turned out not to be true."

"So they started over with Light Source Ventures, apparently."

"Apparently. I'm wondering where they got the cash to fund themselves. The jury awarded enough damages to send InTech belly up. I will say this, if those two are involved in Light Source, you can bet there's something illegal going on."

"But Matt's file didn't give me any clues about what it is."

"The U.S. Attorney is the person you need to talk to."

"His name is Eric Franson, and he no longer works for the Department of Justice. I was getting ready to run a search for him through the D.C. Bar when you came in."

"Sounds like a good idea. I'll go back to my office and call some of my old colleagues and see if I can come up with anything."

"Thanks."

"I came to tell you that it looks like Axel is going to offer Andy a plea to voluntary manslaughter with the low term of three years. So he'd be out in eighteen months."

"That would be a great deal," Charlotte said. "But you realize Andy won't think so."

"I was counting on his parents to lean on him."

"And you were hoping I would talk to Lucas?"

"Unfortunately, you're the logical person to do it."

"How soon do I have to?"

"Not until we get a formal offer. Axel hasn't gotten formal

approval from Bart Stephenson, yet. But he's optimistic that a definite yes is coming any day now."

"Well, I'll deal with that when I have to," Charlotte said. "Right now, I'm a lot more interested in talking to Eric Franson about his dealings with Matt and Rosemary Spencer."

* * *

Monday October 8, 2018, 4280 Caminito Azur, La Jolla, California

That night, Charlotte curled up in her sunroom with a cup of tea and her laptop, obsessed with finding Eric Franson. After twenty minutes of searching, she found him. He was a partner in the Chicago Office of King and White. His specialty was defending financial crimes.

She sipped her tea and studied Franson's picture. He was wearing a navy suit, white shirt, and deep-maroon tie. His arms were folded across his chest, the classic litigator's power pose. He had a long, thin face and serious dark eyes that seemed incompatible with the smile that he'd clearly put on only for the camera. His dark hair was peppered with gray. She guessed that he was in his mid-to-late forties and that he had almost no sense of humor and no patience with people who wasted his time. But she hoped that he could tell her what Rosemary Spencer had been planning to offer the government because undoubtedly Matt had been killed to prevent that disclosure.

She picked up her phone and called Sean at home. "I've found him."

"Franson? Really? Where?"

"He's followed in your footsteps and left the government for big money. He's a financial crimes partner at King and White in Chicago."

"Let me pull him up on my computer. Maybe I've met him. I used to go to the D.C. office quite a bit."

Charlotte waited for Sean to find the King and White website.

"No," Sean said a few seconds later. "No luck. I've never met him."

"Too bad. I was hoping for an in. I need to talk to him."

"He won't be able to tell you anything if he agreed to keep Rosemary Spencer's proposed proffer information confidential."

"Are you sure?"

"I was an Assistant U.S. Attorney in my other life."

"But I don't have any other way to find out why Matt was killed. I'll take the red-eye to Chicago tomorrow night and take my chances that he'll tell me what he knows."

"Don't you think you should call ahead and find out if he's in town?"

"Of course."

"You shouldn't go alone."

"Why not?"

"Have you forgotten that they are after you, too?"

"Not forgotten. But nothing's happened recently. And I've been running again. No one's following me."

"Or so you think."

"I've been watching very closely."

"Tell you what, I'll go with you."

"Okay. Since you're one of his tribe, he might be more willing to talk to you."

"Did you get your husband's file on that Spencer woman out of your house?"

"Not yet. But I'm assuming Matt met with her to find out what she was going to say; his notes are not in the file."

"That is, if he took notes."

"Matt always took notes."

"Not if he realized that what she knew endangered both of them."

CHAPTER THIRTY

Monday, October 8, 2018, United Flight 1589, San Diego to Chicago

At ten fifteen p.m., fifteen minutes after it was scheduled to take off, United Fight 1589, hurled itself into the night sky, bound for Chicago. Charlotte closed her eyes and wished for a drink. But the flight attendants wouldn't be around with the cart for ages.

Her nerves were frayed, and she was completely exhausted. She'd made a mistake to take the red-eye. Instead of keeping her appointments that were already on her calendar for today, she should have left for Chicago this morning. She'd be sleeping in the suite that she had booked at the Fairmont right now, gazing out at the lights of Millennium Park and the city, instead of flying through the night and condemning herself to function on caffeine and courage in the morning.

"We've got to postpone the trip," Sean had said at four that afternoon. He'd come into her office with a long face and plopped down in one of the chairs in front of her desk.

"We can't. Eric Franson will see me tomorrow morning at ten. Then he's leaving for Zurich for ten days."

"Well, you can see him in ten days when he comes back."

But she shook her head. "No. I can't wait to find out what he knows."

"Bad idea," Sean said.

"Well, bad idea or not, it's my idea. And I'm going to Chicago at ten o'clock tonight on the red-eye."

"But we have to be here tomorrow," Sean insisted. "Axel has called a meeting in the morning."

"About what?"

"No idea."

"Did he mention the plea offer?"

"No, he didn't. But I'm guessing that's what it's about. He's going to make a formal offer. We'll just have to wait and see."

"*You'll* have to wait and see. I'm going to Chicago tonight as planned."

He looked exasperated. "Charlotte, we talked about that. It's dangerous for you to be traveling alone."

"I'll be in public places."

"Not in your hotel room."

"I'll lock the door."

"Charlotte, someone killed your husband. And someone's been trying to kill you ever since."

"Not someone. Rosemary Spencer. I'll keep an eye out for her. Don't worry."

"Of course I'm going to worry. And you should, too. And you shouldn't go without me!"

"Probably not. But I'm going anyway."

* * *

Tuesday, October 9, 2018, Offices of King and White, Chicago

The attractive red-haired receptionist who presided over King and White's vast reception area like an empress summoned her minions to seat Charlotte comfortably on one of the plush white sofas by a wall of glass that allowed her to survey the view from the fiftieth floor of the Blue Shield Tower. Chicago's forest of skyscrapers marched in lockstep toward the horizon. One of the minions brought her coffee in a simple white mug with the cream she had requested.

She'd arrived fifteen minutes early for her ten o'clock appointment. She'd had little sleep on the plane. She'd blocked out her anxiety over Sean's warning that she shouldn't travel alone and had focused on her overwhelming need to get to the bottom of Matt's death. But as she had settled in for the flight, the fear that had gripped her when she'd heard the gunshot that day at the canal suddenly hit her out of nowhere. When the drinks cart had arrived, Charlotte had ordered a scotch because that had been Matt's drink of choice when he was deeply upset. But the whiskey tasted like bitter medicine, and it did nothing to allay her anxiety. After two sips, she summoned the flight attendant to take it away.

There had been no sign of dawn when her plane landed at four forty a.m. She had made her way to ground transportation where the driver of a black town car approached and offered her a cut-rate fare to the city. She had considered his offer because there were no taxis at the cab stand at that moment and summoning an Uber would take longer. But she had thought better of it because heading off into the dark with a stranger under the present circumstances was asking for trouble.

So she had taken the next bright-yellow taxi that had pulled up to the curb and had settled back for the thirty-minute ride to the city. The first pink streaks of dawn had been visible when she had checked into her suite at the Fairmont on the edge of Millennium Park.

She glanced at her watch. It was exactly ten o'clock. Where was Eric Franson?

She hadn't been able to sleep even after she'd reached the hotel. Her mind had whirled round and round thinking of ways to persuade Eric Franson to tell her about the disclosures that Rosemary Spencer had been prepared to make.

A half hour passed without being summoned to Franson's office. She got up and went over to the marble reception desk that occupied an entire wall. A placard announced that the young ruler's name was Ms. Lipon.

"Yes, of course. Mr. Franson does seem to be running late," Her Majesty agreed. "I'll call his secretary. In the meantime, I'll have someone bring you a fresh cup of coffee."

Charlotte resumed her seat and took out her iPhone. It was eight thirty in San Diego. The day's emails were stacking up. Best to get a start on them while she waited.

A few minutes later, Ms. Lipon herself appeared with another mug of coffee.

"I'm so sorry, Mrs. Estes. There's no word from Mr. Franson. This is highly unusual. Would you like to continue to wait, or would you like to reschedule your meeting with him?"

"I flew in from San Diego overnight just to see him," Charlotte said, trying to keep emotion out of her voice. "This is the only reason I'm in Chicago. I'll wait. Does anyone have any idea when he might be coming in?"

Her Majesty had stopped looking regal and now looked sympathetic. "I'll talk to his secretary and see if she knows what's going on."

Charlotte watched her go back to her throne and pick up the phone and have an earnest conversation with whoever was on the other end. Then she went back to trying to focus on her emails. There was one from Sean asking her to call as soon as her meeting with Franson was over.

Ten forty-five became eleven fifteen. Charlotte suppressed her desire to go back to the reception desk and demand to know the outcome of the call to Franson's secretary.

At eleven twenty-five, the door to the inner offices opened, and a thirty-something brunette with large dark eyes came over to Charlotte.

"I'm Terry Milton, Mr. Franson's secretary," she said. "I don't know what's happened with Eric. He had an eight a.m. breakfast meeting at The Langham Hotel and then your meeting with him at ten was on his calendar. He should have been back in plenty of time to keep his appointment with you, but we haven't heard from him."

"I see." Charlotte's stomach tightened, and her heart began to race.

"It's not like Eric to forget a meeting," his secretary said, "especially with someone from out of town. I tried to call his wife to see if there was some sort of family emergency, but she's not answering. It could be one of their children. I expect he'll be in eventually or call and let us know what's going on. How long are you staying in Chicago?"

"I've scheduled a return flight at ten thirty tonight," Charlotte said. She struggled to keep her voice emotionless, but she was overcome with disappointment and anxiety. "I didn't sleep much last night. I'll go back to my hotel and rest and wait for news. If he does come in later, would you ask him if he will still see me?"

"Of course."

* * *

Tuesday, October 9, 2018, The Fairmont Hotel, Chicago

Charlotte went back to her suite, took off her suit jacket, and paced her room. She felt driven to do something, but she couldn't think of what she could do. Trying to make up for lost sleep was out of the question. She'd picked at her croissant and fruit breakfast that morning. But food didn't sound appealing either.

Where was Eric Franson? He'd agreed to a meeting when she'd phoned him. She felt certain that he wouldn't have let her fly all the way to Chicago just to stand her up. He'd have told her before she left San Diego that he wasn't going to see her.

His secretary had said he was meeting a client at The Langham. The hotel was about a fifteen-minute walk from the Fairmont. It didn't seem possible that Eric Franson was still there. But sometimes meetings ran long, and he could have forgotten that his phone was turned off. It was the longest of shots, but it was better than sitting in her room, waiting for a phone call. And it was unseasonably warm for Chicago and therefore inviting walking weather. So she put on her suit jacket and headed out, hoping that her gamble would pay off and that she'd find Franson.

* * *

Breakfast service had ended in Travelle, the concierge informed her, but lunch was underway. Charlotte made her way to the restaurant on the second floor and ordered the quinoa salad. The soft neutrals were soothing. The room was populated with light-wood tables and sleek versions of traditional captain's chairs. She found that she was actually hungry by the time her lunch arrived.

But there was no sign of Eric Franson. She recognized her trip to the hotel for what it was, denial and desperation. She paid her check and decided to go back to the Fairmont. She was tempted to go back to King and White, instead, to ask in person for news, but she knew she'd have received a call if there was any.

She was crossing the nearly deserted lobby, headed for the street, when her attention was drawn to a man and a woman sitting in the large square club chairs to the left of the hotel's front door. They were glancing at the door, as if waiting for someone. The man's back was toward her, but the woman was facing her.

The woman glanced up, and Charlotte suddenly felt as if she'd been hit by a rock. Rosemary Spencer looked away quickly, and Charlotte knew she'd been recognized. She said something to the man, but he did not turn. The two of them got up and headed toward the elevators so quickly that Charlotte barely got a glimpse of Spencer's companion. He was about six feet tall with light-blond hair. He was wearing a gray suit. Charlotte wondered if he was Rosemary Spencer's business associate or another unlucky attorney hired to represent her.

She was so upset that she hailed a cab for the four-minute journey back to the Fairmont. But her legs were shaking, and her heart was pounding. And she wished she'd listened to Sean and stayed home.

* * *

Charlotte fumbled with her keys and managed to open the door to her suite. She sat down on the sofa in the living room and breathed deeply, trying to still her racing heart. For a minute, she tried to convince herself that she'd been mistaken. But the blond woman was definitely Rosemary Spencer.

Charlotte took her cell phone out of her purse and called 9-1-1.

"Nine-one-one, what's your emergency?"

"I've just seen the woman who's wanted for the murder of my husband at The Langham Hotel."

"And your name is?"

"Charlotte Estes. I'm an attorney. I live in San Diego. I'm in Chicago to meet with another attorney who may have information about why my husband was murdered."

"I'm sorry, Ms. Estes. That's not an emergency. I'll transfer you to our routine reports line."

"Please! Wait!"

But her call rolled to hold and then a minute later, Charlotte realized she'd been cut off. She took a long breath and stared at her phone. She considered trying again. Maybe she'd reach a dispatcher more willing to listen. But maybe the story without the rest of the facts did sound too crazy to be believed. As much as she hated Detective Merrill's cold, piggy-eyed stare, he alone would understand the significance of her news. She found him in her phone contacts and hit call.

His phone rang and rang and eventually rolled to a voicemail that announced it was full. She called back and hit the button that promised to connect her with a live person.

"Detective Roberts."

"I'm Charlotte Estes. I'm trying to reach Detective Merrill."

"He's out of the office until Monday. You should call back and leave a voicemail."

"No, his is full. I've just seen the woman who's the suspect in the homicide of my husband, Matt Estes. She's here in Chicago."

"Then report it to the Chicago Police Department."

"I tried. They wouldn't listen."

"Are you sure you've seen the actual suspect, Mrs. Estes? Isn't this quite a coincidence?"

"Maybe. Not exactly. I'm not sure." She was growing more nervous by the minute as she tried to convince him to move on her news. "I live in San Diego. I flew here to talk to an attorney who may know why Matt was murdered. But he didn't show up at the office this morning to see me as scheduled."

"Who did you say you are?"

Charlotte could tell that she was losing her credibility with him every time she opened her mouth. "Charlotte Estes. My husband Matt died last November. The coroner thought it was a heart attack. But Detective Merrill came to see me in San Diego in September to tell me that Matt had been poisoned."

"I see. And how do you know that this Spencer woman is the suspect?"

"Because Detective Merrill told me so!" She couldn't hold back her frustration any longer. "Because I saw her in the hotel room the night my husband died. The woman at The Langham just now is the same woman. There was a man with her. I didn't get a good look at him, but if he's her attorney, his life could be in danger, too."

"Okay," Detective Roberts said. "I've pulled up your husband's file in the computer. Matthew Estes, right? It says suspect is a British national. Rosemary Spencer."

Charlotte wanted to scream *I just told you that*. But she managed to hold her anger in check. "That's right. Detective Merrill said Scotland Yard has been looking for her without any success. Well, she's here. Now. In Chicago."

"Okay, Mrs. Estes. I'll phone the department there and get them to check out your tip. You said The Langham Hotel? Do you know if she's staying there?"

"I don't. But the attorney who I was supposed to meet at ten this morning was going there at eight to see a client. He never made it to his office."

"And you said he had information about your husband's death?"

"I think so. I'm here to find out."

"Okay, I'll text you my direct number in case you get to meet with him. Call me if he tells you anything we should know."

"I will. Thank you."

Charlotte sat back on the sofa and closed her eyes for a few seconds. She had that edgy feeling that only a good long run could cure. But she hadn't brought her running clothes, and she was still waiting for news about Eric Franson. Surely King and White had heard from him by now. She picked up her phone again and dialed the number his secretary had given her.

"I was just getting ready to call you," Terry Milton said. "We've had some really bad news about Eric."

"What's happened?"

"He became ill this morning during his breakfast meeting. The hotel summoned an ambulance, and they took him to Northwestern Memorial." Her voice broke.

Charlotte realized that her hands were clammy and shaking. She knew the answer even before she asked the question. "Is he going to be all right?"

"No, Mrs. Estes. He passed away about an hour ago. His wife just called a few minutes before you did. He had a heart attack."

* * *

Tuesday, October 9, 2018, The Fairmont Hotel, Chicago

Charlotte stared at her phone for a long time after her call with Terry Milton ended. Her thoughts were racing. Rosemary Spencer had killed again. And Rosemary Spencer knew that Charlotte was in Chicago. For a minute Charlotte felt safe because at least no one knew where she was staying. But then she realized that she'd been seen in the area, and it would be easy for Spencer and her cohorts to call all the nearby hotels and discover that Charlotte was at the Fairmont.

Her phone began to ring again. Charlotte willed her shaking hands to be still enough to let her answer it.

"Charlotte, it's Sean. I've just left the meeting with Axel. I've got bad news."

She glanced over at the clock on the end table. One thirty. So it was only eleven thirty in San Diego. She'd forgotten all about the meeting with Axel.

"Charlotte? Are you there? Can you hear me?"

She struggled to find her voice. "Yes, Sean. I'm here. I've had some bad news, myself."

"So your meeting didn't go well?"

"There was no meeting. Without going into all the details, the woman who killed Matt, killed Eric Franson this morning over breakfast at The Langham Hotel."

"Oh, God! Charlotte! I told you that you were being watched. Rosemary Spencer knew exactly why you were going to Chicago. And she got there ahead of you."

"And she saw me, Sean. She knows I'm in Chicago."

"Good, God. Where did she see you?"

"At The Langham. I went there for lunch. I had a crazy idea that I might run into Franson."

"I agree that was a crazy idea. And dangerous. When is your return flight?"

"Tonight at ten thirty. But I'm going to head for O'Hare now and see if I can get an earlier one."

"You shouldn't be there alone."

"I've come to realize that. You can say 'I told you so' when I get back."

"I can say it, but I won't. I've got something far more important to tell you. That's why I called."

"What is it?"

"Bart Stephenson didn't want to extend an offer to Andy. He was afraid that he'd be accused of taking a payoff from the parents. So he made Axel send the cops back to search *The Escape* again."

"And?"

"They found an expended bullet casing. A nine-millimeter."

CHAPTER THIRTY-ONE

Tuesday, October 9, 2018, Lindbergh Field, San Diego

At ten thirty, Charlotte stepped out of the secure area of the Lindbergh Field terminal into the public lobby, almost too tired to pull her suitcase behind her as she headed for the taxi stand. She hadn't been able to get an earlier flight, and her body felt as if it was well past midnight because she was on Chicago time.

"Here, I'll take that." Sean reached out to take her bag.

"What are you doing here?"

"Making sure you're safe. You said I could say 'I told you so' about traveling alone when you got back. In case you need a reminder, someone is trying to kill you."

"How did you know I wasn't on an earlier plane?"

"Bribery. And that's all I'm going to say about that. Come on. You look too tired to be questioning my methods. We're headed this way. I got lucky and found a parking space close by."

She followed him to his black BMW which was not far away as he'd promised. He put her bag in the back seat and opened the front passenger door for her before walking over to the driver's side and getting in.

"I'm taking you to my place for the night," he said as he started the engine and began moving toward the exit. "I've got a spare room with a bath, and you've got your pj's with you."

"Thanks, but I'd rather go home."

"I'll overlook your slight to my hospitality," he said. "You know for sure that you're being followed because the man you went to Chicago to see was killed this morning. And someone wants to make you next. So it's my place for now. You can sleep in because I'm so close to the office. Consider it a dry run for my new career as the host of an Airbnb if we get slammed in the Owens case. And we can talk about that tomorrow."

* * *

Charlotte woke to the smell of coffee brewing. For a minute she thought she was still at the hotel in Chicago. Then she remembered this was Sean's spare bedroom, and she was here because Rosemary Spencer had killed Eric Franson yesterday. For a moment, the full horror of what surrounded her overwhelmed her, and tears welled up in her eyes. But she fought off the urge to give in to emotion. Instead, she checked her phone for the time. Eight fifteen. She got up and put on her robe and went to the kitchen, hoping there was enough coffee for two.

Sean was already dressed for the office in a gray suit and dark-blue tie. He was filling up a travel mug with coffee. He smiled when she came in.

"I was hoping you'd wake up before I left. I've got to be in superior court this morning for a status conference. I made extra coffee, and here's the Omni's room service menu. Order whatever you want. It's on me."

He finished pouring coffee for himself and poured a cup for her.

"Thanks."

"How did you sleep? Asking for a friend who might be my first Airbnb guest."

"Very well, thanks. Are you serious about becoming an innkeeper?"

"Host. The word is 'host.' And definitely yes if we don't pull off a miracle for the Owens kid."

"Maybe we should call him 'Andy' instead of 'kid.' He's thirty-two."

"Maybe."

"When do you want to talk about the news from Axel?"

"Not now. I want you to enjoy your breakfast. Take your time. This status conference has six plaintiffs, and I'm the lone defense attorney. So it's going to last a while. I'll come to your office after I get back from court, and we can wring our hands together. I recommend the Eggs Benedict by the way. And the green smoothie isn't bad if you're determined to sacrifice taste for nutrition. See you later."

He smiled again as he headed for the front door. A few seconds later, she heard it close behind him. Suddenly there were tears in her eyes again. Mornings with Matt had been like this. One of them leaving for the office early, telling the other they'd meet up later to discuss a case.

But she didn't want to cry. Crying wouldn't change anything. The coffee was perfect, dark and rich. She found half and half in the refrigerator and added a drop. She ordered the Eggs Benedict and studied the view of Coronado from Sean's living room while she waited for her food. Had the Chicago police caught up with Rosemary Spencer by now? Detective Merrill had promised to let her know when they took her into custody. He'd seemed certain that she wouldn't be able to slip out of the country undetected this time. She checked her phone for messages. But there were none.

* * *

It was one o'clock before Sean appeared in her office.

"How was breakfast?"

"You were right about the eggs. And you were right about the length of that status conference."

"What can I say? Six plaintiffs beating up one defense attorney. I was tempted to drink my lunch."

"And that doesn't mean a green smoothie I take it?"

"No, but I settled for a salad instead. You might be a good influence on me."

"Thanks for picking me up last night. And thanks for the hospitality."

"If you want my honest opinion, I think you should take out a lease on that room for a while. Or rent one of the empty condos in my building. You'd be safer."

"I'll be fine at the house. Detective Merrill is going to call me when they pick up Rosemary Spencer."

"And has he called you?"

"No."

"My point exactly."

"So where are we on Andy's case?"

"It's more like where Axel is. Because the cops found that

casing, Dr. Gus has changed his mind about the cause of death. It's now homicide by gunshot wound."

"Not surprising. Did they find the gun, too?"

"No. They've been back to look, but they haven't found it."

"But how can that be?" Charlotte's tone was skeptical.

"Well, if you recall, we almost missed it."

"But unfortunately for us, we didn't."

"Now don't start throwing Rules of Professional Responsibility at me," Sean warned. "We both know that we have no idea whether that's the murder weapon or not."

"I'd like to believe you, but honestly, what are the chances that it's not?"

"It doesn't matter if it is or isn't as long as Axel doesn't have it."

"But at this point I think we have an obligation to tell Axel about what we found and recuse ourselves."

"No!" Sean's voice rose. "If we hand off this case under those circumstances, we'll be putting the kid under a cloud. And as much as I don't like him, I don't want to do that. Our coroner says the damage shown on the head X-ray is from the heavy surf that night."

"But Dr. Cerna didn't say that," Charlotte reminded him.

"But no one else knows that, and we aren't under any obligation to reveal Dr. Cerna's opinion to Axel."

"True."

"Unless Axel finds the gun, I think we can still use our accident defense," Sean said.

"How so?"

"Using Dr. Walsh's testimony, we can show the jury that

there's reasonable doubt about Dr. Gus' finding and that Dr. Gus changed his mind just to make the prosecutor happy. And the rest of the evidence that we've put together in the defense case lines up with Nate's death being an accident."

"So how do we explain that nine-millimeter bullet casing?"

"We don't. We have no burden of proof. It's Axel's job to tie the gun and the casing and Andy together. And he can't do that. Without the gun, Axel's chances of getting a murder conviction aren't very good in my professional, ex-prosecutor opinion. If this case goes to trial, the jury will have to choose between Axel's version of the facts, gunshot wound with no gun and no proof our client used the missing gun, and our version, Nate fell off the boat when it hit that buoy because Andy was driving drunk. Our version fits what happened in New York. Andy's a careless child of wealthy parents with a serious drinking problem, but he doesn't intend to kill people. That should get him involuntary manslaughter and minimal prison time or even probation. I think the jury will go for our story. At least, as long as Axel doesn't find that Glock."

"But what if Andy has gone back to the villa and disposed of it? Lucas turned the surveillance tapes back on, so he might be on tape with that gun."

"Right," Sean agreed. "Axel is going to ask for those tapes. We'd better have a look at them first to see if there's anything incriminatory on them. Let's set up a meeting with Lucas ASAP."

CHAPTER THIRTY-TWO

Friday, October 12, 2018, The Italian Kitchen, La Jolla

But Lucas refused to meet with the two of them at Charlotte's office. Instead, he insisted on a dinner meeting with Charlotte alone. She resisted, but in the end, she had to give in.

"I know how you feel about him," Sean said, "and I don't blame you. But we've got to get those tapes even if it means you have to listen to what's on his agenda alone."

But, of course, Lucas' agenda was exactly what she didn't want to hear.

He had already settled into one of the red leather banquettes at La Jolla's famed Italian Kitchen, nursing a glass of red wine and nibbling on the legendary antipasto platter when she arrived at seven thirty. He was hitting on a very young, very blond waitress who was laughing at his jokes, but whose eyes said she wanted to run away. Sleazy. The word popped into her head as she surveyed him in his dark polo shirt, unbuttoned enough to reveal some dark chest hair and a matching blazer. He was laughing at his own jokes and patting the waitress on the shoulder even though she winced at his touch. She looked like the stereotypical aspiring model and actress. At least this gig paid well.

Lucas immediately lost interest in his captive when he saw Charlotte. He stood up as she crossed the room to his table. But when he tried to kiss her cheek, she offered him a firm handshake instead and slid into the seat opposite.

He looked disappointed, but he picked up the bottle of wine and poured a glass for her, apparently trying to show her that he didn't care.

"Antinori Solaia, Chianti, 1999," he said. "There's nothing like it. And I hope you don't mind that I ordered the antipasto platter. The salami and the olives are the best."

She forced herself to smile and took a sip of wine. She wondered how fast she could get to the point and go home.

He settled back in his seat and smiled at her. He said, "I'm glad you finally agreed to have dinner with me."

"I've come to talk about Andy's case." *Best to disabuse him of the notion that this is personal right away.*

"Of course. But it gives me an opportunity to say that I've missed you. It's just so good to see you again."

Charlotte was relieved that the waitress interrupted with an offer to take their order. She acquiesced in Lucas' seafood pasta choice to hurry the evening along.

"So I was saying that I've missed you," he repeated when the waitress retreated.

"Lucas, I've already told you that the past is the past. I'm not interested in going over old history."

"I'm not, either. I'm interested in making some new history. What do you think?"

"I think I'm your son's attorney, and this is why I agreed to meet you for dinner."

His face fell. He sipped his wine and ate a few olives. Charlotte was relieved by his silence. But he was a man used to getting his way, so she braced herself for his next attempt.

"Would it make any difference if I told you how unhappy Ella and I have been together?" His dark eyes searched her face, looking for any chink in her armor of indifference.

"No, it wouldn't."

"The disaster of my marriage is obvious, isn't it?"

"Lucas, we need to focus on Andy. There's a new development in his case, and it's not good news."

He sighed, drank some more wine, and then topped off his glass before he asked, "What's the bad news, then?"

The waitress arrived with salads. When they were safely settled on the table, Charlotte said, "The prosecutor sent the police back to search *The Escape*, and this time they found a nine-millimeter bullet casing. So Dr. Tavoularis has changed his theory about the cause of death. Now it's a gunshot wound to the head."

Lucas looked stricken. "I don't know what to say."

"Does Andy own a nine-millimeter firearm?"

"Not exactly. I had a Glock 26 that I kept at the villa. Andy and I have used it to shoot off rounds to celebrate New Year's. When he was in high school, we used to go to the shooting range. Ella and I both neglected him. Teaching him to shoot was my belated effort at father-son bonding time."

"Did you ever use the gun to celebrate New Year's on *The Escape*?"

"No. I got *The Escape* in March. I'd only had it three months when Andy wrecked it."

"And Nate was killed." *Always focused on yourself, aren't you?*

"Right. And Nate was killed," he dutifully repeated.

"Where was your gun that night?"

"I thought it was at the villa, but apparently it wasn't."

"What do you mean?"

"I always kept it in the locked drawer of the desk in the bedroom that I used as an office. When I realized that the cops were coming, I checked the drawer, thinking I'd better get rid of it because I didn't want them to find a gun in the house even though it had nothing to do with Nate's disappearance. But the gun wasn't there. I just figured someone had taken it out without telling me, and I was relieved that it wasn't there for the cops to find. After the coroner's report, I realized it wasn't important in Andy's case, anyway, so I forgot about it."

"But if you kept the drawer locked, how could someone have taken the gun out?"

"The key to the drawer was in a metal box on the desk. Andy and all his friends knew the key was there." He paused and focused on the candle in the center of the table. His dark, sad eyes, seemingly lost in the flickering flame, suddenly reminded her of the boy she'd loved. Finally those eyes met hers, still thoughtful and sad. He said, "Andy was devastated when that girl stopped seeing him, but up until this minute, I didn't think he was capable of murder."

She studied his face. The one thing he hadn't had was plastic surgery. In the low light, the wrinkles were visible. They made him look tired and old and sad. Whatever heartache he had caused her was long gone. Suddenly she felt sympathy for him. He'd paid for his greed with his unhappy life.

"Of course you can have the tapes. But why do you need to see them?"

I'm not going to tell him Sean and I broke into the villa and found his gun.

Instead, Charlotte said, "The police have searched the villa several times. The most recent search was this week. And they haven't found your gun."

"But surely Andy didn't take it back to the villa after—" She could see that he couldn't bring himself to finish.

"Sean and I don't know," she lied. "But we do know that Axel is going to ask for any surveillance tapes you have. We need to see if Andy's on them with the Glock. If he took it back to the villa that night, he probably came to get it and dispose of it at some point. If he did and the tapes show that, our accident defense goes out the window. Andy is as good as convicted."

"I didn't know that the police were at the villa this week."

"Didn't Sean call to tell you they were coming?"

"He probably did, and I didn't take the call. I told Jeanne I only wanted to talk to you about Andy's case."

"Well, you can't do that. I was out of town while all this was going on. If Sean calls, you have to talk to him."

"I apologize." All at once, Lucas had tears in his eyes.

She crossed her knife and fork across her plate, signaling she was finished with the entree, and put her hand over his sympathetically. For a moment, her burst of sympathy for him returned. At that moment, he wasn't the arrogant man she despised. He was the boy she and her father had loved. And his son was in trouble, and it was her job to keep him from going to prison for life.

He looked at her and said, "Thank you."

She removed her hand from his as he wiped his eyes with his napkin. She could see that the tears had embarrassed him.

"How do you feel about coffee and dessert?"

She decided she was willing to stay a little longer because the sudden emergence of his genuine pain had touched her. "Decaf," she said and smiled again.

After they had settled with their coffee, he said, "I apologize for the waterworks."

"It's okay. It's understandable."

"It's just that I know this is all my fault. Ella didn't want children. I insisted. Then I was too busy to give him what he needed." He paused as if considering how to explain his feelings. Then he said, "I need another chance, Charlotte. To be there for him. To spend time with him. To tell him I really do care about him. If he goes to prison, I won't have that chance. Please, give me that chance."

His eyes were wet with tears again. Charlotte gave his hand one more quick squeeze and then stood up. Suddenly, she wanted to be away from the intensity of his emotion. "Sean and I are trying as hard as we can. Get those tapes to us on Monday if at all possible. We have to know what's on them."

"I will. Let me walk you to your car."

"No, Lucas, that's fine. I'm parked close by."

But as Charlotte hurried away from the restaurant in the dark, she heard rapid footsteps behind her. And they stayed behind her. Whoever it was, wanted to follow without overtaking her. She didn't turn around because she didn't want to see who was there. She breathed a sigh of relief when she got into her Mercedes and drove off.

BEING GUILTY

CHAPTER THIRTY-THREE

"You've brought the wrong financial report," Elliott Shafer, the president of the Owens Small Business Foundation, told Andy condescendingly at eight thirty on Monday morning as they sat in the small conference room near Andy's office.

Andy looked down at the document he'd pulled out of his file marked "Owens Financial Docs" and frowned. "No, I didn't. This is the 'Comprehensive Financial Report of Owens Commercial Real Estate and Construction.' The Foundation is part of my father's business, not my mother's." He didn't add that this was the statement he'd taken off his father's desk under protest from Jeanne.

"But ours is separate from the rest of the company because we're a nonprofit. Here," Elliott tossed a stapled set of papers toward Andy, who was trying not to let his resentment overwhelm him. Elliott was only a couple of years older than he was, but he had been far more successful with his business degree from San Diego State than Andy had been.

Feeling humiliated, Andy picked up the report and studied it. After a minute or two he said, "There's no individual listing of accounts here for the businesses that the Foundation has assisted."

"That's broken down here." Elliott pulled a thicker report out of the stack of papers that he had brought with him and shoved it across the table to Andy, who picked it up and began to turn the pages. He felt Elliott's blue eyes watching him with amusement. He struggled to contain his anger and resentment.

Elliott said, "I think I can save us a lot of time by telling you that the Hernandez Moving account is on page ten, and it shows that it's in default."

Andy turned to page ten, saw the default entry, and looked up at Elliott. "It was my understanding that Mrs. Hernandez, who keeps the company's books, took the Foundation to small claims court and showed that the payments on the trucks' leases had been made."

"And I assume the said Mrs. Hernandez told you that?"

Andy tried to tell himself that Elliott's smile was meant to be friendly, but it looked more like a smirk. He didn't want to admit that Letty Hernandez had sworn never to speak to him again and that all his information had come through her sister, Esmeralda. "That would not be correct."

"Well, wherever you got that idea, it's not true. I was the one who represented the Foundation in small claims, and the only evidence Mrs. Hernandez produced was her check ledger. There were no canceled checks. Look, Andy, I'm busy, and I don't have time to waste on your amateur efforts to play lawyer. The truth is your mother got into some kind of snit over the way your ex treated her. I don't know the details. But we received orders to lose the Hernandez payments and throw the account into default."

That day my mother went to Salk to bribe Tina, and she had her thrown out. But he couldn't resist giving Elliott a hard time. "I thought you said the Foundation was an independent entity."

"Don't play games with me, Andy." Elliott stood up and gathered his papers even though Andy was still seated and hadn't given any indication he was ready to end the meeting. Elliott picked up his folder and walked toward the door. With his hand on the knob, he said, "Everyone knows who calls the shots in both companies. You've wasted enough of my time this morning. I came as a courtesy to your parents."

Andy was even more angry because of Elliott's rudeness. He wished he had the authority to terminate him on the spot. But he didn't. Instead, he stood up and said, "So what if I give the Hernandezes my sworn statement that their payments were deliberately lost?"

Elliott began to laugh as he opened the door. He stopped in the doorway long enough to say, "You go right ahead. And see if anyone will believe you."

* * *

Still seething at the way Elliott had treated him, Andy walked back to his own office and tried not to slam the door even though he wanted to. Powerless. He felt as if that word was etched on his forehead because everywhere he turned someone or something reminded him of that fact.

He sat for a while using Tina's meditation breathing to try to calm himself. He considered the still-unopened vodka bottle in his bottom drawer but was relieved to find that the idea of a drink remained unappealing.

His eyes were still closed when he heard the knock on his open door.

"Praying again?"

Andy wished he could punch his father.

"Not now, Dad. I've just had a meeting with Elliott about the Foundation."

"Still trying to save that bunch of Hernandez clowns?"

Andy wanted to slam his hand down on his desk and scream at Lucas to stop insulting Tina and her family, but he didn't want to give his father an opportunity to call him childish. Instead, he kept his face expressionless and asked quietly, "What do you want to talk to me about?"

Lucas walked over and sat down in the chair in front of Andy's desk. "Have you talked to your attorneys this morning?"

"I have a message from Charlotte Estes that she wants to talk to me. I was going to call her after I calmed down from the meeting with Elliott."

"Elliott's a bright guy."

"If only he'd been your son."

"Don't, Andy. But Elliott is a good role model for you."

"As you've let me know many times. And him, too, given the way he treats me."

"Elliott isn't the point, right now. I had dinner with Charlotte on Friday night."

"Something you've been trying to make happen since she took on my case. Is she finally starting to give in?" His father had punched him in his weak spot. He couldn't resist punching back. He knew Charlotte's refusal to let him into her life had infuriated him since Day One.

"Cut the barbs," Lucas growled. "If you'd called your attorney the way you were supposed to instead of sitting here being useless, you'd know by now that the coroner has changed his theory about the cause of Nate's death."

"So? Has he finally figured out that I didn't kill him?"

"To the contrary. The cops found a nine-millimeter casing on the boat, and the coroner sees a bullet path in Nate's head."

Andy felt his stomach drop. Who could possibly have had a motive to execute Nate? "Now they think I shot him?"

"Didn't you?"

"God!" Andy couldn't keep the anger and anguish out of that single word. He swiveled his chair so that his back was toward his father and tried to control his tears. But the picture of Nate standing helplessly with a gun to his head was like a knife to his heart. He began to sob uncontrollably.

The sound of fabric sliding across leather told him that his father had risen from the chair. Lucas said, "Don't think those crocodile tears are going to do you any good. I'm not impressed, and a jury won't be either. Your life is hanging by a thread. If the police go back to the villa and find my gun, you're finished."

Andy summoned self-control that he didn't know he had, wiped his eyes, and turned back to his father, who was now standing in front of his desk.

"I haven't had my hands on your gun since we went to the shooting range in December."

"Don't lie to me, Andy. Charlotte wants to know if the gun is still at the villa. The day Nate disappeared, it wasn't in my desk drawer. If you hid it at the house and if the cops find it the next time they search, Charlotte can't tell the jury Nate's death was an accident. Charlotte wants the surveillance tapes from the house to see if you're on them taking the gun away to dispose of it."

"That's ridiculous." Andy was shaking with anger and grief now. "I told you. I haven't had my hands on the Glock since before Christmas. And how do you know that Nate was killed with your gun?"

"I'm assuming."

"God, Dad! You don't have any faith in me at all. First you buy the crazy theory I beat Nate to death, and now you think I shot him in the head. How low can your opinion of me go?"

"As low as thirty-two years of living with you has proven who and what you are."

"It's time for you to leave my office," Andy said levelly, proud of the fact that he wasn't screaming at his father to leave.

"I'll go when I'm ready."

"You're ready."

"If I stay, will you shoot me, too?"

* * *

Andy got up and closed the door behind Lucas. He was still shaking all over. He paced back and forth and tried to breathe deeply. He didn't see the point of calling Charlotte. She'd just accuse him of using the Glock and ask him where it was. Wasn't it obvious that the killer would have thrown it into the Pacific along with Nate's body? Why were they obsessed with searches of the villa? There was nothing there to find.

Suddenly his cell phone rang, and he could see the call was from Erin Mahoney. Maybe she'd discovered a way to end his nightmare.

"Hello."

"Hey, Andy. I've got some news."

"As in 'good,' I hope."

"At this point, I'm afraid it's just news. You sound as if you've had a rough morning. Have Charlotte and Sean been after you again?"

"Not yet, but it's coming. I started my day by trying to find out why the Owens Small Business Foundation double-crossed Tina's family's business. And I found out."

"Would it help to tell me what happened?"

"Not all of it. It's too depressing. It's enough to say my mother got them in her crosshairs because Tina stood up to her."

"If it makes you feel any better, my father bankrupted an entire law firm that he only imagined had undermined him. Of course, he's terribly sorry now."

"Well, it's unlikely that anyone like Kathryn Andrews is going to come along to wake up my mother's conscience. I'm pretty sure she was born without one. And if my father ever had one, and that's dubious, my mother erased it. God, Erin, if only I'd passed the bar. I'd take my parents to court over what they did to the Hernandezes and Tina and make them pay."

"Well, you may yet pass the bar and get your chance."

"Not likely. When I got back from being insulted by the president of the Foundation, my father was here to accuse me of shooting Nate in the head."

"What?"

"The cops found a nine-millimeter casing on *The Escape*."

"Did they find a gun, too?"

"No. My father assumes that I used the little Glock that he keeps at the villa. Apparently, it has vanished from the drawer where he kept it. Supposedly, I took it out of the drawer, used it to kill Nate, and then hid it at the house. And now the cops have searched multiple times and haven't found where I hid it."

"That's ridiculous," Erin said. "If anyone used that gun, it's long gone into the ocean."

"Thanks for saying that. I thought that was pretty obvious, too. But Charlotte wants the surveillance tapes from the house to see if I'm on them taking the gun out after the fact."

"Well, she's on a fool's errand. I wouldn't worry about her inability to see that if I were you. Actually, this is a good development. If Axel Saldana goes to trial accusing you of murder without a gun, your chances of being acquitted go up quite a bit."

"But Sean and Charlotte are still going to say that I killed Nate. They refuse to put on a defense that says he was alive when I left him at one a.m."

"Well, that's where my news comes in; but I'll tell you up front, it's mixed. I've received another surveillance tape. This one is from the guy who keeps his boat in the slip next to your father's. It does show you leaving *The Escape* at one a.m. The time stamp is even accurate on this one unlike the others we've received."

"I'm guessing the news is mixed because it shows me but not Nate."

"Right. But here's the encouraging part. The tape shows you turning around as you're leaving and waving in the direction of the boat. *The Escape* isn't well lit, so we can't see who you're waving to. I'm going to talk to the digital techs to see if it can be enhanced."

"Okay, thanks." He couldn't keep the disappointment out of his voice.

"We're not giving up, Andy. We haven't heard from all the owners with cameras that could have picked up the activity on *The Escape*. And the boat owner who sent this tape has more. He's in the process of sending them to me. Plus, you've still got Russell Blake working to recover the tapes your mother erased."

"That's a really long shot."

"I know. Look, I'll send you a copy of this. Maybe you'll see something I haven't noticed."

"Thanks, Erin. And thanks for being the only person who believes in me."

CHAPTER THIRTY-FOUR

Monday, October 15, 2018, The Owens Tower, San Diego

After he hung up with Erin, Andy sat for a while, staring at his folder of financial documents and fuming about the arrogance of Elliott Shafer. He hadn't deserved to be treated like a child. He had a business degree. He knew how to read a financial statement.

He opened the folder and began to read the "Comprehensive Financial Report of Owens Commercial Real Estate and Construction." Suddenly, he realized why he hadn't been meant to have a copy of this report. His father's entire empire lay exposed. And the news wasn't good. The Construction and Commercial Real Estate sides of the business were deeply in the red. The Property Management Division and the Residential Real Estate Divisions were breaking even, but barely. The only side of the business that was showing a profit was the REIT Division, the private real estate investment trust which took in private investors' money, invested in various real estate projects, and paid high yields to its investors.

Andy leaned back and closed his eyes for a moment while he processed what he had just read. Could his father's business be nothing more than using investors' money to keep the other divisions afloat and to pay off the investors who wanted to cash out their holdings?

He opened his eyes and began to turn through the remaining pages of the report. Page after page confirmed his suspicion. And he could see investors whose names he recognized from his days of working for Wentworth Investment and from his summers interning for Lawrence Securities and Investments during college. Two things were obvious. His parents were luring investors into a gigantic Ponzi scheme. And he was never meant to see this report.

Suddenly he realized that it was lunchtime, and he was starving. He'd skipped breakfast this morning to be on time to be humiliated by Elliott. He needed comfort food.

"Where are you going?" Jeanne barked as he came out of his office with his suit jacket on.

"To McDonald's. Unless you want to bring me two Egg McMuffins and a large coffee yourself."

She turned up her nose. "Can't stand the smell of all that grease. Besides, I'm your father's executive assistant, not your waitress."

He didn't bother to say that she never stood on the ceremony of her position when his father required her to go for takeout. Instead, he just gave her a cheerful smile and headed for the elevator. He was relieved to find her chair empty when he came back fifteen minutes later.

He sat down at his desk again, unwrapped his first sandwich, and picked up the Comprehensive Report, hoping that the loss numbers had disappeared. But they were still there, and they told him that he was not the heir of a vast real estate/securities brokerage empire as he had been raised to believe.

He bit off a piece of McMuffin and savored the taste of gooey cheese and egg, which he then washed down with a swig of black coffee while contemplating the fact that his parents were a pair of crooks. He bit off another piece of egg and cheese, this bite accompanied by the rubbery Canadian bacon that came in the sandwich. He tried on the fact of his parents' criminality for size as he chewed. It seemed to fit. Them, not him.

He wondered when, if ever, they had planned on letting him know that the family business was a scam. Had they actually believed that they could outrun the investors that they were defrauding forever?

He sipped his coffee and considered what it would be like to spend twenty years evading investors' requests to withdraw their investments plus profits. Had his parents ever planned to train him in the art of defrauding their rich friends? He took another bite of Egg McMuffin and savored a crisp edge of toast and cheese minus egg. He washed this down with another sip of coffee.

He could be pretty sure that his parents thought he was too intellectually challenged to run a real estate/securities Ponzi scheme. He wadded up the first McMuffin's bright-yellow paper wrapper, threw it in the trash, and began on McMuffin number two. As he savored the second combination of toast, melted cheese, and egg, he considered what to do next. He wished that he hadn't grabbed this report off his father's desk on the morning of his meeting with Peter. And he wished he'd obeyed Jeanne and put it back, sight unseen. But his already upside down world was even more upside down now.

He chewed his way through his final sandwich and sent the second bright-yellow wrapper into the waste basket. There was only one person who knew the real truth about what was going on in the Owens/Lawrence Empire: his godfather, Bert Campbell. He picked up the phone and called Uncle Bert.

"Yes, Andy, I was expecting you to call me today. Elliott said the two of you met this morning. He saw that you had the Comprehensive Report, the one that no one but your father and mother are supposed to see."

"I grabbed it by mistake."

"Well, I'm sure you have a lot of questions for me now because you've seen it. But I'd much rather talk to you about it over a nice dinner at Over the Moon in Seaport Village. The jazz and the food are unbeatable. How about six thirty tonight?"

* * *

Monday, October 15, 2018, Over the Moon, A Jazz Club, Seaport Village

Bert was already at a table near the stage when Andy arrived. He was sipping his favorite Jack Daniels and listening to the first act of the night, a beautiful brunette playing jazz piano in a form-hugging dress. He was wearing his suit and tie, which meant he had come straight from work. Andy, too, was still in work clothes.

"Glad to see you!" Bert stood and gave him a warm hug. "You look great, and your numbers on the Carmel Valley Project are fantastic!"

"Thanks." He smiled and gently freed himself from his godfather's embrace. He sat down at the table topped with white linen and a vase of red roses and ordered a tonic with lemon.

Bert's eyebrows went up. "Ella got you on the wagon?"

"Not really. Just not in the mood for alcohol right now."

"Got it." Bert sipped his whiskey and smiled. "She's a hell of a piano player, isn't she?"

"She is." In truth, Andy had no idea about the performer's skills. But he didn't want the discussion to sidetrack into Bert's efforts to convince him of the musician's chops.

They worked their way through another whiskey for Bert, a charcuterie platter, and a filet with roasted potato puree and tiny peas in butter sauce before Andy found an opening to talk about the financial statement, an opening that vanished almost immediately.

The piano player gave way to a trumpet player who brought the diners to their feet several times. When he finished his last set at ten p.m., a tall, gorgeous redhead in a bright-blue evening gown approached Bert who stood to hug her.

"Carrie!"

"Bert! So glad to see you again at Over the Moon!"

"This is my godson, Andy Owens."

The goddess smiled and shook his hand. "Happy to have you, too, Andy."

"Stan was on his game tonight," Bert said.

"He was!" Carrie agreed. "I'm tearing up your check and sending you two a bottle of champagne for whatever you're celebrating. Come back soon, Andy."

She turned and hurried toward the stage where the trumpet

player in his white dinner jacket was waiting to give her an embrace. Arm in arm, they walked toward the kitchen. A few minutes later, the champagne arrived.

"Who is that?" Andy asked.

Bert smiled. "Would you believe she used to be a superior court judge? And before that, she was the top-billing corporate partner at Warrick, Thompson. Marcy worked with her."

His godmother Marcy had been dead for two years. She'd devoted herself to her career as a corporate lawyer at Warrick, Thompson. As a result, she and Bert had never had children, so Andy, in many ways, had found solace in their willingness to parent him in the absence of his preoccupied parents.

"She left law to run a jazz club?"

"It's her club," Bert said. "She and the trumpet player have a history that goes way back. She left Howard Morgan for him, and Morgan made the divorce especially nasty."

"I've heard of Howard Morgan. He's supposed to be a pit bull."

"Marcy didn't like him." Bert smiled. "Ever a romantic, she sided with Carrie."

"The club is beautiful." Andy wondered if Erin would ever consider coming here with him.

"It is. And now we have champagne on the house. What are we celebrating?"

"From what I read this morning, nothing. Apparently, Dad's business is a gigantic Ponzi scheme. And it looks as if my mother's investors are funding it. And I'm guessing that she might be in trouble, too."

Bert sighed and said, "It's not quite that bad."

"But it's bad, isn't it? Has it been this way the whole time? Have my parents always been crooks? And why haven't you blown the whistle on them?"

"Whoa! Too many questions at once. First, Andy, your mother and I go way back. I mean, way back. Our parents were friends, and everyone expected us to get married one day."

"Really? I never knew that."

"I haven't wanted to talk about it," he said. "Your mother met your father, and she was determined to have him."

"To their eternal misery. And mine."

"I know." Bert smiled reassuringly and patted Andy's hand. "But it turned out well for me. I met Marcy, and you know how happy we were."

"I do." Andy smiled. "And I'm glad. But were either of my parents' businesses ever legitimate?"

"Oh, yes," Bert said as he poured more champagne for them both.

"Which one?"

"Both in the beginning. At least, more or less. Your grandfather Lawrence did use new investor money to pay off old investor's interests at times when Ella and I first started at the company. Hugh Mahoney got wind of that and advised your grandfather to put a stop to it."

"And as far as your father was concerned, Old Man Lawrence wouldn't give him a nickel to start his real estate business. Your dad got his first business capital on the strength of his own name and business plan."

"So that's why there's always been that bitterness over how Dad got started."

"Right," Bert agreed. "He thought by marrying Ella, he'd have access to the Lawrence millions. But it didn't turn out that way."

"So Dad's business was legitimate for a while, right?"

"Yes. Your father was turning a good profit for many years. But the downturn in 2008 hit him pretty hard."

"So he decided to take in investor money, knowing he couldn't pay it back?"

"It's not that simple."

"What do you mean?"

"Around 2008, when things were going south for your father, Sam Wentworth came to your mother with clients who had money to invest. At first, she put them in investments that had nothing to do with your father's business. She had her father's prejudice against helping him. But by and by, it became clear that he was going under without capital. And Sam had more and more clients, a lot of them tech companies, with surplus profits to invest. So Ella began to direct them into your dad's business. With full disclosure of the relationship, of course."

"So why, then, does the financial statement say that my father couldn't pay off all his investors if they called in their money?"

"Because he can't. And neither can your mother. They've allowed both businesses to become dependent on cash infusions from new clients referred by Sam Wentworth."

"It sounds bad. All Ponzi schemes collapse in the end."

"I've warned them. And so have the outside accountants. But the two of them are convinced they can outrun any shortfall. And so far, they have."

"I don't like what I'm hearing," Andy said.

"And you shouldn't. They're engaged in illegal activity."

"Where will it all end?" Andy asked.

Bert shrugged. "I can't say. The stock market has been doing better lately. That helps your mother if anyone wants to cash out an investment. Your father's office building projects, particularly the one you've been in charge of, are bringing in a good return."

"But not enough to cancel out the existing debt?"

"Not yet. If I were you, Andy, I wouldn't let on to either of your parents that you know about this. You've got your own legal troubles to worry about. Whatever they're doing has nothing to do with you."

"I wasn't planning on bringing it up. But Jeanne saw me take that report off my father's desk and put it back."

"Well, then, if Jeanne saw you take the report, your father at least knows you've seen it."

"I know. But he doesn't think I'm smart enough to understand it."

"They're going to have to stop underestimating you one of these days," Bert said.

"Not if I get convicted of murdering Nate."

CHAPTER THIRTY-FIVE

Wednesday, October 17, 2018, The Owens Tower, San Diego

Lucas never mentioned Andy's access to the comprehensive report. On Tuesday morning, he merely asked if he'd enjoyed dinner with his godfather. Andy guessed that his father and Bert had agreed on the explanation that Andy was to have received, but Bert had decided to tell him the truth, instead. Andy decided to forgive his godfather for failing to prevent the Hernandez debacle because, in truth, once his mother had set her sights on ruining Hernandez Moving, no one could have prevented her from succeeding.

Now it was Wednesday morning, and he was struggling to keep his mind off Bert's revelations and to focus on reviewing a draft lease for a prospective tenant of one of the Carmel Valley office buildings. His cell phone began to ring.

"Hi, Andy, it's Brian McClellan. I've had a call from the Hernandez brothers."

"Yes?" Andy felt his heart pounding.

"And they've agreed to let you see Nate's file on their case. I'll have it available for you to inspect in my conference room at one p.m. this afternoon."

"Thank you," Andy said, his voice full of relief and gratitude. "You have no idea what this means to me."

"Actually, son, I do."

* * *

He had expected to see Brian McClellan when he arrived at the offices of McClellan and Wyatt at 600 West Broadway that afternoon, but he did not appear. A secretary led Andy to the conference room where a two-inch-thick folder lay in solitary splendor on the polished mahogany table. She asked him if he wanted something to drink and then left him alone after he shook his head.

He sat for a few moments with his hand on Nate's file, picturing Nate as Andy had left the boat that night. He'd been holding his beer and looking thoughtful, and Andy wondered if he'd stayed with him a few minutes longer, if he would have told him about his feelings for Tina. They'd been so close that he half believed Nate would have.

But mid-June seemed a lifetime ago, and speculation about what might have been was useless. He opened Nate's file and turned to the back so that he could read the oldest documents first, wondering how Nate had managed to get the D.A. to dismiss the possession charges against Jose and Sebastian. In less than an hour, he knew everything. And he knew who he had to talk to right away.

* * *

Wednesday, October 17, 2018, 1512 Caminito Mexicali, Chula Vista

Andy inched along the 805 in the late afternoon traffic until he came to H Street. His GPS told him to exit and go four miles before turning right on Hacienda Way. Hacienda Way wound up a hill and down and then twisted left and right through a neighborhood of small run-down pink stucco houses, none larger than twelve hundred square feet. Andy's real estate eye appraised the whole community as ripe for razing and replacing with five-thousand-square-foot mansions. The proximity to the 805 would attract high-end commuters who worked downtown.

Just when he was sure his GPS had taken him on a fruitless search for 1512 Caminito Mexicali, he rounded the last curve and saw the turnoff. Number 1512 was the second house on the right. He parked, went up to the weather-worn red door, and rang the bell. A few seconds later, a fiftyish man in jeans and a white-T shirt opened the door. His dark eyes appraised Andy carefully. His face was tanned and deeply lined, and Andy guessed he had spent a considerable amount of time outdoors. He had a slight paunch but otherwise was in good shape.

"I'm looking for Mateo Reinaldo," Andy said. "I called earlier. I'm Andy Owens."

"I'm Mateo," the man said. "Come inside."

They walked through a narrow hall to a living room in the back furnished with a shabby brown couch and an equally shabby gray chair. The room smelled of stale air, old grease, and cigarette smoke. Mateo had been watching television. He turned it off and sat down on the chair. Andy sat on the edge of the center sofa cushion.

"You said you wanted to talk about the arrest of the Hernandez brothers."

"Nate McClellan was their attorney. And one of my best friends. I read his file this afternoon. You planted meth on them at Club Red and called the cops."

Mateo nodded. "Your friend found out about me."

"How?"

"He studied the surveillance videos from the club. I made the mistake of standing too close to a camera when I dropped the meth on those two."

"I realize he saw you make the plant, but how did he identify you?"

"Damn, if he wasn't the most determined attorney on the planet. He isolated the frames that showed my face and took them down to the club. A couple of waitresses did the rest."

"So you were a regular there?"

"Right."

"Posing as an undercover cop?"

"Not exactly." Mateo pulled out a pack of cigarettes. "Mind if I light up?"

Andy minded, but he wanted maximum cooperation, so he said, "Go ahead."

Mateo made a production out of taking out a cigarette, lighting it, and taking a few long drags while Andy watched, choked by the smoke and the smell, but doing his best not to show his discomfort. He decided it was time to bring Mateo back to the point.

"You do admit, don't you, that you were posing as an undercover cop the night the Hernandez brothers were arrested?"

"Sure. That was my MO."

"MO for what?"

"Okay, so here's the story. I was a private investigator for twenty years until I lost my license."

"How'd you manage to do that?"

"Perjured myself on the stand for a lying SOB who promised me a million bucks to say he didn't kill his wife. I didn't get the million bucks, and I lost my license. After that, I had to regroup, and my only opportunity was to do side jobs for Joey Menendez."

"Who's Joey Menendez?"

"He's the sole proprietor of the Menendez Drug Cartel. You're not a criminal lawyer, I take it, so you've never heard of him."

"I'm studying for the bar right now," Andy lied.

"Well then, kid. Let me broaden your education. The Menendez Cartel is a worldwide distributor of street drugs, primarily meth, cocaine, and marijuana. One of the biggest in the world."

"Okay. So what kind of 'side jobs' were you doing?"

"Joey had an unorthodox approach to disciplining his drug dealers. Instead of sending a hitman to put the fear of God into them, he often used the law instead."

"You're saying the head of a Mexican drug cartel used U.S. law to get even with his rogue dealers?"

"Yep, that's exactly what I'm saying. If one of his guys wasn't living up to Joey's standards, he'd find himself arrested. Then Joey would play cat and mouse with the poor guy."

"What does that mean?"

"It means that Joey used to have this Senior Assistant D.A.

in his pocket. A guy named Noah Hendricks. If Joey actually wanted his dealer prosecuted, Hendricks would go ahead and put the guy in prison. But if Joey decided an arrest was enough to bring the guy back into line, he'd have me plant on the guy to get him arrested, and then he'd give Noah the word, and a dirty cop named Tony Lopez would make sure the goods disappeared from the evidence room. Joey had a great system going until Tony and Noah tried to frame this young hotshot attorney named Jeff Ryder. Ryder eliminated Hendricks and Lopez, so when I planted on the Hernandez brothers, it meant they'd for sure be prosecuted."

"But they weren't."

"Right. Because your friend found out about me."

"But why didn't the real police expose you as a phony undercover cop right from the beginning?"

"Because I was playing both sides of the street. Sometimes the cops used me to plant on guys who they knew were guilty but couldn't get any other way. And they had no problem arresting Joey's people even if the arrest was illegal because every dealer off the street was a good thing in their view."

"So the cops let you set up illegal arrests?"

"Yep. And they turned a blind eye when I was dealing, too."

"You were dealing?"

"Right. Joey set me up with product."

"What kind of product?"

"Meth, marijuana, cocaine was a specialty."

"So why'd you pick Jose and Sebastian Hernandez to set up? Surely they weren't dealing for the cartel."

"I didn't pick them. Joey did."

"But why?"

"He was doing a favor for a woman who launders money for the cartel. Joey funnels dirty money to her through a guy in New York named Went-something. This woman runs a fancy securities firm. Her name is Ella Lawrence. Joey told me she wanted those two Hernandez guys framed because their sister had disrespected her."

Andy felt as if Mateo had just delivered an electric shock. His mother was money laundering for a drug cartel to support the family Ponzi scheme. And his old boss, Sam Wentworth, was funneling the dirty money to her. *Thank God Mateo doesn't know about the Lawrence/Owens connection. He wouldn't be telling me this if he did.*

Andy struggled to keep his face neutral as he asked, "So how did Nate find out that you were a phony undercover cop?"

"I told him. After the girls at the club ID'd me, he traced me back through the Bureau of Security and Investigative Services and found out that I was a PI who'd lost his license."

"Why'd you confess to him?"

"Because it was clear that he was going to expose me if I didn't admit to framing the Hernandez brothers. He agreed to keep quiet if I helped him get those guys off."

"Did you tell him Ella Lawrence was responsible for what you did to Jose and Sebastian?"

"I did."

"Why?"

"He said if I didn't explain who had hired me to plant on them and why, he wouldn't keep quiet. So I told him that the Lawrence woman had talked to Joey about a favor, and he'd agreed to help her because the work she does for the cartel is very valuable."

"Did he tell the D.A. about Ella Lawrence's connection to the cartel?"

"No, he didn't have to in order to get the charges dismissed. He went to the D.A. in charge of the Hernandez case and told him he'd found out that I wasn't an undercover cop. And I'd admitted to planting the drugs.

"At first the cops didn't want to admit that they knew who I was and that I'd worked for them in the past. But your friend threatened to go to trial for the Hernandez brothers and to put me on the stand. Of course, he knew that I wouldn't have perjured myself again, so I would have admitted my role in arranging all of those illegal arrests. The D.A. caved because the cops didn't want to lose me as an asset, and the D.A.'s office didn't want the bad publicity. And they didn't want any of those drug dealers who I'd set up to get out of prison."

"So what happened?"

"Everyone agreed to stay quiet about me in exchange for letting the Hernandez brothers walk."

"Are you still working Club Red?"

"Not right now. After your friend got killed, I decided to cool it for a while."

"Any idea who killed Nate?" Andy held his breath waiting for an answer.

"I have two theories," Mateo said as he stubbed out his cigarette. "Obviously Joey wasn't happy that your buddy found out about my connection to the cartel. Joey doesn't like to leave anyone walking around with information about his operation who isn't completely loyal to him. So it could have been a hitman that Joey sent.

"But it could also have been that Lawrence woman. She's pretty high society, I hear, and being connected to a drug cartel wouldn't fit her image. Personally, I think she arranged for the hit because after the D.A. dropped the Hernandez charges, she called me and asked if I'd be interested in a side job for her. At the time, I thought she wanted me to do a hit on the brothers. I said no because I'm not a hitman. But after your buddy died, I realized he was the one she wanted to get rid of."

CHAPTER THIRTY-SIX

Wednesday, October 17, 2018, Rancho Santa Fe

It was dark by the time Andy got back into the Camry and headed north on the I-805. His head was spinning. It had been one thing to learn that his parents were running a Ponzi scheme, risking other people's money for their own profit. It was quite another to learn that his mother had solicited someone to kill his best friend. And then allowed Andy to be charged with his murder.

It was like her, he realized as he headed toward Rancho Santa Fe in the dark, to take such an outrageous risk. She had infinite faith in her wealth and influence to get exactly what she wanted. That was, after all, the way she'd captured Andy's father and imprisoned him all these years. And she would be just as certain that her son would escape the consequences of being charged with murder because she had the money to buy the legal team that would get him off. Except, his legal team seemed bent on doing nothing of the kind.

He drove on through the dark, wishing he didn't have to go back to the Mansion of Doom. He was determined to confront her when he got home. But first, he wanted to make sure that

Brian McClellan knew the truth about Nate's death.

The housekeeper admitted Andy to Brian's study where he was reading a stack of legal documents in front of the fire. He didn't get up when Andy came in, but he motioned for Andy to take a seat on the chair opposite his.

"You shouldn't be here," he said. "I received a subpoena today from the District Attorney's Office. I'm going to be called as a prosecution witness at trial."

"I just wanted you to know that I found Mateo Reinaldo and talked to him."

"The guy who impersonated an undercover cop to get the Hernandez brothers arrested?"

"Yeah."

"Nate found out he is connected to Joey Menendez," Brian said. "You don't want to mess with that cartel, son. I suppose this Mateo character told you that?"

"He did. But he told me something else. He said my mother is money laundering for the cartel. You don't look surprised."

"I've had a suspicion for a long time that there might be cash flow problems for your parents. It's never been any of my business."

"I saw a financial report, by mistake. Bert told me the rest."

"Are you saying your mother had something to do with Nate's murder?"

"Mateo thinks so. She called him about a hit on someone. He thought it was the Hernandez brothers."

Brian was silent as he studied the fire. "I wish I could help you, son. But I'm not part of your defense team. I can't give you any legal advice. And I'm in a more difficult position now

DEBORAH HAWKINS

because of this subpoena. If the D.A. finds out you've been here, he'll accuse you of witness tampering."

"I know. Charlotte and Sean have drilled that into me. It's just that I wanted to make sure that you know I didn't kill Nate."

Brian sighed. "The truth is, Andy, I don't know if you did or you didn't. You're attributing a lot of credibility to a man who's admittedly dishonest. I can picture your mother doing a lot of things, but not looking for a drug hitman to set up the murder of my son. I've been friends with your parents for a long time. They know that Nate wouldn't disclose anything without telling me first. And they know I wouldn't have let Nate take this information to the authorities. We're criminal defense attorneys. We know how to keep quiet.

"I have to be honest with you, son. After what happened in New York and since you're still drinking and since I know how you felt about Tina, I can't rule out the possibility that you did kill Nate. You don't remember a lot about the night he died. Be honest about that."

"I—" Andy was about to repeat his memory of seeing Nate as he left the boat. But suddenly he wondered if he could be filling in gaps instead of actually remembering as Charlotte had said. If Nate's image was on the surveillance tape that Erin had found, it was impossible to see.

"It's okay, son," Brian said. "I understand. You'd better go. And don't risk coming again. Things aren't the same now between us."

* * *

330

Brian's rejection hurt more than if he'd slapped Andy in the face. Reeling from Brian's failure to believe in his innocence, Andy managed to make his way to the Camry and get in. He turned on the ignition and considered driving all the way to Erin's cottage in Coronado. At that moment, he needed to be with the only person in the world who believed in him.

But it was an hour's drive to Erin's place, and he hadn't been invited. He hoped that she wasn't seeing anyone, but he didn't know for sure. As much as he wanted her company, he knew that he shouldn't invade her privacy. He drove back to the Mansion of Doom and locked himself in his room. He opened his chest of drawers and looked at the vodka bottles inside. Then he closed the drawer and called Erin.

"What's up?"

The sound of her voice filled him with hope. And something else he didn't want to acknowledge.

"Brian McClellan let me see Sebastian and Jose's file today. The one Nate kept on their case."

"What did you learn?"

"It's a long story. But, in a nutshell, my mother has been money laundering for the Menendez Cartel, and either she hired the hitman who killed Nate or Joey Menendez did."

CHAPTER THIRTY-SEVEN

Friday, October 19, 2018, Offices of Goldstein, Miller, Emerald Shapery Center

Charlotte now deeply regretted everything: the merger with Goldstein, Miller; her decision to leave Hayden and Ian in D.C.; giving in to the pressure to take Andy Owens' case; and, above all, dinner with Lucas and her alcohol-infused impulse to offer him sympathy. Ever since that night, he'd been bombarding her with calls and embarrassing her by sending dozens and dozens of roses, not only to her house, but worst of all, to her office. On Friday morning, her office was once again full of flowers when she arrived at nine a.m. She summoned her hapless secretary.

"Didn't I tell you to refuse delivery of any more of these?"

"Sorry, Mrs. Estes. They were already here when I arrived this morning."

"Well, call the cleaning people to get them out of here, and then call that florist and put a stop to this. And you're fired if I come to work on Monday morning and find even one rose petal in my office."

"Yes, Mrs. Estes."

Fuming, Charlotte sat down at her desk, took a sip of the latte she'd brought with her, and turned on her computer. Someone knocked on her door, and she looked up to see two members of the cleaning team. They entered and began piling the flowers on the cart they had brought with them.

A second knock. This time it was Sean.

"That must have been quite a dinner," he observed from the doorway as the cleaning staff finished filling the cart. "Isn't this the fifth day in a row?"

"Don't remind me. I might be looking for a new secretary on Monday if she can't put a stop to it. Maybe I should blame you, too. You were the one who made me have dinner with him."

"True. But it was a sacrifice worth making. We got those surveillance tapes, and our client is not on them carrying away a gun for disposal. I just finished reviewing all of them last night. Axel still has no murder weapon. And I have even more good news."

"I'm glad to hear that. Come sit down."

He waited for the cart loaded with the unwanted flowers to go through the door and then came in and took the chair in front of her desk.

"Bart Stephen has changed his mind about refusing to allow Axel to offer Andy a plea bargain."

"Why?"

"Because Axel doesn't have a murder weapon. He made Bart see that he probably wouldn't get a conviction without the gun. So they're offering Andy a deal."

"Is it something we can recommend?" *She cautioned herself*

not to get too excited about an end to this case.

"Absolutely. Axel will let him plead to involuntary manslaughter for a term of three years. With sentencing credits, he'll only be in prison for eighteen months."

"That's the best we could have hoped for."

"Exactly. I've run it by Hugh, and he's ready to offer us congratulations."

"But first, there's the hurdle of getting our client to accept the offer. Please don't say I have to spend any more one-on-one time with Lucas."

"No. Once was a big enough sacrifice. I can see that." Sean smiled. "I've called Andy, and he's agreed to come by the office at two. What if we have dinner tonight at The Italian Kitchen to celebrate? We can erase that dinner with Lucas. And I promise not to fill your office with flowers on Monday if you say yes."

"What if I say no?" She smiled. Working with him was the only thing she didn't regret about the merger and about having to represent Andy Owens.

"No flowers, either way. But you won't say no. I'll go make a reservation. I told Andy we'd meet him in the small conference room."

* * *

"But I didn't kill Nate," Andy said after Sean had finished outlining Axel Saldana's offer.

He's lost more weight, Charlotte reflected. *He looks older now. But he still hasn't grown up enough to accept responsibility for his conduct.*

"Andy, you need to be reasonable," she said gently. "If you go to trial, you could be convicted of first-degree murder and go to prison for life."

"Eighteen months is nothing compared to life," Sean added.

"The Menendez Cartel killed Nate," Andy said.

"Andy, that's ridiculous." Charlotte shook her head.

"No, it's not. My mother and father are money laundering for the Menendez Cartel. My old boss in New York, Sam Wentworth, is involved, too. Nate found out about it when he represented Tina's brothers. Either the cartel or my mother, or both together, arranged for the hit on Nate."

Charlotte exchanged a look with Sean, who said, "I hope you realize how crazy that sounds, Andy."

"No, it doesn't. Mateo Reinaldo told me everything."

"Mateo Reinaldo?"

"My mother hired him to set up Tina's brothers to get back at Tina because she stood up to her. He's a private investigator who lost his license. He deals drugs for the cartel and informs for the police. You have to go talk to him. He'll tell you exactly what he told me."

"Andy, your parents are long-time clients of the firm who run well-respected businesses in San Diego," Sean said.

"They're running a Ponzi scheme in addition to money laundering," Andy shot back.

"And I suppose this Mateo Reinaldo told you that, too?" Charlotte asked.

"No, Bert Campbell, my mother's Chief Financial Officer and my godfather, told me that. And I've got a secret balance sheet that proves it."

CHAPTER THIRTY-EIGHT

Friday, October 19, 2018, The Italian Kitchen, La Jolla

It wasn't a date, Charlotte told herself, but it felt like one. Sean had picked her up at eight, and now they were sitting in one of the famous red banquettes, bathed in the glow of candlelight, sharing a bottle of wine. But unlike the evening with Lucas, she felt happy and relaxed and as if she didn't want this evening to end.

"So how am I doing?" Sean smiled. "Am I redeeming the place for you?"

"You are." She smiled back. *He has such kind eyes.*

"If I order the antipasto platter as an appetizer, will that ruin it for you? Everyone orders that here, so I'm guessing Lucas did, too."

Charlotte laughed. "I'd love to share one with you. Speaking of the devil, any progress on getting Andy to accept the plea offer?"

"Zip. None. I called Lucas before I left the office. Andy won't be budged. You know, maybe we should make a motion to suspend the proceedings because he's incompetent to stand trial. That was a crazy story he told us today."

"But he isn't mentally ill." She shook her head. "He's just immature and in denial about being responsible for another death."

"I wish we could force him to take Axel's offer."

"I do, too. But we can't. Did you tell Hugh that no one can make him see reason?"

"I did. He thinks we've got a good shot at winning. And I do, too. As long as Axel doesn't find that gun."

The array of aged cheese, thinly sliced bits of cured prosciutto, and mild, sweet Castelvetrano olives arrived.

"Thanks for being the point man with Lucas," she said as she put cheese and olives on her plate.

"I apologize again for making you spend the evening with him."

"Those flowers were embarrassing."

"Has he always been like this?"

"No, he was different in college. For one minute the other night, I saw that side of him. And offered my sympathy for what he's going through. I wish I hadn't."

Sean put his hand over hers. His empathetic gesture startled her at first. But then she realized how right it felt. *I keep thinking it's too soon after Matt. But maybe it's not.*

"You shouldn't have any regrets about being kind even if Lucas tried to take advantage of your kindness."

"Thanks."

They finished the appetizer, and the entree arrived, a lasagna to share.

"Have you heard from Detective Merrill?" he asked.

"Yes, and I wish I hadn't."

"So all bad news?"

"Yes, but news I expected to hear. Eric Franson's autopsy showed Nerine in his system. And Rosemary Spencer is nowhere to be seen. So Detective Merrill thinks she's made it out of the country again."

"Well, you're safer with her an ocean away, so I'm taking that as good news."

In the soft light, his eyes held hers and told her that what he felt was more than friendship. He reached out and took her hand again, and this time he gave it a gentle squeeze.

"I'm fine."

When he released her hand, she was surprised to find that she was sorry.

If I'm honest, I'll have to admit I'm feeling something for the first time since Matt. It's too soon. No, it's not.

"Have you given any more thought to moving into my building? I was hoping after spending the night at my place, you'd see how much safer you'd be there."

She chuckled. "I didn't think you were really doing a trial run as an innkeeper."

"Host. Airbnb calls us hosts."

"I've given it some thought. But I love the sunroom at my house. And the view of the sea. I'm seriously considering buying it when the lease is up."

"So you're not going back to D.C.?"

"Sometimes I think about it. I miss Hayden and Ian."

"But now you have reasons to stay here."

It was a simple, matter-of-fact statement, but she felt that warm glow in her heart again.

"Yes."

The impulse to ask him to stay the night grew stronger and stronger as they lingered over wine and dessert. The waiter returned several times for the check which remained unpaid.

"I think he wants us to leave," Sean said after the waiter's third unsuccessful attempt to collect the bill.

She looked at her watch and was surprised to find that it was eleven forty-five. "It's nearly midnight. He wants to go home."

"We'd better go, then."

She was torn by indecision on the ride home. *I want to ask him to stay. But we have to try a case together in two weeks. It needs to stay professional until after that. And it's too soon after Matt.*

He walked her to the front door, and she was tempted to relent. But she unlocked it and smiled up at him. She could see he wanted to come in.

"So I redeemed The Italian Kitchen?"

"You did."

"You're sure?"

"I'm sure."

I want him to kiss me. The thought surprised her. *But no. It's too soon.*

She saw regret in his eyes as he turned away. She stood in the doorway and waved goodbye as he backed his BMW out of the driveway. He paused and gave her a wave before he went around the cul-de-sac and then headed off down the street. As she saw his taillights vanish, she realized she'd been wrong. *It wasn't too soon. It wasn't too soon at all.*

CHAPTER THIRTY-NINE

Monday, October 22, 2018, Offices of Goldstein, Miller, Emerald Shapery Center

On Monday morning, he was still disappointed that she hadn't asked him to stay on Friday night. He'd felt certain all through dinner that she had feelings for him, too, and that she would. To assuage some of his lingering disappointment, he'd reminded himself that he hadn't had the least intention of even liking Charlotte Estes in the beginning. But she was charming and smart and funny; and bit by bit, his barriers had crumbled. As he'd driven away, he'd had to admit that he cared about her far more than he wanted to.

By Saturday morning, he'd wanted the reassurance of the sound of her voice. He was suddenly worried that allowing his feelings to show had put her off. He worried even more when she didn't answer any of his calls or voicemails.

And it was the same on Sunday. Surely she wasn't angry enough to refuse to speak to him. They had a trial to get through together. Now he wished he hadn't let her see his feelings.

He was nearly frantic by Sunday afternoon. Something had happened to her. He felt certain. He got in his car twice, determined to drive by and check on her. But each time he got out again, reminding himself that he was the first person she would call if she needed help. And she hadn't called. And he shouldn't invade her privacy.

But now it was ten o'clock on Monday morning, and they were scheduled to meet with their expert on the tides and currents in San Diego Bay. Sean's secretary had informed him ten minutes ago that Dr. Abernathy had arrived and was in the reception area. But there was no sign of Charlotte. She was never late. And Sean was worried.

But just as he was about to pick up his phone and call her yet again, he heard rapid footsteps coming down the hall. A second later, she called from the doorway.

"I know I'm late!"

Sean got up from his desk and hurried over to her. At the last minute, he realized that he'd been intending to hug her and that wasn't appropriate. Instead, he said, "I was worried. I tried to call you several times over the weekend, but you didn't answer."

"Sorry." She smiled. She didn't seem upset with him. But he felt a distance that he hadn't felt on Friday night, a distance that he wished wasn't there. "I dropped my phone when I got home after dinner, and I ordered a replacement, but it didn't come until this morning. I had trouble activating it, so I had to stop by the store. I didn't think that would make me late."

"I'm just glad that you're okay." He hoped he was successfully hiding just how relieved he felt. "But you should have replaced your phone immediately. There are people out there trying to kill you, you know."

Her smile faded, and he could tell she wanted to change the subject. She said, "I told your secretary to take Dr. Abernathy down to the conference room and tell him we'd be right along."

"Then we'd better get going."

Thank God, it was nothing worse than a broken phone. But she was keeping her distance. Had he been wrong to let his feelings show, even a little bit?

* * *

"We've been over your report, Dr. Abernathy," Charlotte began after the three of them were settled in the conference room. "Sean and I just wanted to make sure we understand your findings."

"Of course." Dr. Abernathy smiled.

He looked like an outdoor person, Sean thought. He had dark hair and dark eyes, and his face was weathered by the sun. He was tall and thin, and he looked uncomfortable in his suit. His resume said that he was forty-five. He'd been born and raised in Australia but had been in San Diego since his college years. His accent would lend authority to his opinions, Sean thought. They had agreed that he was Charlotte's witness, so Sean could sit back and watch the meeting unfold.

"I think the thing we are most concerned about is persuading the jury that the tides and currents were strong enough that night to account for the damage to Nate's body. The District Attorney is going to argue that the autopsy X-rays of his head show a bullet wound. We say the time in the water caused that injury after he was dead."

"My findings make a case for that," Dr. Abernathy said.

"The tide in the bay was beginning to go out at midnight. The currents were strong, and the wind was, too. Anything in the water would have been thoroughly bashed around."

"And that would be true even if the body was in the water for just a few hours?"

"Yes. The sea was churning that night in the wind."

"Thank you so much, Dr. Abernathy," Charlotte said. "Andy's trial begins in two weeks. And there's a possibility that we might not need you because the District Attorney has made an offer to let Andy plead to a lesser charge. But either way, we'll be in touch to let you know."

* * *

Sean walked Charlotte back to her office after they escorted Dr. Abernathy to the elevator. She sat down on one of the sofas in the corner, and he took the chair opposite. She smiled at him in her usual friendly way, but there was still that air of distance.

He decided he should clear the air. Showing his feelings on Friday night had been wrong. "I wanted to say how much I enjoyed dinner the other night, but if I—"

Suddenly his cell phone began to ring. He looked down, determined to silence it and finish his apology, but the caller ID said "Axel Saldana."

"Hello, Axel."

"Good morning, Sean. We've found the gun."

RECKONING

CHAPTER FORTY

Wednesday, November 14, 2018, Rancho Santa Fe, California

It was raining. Andy sat in his bedroom in the Mansion of Doom at nine p.m. and listened to the steady downpour. The bottles of vodka in his chest of drawers still held no interest for him. Although Charlotte and Sean had thought he was guilty from the beginning, they had held out hope that he wouldn't be convicted of murder. But now that the prosecutor had his father's gun, they had no doubt that he was both guilty and that he was going to prison for the rest of his life. No amount of alcohol could dull the terror of that realization. Being sober and alert was the best way to defend himself against what was coming because the knowledge that he was innocent was the slender thread that his life was hanging by. He was still looking for a way to stop what was coming.

His trial had been underway for a week before Judge Carter, the judge who'd presided over the preliminary hearing. His Honor still wasn't a fan of the defense. Andy had asked Charlotte and Sean why they hadn't recused him and had been told no one else would view a defense case any more favorably. The judges were all ex-prosecutors. He shivered at the thought.

So as of last Monday, November 5, and on all the following mornings, Andy had put on a suit, black or navy, a white shirt, and a conservative red or maroon tie. Then he had joined his parents in the dining room by seven a.m. His mother sat at the head of the table. His father sat at her left, across from Andy. The two of them talked to each other while Andy stabbed at two soft boiled eggs in china cups with a silver knife and fork and wished for an Egg McMuffin. Afterward, they stuffed him into the backseat of his father's obnoxious Mercedes and drove to the courthouse where the photographers were waiting to take his picture as he got out of the fabulously expensive car.

On that first day, his parents had talked about how sure they were that Charlotte and Sean would quickly convince his jury that he had thrown Nate overboard and then driven off into the night because he was drunk. Andy listened in horrified silence as his parents recited their litany of why such a callous defense would succeed in front of an unbiased jury who was also going to hear that Andy had executed Nate with his father's gun.

On November 6, the second day, they had begun to select a jury. Andy noted with interest how the prospective jurors reacted to him from the jury box. Some refused to look at him. Some looked but were obviously hostile. Some looked and were obviously sympathetic. The prosecution eliminated the sympathetic ones immediately and resisted Charlotte and Sean's attempts to eliminate the hostile ones. Those tactics made Andy angry, but he kept his expression absolutely neutral as he watched the people who seemed capable of understanding his story being sent away. Sometimes, Axel Saldana's Number Two, the perfectly groomed Kaitlyn Green, would shoot Andy a triumphant look as another sympathetic prospective juror was shown the door. Andy felt as if she were sticking pins into him, and he was powerless to stop her.

As that second afternoon wore on, Andy also became aware that Axel and the relentless Ms. Green were removing all the young female jurors. Charlotte and Sean argued extensively against this, citing a United States Supreme Court case that Andy had never read in law school called *Batson v. Kentucky*. Apparently, the Supreme Court had declared that a defendant is entitled to a jury of his peers and removing one class of individuals violates that right. But the jurors removed in *Batson* had been African American, not young and female. When called on his strategy, Axel protested loudly to Judge Carter that *Batson* didn't prohibit him from removing these prospective jurors. And besides, he went on, young women jurors would likely vote for acquittal in hopes that a romance would bloom into a rich marriage for the lucky juror who saved the defendant from life in prison. It was a completely ridiculous theory, but because the prosecutor was arguing it, Judge Carter endorsed it.

And that, Andy learned on day two, was going to be the theme of his trial. In between selecting jurors, the attorneys argued about the admissibility of various pieces of evidence. It quickly became obvious that if the prosecutor wanted the evidence admitted, Judge Carter was all for it. If the defense wanted the evidence before the jury, Judge Carter found it completely inadmissible. The biggest loss for the defense so far had been Judge Carter's refusal to keep Tina's text message out on the grounds that it was both hearsay and the product of an illegal search. It was clear to Andy that the trial was being shaped by a pro-prosecution bias in favor of conviction even before a single witness took the stand. Judge Carter knew what Axel Saldana needed to convict, and he was going to make sure he had it.

Andy listened to the rain and wished he had someone to talk to. The isolation and loneliness that had surrounded him for his whole life bore down harder now. He felt as if he was carrying a hundred-pound weight all alone. Monday had been a court holiday. Tuesday had been more arguments about the admissibility of evidence. They'd finished selecting a jury this afternoon. And Andy didn't think it looked good for the defense. Nine of the twelve jurors were around his parents' age. For the most part, their faces were expressionless, but when they looked directly at Andy, he thought he saw the same contempt for him in their eyes that he saw in his parents' each day as they came and went from court. He was just a miserable screwup who had gotten into trouble way over his head, and despite what his attorneys were going to tell these hostile jurors, there really was no defense for what he'd done. Except, of course, he hadn't done it. But no one believed that. Except Erin. She'd been watching the proceedings every day from the public seats.

Of the remaining three jurors on his panel, one was a woman, a King and White civil lawyer, caught by the snare of jury duty. Andy guessed she was mid-thirties and probably Axel's way of keeping one young female on the jury to withstand a *Batson* claim on appeal. She looked confident, crisp, and professional in suits more expensive than even Kaitlyn Green's. Andy was pretty sure that she was going to identify with Ms. Green and be quick to adopt her view of him. And he was sure that Axel thought she had enough money in her own right to keep her from saving him from prison and putting a ring on her finger.

The remaining two jurors were accountants, both mid-forties, one an Asian female the other a Hispanic male. They had said little about themselves during the jury selection process, and Andy thought this was the reason that Charlotte and Sean had left them on the panel. They were the equivalent of a Hail Mary pass. Maybe one of them would side with the defense and hang the jury. But that, of course, would only send Andy back through this whole horrible circus all over again. He didn't see how he could endure what was unfolding around him even once. A hung jury wouldn't be a victory in his opinion.

He picked up his laptop and played the surveillance tape that Erin's tech people had tried to enhance for clarity. It was the only thing that made him feel better, but Charlotte had nixed using it because she said she couldn't see anyone waving back to him as he left *The Escape*. Andy had pointed to the dim image of a hand and an arm just left of the center of the screen. He could see Nate's face dimly, too. But Charlotte had shrugged and said if she couldn't see it, the jurors couldn't either.

He had begged them repeatedly to play it for the jury. But Charlotte had continued to refuse. Sean had said he'd take a closer look and ask Russell Blake to see if he could improve the image quality, but Andy was certain that this was just an empty promise to make him stop begging. This tape was his only slender hope of being acquitted. And his jury was never going to see it.

Suddenly there was knock on his door. A second later his father's voice called out,

"Andy? How about a beer?"

"No, thank you." The last thing he wanted was to deal with either of his parents at that moment.

But Lucas knocked again, harder. Andy could tell that this wasn't a request. He sighed and got up from his chair by the window. He went to the door and opened it. His father was standing there in one of his favorite tracksuits, two Ballast Point IPAs in his hand.

"Here." He offered one to Andy. "It's your favorite Sculpin."

"No, thanks."

"It'll help you calm down and sleep. You'll need some sleep before tomorrow."

Andy sighed and took the beer. He walked over to the table by the sofa and put it down. He wasn't going to drink it because he needed restful sleep, and alcohol never brought restful sleep. But he wasn't going to debate that with his father, who relied on both alcohol and sleeping pills every night.

Lucas sat down on the sofa and took a long swig of beer. Andy repositioned his chair so that he was facing Lucas and not the window. He steeled himself for a conversation he didn't want to have.

"I just came to see if you needed anything."

"Those surveillance tapes that you and my mother erased."

Lucas flinched, and Andy was happy to see that he'd gotten a rise out of him right away.

"I didn't erase them."

"Well, I need them."

"I gather Russell Blake couldn't recover them."

"That's right. I got a call from him today."

"I told you not to waste your money."

"I didn't. He refunded it. He said he wouldn't feel right keeping it because he hadn't been able to help me."

"Well, you were lucky. Most people wouldn't have done that."

"Okay, now that we've established that between one or both of my parents, the evidence I need to keep from going to prison for life has been destroyed forever, I have nothing further to say to you."

Lucas drank some more beer and then set his bottle on the table. He leaned toward Andy and said earnestly, "Your mother thought she was helping you. I told her not to do it."

"Like I really believe that."

"Charlotte's got a strong case to put on for you."

"Not just Charlotte, Dad. Sean, too. There are two lawyers on my case. Just because you've carried a torch for years for one of them, doesn't mean there's just one. And she's not trying very hard to keep me from being convicted."

"Don't be ridiculous!" Lucas scoffed and drank some more beer. "She knows how much revenue Goldstein, Miller will lose if she doesn't keep you out of prison."

"So that was the plan, wasn't it, Dad?"

"What do you mean?" Lucas took another swig of beer nervously this time.

"I mean you and Mother arranged for someone from the cartel to kill Nate because he found out about what the two of you were up to. Then you pinned it on me and figured your money would keep me out of prison. Except it won't."

"What?" Lucas polished off his beer and put the bottle on the sofa table. "That's crazy."

"No, it's not. You know very well that I've seen the balance sheet that shows your real source of income. Bert told me about the Ponzi scheme, and Mateo Reinaldo told me about the money laundering."

"Who is Mateo Reinaldo?"

"You know."

"I do not. Look, Andy. There's no Ponzi scheme and no money laundering."

"That's not what your Comprehensive Financial Report shows."

"That report isn't accurate. It's the product of Bert's conservative application of the accounting principles. He's wrong. You heard me raising my voice with him that morning in my office. I was telling him he'd grossly undervalued the assets of my business."

"That's not what Bert told me."

"Well, he didn't tell you the truth, then. And your mother and I aren't money laundering. Don't be ridiculous, Andy. Sam Wentworth sends your mother companies who have profits they want to invest. She directs some of the money into my businesses. Most of the investors Sam sends are tech start-ups who've done well. Everything we do is strictly legitimate."

"That's not what Mateo Reinaldo told me."

"I've already told you that I've never heard of him."

"Sure you have. Mother hired him to plant drugs on Tina's brothers to make the family look bad. And then, when Nate took their case and found out that the two of you were connected to the Menendez Cartel and its dirty money, Mother asked Mateo to do a hit on Nate."

"This conversation is becoming more and more ridiculous. Nate was part of the family. Your mother would never have wanted any harm to come to him. It is true that your mother offered Tina money to break up with you. But the girl wouldn't take it, and apparently she insulted your mother."

"No, my mother insulted her."

"I don't know much about the rest of it. I think your mother set out to punish Tina through her family."

"You knew the day I came to you when the Foundation repossessed the trucks that Mother was behind that, and you lied to me."

"Okay, I knew, and I lied. But look, Andy, don't you see they deserved it? Tina left you for Nate. She's going to testify against you. She's on the prosecution's witness list."

"She didn't leave me for Nate. Mother drove her away. And she's refused to cooperate with the prosecution."

"Wishful thinking, kid. She's been subpoenaed, and she's not on your side."

"And you are? Because you made sure the gun your hired goon used to kill Nate had my fingerprints on it? And then you erased the evidence that showed he was alive when I left him that night?"

"Andy, I had no idea that gun was hidden at the villa. And I've told Charlotte why it has your prints on it."

"Yes, but yours aren't on it. And you've fired that gun a lot more often than I have."

"I didn't kill Nate, if that's what you mean."

"Yes, you did. Even if you didn't pull the trigger, you and Mother hired the person who did, and the two of you made sure he had access to that gun."

"Really, Andy. It's long past the time when you should be functioning as a grown-up. You're in serious trouble now. Maybe your fantasies about hitmen and drug cartels make you feel better about driving the boat drunk and leaving Nate behind, but they're just fantasies. Neither I nor your mother had anything to do with Nate's death."

"I don't believe you."

"Do you really think that your mother and I would risk putting you in prison for life by framing you for a murder?"

"Of course you would. You'd do anything to protect yourselves, and I've never been anything more than an afterthought in your lives. And both of you thought I'd be too dumb and drunk to find out the pair of you were responsible. And now that I've found out what you were up to, you're telling me that your money can keep me out of prison. But it can't."

"It did in New York."

"This isn't New York."

"God, Andy! I swear I had no part in this. Charlotte and Sean will get you off. You'll see. Drink your beer. It'll take the edge off your anxiety."

But after Lucas left, Andy poured the Sculpin down the drain in his bathroom. Then he sat and watched the video of Nate waving goodbye, over and over, trying to think of a way to persuade Charlotte and Sean to play it for the jury.

CHAPTER FORTY-ONE

Thursday, November 15, 2018, The Metropolitan, 165 Sixth Avenue, San Diego

At ten o'clock, Sean didn't feel like going to bed. He never slept well during a trial; but, in truth, he hadn't had a good night's sleep since the police found the gun at the villa. The pressure of needing to win this case was bearing down on him. And the first day of witness testimony had gotten off to a mixed start. His anxiety put sleep beyond reach. Instead, his mind kept replaying the day.

Axel had chosen Marilyn Becker Smith to lead off the prosecution's case. She was the seventy-year-old tourist who, with her husband, had discovered Nate's body that terrible Sunday morning. Axel had delegated presenting her to his second chair because her softer approach would heighten the sympathy he wanted to evoke from the jurors. And to that end, he and Charlotte had agreed that she would cross-examine Mrs. Smith. But then, she hadn't.

"What brought you and your husband to San Diego in June of last year?" Kaitlyn began.

"We came to celebrate our fiftieth wedding anniversary at the Hotel Del."

"And where is your home?"

"Phoenix."

She was a good lead-off choice, Sean reflected, because she was the kind of witness who immediately grabs a jury's sympathy. She had a round face and pink cheeks and was wearing a simple navy dress with a white collar and a matching navy jacket. Her white hair and pearls and wire-rimmed glasses made her the quintessential, pleasant-faced grandmother.

"And what were you doing on the morning of Sunday, June 10?" Kaitlyn asked.

"My husband and I had an early breakfast on the terrace at the hotel, and then we decided to take a walk on the beach. I have a heart problem, and I'm supposed to exercise every day."

Her heart problem is just an irrelevant ploy for sympathy. Sean looked over at Charlotte, expecting to hear an objection, but she hesitated, and the opportunity passed.

"So you were taking a walk on the beach," Kaitlyn Green went on, "and then what happened?"

"We walked all the way to the fence that closes off the beach from the Navy base. We turned around and walked back toward the hotel. We had almost reached the hotel when I saw someone lying on the beach at the water's edge."

Suddenly Mrs. Smith's eyes were full of tears. *The prejudicial sympathy factor is going up way too fast.*

"Do you need a minute?" Judge Carter asked as he handed her a tissue.

Too overcome to speak, she nodded as she wiped her eyes. "I'm sorry," she whispered. "It was just such a shock. I'm okay now." She finished wiping her eyes and balled the tissue up in her fist and hung on to it tightly.

"So you saw someone lying on the beach?"

"Yes. But when we got closer, we realized it was a young man, and he was dead. His head was injured, and his face was very swollen."

"What happened next?"

"I had the only phone, so I called nine-one-one."

"And did something happen to you, too?"

"My husband summoned medical aid for me. The sight of that poor young man upset me and triggered my heart problems."

That's irrelevant and prejudicial. Charlotte should object.

"But you are all right now?" Kaitlyn gave her a reassuring smile.

"Yes, just fine. But I'll never forget the sight of that poor young man's body."

Kaitlyn turned her back to the jurors as she returned to the prosecution's table and shot the defense team a look of triumph that the jurors could not see.

We should move for a mistrial, Sean thought. *That was a deliberate appeal to passion and prejudice right out of the box.*

But instead of making a motion, Charlotte stood up and said, "No questions for this witness, Your Honor."

* * *

Next up was Dr. Gus Tavoularis, and he was Sean's witness. On direct examination, Dr. Gus droned on about the gunshot wound he'd discovered in Nate's temple, and why he hadn't found it during his initial examination of the body. That gave Sean the opportunity he wanted to go after Dr. Tavoularis aggressively on cross-examination. He led him, step by step, through his preliminary hearing testimony about the supposed fistfight and the blunt force trauma that he claimed had been Nate's cause of death. Then he closed in, trying to discredit Dr. Gus in front of the jury once and for all.

"So isn't it true, Dr. Tavoularis, that you've given contradictory opinions about the cause of Nate McClellan's death. He can't be both beaten to death and shot to death, can he?"

"I've already explained why I missed the evidence of the gunshot wound. The body was in the surf long enough to be damaged by the waves."

"But isn't it also true, because of the damage to the body, you can never be certain about the cause of death in this case?"

"No, I'm certain the young man died from a gunshot wound to his temple."

"Just as you were certain last July that he died from blunt force trauma, Doctor?"

It was, Sean reflected with satisfaction, a wonderfully dramatic ending to his cross. Of course, Axel had rehabilitated Dr. Gus' opinion about the gunshot wound on redirect. But the look on the jurors' faces told Sean that by pointing out Dr. Gus' wishy-washy shift in his opinion, he had definitely planted seeds of doubt in their minds.

But he was haunted by Charlotte's failure to combat the prejudice that Marilyn Smith had created. Maybe eleven o'clock was too late to call. But maybe she wasn't sleeping well either.

"Did I wake you?"

"No, I was thinking of calling you. I didn't do a good job with Marilyn Smith this morning."

"I wondered why you didn't object to that testimony about her heart condition and move for a mistrial after all those tears."

"I should have. I can't really explain it other than I didn't realize how much strain I was going to be under after...everything that's happened since Matt died."

"I saw Lucas harassing you this morning about those flowers when you sat down at the defense table."

"He wanted to know why I'd stopped the deliveries."

"That should have been obvious. I'll deal with him for the rest of the trial."

"Thanks."

"What's the latest on Rosemary Spencer?"

"No news."

"I see why you're preoccupied. I'm worried about you. I wish I could talk you out of staying in that house all alone."

"I'm okay. I just wish I'd cross-examined Marilyn Smith this morning."

"It's probably just as well that you didn't. You couldn't have shaken her credibility and crossing her would have given her another chance to add to the prejudice that she'd already created. You couldn't have changed the fact that she was a sympathetic witness for the prosecution."

"At least you did a good job on Dr. Gus."

"Thanks. I think we scored some points with the jurors on that one."

"*You* scored the points." Her voice was raw with anxiety, not jealousy.

"Try to get some sleep." He wanted to reassure her and himself.

"You, too." She sounded relieved.

The conversation had made him feel better. He turned off the light and went to sleep.

CHAPTER FORTY-TWO

Thanksgiving was only six days away. Could Sean and Charlotte pull off the miracle of acquitting him by then? Andy pulled his chair up to the window in his room so that he could study the night. The rain was over. The moon was not yet full, but there was plenty of light at midnight on his parents' lush green lawn. What if a week from tonight when the moon was full he was in jail, waiting to be sentenced to life in prison? The thought was terrifying. He couldn't sleep. He kept replaying the scenes from the courtroom today over and over in his head. Yesterday Sean had made Dr. Tavoularis and his conclusions look shady and that had given Andy some hope. But today hadn't been a good day for the defense.

Officer Perkins had been the prosecution's first witness that morning. He looked much younger than Andy remembered him. His blond-haired good looks made him seem likeable, but his dark blue uniform lent an air of authority to his answers. His clear blue eyes focused on the jurors as he explained what he'd seen at the villa and on *The Escape* that June morning.

Eventually, they came to the discovery of Nate's cell phone. Tears stung Andy's eyes as the prosecutor handed it to Officer

Perkins to examine, still in its leather case.

"Do you recognize this, Officer?"

"Yes, it's the cell phone that belonged to the victim. I found it near the swim platform on the boat."

"What is the swim platform?" Axel asked.

"It's an electric platform on the back of the yacht that raises and lowers. It's designed to create easy access to the water for swimmers."

"And could that platform be used to lower a body into the water?"

"Yes."

Sean stirred and looked over at Charlotte, who was in charge of this witness. Sean's look heightened Andy's anxiety.

"Now, turning to the victim's phone which was near this platform," Axel went on. "Did you find anything of immediate interest on the phone?"

The speculation about the swim platform made Andy angry, but he didn't let it show.

"Yes, a text message that came in at ten thirty p.m."

It was more difficult to keep his face impassive as Officer Perkins read Tina's words to Nate which were never intended for anyone else to hear.

"Family is everything and yours would never understand. And I don't think you want to destroy your relationship with Andy. But I will meet you for breakfast in the morning to talk. Love, Tina"

"And did you learn the identity of Tina through your investigation?"

"Yes. She's the defendant's ex-girlfriend."

* * *

"I think we should have objected to the testimony about the swim platform," Sean said to Charlotte at the break. "It was all speculation."

"Maybe you're right," she agreed.

But it was too late to go back, Andy reflected. *It had been nothing but a parade of horrors after that.*

Officer Brooks was called to tell the jury about finding the gun at the villa. As he talked about opening the broom closet, Axel had strolled over to the jury box to give the jurors a closer look at the little Glock.

Sean, now the point man for objections, had put a stop to it. But the looks on the jurors' faces said the damage was done.

Next Axel called a DNA expert who told the jurors that Andy's DNA profile matched the profile found on the gun. He was Charlotte's witness. She had cross-examined him without asking if he had found other DNA profiles. This time, Sean jumped in.

"One additional question from the defense, Your Honor."

"That's fine, Mr. Donovan."

"Mr. Simpson, were other DNA profiles found on People's Exhibit No. 82?"

"Not complete ones."

"But the profile that matched my client was not the only one recovered, correct?"

"There were traces of others, but nothing complete. Your client's was the only complete profile that I found."

"And are you able to say when that complete profile was deposited?"

"No."

"And you can't rule out the possibility that others have handled that weapon, can you?"

"That's true. I can't."

But on redirect, the expert opined that the completeness of Andy's profile suggested that he had handled the gun recently.

* * *

Three a.m. The bright silver moonlight had faded. Andy tried to imagine what the rest of his life would be like if he was never able to see moonlight again. And that was very likely to happen because things had only gotten worse for the defense during the rest of the afternoon.

A fingerprint expert testified that the only fingerprints on the gun were Andy's. A ballistics expert told the jury that the casing that was recovered on *The Escape* near the swim platform had been fired from his father's gun. Sean then tried to cast doubt on the expert's testimony with some complicated scientific questions about the reliability of ballistics evidence. But Andy saw the jurors' eyes glaze over. It was clear that they bought the expert's story that the markings on the casing matched the markings on the inside of the Glock's barrel, and nothing from the National Academy of Sciences was going to change their minds.

The day ended with the prosecutor from New York testifying about the deal that had been reached in Andy's drunk driving case. Andy felt the jurors' eyes boring into him as they heard how a rich and entitled party boy had escaped prosecution for killing a college student on his way home from an overnight shift as a hotel desk clerk. And that gave them another reason to convict him: to make him pay for his past, too.

* * *

When Andy woke up the next morning, it was seven a.m. He'd barely slept, but he didn't care. If things kept going the way they had on Friday, this was likely the last Saturday that he'd ever spend outside of a prison cell. He didn't want to waste it by sleeping.

He showered, pulled on blue jeans, a T-shirt, and a navy hoodie. Then he called Erin.

"Did I wake you?"

"No, I'm headed into the office this morning. It looks like Axel is going to wrap up his case on Monday."

"He has one witness left. Tina."

"That will be hard for you."

"And for her. Erin, it's not going well."

"I know. Charlotte's off her game. She's letting the prosecution paint a picture of you shooting Nate by the swim platform and then disposing of the body. And there's no evidence that happened."

"And she's dead set against playing our surveillance tape."

"How does Sean feel about it?"

"He thinks using it is too big a gamble because it undermines the defense they've developed. If they put on the tape, they can't put on their coroner who says Nate's death was an accident and their oceanographer who says the currents just made it look like he was shot in the head. I'd rather gamble on a surveillance tape that shows him waving goodbye to me at one a.m. Listen, I called to ask a favor. I hope you don't mind."

"Anything. I'll talk to Charlotte about playing the tape if you want. Or I'll ask Dad to talk to her if you think his opinion would carry more weight."

"It's not that. Don't go to work today. Spend it with me."

She didn't answer, and Andy was embarrassed. "Erin, I'm sorry. I didn't mean—

It's just that—"

"I know," she finally said, her voice still warm and sympathetic. "I hesitated because I was thinking over the work that won't get done today if I don't go to the office. But this is more important. Let's have breakfast at my place and then go back to the yacht club one more time. Maybe there's someone we haven't talked to yet who has evidence that would help."

"Erin, thanks."

"Of course."

CHAPTER FORTY-THREE

Monday, November 19, 2018, San Diego County Courthouse, 330 West Broadway

Tina Hernandez, the prosecution's last witness, was already in the courtroom, sitting in the public seats, when Sean arrived with Charlotte that morning. Charlotte had told him that she was beautiful, but he hadn't been prepared for just how strikingly lovely she was. He scrupulously avoided eye contact with her, all the while hoping that she'd knock out Axel's motive for murder.

His anxiety was on high alert the minute Andy appeared, escorted by his parents. Charlotte had cautioned Andy not to try to make any sort of contact with Tina, even eye contact, in the courtroom. Andy had behaved well so far in all of his court appearances, but Sean always regarded him as a wild card.

And he lived up to that reputation as soon as he was seated at the defense table next to Sean. He didn't look at Tina, but he leaned over and began babbling to Sean and Charlotte about someone he and Erin had talked to at the Cays on Saturday who claimed to have seen a man leaving *The Escape* at some undefined time on the night of June 9-10. And not only was

Andy babbling nonsense, the nonsense was loud enough to get Axel and Kaitlyn Green's attention.

"Not here," Charlotte said.

"But I have to tell you!" Andy protested. "Erin—"

Sean looked over at the public seats and saw that Erin had just entered the courtroom.

"Let's get Erin and take this out in the hall," he said, and Charlotte nodded.

The four of them assembled in a deserted area where no arriving jurors could overhear them.

"Okay," Charlotte began. "First rule of being a smart criminal defendant, don't let the prosecutor hear what you're saying to your attorneys."

"Sorry." Andy looked down at his polished loafers.

"What's this about, Erin?" Charlotte turned to her.

"Andy and I canvassed the Cays on Saturday just to see what else we might turn up. We found a man whose house has a view of the Owens' boat slip. His name is Mark Rollins. He remembered seeing a man leave the boat sometime after midnight in the early hours of June 10."

"Don't you see?" Andy broke in. "That's the cartel hitman my mother sent to kill Nate."

Sean tried not to roll his eyes. He looked at Charlotte, who shook her head slightly.

"So if you call Mark Rollins as a witness, and you play the tape of me waving goodbye to Nate on the boat, the jury will see that I didn't kill him," Andy insisted.

Oh, God. The only person I want to kill right now is Erin for stirring this up.

But maybe she deserved to be forgiven. She said calmly, "I apologize to both of you. I told Andy I'd tell the two of you about this, but I didn't think it would change anything. Mr. Rollins just isn't sure about the time he saw the man leaving."

"And it's very likely that the person he saw was Andy on the way to open up the house," Charlotte said.

"I think the time was later and that he saw someone else," Erin told them. "Mr. Rollins thought it was around three thirty, but he couldn't say for sure. He was up because he and his wife had a newborn, and they were taking turns caring for the baby. His wife had had the early shift, and he had taken the later one. So it's likely that he saw the man around three thirty. But he just couldn't be sure of the time. I told Andy putting him on as a witness with that much uncertainty would be too big a gamble, and the two of you wouldn't want to do it."

"You should have listened to Erin." Charlotte turned to Andy. "And above all, you shouldn't have brought this up in hearing distance of the prosecutors."

"I—"

But Charlotte cut him off. "We have to go back now. Judge Carter will be ready to start at any minute."

"You go back with Andy," Sean told her. "I want a minute with Erin." *She might be the boss' daughter, but she needs to stop meddling.*

"I apologize again," Erin said as Charlotte and Andy walked down the hall toward the courtroom.

"Why did you get mixed up in this, anyway?"

"He came to me because I was there that first Sunday with Dad when the police found the body and searched the house and the boat. He felt that you and Charlotte weren't listening to him. And he felt that you weren't doing anything to try to find evidence that he wasn't guilty."

"We've listened. And we've looked for evidence that he didn't do it. But we haven't found any. And all we've heard from him is this Menendez Cartel hitman fantasy. Come on, Erin. You know how long your father has been friends with Lucas and Ella. And you know what their business means to the firm. Do you seriously believe they've been involved in an international drug ring for years, all the while hiding that from Goldstein, Miller?"

Erin sighed. "No, I don't believe that. But I don't think Andy's guilty, either. Nate was a criminal defense attorney. It's not impossible that someone else had a motive to murder him."

"Well, as you know, we can't use that as a defense." He knew he should keep the hostility out of his voice. But he didn't.

"I honestly didn't mean to stir up Andy," Erin said. "But I do innocence investigations, and I think Andy deserves one." Her tone was still friendly, and she smiled.

Anyone else would be furious with me for lecturing her.

"Well, all I can tell you is how much Charlotte and I have wished to find evidence that he's innocent. But it's just not there."

"Look, I know he shouldn't be interviewing witnesses," Erin said. "I didn't really think we'd run into anyone like Mark Rollins."

"Keep Andy away from him."

"Of course. But I did leave Mr. Rollins my business card and asked him to get in touch if his memory improves about the time he saw the man. Do you want to know if I hear from him?"

"Of course. And thanks, Erin. We'd better get back inside."

She walked down the hall with him companionably as if he'd never spoken sharply to her.

I admire her for her confidence and self-control. And she's not reminding me that she's Hugh's daughter. I don't know why she's so set on the kid being innocent. All the evidence points the other way. But we need a Hail Mary pass. If this guy thinks he saw someone else at three thirty, I hope his memory improves before this trial is over. And I hope Tina throws us a bone this morning by killing their motive theory. Come on, Universe. Charlotte and I need a break.

* * *

Tina Hernandez took the stand with the air of a young queen who had deigned to come down from her throne to answer her subjects' questions. But only for as long as it pleased her. Her simple black dress and short jacket displayed her graceful, athletic figure to perfection. She was poised as she took the oath and sat down on the witness stand. Her hair was pulled back into a tight, glossy bun that added to her air of authority. She settled herself in the witness chair and fixed her large dark almond-shaped eyes on Axel Saldana as he stood at the podium, ready to question her. The expression on her face said that she was more than prepared to meet any challenge he could throw at her.

I hope he can't shake her. But she's so gorgeous. The jurors are certainly going to believe that jealousy could drive a kid like Andy to kill his best friend for her.

"Good morning, Miss Hernandez."

"Dr. Hernandez."

She's tripped him up right out of the gate. That's a good sign.

"I apologize. Where are you employed, Dr. Hernandez?"

"I was formerly a research scientist at The Salk Institute. As of January, I will be enrolled as a medical student at Stanford University."

"And are you acquainted with the defendant?"

"I am."

"For how long?"

"About a year and a half."

"And did that acquaintance include a romantic relationship with him?"

"At one point, yes."

"And when did that relationship end?"

"Last March."

"And did you or the defendant end it?"

"I did."

"And were you acquainted with the victim at the time you ended your relationship with the defendant?"

"Yes."

"How about after you ended your relationship with the defendant? Did you go on seeing Nathan McClellan?"

"He was my brothers' attorney."

Axel isn't going to bring up the false arrest because that will make his office look bad.

"Would you read this aloud, Dr. Hernandez?" Axel handed her a copy of the text that she'd sent Nate.

"Objection!" Sean was on his feet. "This message has already been read to the jury and entered into evidence." *It was prejudicial enough the first time.*

"Overruled." Sean hated the way Judge Carter smiled condescendingly when he overruled defense objections.

Tina read the text in a steady voice and then looked up at Axel as if challenging him to make something out of her words. Sean hoped he wasn't ready for the challenge, but he was.

"And is this a text message that you sent to Nathan McClellan on June 9, 2018, at ten twenty-nine that evening?"

"Yes."

"And are you in the habit of ending messages to your brothers' attorney with 'Love, Tina'?"

"Nate was a family friend, too."

She's starting to sound defensive. That's not good.

"And did you go on dates with this family friend after you broke up with the defendant?"

"I don't recall."

"You never met for coffee?"

"I don't recall."

"What about dinner? Did Nate McClellan ask you out to dinner?"

"I don't recall."

"You refused all of my requests to meet with you, didn't you, Dr. Hernandez?"

"Objection, leading," Sean said.

"I'll permit it."

The appellate attorney can raise judicial bias on appeal. But she's not being forthcoming. That's making her look as if she's covering up for Andy.

"I don't recall."

"And you refused to come to testify unless I issued a subpoena?"

"I received a subpoena."

"And you don't want to be here today, do you?"

"I don't want to be involved, that's true."

"Your Honor, I'd like permission to treat Dr. Hernandez as a hostile witness."

"Granted. You may use leading questions."

She's trying to help Andy, but she's hurting him. The more hostile she is, the more the jurors are going to believe that she was involved with Nate and doesn't want to admit it.

"Now going back to the message that you sent the victim on the night of his death. You signed it 'Love, Tina,' but you say you weren't dating him?"

"I said I didn't recall."

"Did the victim think that you were only close friends?"

"Objection!" Sean was on his feet again. "This witness can't testify to what's in someone else's head."

"Overruled," Judge Carter said with that irritating smile. "You may answer."

"I always told Nate that we were friends."

"And isn't it true that you have had contact with the defendant since he was arrested and charged with the victim's death?"

Sean wished he could pound the table in frustration at Andy's stupidity. *We warned him about interviewing witnesses himself.*

"I don't recall."

"And isn't it true that the defendant asked you to deny that you had a romantic relationship with Nathan McClellan?"

"No, he did not."

"You can recall a conversation with the defendant, Dr. Hernandez, but you can't recall your contacts with the victim?"

"Objection. Argumentative."

And I'm right about that.

"Sustained. Next question, Mr. Saldana."

"Your text said, *'Family is everything, and yours would never understand.'* What would Nathan's family never understand, Dr. Hernandez?"

"I don't recall."

"Weren't you the reason that the victim wanted to call off his wedding to his fiancée?"

"No!"

He's finally gotten to her.

"Isn't it true, Dr. Hernandez, that you didn't leave The Salk Institute voluntarily?"

"No, that isn't true. I left to apply to medical school."

"But isn't it true, Dr. Hernandez, that you were fired for embezzling research funds?"

"Objection!" Sean roared. *Axel is getting to me, too.* In a calmer tone he said, "The defense is asking for a sidebar."

"That isn't necessary," Judge Carter said. "I know Mr. Saldana. He's been in front of me numerous times. He wouldn't ask that question if he didn't have a good faith belief that it's true. Goes to witness credibility."

Here's another one for the appellate attorney. But the odds of reversal on appeal are never very good. I should start looking for a new job.

"Thank you, Your Honor." The prosecutor and Judge Carter exchanged smiles.

"Answer the question," Judge Carter said.

"My accounts were hacked. I didn't take anything that didn't belong to me. I received a full apology."

"Yet you still left the Salk Institute?"

"I was insulted because the administration had impugned my integrity." The young queen was back on her throne.

"No further questions."

Sean took a deep breath and replaced Axel at the podium. *I've got to be careful. This is the most important cross-examination of the trial.*

"Good morning, Dr. Hernandez. I only have a few questions. Were you engaged to marry Andy Owens?"

"No, I was not."

"And did you have hopes of an engagement to him?"

"No, I did not."

"What about Nathan McClellan? Were you engaged or did you hope for an engagement to him?"

"No."

"So isn't it true that your relationship with Nathan was not in any way a threat to my client?"

"Objection."

I could have predicted that.

"Sustained."

I could have predicted that, too.

"No further questions." *Judge Carter isn't going to let me make any points for the defense.*

"You may step down, Dr. Hernandez."

CHAPTER FORTY-FOUR

Monday, November 19, 2018, San Diego County Courthouse, 330 West Broadway

The afternoon felt endless. Finding Mark Rollins at the Cays had raised Andy's spirits over the weekend. But Erin had warned him that Charlotte and Sean would consider those observations too uncertain to call him as a witness. Andy had still pumped himself up with optimism that this time his attorneys would take him seriously. But, of course, they hadn't. Charlotte's reprimands had stung, as they were meant to. And then right after being put in his place yet again, he'd had to sit through Tina's testimony. He had wanted to punch Axel Saldana for dragging her into this and insulting her. He'd had to hold back tears when Axel brought up the embezzlement accusations.

Now he, along with the jury, was being put to sleep by the defense experts. Andy had no faith in the defense story no matter who was telling it. After all, he knew the truth. If the police had done their job and investigated Nate's death, his parents would be sitting here instead of behind him. All his life, they'd thought that he wasn't very bright and he couldn't take care of himself. But he'd done it this time. He not only had taken care of himself, but he had uncovered the truth about his parents. However, in the end, it hadn't been enough because no one would believe him.

At least Sean was trying to run through the very technical defense quickly to salvage what attention was left from the jurors. The accident investigator said the boat hit a buoy marker near the bridge and brought the paint samples to prove it. The coroner said Nate drowned when the impact of the accident threw him overboard. The tides expert said the damage to the body from the currents only made it look like there was a bullet wound to the head. The blood alcohol expert said Andy was in a blackout from ten thirty p.m. on although his blood alcohol numbers the next morning didn't support that conclusion, even with generous backtracking allowances. The ballistics expert, who had never fired the Glock 26, critiqued the prosecutor's expert, and said the bullet found on the yacht hadn't been fired from Lucas' gun. Kyle testified to Andy's good character, and Gavin told the jury that Andy was a great guy with a drinking problem who loved Nate. Finally, Lucas tearfully confessed his shortcomings as a father and explained why Andy's DNA was on the gun. Axel Saldana was so convinced of the strength of his case that he barely cross-examined the defense witnesses except for asking Lucas to admit that he couldn't explain how a nine-millimeter shell casing wound up on *The Escape.*

Andy was thankful that it went by quickly. No juror looked the least bit impressed.

Judge Carter dismissed everyone at five o'clock, slightly later than usual to allow the defense to finish that day. The judge announced that closing arguments would begin in the morning.

But Andy knew that closing arguments didn't matter. His fate had been sealed ever since the cops found that gun. As he left the courtroom that afternoon, sandwiched between his parents like the useless child they thought he was, Erin shot him a look of deep sympathy. Her eyes told him how bad the defense story had sounded. And she knew what was coming.

CHAPTER FORTY-FIVE

Tuesday, November 20, 2018, The Metropolitan, 165 Sixth Avenue, San Diego

Sean was wide awake at midnight. He'd been trying to sleep since eleven o'clock without success. He wouldn't let himself drink alcohol. He had to be up early and on his game. While Charlotte delivered the closing argument for the defense in the morning, his job would be to focus on the jurors' twelve stony faces to see if there was a ghost of a chance of getting an acquittal for Andy. Or at least a voluntary manslaughter verdict. A hangover would hamper his performance.

He was anxious and nervous and miserable. Normally, he'd have had at least one double scotch at bedtime to soothe his jangled nerves. But his months with Charlotte had made him more cautious about alcohol. She was a good influence on him. He'd taken up running, too.

His phone rang. He picked it up, hoping to see Charlotte's number on the caller ID. But he saw Hugh's private line, instead.

Oh, God, not now. This isn't going to be good news. Is he calling to tell me that I'm finished at the firm? "What's up, Hugh?"

"Sorry it's so late. Erin just called and told me Charlotte is closing for the defense tomorrow. Given the way things are going, Erin doesn't think that's a good idea. I want you to close."

"But Charlotte wanted to do it, and we agreed."

"But she's made too many mistakes. The last one about the DNA profile on the gun was really serious. She forgot to question their expert about the other profiles."

"I know. But I took care of it."

"But the evidence that other people are connected to that gun lost its impact. I know because I was there that day, watching. It's better if you close. Look, this is my fault. I forced Charlotte to take on this case. It was too soon after Matt's death. She wasn't emotionally ready. Erin's been there every day. She says Charlotte doesn't come across as believing in Andy."

"Neither of us think he's innocent, Hugh."

"Charlotte has made more than one mistake in this trial. You should close."

"Have you called Charlotte and told her?"

"I tried to, but she didn't answer. I sent her a text and an email. They'll be waiting whenever she turns her phone back on."

"She's not going to be happy."

"I don't care. I need Lucas and Ella to be happy. We need to get Andy acquitted."

* * *

She wasn't answering her phone. Sean was frantic. It was a brand-new phone. Maybe she just hadn't wanted to talk to Hugh.

But she didn't answer when he tried at repeated intervals

throughout the night. He tried to organize his thoughts to prepare a closing argument, but he was panicked over Charlotte's silence. Was she all right? Should he call the police? He wasn't in any shape to deliver a closing argument, he decided, as he dressed for work at six thirty.

Relief flooded him when he found her waiting in his office at seven fifteen. She looked pale and tired, but calm and authoritative in her navy suit and white blouse.

"You don't look as if you've slept," she said. "What's wrong?"

"I've been up all night worrying about you. Hugh tried to call you last night, and you didn't answer. And then I tried multiple times. Same result."

"I'm sorry. I turned off my phone to work on my closing argument. And then I found Hugh's text and email this morning. Why does he want you to close? It's because I've made mistakes at trial, isn't it?" She suddenly looked anxious, and Sean was angry with Hugh for doubting her.

"Look, we all make mistakes," he said. "Honestly, I'm in no shape to argue this morning. And you're prepared. Hugh's not in charge of this case. We are."

But she hesitated. "I don't want to put you in a bad position with Hugh. It's okay if you want to do it. I've already admitted that I didn't realize until we were in trial that I've jumped back in too soon after losing Matt. But I thought if I did a good job today, I could make up for my mistakes."

His heart turned over with love and sympathy as he studied her face. She was a good lawyer, and she'd been unfairly drawn into a major case at a time of deep personal grief. Maybe he owed it to his own career to follow Hugh's directive and close. But her anxious eyes told him how much the chance to redeem herself meant. He wasn't going to deny her that.

* * *

"Good morning, ladies and gentlemen," Axel began at nine a.m. "This case is about a spoiled young man who thought he had the right to remove anyone in the way of what he wanted. And what he wanted was Tina Hernandez. The person in the way was Nathan McClellan. Andy Owens used this Glock 26 to get what he wanted."

Sean was glad that Andy was able to keep his face expressionless as Axel started through the litany of damning evidence. He could see that the jurors' eyes were focused on Andy's face. It helped that his natural expression was softened by his large dark eyes. Even in repose, he looked likeable and sympathetic. And there were tears in his eyes, but Sean was pretty sure the jurors were too far away to see those.

"So what does the evidence tell us?" Axel went on. "It tells us that Andy has lived in the lap of luxury all his life. He's had everything he's ever wanted. And it tells us that he's killed before. Three years ago, he went to an exclusive gathering in the Hamptons at Christmas. Now remember, only rich people like the defendant are invited to parties in the Hamptons. The defendant partied hard that night. And then he went out and got into his car and took the life of a young man whom he'd never even met. A young man, about to graduate from college, who had his whole life ahead of him until the moment when he met an eighty-thousand-dollar Mercedes coming hard and fast on the wrong side of the road with the defendant at the wheel."

Charlotte was on her feet. "Objection, Your Honor. Mr. Saldana is appealing to passion and prejudice."

"Overruled. You may continue."

At least she tried, Sean thought.

"Thank you, Your Honor."

Axel's tone of voice makes it sound like the judge is on his side. And he is.

"And what did the defendant learn from that experience, ladies and gentlemen?" Axel went on. "Did he learn to be sorry? Did he learn to stop drinking? No, he learned that with enough money, he could get away with murder."

"Objection." Charlotte stood up again. "Andy Owens was not convicted of vehicular homicide."

"Overruled."

The appellate attorney will be all over that one, Sean thought. *But by then it will be too late.*

"Now the defendant's father owned a yacht. And the defendant's father owned a gun. And on the night of June 9, 2018, the defendant used both to kill his childhood friend because Nate McClellan wanted to marry the woman the defendant was in love with. The evidence tells the story, ladies and gentlemen. The DNA on the gun is unshakeable proof that it was in the defendant's hand at the moment Nate McClellan died. And the navigation log is unshakeable proof of the trip that the defendant took to dump the body. He threw what was left of Nate into the Pacific to float like a piece of garbage. A piece of garbage that he thought would never be found. The defendant has killed two innocent young men, ladies and gentlemen. Two young men who had their whole lives ahead of them. Don't turn the defendant loose to kill again."

"Thank you, Mr. Saldana," Judge Carter said with his inevitable smile for the prosecutor. "Ladies and gentlemen, it is noon, so we'll take our lunch break now. When you return at one o'clock, we'll hear from the defense."

Sean studied Charlotte's profile as the jurors left the courtroom. Her eyes were fixed on the judge. She looked like a cheetah ready to spring. As soon as the door closed behind the last juror, she stood up.

"Your Honor, the defense would like to move for a mistrial."

"A mistrial, Mrs. Estes?" Judge Carter raised his eyebrows but otherwise maintained his genial expression. "On what grounds?"

"Prosecutorial misconduct. Mr. Saldana was inviting the jury to convict based upon the defendant's economic status and a tragic accident that is three years old."

"What's your answer, Mr. Saldana?"

"The only prejudice to the defendant comes from his own conduct," Axel asserted as he rose to his feet and folded his arms confidently across his chest. "I've merely argued the evidence."

"Mrs. Estes?"

"The cost of the defendant's vehicle, the guest list for a party in the Hamptons, the cost of Lucas Owens' yacht are not in evidence, Your Honor. And the description of the youth of the victims was entirely unnecessary."

If His Honor blows this one off, there's going to be a good chance of reversal on appeal, Sean thought. *Axel laid it on too thick. Maybe I'd better hope Judge Carter continues to favor the prosecution.*

DEBORAH HAWKINS

"I think the defense has a valid point, Mr. Saldana," Judge Carter said.

Damn, he sees the danger of a reversal, and he's not going to let that happen.

"I'll admonish the jurors when they return from lunch and remind them that they cannot convict the defendant based upon the incident in New York or because he is the son of wealthy parents."

"Yes, Your Honor."

* * *

"Good afternoon," Judge Carter said after everyone was seated for the afternoon session. "Before we recessed, Mr. Saldana referred to facts that are not in evidence when he described the defendant's previous conduct in New York. You can consider that evidence, ladies and gentlemen, only as evidence of propensity and you cannot render a guilty verdict based solely upon that evidence."

Legal speak for the prosecutor made a mistake. I doubt that lay jurors are going to get that. But Judge Carter has protected Axel's conviction. If he gets one. It's up to Charlotte to see that he doesn't.

Judge Carter gave the defense table his friendliest smile and said, "Mrs. Estes, you may now deliver the closing argument for the defense."

"Thank you, Your Honor."

Sean watched Charlotte take her place at the podium. She looked serene and supremely confident. Whatever her demons were, she'd left them behind. The jurors regarded her with interest. *That's a good sign.*

Sean glanced back over his shoulder and saw Hugh sitting next to Erin. His stomach tightened. *This better be good.*

"Good afternoon," she began. "This morning, Mr. Saldana painted the pictured of an entitled and callous young man with no regard for the rights of others. But the truth, ladies and gentlemen, is an entirely different matter. You heard it from his father, Lucas, who loves his son, but who admitted tearfully, that he and Andy's mother were always too busy to be there for him. Andy tried and tried to be the scholar and the son they wanted him to be. But when he failed over and over again, his parents were just too busy with their own lives to give him the guidance and support he needed.

"Andy turned to alcohol because it was the friend that was always there for him.

"He drank because it numbed the pain of always being alone. This morning Mr. Saldana implied that rich people are always bad people. But the truth is, riches do not make people good or bad. And they don't always make people happy. And they didn't make Andy Owens happy.

"The truth is, Andy made a mistake in early 2015. He went willingly to rehab for an entire year. Then he came back to San Diego and worked to rebuild his life. He studied for the bar exam. He met Tina Hernandez and fell in love, really in love for the first time in his life.

"But then Dr. Hernandez ended their relationship. Andy accepted that. He was hurt, but he carried on with his childhood friends. On the night of June 9, Nate McClellan, his oldest friend, was upset. Andy didn't know that Nate was torn between the marriage that his family wanted and the marriage that Nate wanted. Andy only knew that his best friend was unhappy, and Andy was determined to be there for him. Nate wanted to go for a ride around the bay on the yacht to forget his troubles. And on that ride, there was a tragic accident, and Nate lost his life.

"The evidence, ladies and gentlemen, does not show a bullet wound in Nathaniel McClellan's skull. Nate's body wasn't in the water long, but it was there long enough to be damaged by the currents. You've heard the defense expert explain what currents can do to a body.

"The navigation log shows an impact with a buoy near the Coronado Bridge. Andy, for all his good intentions to make his friend feel better, didn't know how to drive a yacht like *The Escape*. Nate was thrown overboard, and Andy, who had been drinking heavily, didn't realize what had happened.

"Ladies and gentlemen, you've heard from the defense how speculative ballistics evidence really is. The scientists at the National Academy of Sciences have demonstrated that the interpretation of test fires from a suspected murder weapon depends completely upon the bias of the examiner. These interpretations aren't really scientific evidence at all. And obviously the prosecution's ballistics examiner was biased, no doubt about that. In truth, we have no idea when that bullet was fired. And we have no idea who fired it. And we have no idea if it actually came from Andy's father's gun.

"Tina Hernandez, herself, told you that she had no intention of marrying Andy or Nate McClellan. The state's motive for murder is nothing but speculation that is totally false. The death of Andy Owens' childhood friend was a tragic accident. Andy should be acquitted of the murder of Nate McClellan."

Sean smiled at Charlotte as she resumed her seat at the defense table. He wished he could hug her.

Judge Carter turned to Axel.

"Rebuttal, Mr. Saldana?"

Axel rose from his seat, looking sleek and powerful as he replaced Charlotte at the podium.

"Ladies and gentlemen, don't be fooled by the defendant's bought-and-paid-for defense. Don't let him use his history of alcohol abuse to hide his cold-blooded murder of his oldest friend. Tina Hernandez may be a scientist, but she's also an exceptionally beautiful woman. There's no speculation involved. Andy wanted her for himself, and he was willing to kill to eliminate his rival. The verdict is simple in this case."

CHAPTER FORTY-SIX

Tuesday, November 20, 2018, Rancho Santa Fe

At eight thirty, Andy sat by the open window in his room, breathing in the cold night air. The contrast with the atmosphere in his overheated room was exhilarating. His escape was imminent. He'd be on his way out of this window in just a few minutes. Down the hall, his parents were planning a victory party for the following evening. Clearly, they hadn't watched the same trial that he had.

At three o'clock that afternoon, the bailiff had taken charge of the solemn jurors and escorted them to the jury room. Andy had waited tensely with Erin in the courthouse coffee shop, expecting to be called back to hear the guilty verdict at any minute. She'd talked to him about appeals and had recommended some appellate attorneys as they had sipped stale coffee. She hadn't tried to tell him everything was going to be all right. He'd appreciated her honesty. Not to mention he was hopelessly in love with her. Oddly, his unrequited emotion buoyed him up instead of depressed him. He could delude himself that one day he would ask her to marry him. Of course, other than getting out of prison and returning to San Diego, the next biggest part of his delusion was she wouldn't laugh at his proposal. In his lucid moments, Andy knew that an accomplished woman like Erin would never settle for a loser like himself. His experience with Tina had already taught him that. But most of the time, he preferred to suppress those thoughts and pretend that Erin felt more than friendship for him.

He'd been surprised when the jurors had returned after an hour and a half of deliberations and announced that they had not yet reached a verdict. When the court had sent them all home at four thirty, his parents and Charlotte and Sean had seen this as a sign of hope. But Andy had known better. He'd endured dinner with Lucas and Ella in the dining room of the Mansion of Doom and then retreated to his own room to nurse his wounds.

He wasn't taking anything except the clothes on his back. Yesterday, he'd managed to buy a burner phone because his own phone's GPS could be tracked. And he'd parked the Camry in a service alley behind the mansion a half mile down the road from his parents' place. Now he was going to execute his plan. He was lucky that the downstairs windows in the Mansion of Doom were floor-length. In just a few seconds, he was going to slip through this one and walk to the spot where he'd parked the Camry. He'd drive to the border at San Ysidro where he'd ditch the Camry and take his chances on getting across before the checkpoint closed at ten p.m. After he made it across, he'd take a taxi to Tina's uncle who lived in Tijuana. Although Uncle Alejandro didn't know Andy was coming, Andy was pretty sure that he'd hide him for a few days until the search for him died down. From there, if his luck held, he'd head on to Mexico City where he'd figure out his new life. He fervently thanked all of his Latina nannies for his practically native Spanish. He watched the minutes tick away. At eight forty-four, there was a knock on his bedroom door, followed by his father's voice.

"Andy?"

Damn. "Not now, Dad. I'm getting into the shower."

The door opened anyway.

"Not in your clothes. What's going on?" Lucas' eyes went from Andy's face to the open window and back again. He walked over and slammed the window.

"Don't be stupid! You're not going to get convicted."

"Bullshit."

"If you do, your mother and I will get you out."

"Bullshit."

"We'll get you out, Andy. We'll buy a pardon if we have to."

"And how many years will that take?"

"Don't be ridiculous. You're going to be acquitted. Charlotte did a brilliant job today."

"Too little, too late. I'm leaving now!" Andy pushed open the window only to have Lucas slam it shut again.

"No way. Your mother would have gotten you out of the country in a heartbeat if either of us had seriously believed that you were going to be convicted. Charlotte has gotten you off. You'll see. I shelled out four million dollars for that screwup in New York. If you run now, it will cost your mother and me another five million in forfeited bail. Nine million to cover your irresponsibility is too much. You're not going to be convicted. You'll see."

Andy sat very still after his father left, waiting to hear his footsteps retreating down the hall. As soon as Lucas was out of earshot, Andy was going to open the window and escape. But there were no retreating footsteps. Instead, Andy heard his father calling one of his gardeners to nail Andy's windows shut.

* * *

Wednesday, November 21, 2018, San Diego County Courthouse, 330 West Broadway

The next morning, Andy stood between Charlotte and Sean at the defense table at eight thirty and watched the bailiff once again lead the jurors into the jury room to resume deliberations. Andy prayed they didn't hate him as much as their faces suggested that they did.

After the jurors left, Judge Carter dismissed everyone. Hugh Mahoney himself had come to take charge of Andy's over-confident, but still anxious parents. Lucas and Ella accepted his invitation to go back to his office where decent coffee and pastries awaited. Charlotte declined to join Hugh's watch party, pleading pressing business in her office. But Sean joined Andy and Erin as they once again drank over-brewed coffee in the courthouse coffee shop.

As the hands of the cheap plastic clock above the condiments table crept from nine to ten and then from ten to eleven, Andy allowed himself to hope that at least one juror had bought Sean and Charlotte's accident defense. The longer the jurors stayed out, the more likely it was that at least one, and maybe more than one, was voting for the defense.

At eleven twenty, the jury sent a note to the judge saying it had reached a verdict. A mad scramble ensued to get all of the lawyers on both sides back into the courtroom. At five minutes to twelve, Andy once again stood between Charlotte and Sean at the defense table with his parents seated directly behind him to hear the verdict. Andy could feel the sweat trickling down his back between his shoulder blades.

"I understand that the jury has reached a verdict," Judge Carter intoned.

"Yes, Your Honor." The bailiff handed an envelope to the judge who opened it and studied the papers inside.

After what seemed an eternity, Judge Carter announced, "The verdicts are complete. The clerk may read them."

Andy felt as if he were having an out-of-body experience. The clerk, a middle-aged woman with gray hair and thick glasses, wearing an ill-fitting maroon suit, stood at her desk and began to read. "We, the jury, find Andrew Lawrence Owens, guilty of the murder of Nathaniel Reyes McClellan on June 9, 2018. Further, we find that the murder was deliberate and premeditated. We further find the lying-in-wait special circumstance to be true."

That meant life without parole. Andy began to shake as if he'd just been placed in an icebox. He'd expected this. If his father hadn't been such a jerk last night, he'd have been in Tijuana by now. He told himself to be calm, but it was impossible. Being taken to prison for the rest of his life was a waking nightmare.

"Thank you, ladies and gentlemen of the jury." Judge Carter smiled. "Your jury service is over, and you are discharged." He turned to Charlotte and Sean. "The defendant has the right to be sentenced within twenty days."

"We ask for thirty," Andy thought he heard Charlotte say.

"Mr. Owens, do you give up your right to be sentenced within twenty days?"

Andy wasn't sure what he answered. The handcuffs were already on his wrists and the deputy sheriffs were leading him away. His life was over. He managed to look back at Erin before the door to the courtroom closed behind him. Her eyes were full of tears.

CHAPTER FORTY-SEVEN

Wednesday, November 21, 2018, San Diego County Courthouse, 330 West Broadway

Sean watched the sheriff's deputies put the handcuffs on Andy and lead him away. Charlotte answered Judge Carter's question about setting a date for sentencing in December. Sean's head was spinning with ideas for an appeal as he gathered his trial documents into his briefcase. He'd expected this verdict, and yet he'd held out hope for an acquittal.

Erin and Hugh and Ella and Lucas were waiting for him and Charlotte in the hallway where a throng of reporters were also swarming. Hugh told them that a notice of appeal would be filed later that afternoon, and the entire firm of Goldstein, Miller was certain that Andy's conviction would be reversed. *A complete fiction, of course,* Sean thought. He looked down at Charlotte who appeared pale and drained.

"Don't worry," he whispered. "We did our best. We knew from the beginning the kid was guilty."

She gave him a wan smile.

The six of them worked their way through the hovering reporters and television crews as they headed for the massive front doors of the Hall of Justice. Sean knew they were going to walk back to the firm to get a hefty retainer from Lucas to get Andy's appeal underway. Throwing good money after bad. But it would make everyone feel better.

Sean and Charlotte were in the lead with the others behind them. There were more reporters and TV crews outside, asking for reactions from the Owens defense team. Sean and Charlotte were still standing on the top step when Hugh stopped to talk to a reporter.

Suddenly, Sean heard tires squealing and people screaming. He looked to his left and saw a black Escalade speeding down Broadway toward them, honking its horn. Traffic moved over to the curb to get out of its way. It was running stoplights, and pedestrians were scattering in its wake. In a matter of seconds, the Escalade was directly opposite Sean and Charlotte. He saw a hand reach out of the front passenger window and then, in a split second, he saw a flash and heard three pops in rapid succession.

His eyes were fixed on the car, trying to read the license plate as it sped away. But when he looked back at Charlotte, he saw red stains on the front of her navy suit. She was staring at them as if she didn't believe they were there. Then she looked at Sean and moved her mouth, but no sounds came out. A second later, she began to fall. Sean grabbed her to keep her from hitting the marble steps.

He heard Erin, who was behind him, calling 9-1-1. Cameras were flashing all around as he held Charlotte. His thoughts were racing.

An ambulance seemed to appear out of nowhere, and paramedics with a stretcher surrounded Sean as he held Charlotte.

"You've got to let go, buddy, so we can get a look."

He stepped back and watched them hovering over Charlotte. He was terrified that she had stopped breathing. The bullets had hit close to her heart. He heard Hugh talking to one of the police officers, but he couldn't focus on what he was saying.

The back doors of the ambulance were open, and the paramedics were picking up the stretcher. Sean tried to follow them.

"You can't come in the ambulance," one of them called to him.

"Where are you taking her?"

"U.C. Medical Center. Hillcrest. It's the closest place. We haven't got much time."

* * *

Wednesday, November 21, 2018, U.C. San Diego Medical Center, Hillcrest

The ride to the hospital with Hugh and Erin in the first taxi they could find was a blur. He kept seeing the black Escalade heading toward them, horn blaring, guns blazing. He realized he was crying, and he couldn't stop.

Erin, who was sitting beside him, put her hand on his arm. "It's okay. We're almost at the hospital. Oh my God, Sean, look at your hand."

He looked down and saw that his left hand was covered in blood. He heard Hugh say, "He's been shot."

Sean let Erin and Hugh lead him into the Emergency Room. He hoped he'd stopped crying. He was shaking uncontrollably now.

He didn't resist when they put him in an exam room and started an IV. But all he could think about was Charlotte. Where was she? Was she going to be okay? Now he wished he'd refused the IV, so he could get up and go find someone who could tell him how she was.

The door opened and Erin appeared. "The nurse said I could come in. Dad's outside talking to the doctors, and there's a couple of police officers here. How are you?"

"I'm okay. I shouldn't have let them tie me up like this."

"Yes, you should have. You were going into shock."

"Did you call Charlotte's children?"

"Yes, they're on their way. They're taking care of calling their grandmother. If she wants to come to the hospital before they arrive, I volunteered to go and get her. She's in Allied Gardens."

Suddenly, he realized how alone he felt, and he didn't like the thought of her leaving. But the antidote to his loneliness was to get out of the hospital and start looking for who was responsible for that black Escalade.

"Do you have any news about Charlotte?" he asked.

"They took her straight into surgery. It looks like it's going to be a while before we know. The police told Dad that her husband's death was a homicide, and there have been several attempts on her life since then. Did you know?"

"I did. I think I'm the only one she told. Matt had a client named Rosemary Spencer who told him some secrets for a proffer session with the U.S. Attorney. Then she changed her mind about turning herself into a government witness and killed Matt."

"So she would be the one behind what happened today?"

"I think she's just a cog in a bigger wheel. Whoever she's mixed up with is responsible for Matt's death and for today."

"Any idea who?"

"None. Charlotte's been trying to find out."

The door opened and a doctor in blue scrubs came in.

"I'm Dr. Doyle. I've come to take a look at your hand."

"I'll go find Dad," Erin said, "and see if I should go pick up Charlotte's mother."

After the door closed behind her, the doctor proceeded to examine Sean's hand, listen to his heart and lungs, and look for signs of any other injuries.

"I don't see any other signs of trauma," he said when he completed the exam. "That's a pretty deep wound. I'm going to put in a couple of stitches. I think it's a ricochet wound. I don't see any fragments in there."

"I'm ready to go home," Sean said.

"You should stay overnight. You were on the verge of going into shock when you came in."

"I'm fine now. I'll sign myself out against orders if I have to."

"Well, then, I'll stitch you up and get the forms for you to sign."

* * *

Once he was dressed, Sean realized that he still wasn't thinking clearly. He had no car, and the hospital refused to release him to a taxi or an Uber. He found his way to Erin and Hugh in the waiting room on the surgical floor where they were sitting side by side on a plastic sofa. They were the only ones there. A television in the corner was tuned to a house renovation show with the volume turned down low.

Erin frowned when he came in. "You were supposed to stay overnight, the doctor said."

"I need a ride home."

"Where you're going to rest," Hugh said.

"Yes, okay. Maybe. Any news about Charlotte?"

"A nurse was just here. She says the surgeon will be out to talk with us in a few minutes."

"After he talks to us, I'll drop you at your place on my way to pick up Charlotte's mother," Erin offered.

Sean sat down on the sofa across from them and tried to calm his nerves. He knew exactly what he was going to do the minute he got home. He was going to grab his keys and head over to Charlotte's house to look for answers.

The door opened and a middle-aged man in blue scrubs with a tired face entered.

"I'm Dr. Martin, one of the trauma surgeons. I'm looking for Mrs. Estes' family."

"We're her law partners," Hugh said. "Her family is en route from the East Coast. What can you tell us about her condition?"

Dr. Martin sat down next to Sean and began quietly. "I've got to be honest with you. She's still with us, but I can't say for how much longer."

Suddenly Sean's eyes were full of tears again. Erin patted him on the shoulder.

Dr. Martin went on. "The bullets missed her heart, but they nicked her aorta. I've done my best, but these injuries are almost always fatal."

I'm not going to believe that. I'm going to believe she'll be okay. She's got to be okay.

"Can I see her?" Sean asked.

Dr. Martin studied his face, and Sean thought that he was going to refuse his request. But finally, he said, "She's in ICU. I'll tell the nurse you can go in for five minutes. But no more."

A few minutes later, a nurse led him down the hall and into Intensive Care. His heart sank when she let him go into the cubicle where Charlotte lay tied to tubes and monitors. He began to cry as he walked over and laid his hand against her cheek, the only part of her that he could touch. *How could it all come to this?* She was one of the most vital, alive people he had ever met. Suddenly he could see her out for a run, strong and confident as she did the thing she loved best.

His shoulders began to heave. He'd kept his feelings bottled up for all the years since Sherrie left. He'd told himself that he'd never allow himself to feel anything for anyone again. But he'd been wrong.

"Mr. Donovan?"

He felt the gentle pressure of the nurse's hand on his arm.

"You've had your five minutes. You'll have to leave now."

CHAPTER FORTY-EIGHT

Thursday, November 22, 2018, The Metropolitan, 165 Sixth Avenue, San Diego

Sean woke from a heavy sleep at six the next morning and felt his hand throbbing. For a minute, he did not remember why he was in pain. And then the nightmare washed over him in vivid detail.

A wave of fatigue had hit him as soon as he walked into his living room yesterday at four thirty. They'd given him pain medication at the hospital, and it had made him sleepy. Reluctantly, he had admitted to himself that he was in no shape to drive to Charlotte's.

Now he sat up slowly because he was stiff and sore. He reached for his phone and called Erin.

"No change," she said. "We're all at Dad's place. I persuaded Hayden and Ian and Charlotte's mother to stay here last night. We're going back to the hospital at eight. I'll call you with any news."

He made coffee and watched the sun rise. Guilt overwhelmed him. He thought of going to the hospital, but he knew he'd feel even more guilty if he did. He'd known her life was in danger, but he hadn't done enough to protect her. Being with her children would make the burden of his guilt that much heavier.

His phone rang.

"I'm Detective Robert Rodriguez," a deep voice said. "I'm in charge of the investigation into the attempted murder of your colleague yesterday. I didn't get a chance to talk to you at the hospital."

"Did you find that Escalade?"

"No. It had stolen plates, and it vanished over the border within minutes of the shooting. It's likely in pieces somewhere in Tijuana now. This looks like a Menendez Cartel hit. Do you know why your colleague would have been targeted by the cartel?"

"She's never mentioned the cartel. I understand your office knows about her husband's murder last November in D.C. Rosemary Spencer, who was a client of Matt's, poisoned him. She killed again, last month, this time in Chicago. Detective Merrill of the D.C. police is in charge of the investigation. He can tell you everything."

"We're working with him. Do you know if this Spencer woman is connected to the cartel?"

"No, I don't. But it certainly looks like she is. After seeing that Escalade yesterday, I was pretty sure that she wasn't working on her own."

"We'll need a statement from you at some point."

"Of course."

He hung up and realized that he was hungry. He hadn't eaten since yesterday. His eyes filled with tears when he picked

VENGEANCE

up the room service menu because it made him think of the night Charlotte had spent with him after the Chicago trip and how he'd teased her about breakfast.

When his scrambled eggs arrived, he ate them from a tray in the living room as he studied San Diego Bay and the city below sparkling in the early morning sunshine. Detective Rodriguez's question about the Menendez Cartel brought back Andy's crazy cartel story about his parents and the reason for Nate's death. But had it really been crazy? Suddenly, he not only felt guilty about failing to protect Charlotte, he felt guilty about brushing off Andy.

His hand throbbed. He didn't want any of this to be true. He didn't want to believe that Charlotte was fighting for her life at that moment, and he didn't want to believe that he could have participated in the conviction of an innocent client. He was seized with the overwhelming urge to do something immediately. But what?

His cell phone began to ring, and a wave of anxiety washed over him. *Erin with news. I just hope it's good.* But Russell Blake's name was on the caller ID.

"How's Charlotte?" he asked.

"The news isn't good."

"I realize this isn't a good time to talk about work, but I saw that Andy was convicted yesterday, and I wondered why that evidence of the yacht's second trip that night didn't swing the jury your way. It supported Andy's story that he went back to the party and didn't return to the boat. And it raised the possibility someone else killed Nate McClellan."

"What evidence of a second trip?"

"The evidence I recovered from *The Escape*'s navigation log. I couldn't recover the surveillance tapes that Andy's mother erased. But he asked me to look at the navigation log again, and I found a second trip that hadn't been erased. I called Charlotte on Sunday night and told her about it, and I emailed her a copy of the animation that I created from the log."

"She never mentioned it."

"I thought for sure you two would use it."

"Charlotte never said a word to me about it. What did it show?"

"Well, if you remember, the previous log showed the yacht back at the Coronado Yacht Club at twelve thirty-two p.m. This additional log shows *The Escape* leaving the dock again at one fifty-five a.m. It traveled north once more toward the bridge, then it went on around the island and into the Pacific toward those small uninhabited islands offshore from Coronado. It paused close to one of them and then turned back. As it passed close to the bridge on the return journey, there's a pause. I think that's where the collision with something, probably a buoy, took place. The yacht seems to go forward and then back up and then go forward again. It was back at the Cays at three thirty."

"God, Russell. You're right. That second log was really important evidence. Andy kept saying there was a second trip, and we kept calling him a liar."

"Well, he wasn't lying about that."

Sean felt as if he'd just been punched in the stomach. Andy hadn't been the dumb, irresponsible kid they'd made him out to be. And Charlotte for some reason had suppressed exculpatory evidence. *No, that's impossible. She would never do that.*

"So I'm thinking you never saw the animation of the second trip that I sent her on Monday morning?"

"That's right."

"She said she was going to talk to you and Andy about it."

"Not a word."

"I'm sending you a copy now. Call me back if you have any questions."

Sean turned on his computer and opened the animation. He saw the path of *The Escape* as it went out to the tiny, uninhabited islands across from Coronado and then back to the Cays. Russell had enhanced the spot on the return trip where the yacht appeared to collide with something very close to the bridge. The killer had taken the body out to the deserted islands to dispose of it. That would explain why it washed up on the beach near the hotel.

His stomach was churning. Why hadn't Charlotte told him about this? The defense case had started on Monday, right after Tina Hernandez testified. They could have called Russell as a witness. She'd made a lot of mistakes during trial. She'd been honest about them. But Sean couldn't believe she would have forgotten to tell him about new evidence that supported their client's story.

Was this the only thing she hadn't told him about? Something was wrong. He thought back to the dinner at the Italian Kitchen. They'd grown close that night. And then she had resumed her distance. Why? The medications had worn off. It was time to go looking for the answers in the house she'd loved and refused to leave. For now, he would take no news from the hospital as good news.

* * *

It was easy to get in. She had given him a key. But he wasn't prepared for the emotional impact of going into her house knowing it was just as she'd left it a little over twenty-four hours ago. He stood paralyzed in the front hall for what felt like an hour but in reality could only have been a few minutes. He walked into the sunroom, her favorite room, but saw nothing to explain why she hadn't told him about Russell Blake's new evidence.

Upstairs, he took a quick look around her bedroom, but nothing gave away any secrets. He walked down the hall to her office, sat down at her desk, and powered up the laptop that was sitting there. She didn't use a password, so he could open both the computer and her email.

At first, he didn't see an email from Russell, but he went to the Trash folder and found it, unopened. Sean sat back in Charlotte's chair and closed his eyes, overwhelmed by grief, anger, sympathy, and outrage. An attorney owes the utmost duty of loyalty to his or her client. Andy was their client. To violate that duty was unthinkable. Yet, she'd suppressed evidence that would have helped Andy's defense. Surely her hatred for Lucas and his ridiculous roses wasn't strong enough to make her commit malpractice.

He opened his eyes and looked at Russell's email again. He reminded himself that there are two sides to every story. Even the worst ones. And now that he thought about it, Sean didn't see the second navigation log as evidence that Andy was innocent. Charlotte had been right to say nothing about it. Andy had lied to them from the get-go about who'd been operating the boat that night, but the DNA and fingerprint evidence had showed that he, and only he, had touched the controls.

Sean didn't want to believe that this navigation log had any value. The facts weren't complicated, he told himself. He didn't have to strain to make up cartel theories.

Nate had confided his involvement with Tina to Andy on that first joyride. Even if Erin's blurry tape showed Andy giving Nate a friendly wave as he left to open the house for the others, in truth, he'd been burning with anger and disappointment. He'd hung out inside while he fueled his courage with alcohol. Then he'd retrieved his father's gun and disposed of Nate. Axel would have used this log of the second trip to invite the jury to reach the inescapable conclusion that Andy had known about the second trip because he'd taken it. With Nate. The result would have been just the same: conviction.

Love and sympathy for Charlotte surged through him. He studied a picture of her with Matt on her desk. They were dressed in jeans and T-shirts and had their arms around each other and were very obviously in love. She'd been lucky to have a marriage like that. Would she ever consider trying again? And with him? The thought just popped into his head and surprised him. But, of course, this wasn't the time to think about that.

He was relieved that Russell's new evidence didn't matter. But even as he reassured himself, his eyes fell on a slip of paper lying next to the photograph. His stomach began to churn again as the print came into focus, a receipt from Walmart for a burner phone with the phone number for the District Attorney's tip line in Charlotte's handwriting across the bottom.

No. It's not possible. She wasn't the reason Axel found the gun.

He told himself to stop snooping. When she recovered, he'd be embarrassed to explain why he'd violated her privacy. But he couldn't stop himself. He had to find an explanation. And the history on her laptop told the story. First, she'd searched for burner phones. Then she'd searched for the tipline.

Ineffective assistance of counsel. No, worse than that. Outright betrayal. To get back at Lucas? Or had she harbored some sort of grudge against Ella? But that didn't make any sense. She was one of the best defense attorneys in the business. She wouldn't have let her personal feelings push her into betraying a client. Yet, it was all right there in front of him. Suppressed evidence. And then revealing the location of the gun.

I can't let anyone know about this. I don't know why she did it, but we both knew that Andy was guilty. I'll wipe this computer and destroy this receipt. Someday she'll explain it all to me.

He looked at his watch and saw that it was two thirty. He felt aimless and sad. He didn't want to go home to his empty condo, but now, even more than before, he didn't belong at the hospital. Still no word, so he'd still take that as good news.

But then his phone began to ring.

"Sean, it's Erin. We've lost her."

CHAPTER FORTY-NINE

Thursday, November 22, 2018, Crown Manor, Coronado

Erin persuaded him to join her and Charlotte's children and her
mother at Hugh's that night. No one ate very much, but
everyone, except Mrs. Patrick, drank a good deal. By midnight,
they had all gone to bed, except for Sean who, although he had
accepted the invitation to sleep there for the night, had decided
to go back to his own place. His hand throbbed, and he was too
miserable and restless to sleep, and the burden of keeping the
secret of what Charlotte had done weighed on him.

He was trying to be as quiet as possible as he crept past the
second-floor bedrooms and down the long hall to the stairs. He
had just reached the top of the stairs when a door opened.

"Are you leaving?"

He turned to find Erin standing in the door of her bedroom.
She was wearing gray sweatpants and a black hoodie. She'd
pinned her hair up in a loose bun.

"I—I, yes. I can't sleep. I just thought I'd go home."

"You don't have anyone to talk to at home."

"True."

"And you need someone to talk to."

He started to say no, but he realized she was right.

"Are you hungry?" she asked. "We could go down to the kitchen and make omelets."

Sean shook his head. "No food."

"Okay. Alcohol. My father keeps the premium scotch in his study. Come on."

The lure of companionship was too great. He followed her to the first floor and to Hugh's study at the back of the house. One wall was lined with photographs of Hugh and the various politicians and celebrities he'd rubbed shoulders with over his long career. One wall had photographs of the clients his Innocence Project had freed from prison. There weren't as many photographs on that wall. Yet.

Erin poured him a generous drink and motioned for him to take a seat next to her on the small sofa in front of the window.

Sean took a sip of scotch.

"How's your hand?" Erin asked.

"That's not what really hurts."

"I know."

"Losing her hurts so much that I don't even have any words to talk about it."

"I know."

"I feel so guilty. I didn't do enough to protect her."

"You can't blame yourself."

"Yes, I can." He drank some more scotch. "I didn't even get to say goodbye."

Erin put her hand over his briefly in a silent gesture of sympathy. Then she asked, "Is it too soon to talk to you about Andy?"

"Probably. I know you think he's innocent, but he's not." *I need for him to be guilty so that I can justify what Charlotte did.*

Erin frowned slightly. "I think you should listen to what I have to say before you make up your mind."

"I'm listening." Sean took a long pull of scotch.

"Russell Blake found another navigation log. The boat made a second trip that night. He sent me an email this morning. He said Charlotte knew about it, but apparently she never told you or Andy."

Sean studied her beautiful, concerned face in silence for a few seconds. He wished Russell hadn't involved her. But it was too late.

"She didn't tell us," he agreed. "But I reviewed it this morning after he called, and it would have helped Axel and hurt us."

"Why? Andy said there were two trips. And there were."

"But we don't have any proof that he didn't make the second trip. Axel would have argued that Nate told him about Tina on the first trip, and then Andy went back to the house and drank some more to get up his courage to go back to the boat and eliminate his competition. Charlotte didn't bring up the second trip because it wouldn't have helped us."

"I don't agree," Erin said quietly.

She's the boss' daughter. I shouldn't upset her. But I'm probably on my way out at the firm, anyway.

"Tell me why," he said, praying she wasn't going to change his mind about Andy's guilt.

"Dad and I were the ones at the villa during the police search."

"I remember that."

"Kyle said Andy was with one of the strippers that night after they all came back. He was very drunk, and he fell asleep with his head in her lap."

"Are you sure?"

"Yes. They only knew her stripper name, Crystal Diamond. I'd forgotten about that until Russell called. At first, I thought the same thing you did. The new navigation log wouldn't have helped. But it would have."

"Charlotte and I never considered the possibility of an alibi because we only had evidence of the one trip."

"And because you always assumed Andy was guilty."

"But in our defense, Erin, the murder weapon was found in the villa's broom closet. What are the odds that someone other than Andy took the gun out of his father's desk and then hid it in that closet? A detective called me this morning and said they thought the Menendez Cartel might be responsible for the attack on Charlotte. No proof, yet. But there's some possibility that's true. And there's evidence the cartel has something to do with Matt's death. But Andy's story that a cartel hitman killed Nate just doesn't make sense. A professional wouldn't have brought the murder weapon back to the villa after he did the job."

"He would have if Andy's theory that his parents were involved is true. But there were also a number of people in the house that night besides Andy who knew about Lucas' gun."

"With a motive to kill Nate?"

"Possibly. We don't know."

"But I think we do. Kyle and Gavin had no motive. The

people from the strip club had just met him. That leaves Andy, and only Andy."

"I'm going to see if I can find Crystal Diamond," Erin said.

"I'll do it."

"You will?"

"Sure."

"I'll go with you."

"She works at a strip club, Erin. It'll be uncomfortable for you."

"Okay. But you'll tell me what she says?"

"If I find her, of course."

"You should go back upstairs and get some sleep. Now you've had too much to drink to drive home."

* * *

Sean went back to his room, but he couldn't sleep. His mind was racing. He hadn't the least intention of finding someone who might alibi Andy. To justify Charlotte, Andy had to remain guilty.

But deep down, he knew that it wasn't impossible for a cartel hitman to be the killer. Lucas and Ella or both of them could have provided a key to Lucas' desk and a key to the house. And he could have gone in and out unnoticed because the house had been full of strangers.

Sean had been able to explain why Charlotte had blown off Russell's new evidence. But had there been any other evidence that she'd deliberately ignored? He had to reassure himself there wasn't. Although he was still buzzed from the scotch, he picked up her laptop and opened it. He decided to search her email again.

He'd already found the email from Russell on Monday that she'd deleted unread. He turned to Tuesday, the day she'd delivered the closing argument for the defense. And he found a series of unread emails from someone named Nicole Mann that had begun over the previous weekend. The last one had arrived in Charlotte's inbox on Tuesday morning at one a.m. and had been deleted after being read. It said,

"Dear Mrs. Estes,
I was with Andy Owens all night after he opened the house for us at one a.m. I'm a stripper at The Naked Lady. He couldn't have killed his friend, because he was with me and because I saw Nate at the party at the villa. I've been trying to contact you since Andy's trial began. I came to your house last night after I got off from work, but you wouldn't answer the door.

Nicole Mann"

Sean switched over to the surveillance camera app at Caminito Azur and found the recording for Monday night. A blonde in a dark trench coat was banging on the front door just after midnight. Eventually, she gave up and drove away in a black Honda. Still, he told himself, Charlotte could be forgiven for not answering. She had known that cartel assassins were women, and they were more likely to come in the night.

CHAPTER FIFTY

Friday, November 23, 2018, The Naked Lady, Imperial Beach

Sean had promised himself he wouldn't do this. He hadn't protected Charlotte in life, and he wanted to protect her now. But his conscience wouldn't be quiet. And the sadness in Erin's eyes haunted him. She was a good lawyer and dedicated to the Innocence Project. And she didn't deserve to be lied to. His only option was to find Crystal Diamond and prove that she hadn't been with Andy all night, and she hadn't seen Nate at the party at the villa.

The Naked Lady was an ugly white concrete square in the midst of a parking lot, jammed with expensive cars and clunkers because it was Friday night in Imperial Beach. The marquee consisted of the nude figure of a woman and some martini glasses, all in garish purple. The massive front door had been painted the same shade of purple. But the paint hadn't held, and the chipped and peeling spots revealed the original black metal underneath.

Sean went inside, paid the cover, took a seat at the bar, and ordered a scotch. All the tables were full. He'd worn jeans, a long-sleeved T-shirt, and a heavy navy hoodie, hoping he'd blend in with the crowd. But right away he felt as if someone was sizing him up. He recognized Juan Carlos Aguilar from the preliminary hearing. Thin, forty-something with his dark hair pulled into a ponytail. He was wearing a shiny red tuxedo and a bright-pink shirt with elaborate ruffles on the cuffs. He was standing next to the stage to keep anyone in the audience from attempting to join the performers.

Aguilar gestured to a nearby waiter to take up guard duty and walked over to Sean.

"You seem familiar," he said.

"Sean Donovan. I'm one of the lawyers for Andy Owens."

"Ah, yes. That's where I've seen you before."

"I'm here because I need to talk to one of your employees, Nicole Mann."

"Crystal?"

"I think that's her professional name."

"But isn't the trial over? Wasn't your client convicted? And your colleague killed?"

"Yes, but Miss Mann tried to contact Mrs. Estes before her death. It's important that I find out what she had to say."

"I'll ask if she'll talk to you. You can wait in my office."

Aguilar walked Andy to a small room, just off the lobby of the club.

"Sit there." He pointed to his own desk. "I'll be back in a few minutes."

Sean nursed his scotch and wished for an open window. The room was small and crowded with a large desk and several chairs. The walls were papered with posters of past performers. The air was heavy and stale with old cigarette smoke.

The door to the lobby opened, and Aguilar appeared with a thirty-something blonde in a leopard print robe. Fake silk. Too much makeup. The whole place reeked of fakery.

"Nicole has agreed to give you a few minutes," Aguilar announced. The blonde came in and sat down in the chair in front of the desk. She crossed her legs suggestively and lit a cigarette without asking if Sean minded. The robe hid her figure, but she had a round, plump face with generous, pouty lips that her bright-red lipstick accentuated and wide blue eyes highlighted by long, false lashes. She was probably pretty under all the paint.

"I hear you want to talk to me."

"Nicole Mann?"

"Crystal, here." She took a drag on the cigarette.

"I'm Sean Donovan. One of Andy Owens' attorneys."

"I know who you are." Her tone was insolent and resentful. "Would you have listened if I had tried to get in touch with you? The other one blew me off. The one that got killed in front of the courthouse."

Sean suppressed the urge to reach across the desk and slap her. "You went to her house at midnight on Monday night."

"Right. After I got off from work. But she wouldn't speak to me."

"She had reasons to fear for her safety."

"Not from me." Crystal inhaled deeply again and then let out another long puff of smoke.

"Why did you wait until last week to try to talk to anyone?" Sean asked.

"I didn't wait. Right after it happened, an attorney named Erin Mahoney left her card at my house. But when I called her, a secretary said that the case had been transferred to another attorney, Estes or something like that."

"Charlotte Estes."

"Right. So I called that attorney a couple of times in the beginning, but she never returned my calls. So I figured I was just a stripper, and she didn't think what I had to say was important. Then on Monday, I saw in the paper that the trial was going against Andy. I knew that he never went back to the yacht after he opened the door for us at the villa. So I called Charlotte Estes again and emailed her. But she still never got back to me. So that's why I went to her house. I knocked and knocked and knocked. But I guess she'd gone to bed."

"Like I said, she had reasons not to open her door to strangers after dark. Tell me this, your email said that you saw Nate McClellan in the villa after Andy came back from the yacht. Is that true?"

"Yes."

The single word sent an electric shock through Sean. Now he couldn't justify Charlotte's ignoring Russell's new evidence.

"Tell me about what you saw."

"Andy let us in the house, and we all sat in the living room drinking. Andy was pounding down the beers pretty hard. He passed out in my lap. At some point, I saw Nate walk through the living room and open the front door. He went out and never came back. I assume he left with whoever came to the door for him."

"What time was that?"

"Close to two, I'm guessing. We'd all been at the house for about an hour."

"But you never saw the person that Nate left with?"

"No."

And Ella erased the surveillance tapes that would have showed us who came looking for Nate that night.

The heaviness that had settled over Sean since he'd realized what Charlotte had done deepened. She'd known Andy wasn't guilty.

"Was Andy still in the living room with you when Nate left the house through the front door?"

"Yes. But he was dead to the world. I got him on his feet right after that and put him to bed. He wanted me to stay, so I did. Nothing happened, of course. He was too drunk."

"So drunk that he doesn't remember being with you?"

"Exactly." She exhaled the last puff of smoke and stubbed out her cigarette.

"When did you leave the villa?"

"At five the next morning. Everyone was still asleep. But there's something else I saw that night."

"What?"

"I saw the killer with the gun."

"Are you sure?"

"Absolutely."

"What did you see?"

"I saw a tall man, wearing a baseball cap, holding a small black gun and rummaging in the closet by the fridge. He was wearing gloves."

So that's why Andy's prints were all over the gun.

"Did he see you?"

"No. I went out into the hall to use the bathroom, and I

realized someone was in the kitchen. I looked that way. I was still pretty buzzed myself, and the full force of what I'd seen didn't hit me until all the news came out the next day. I just went back to Andy's room and went to sleep."

"What time was this?"

"Somewhere between three thirty and four. I never really got back to sleep after that, and I left an hour later."

The magnitude of Charlotte's misconduct settled over him like a lead weight. Andy wasn't guilty, and he couldn't go on pretending that what Charlotte had done didn't matter.

"Thanks for talking to me," he said. "My colleague had her reasons for failing to contact you. All I can say is they weren't good ones."

"The thing is, I feel bad for Andy. Even that night, I could tell he was a lost soul. He was still hurting over his breakup with his girlfriend. Apparently, he really loved her."

"Did he tell you that he knew Nate was involved with her?"

"No. He never said anything like that. He said that they'd been broken up for months, and she wasn't coming back. And he accepted that. But he felt as if his life was over because she was the only person who had ever loved him. And he missed being part of her family. He said he didn't have much of a family."

"He doesn't."

"I'd still help him if I could. Is it too late?"

"I'm not sure."

CHAPTER FIFTY-ONE

Saturday, November 24, 2018, The Metropolitan, 165 Sixth Avenue, San Diego

Sean's phone began ringing at eight the next morning.

"Did I wake you?" Erin asked.

"Yes."

"Sorry."

"It's okay."

"Did you talk to her? What did she say?"

Sean sat up in bed and rubbed his eyes. How to avoid telling her the whole truth? Maybe he couldn't. Maybe it was time to confide in someone.

"Quite a bit, actually. But there's more. If you want to come over for breakfast, I'll order room service from the Omni."

"No. Come here. I'll cook something."

"Are you still at your father's place?"

"No, back home at 910 Flora. Not far from Dad. White cottage, green shutters, picket fence. You can't miss it."

* * *

He sat at the table in her small kitchen and watched her scramble eggs while he drank the coffee that she'd poured for him. She was wearing jeans and a light green sweater that accented her brown eyes. She'd pulled her hair back into a ponytail. She wasn't wearing makeup, and she looked tired, but still beautiful.

She divided the eggs between her plate and his and sat down across from him.

"What did Nicole Mann have to say?"

"Andy was with her when Nate was killed."

He'd expected a whoop of joy at the news, but she looked thoughtful as she ate a bite of toast and drank some coffee.

"Good news, but bad news," she said. "She's a stripper; she'd be interested in helping Andy for financial gain, and Judge Carter is not going to be overwhelmed by her credibility even though she's telling the truth."

"Wow, I'm impressed," Sean said.

"Why?" She smiled.

"Well, I'd heard you were a good lawyer, but I wasn't expecting you to see the problems with Nicole."

She shrugged and took a bite of her eggs. "I've been part of the Innocence Project long enough to know how hard it is to undo a conviction. You aren't eating."

"It's not your cooking, Erin. I'll be honest. I'm having a really hard time. There's a lot more to this story that I was hoping not to have to tell you."

"And that would be?"

"Charlotte was the one who tipped off Axel about the location of the murder weapon."

Erin put her fork down and stared at him. "No, that's not possible."

"That's what I thought, too. But it's true." As unemotionally as he could, he explained what he'd found at Charlotte's house on Thursday.

"But why would she use Andy to punish Lucas?"

"That's the part of the puzzle that I haven't discovered yet. Lucas kept trying to revive their old relationship, but that wouldn't have been enough for an attorney like Charlotte to go against her client like this. In her defense, we both were convinced that he was guilty."

Erin nodded slowly. "I know."

"But now we know he's innocent, and his story about the cartel hitman wasn't crazy after all."

"You said that Nicole saw the man at the villa that night."

"In the kitchen. He was fumbling in the broom closet. The trouble is, we don't have a way to prove that Ella and Lucas are mixed up with the Menendez Cartel."

"There's Andy's godfather. Bert Campbell. He's Ella's Chief Financial Officer. He was the one who told Andy they were running a Ponzi scheme."

"But who told Andy that his parents were mixed up with the cartel?"

"That was a down-and-out former private investigator who Ella had contacted about some sort of side job. His name is Mateo Reinaldo."

"We'll have to find him, then. He can't testify Lucas is mixed up with the cartel, but he can tie Ella to it. But I don't like having to do this, Erin. We're going to have to accuse Charlotte of ineffective assistance of counsel in order to put on new evidence."

DEBORAH HAWKINS

"We can show there were extenuating circumstances. She had been the target of multiple attempts on her life since her husband died. And we don't have to say she tipped off the D.A. about the murder weapon. It will be enough if we persuade Judge Carter to consider that second navigation log and let Bert Campbell and that former PI give him a solid reason to believe Nicole Mann saw a cartel hitman in the villa that night."

"I hope you're right," Sean said.

"I hope so, too."

"What have Hayden and Ian decided about Charlotte's memorial service?"

Erin sighed. "It's going to be in D.C. They're heading back on Monday and taking their grandmother with them."

"Nothing here?"

"They're bitter, Sean. They blame all of us for what happened."

"Well, I'm to blame for sure."

"No, you're not." She put her hand over his.

"But I knew she was in danger, Erin. I didn't do enough to protect her."

"You did what you could. She took risks, and none of us could have foreseen an attack in broad daylight in a public place."

"Maybe. I don't know. I just know I'm miserable and guilty, and I can't sleep."

"Let's focus on getting Andy out. That might help."

CHAPTER FIFTY-TWO

Monday, November 26, 2018, Offices of Goldstein, Miller, Emerald Shapery Center

Only Hugh was allowed to go to the airport that morning. Hayden and Ian and their grandmother's flight departed at ten a.m. At five minutes to ten, Sean went down to Charlotte's office, hoping for a personal memorial of his own in a place where he felt close to her. But the door was locked, and a notice from the San Diego Police Department said that no one was to enter without police permission.

Sean went back to his own office and stared aimlessly out his window. He saw an airplane gaining altitude over the sparkling blue water of San Diego Bay, and he wondered if that was Charlotte's flight. His eyes blurred as he realized that she was on her way home to Matt.

His phone rang, and his secretary said, "Detective Rodriguez is calling for you."

"Tell him I'm busy. I'll call him back this afternoon."

But a few seconds later, his personal cell phone rang.

"Sean, it's Axel."

"This isn't a good time," he said. Anything to ward off more bad news.

"Detective Merrill is here from D.C. He assisted us in going through some of the evidence at Charlotte's house. We've found something that isn't exactly *Brady* evidence, but it's something I think I have a duty to make you aware of as Andy Owens' defense attorney."

"I don't understand."

"We've found evidence that Charlotte had a conflict of interest during Andy's trial. Of course, I'll argue that her conflict didn't affect the outcome. But I think it's my duty to show you what we've found."

"Okay. Thanks for being up front, Axel."

"So could you come on over to my office now and view this with Detective Merrill and Detective Rodriguez? They want to know if you knew anything about it."

"What am I coming to view?"

"The security tapes from Charlotte's house from the night of October 19."

Oh, God. The night of our dinner at the Italian Kitchen. The night everything changed.

"Erin Mahoney is working with me now on Andy's case."

"Then bring her, too."

* * *

Erin postponed her meeting with Bert Campbell to accompany him to the District Attorney's Office. Axel and the two detectives were waiting for them in a conference room with a large screen on one wall. Sean was surprised to see Martin Harmon, who had been one of Sean's colleagues in the U.S.

Attorney's Office, whose specialty was Organized Crime.

"It's been a long time," Sean said as he shook Martin's hand. "This is my co-counsel, Erin Mahoney. I didn't realize your office was going to be involved, too."

"I know just as much about this as you do right now," Martin said. "Axel told me he thought he had information my office would be interested in."

Martin, Erin, and Sean took seats at the conference table across from Axel and the detectives.

"The best way to do this is to just start the video and view it until the end," Axel said.

"It's rather long. It begins with Charlotte coming home after midnight."

"We'd been to dinner that night. I had just dropped her off," Sean said.

"Okay. Well, that gives us a little context about where she was coming from. Let's get started."

The tape showed her entering the front hall and walking toward the sunroom where a light was on. A blond woman suddenly appeared from the sunroom. She was pointing a small semi-automatic weapon at Charlotte, who still had her house keys in her hand.

"Don't move!"

Charlotte stopped and demanded. "What are you doing in my house?"

"I've come to talk to you. There are things you don't know about your husband's death."

Sean watched as Charlotte tried to reach inside her handbag for her cell phone. As she pulled it out, the gun went off.

Charlotte threw herself on the floor as the phone slipped out of her hand. The blonde kicked the phone across the kitchen and fired a shot that destroyed it.

"Now get up and do as I say. I won't hurt you, I promise, if you'll listen to me. I didn't kill your husband."

Rosemary Spencer. British accent. And that was the weekend he hadn't been able to reach her by phone. And on Monday morning, she'd been late because she'd gone to get a new one.

Sean watched Charlotte get to her feet slowly. At gunpoint, she walked ahead of Spencer toward the sunroom. The video from the sunroom was spliced in at this point. Sean noticed that a laptop lay open on the sofa.

"You can take your coat off if you don't try anything. Then sit down."

Charlotte slipped out of her coat and sat down on the sofa next to the little computer. The blonde kept the gun pointing at her.

"Pick up the laptop. There's a surveillance tape from the Four Seasons queued up that I want you to see."

Charlotte obeyed. Her eyes teared up as she watched the tape. "I don't want to see this," she said.

"I don't care." The blonde waved the gun menacingly in Charlotte's direction.

A different camera had captured the tape as it played on Rosemary Spencer's laptop. The first frame showed Spencer walking toward Matt Estes, who was sitting at the bar, waiting for her. She hugged him and took the seat next to his. He turned to the bartender and ordered a drink for her.

A few frames later, a man in a dark suit, who seemed familiar to Sean, approached Matt and Rosemary. As the three of them exchanged greetings, Sean realized the man was Lucas Owens.

Charlotte said, "I—I don't understand. I had no idea that Lucas knew my husband."

"He didn't. This was their first meeting. Keep watching."

Lucas sat down at the bar on Matt's right. Rosemary was on his left. The three of them chatted and sipped drinks. After a few minutes, a waiter summoned them, and they rose and walked toward their table in the dining room. Almost as soon as Lucas sat down, he received a phone call, and he left before they placed any food orders.

"Okay, I've watched this," Charlotte said when it ended. "I don't see how this tape proves you didn't kill my husband."

"There's more. You haven't seen that part yet. Open the file again and push play. There's a clip from the camera at the bar."

"I will. But if you honestly are not responsible for Matt's death, will you put that gun down?"

Rosemary Spencer hesitated and then put the gun on the coffee table. She sat down next to Charlotte and opened the next video clip.

"Here, this one's from the camera at the bar."

The camera had caught Lucas' hand slipping something into Matt's drink.

"No!" Charlotte said.

"Yes. Shall I play it again?"

Charlotte looked almost too angry to speak. "This is obscene. Where did it come from? It can't be authentic."

"But it is. I told you. It's from the hotel's security cameras."

Charlotte began to cry uncontrollably.

"I know, I know," Rosemary Spencer said. "I loved him, too. I was devastated. I'm sorry that I had to break in here with a gun to get you to listen to me. But I didn't kill Matt. And I'm tired of being on the run." The desperation and grief in Rosemary Spencer's voice seemed genuine.

Charlotte wiped her eyes and regained control of herself. "I'll put on a pot of coffee, and you can tell me everything. If my neighbors have called the police, I'll find a way to put them off. I want to hear your story."

You're taking a risk she isn't going to pick up that gun again.

Charlotte got up and walk toward the kitchen. Suddenly the doorbell rang, and Rosemary Spencer reached for the gun.

"Put it back," Charlotte said from the kitchen doorway. "I'm guessing one of my neighbors heard the gunshots and called the police. Stay here, and I'll take care of it."

The tape switched back to the camera that covered the front hall. Sean watched Charlotte walk toward the front door and open it. Two uniformed officers were standing on the porch.

"Mrs. Estes?" The taller one seemed to be in charge.

"Yes."

"We received a call for service from one of your neighbors. He thought he heard shots fired. We have a request from Detective Merrill in D.C. to give your residence priority because of the attempts on your life."

"Yes, of course. Thank you." Charlotte smiled. "I'm fine. Nothing's wrong. I just returned from late dinner with a colleague. I have no idea what the neighbors heard. Probably fireworks. People in this neighborhood have a lot of parties."

"That's true," the tall officer agreed. "We're glad to hear that you're okay. If you need anything, call nine-one-one."

"I certainly will."

But her cell phone has just been destroyed.

She closed the front door and activated the security locks. She walked back to the sunroom and paused at the door.

"The officers are gone," she said to Rosemary Spencer. "I'll be back in a minute with coffee."

Sean was glad to see that the gun was still on the table. A few minutes later, Charlotte came back with two mugs of coffee and put one down next to the gun.

"Would you like something to eat, too?" Charlotte asked.

"No. I can't eat. My nerves are shot from being on the run. Food makes it worse. Please sit down and let me tell the rest quickly. I need to tell you all of it and get out of here before the cartel figures out where I am."

Charlotte sat down in the chair opposite the sofa and said, "So you were the one following me? I heard footsteps when I left the restaurant that night after I had dinner with Lucas."

"Yes. I've been trying to find a way to tell you my story. That's why I came to San Diego. To see you."

"Why don't you begin at the beginning?"

"Well, the very beginning is when I was hired by James and Mitchell in 2016. I was desperate for a job. I told them I had experience as a lobbyist. I didn't. They assigned me to a tech startup called Light Source Ventures. The company made security software that they were hoping the U.S. government would buy. I didn't know the rules. I offered a couple of congressmen free vacations at the company's expense in return for their efforts to promote purchase of our products. But my offer was illegal, so I was in trouble and so was James and Mitchell because of me."

She paused to sip her coffee. The lines around her tired blue eyes were deeply etched. She didn't look as if she'd slept for a long time.

"Anyway, you know the story of how I got to Matt. I was terrified of being indicted and sent to prison. A guy in the financial department at Light Source who I'd gone out with quite a bit came to me when he heard that I was in trouble and gave me the lowdown. He said that he was leaving because of what he knew, and maybe the information would help me stay out of prison."

"What did he tell you?"

"Light Source appeared to be a legitimate software developer, but its primary purpose was money laundering for the Menendez Drug Cartel. Apparently there had been an earlier version of the company called Intech. But Intech had to dissolve after it got sued. So it started over as Light Source."

Damn! I remember seeing those sleazy clients on the website Charlotte showed me. They've been crooks all along.

"So I gather you told Matt about Light Source, formerly Intech?"

"Right. And he went to the U.S. Attorney with the information. And that was Eric Franson."

"How did you know that I was going to meet with him?"

"The cartel wanted to keep tabs on him, so they bribed one of his paralegals for any information that might be related to Matt's death and Franson's work on my case. She saw that you had an appointment, so the cartel sent me to Chicago."

"Who killed him?"

"Oh, God!" Rosemary Spencer put her mug on the coffee table and ran her fingers through her long blond hair nervously. "I didn't kill him, but I can't expect you to believe me. You saw me in the hotel."

"There was a man with you."

"His name is Roberto Martinez. He's a lawyer for the cartel. I was instructed to meet Eric Franson at the hotel and to introduce him to Roberto. I was told Roberto needed to hire local counsel in Chicago for some of their legitimate businesses. I left them together at breakfast to talk it over."

"When did you start working for the cartel?"

You shouldn't have trusted her, Charlotte. You shouldn't have lied to the police.

"I never started working for them voluntarily."

"How did that happen, then?"

"One night after Matt had opened negotiations for me with Franson to tell him everything I knew about Light Source, a man approached me at the bar in Georgetown. We drank a lot and danced. I took him home with me. I was lonely and scared, and his interest seemed like a godsend.

"But he worked for the cartel. He said he'd killed my ex-boyfriend, the accountant who'd left Light Source. And now the cartel had sent him to stop me from going through with the proffer session. He said he wouldn't kill me if I kept quiet and drugged Matt and took compromising pictures of him in bed with me, so they could blackmail him to keep quiet about what I'd told him. I didn't want to do it, but I didn't have a choice."

"But where does Lucas fit in all this?"

"The cartel didn't trust me to administer the drug because they knew I cared about Matt."

"So they sent Lucas?"

"Yes."

"And I suppose you're going to tell me that you weren't the one who poisoned that barrister in London after Matt died?"

Sean watched Rosemary Spencer take a deep breath and stare at the dark yard for a moment as if summoning her courage to go on. Then she looked back at Charlotte and said, "After Matt died, I realized I was in too deep. If I didn't follow their orders, I'd be killed. The guy who sends me instructions has been trying to get in touch with me about another hit. I think it's meant to be on you. The cartel thinks you've read Matt's file and you know about the information for the proffer session. I'm on the run now. I've been avoiding his calls. I can't go on like this."

"Why don't you go to the police?"

"Because I can't. I've been involved in three deaths. You're a defense attorney. You know they'd never believe me."

"Where did you get this surveillance tape?"

"The cartel was trying to get it from the hotel, so the police wouldn't have access to it. They sent me to bribe the head of security. I told him I needed a copy, and he gave me one. The cartel got the original, and I kept this one."

"Do you know how Lucas came to be involved with the cartel?"

"His wife. Joey Menendez has been close to a friend of hers in New York for years, Sam Wentworth. My ex-boyfriend told me about seeing Menendez and Wentworth at Light Source. Wentworth funneled some of the cartel's money to Ella's" business and to her husband's."

And I ridiculed Andy for telling us this. Oh, God.

"But why was Lucas sent to poison Matt?" Charlotte asked.

"I can only guess that he and his wife are deep enough with the cartel to be trusted to carry out some of its dirty work. The only conversation that I ever had with him was this one you see on this tape. When I found out that you were defending his son, I wanted to tell you about him. But I couldn't find a way until tonight. I've got to go now." Rosemary Spencer began to close up the laptop.

"But where are you going? It's two thirty in the morning."

"To Scotland. I have a friend who has a sheep farm on North Ronaldsay Island at the ends of the earth. I'm going to hide there while I figure out a permanent place out of sight of the cartel. I'm going to the airport now to wait for my flight."

"But that's not safe. I have a guest room. You can stay here for a few more hours."

"No. I need to leave while it's still dark. My car is parked near the gate in your back garden. That's how I got in. No one will see me leave."

Rosemary Spencer picked up the gun and slipped it into a large bag on the floor next to the sofa. She finished folding the laptop and added it to the bag. Then she stood up and put on an oversized dark brown wool coat.

Charlotte stood, too. "I need a copy of this tape."

"Why? You can't take it to the police. Without me, you can't prove it's authentic. You'll have to find another way to get revenge on Lucas."

The receipt for the burner phone on her desk with the number of the tipline on it. And then she insisted on making the closing argument so that if anyone ever found out she'd tipped off Axel, she could say that she tried to undo the damage she'd done. Only she knew that Andy was always a goner, no matter what the defense did once Axel had that gun.

CHAPTER FIFTY-THREE

Thursday, January 31, 2019, San Diego County Courthouse, 330 West Broadway

Andy struggled to keep his face expressionless as he sat at the defense table between Erin and Sean. He'd been wearing prison scrubs since the day of the jury's verdict, and he didn't feel comfortable in the suit that Erin had brought him. The courtroom was full of reporters. He didn't want any of them to see how alone and frightened he felt.

The national and international media had fixed on his case after the arrest of his father for the murder of Charlotte's husband. The D.C. police had located his accomplice in Scotland and had worked out a deal for her to testify against Lucas. He was now in jail in D.C. Afraid of being arrested herself, Andy's mother had fled to Mexico. The U.S. Attorney was now in the process of bringing her back to San Diego to stand trial on multiple federal charges of racketeering and securities fraud.

"Good morning." Judge Carter smiled. Andy could see how much His Honor was enjoying the press attention. "We're here this morning for the sentencing of Andrew Lawrence Owens.

Sentence, as you know, is set by statute at life without parole. The defense has filed a Motion for Reconsideration of The Order Denying a New Trial, and I have read that motion. Would you like to be heard, Mr. Donovan?"

"Yes, Your Honor."

Andy watched Sean pick up his notes and take the podium in front of Judge Carter. A wave of gratitude washed over him. Sean had explained everything that Charlotte had done, and why, and he had apologized for not believing in Andy's innocence.

"Your Honor, two weeks ago my colleague and I put on five witnesses who gave compelling testimony that supports my client's innocence. Mateo Reinaldo, a former private investigator and police informant, testified that Ella Lawrence was money laundering for the Menendez Cartel. Bert Campbell, the Chief Financial Officer of Ella Lawrence's securities firm, explained the Ponzi scheme that she and her husband were running. He explained her motive for silencing Nate McClellan after he uncovered her illegal activities. Our third witness, Nicole Mann, testified that my client was with her at the time that Mr. McClellan was killed, and she saw the killer with the gun in the kitchen of the villa that night. Russell Blake, a forensic computer expert, presented evidence of a second trip that *The Escape* took while my client was with Miss Mann. And finally, we presented the testimony of Detective Paul Merrill of the District of Columbia Metropolitan Police, who explained the factors that led Mrs. Estes to render ineffective assistance of counsel to my client during his trial. For all of these reasons, the defense is asking the court to reconsider its denial of our motion for a new trial based upon ineffective assistance of counsel."

"Thank you, Mr. Donovan." Judge Carter beamed at the defense table as if he were actually reconsidering his decision. He turned to Axel and Kaitlyn Green. "And now I'll hear from you, Mr. Saldana."

"Thank you, Your Honor." Andy watched Axel replace Sean at the podium. The prosecutor paused for a minute to organize his notes and to make eye contact with the judge. Andy braced himself for what was coming.

"Mr. Donovan's rehash of the evidence from the prior hearing is not persuasive," Axel began. "While the People agree that Mrs. Estes' performance fell below professional norms, the court reached the correct conclusion when it found that the deficiencies in her performance did not affect the guilty verdict in this case. The defense's new evidence merely demonstrates that the defendant learned how to commit crimes from his parents. And, like his parents, he thought that his money made him untouchable by the law. Mr. Campbell, as the People brought out on cross-examination, is the defendant's godfather and that makes his credibility suspect. The family empire is now collapsing, and Mr. Campbell is trying to free the heir to take over from his parents. And Miss Mann is a stripper who never went to any of the investigating officers with her alibi claim. The defendant is in a position to reward her financially if the court should misguidedly believe her testimony. The court's previous decision to deny the defendant a new trial should stand."

Axel knew the truth. Sean had said that he did. Axel knew that Bert and Nicole weren't liars. I've told my share of lies, but the prosecutor is the only one lying now.

"Mr. Donovan, the defense is allowed to have the last word."

"Thank you, Your Honor. Briefly, Ms. Mann did come forward to Ms. Mahoney immediately. And she tried diligently to reach the defense, and we've explained why she failed to reach Mrs. Estes. And Mr. Campbell is clearly not trying to resurrect the Lawrence-Owens' illegal empire. Mr. Campbell faces federal exposure himself, and he's agreed to cooperate with the U.S. Attorney in bringing my clients' parents to justice."

"Thank you, Mr. Donovan. I think you and Mr. Saldana have made excellent points, but absent any actual evidence that the person Ms. Mann saw was not your client, I see no reason to overturn the verdict and grant a new trial. And so, for that reason, I am sentencing the defendant to confinement in the state prison for life without the possibility of parole."

Hearing his sentence spoken aloud was so horrible that Andy felt himself catch his breath. He hoped the reporters hadn't noticed.

The doors at the back of the courtroom seemed to stir as if someone were trying to enter. The bailiff looked up sharply because the room was full, and there were no more empty seats. Spectators and reporters had been turned away before the hearing began. And there were extra sheriff's deputies and police officers posted in the hall because of the attack on Charlotte. Andy wondered who could have possibly gotten through that army and reached the doors.

But, indeed, someone seemed to be trying to get in. With his hand on his holstered gun, Judge Carter's bailiff walked toward the sheriff's deputy at the rear of the courtroom. The two uniformed officers conferred briefly.

"Your Honor," the bailiff said, "the victim's father is here, and he wishes to make a victim impact statement. He apologizes for being late."

"That's fine." Judge Carter smiled once more. "He has the right to speak. Escort him in."

Andy watched Brian McClellan follow the bailiff down to the podium. He was in his best navy suit and maroon tie. He looked ready for trial. Andy could see the gold cufflinks that he and Nate had pooled their allowances to give him for Christmas when they were in middle school. And he remembered sadly what Brian had said to him the last time he'd seen him. *Things aren't the same now between us.*

"Good morning, Your Honor. My name is Brian McClellan, and I am Nathan's father. He was the youngest of five children, and his sisters and I and his mother have been devastated by his loss.

"As Your Honor knows, I have spent my life seeking justice for the accused. I pressured Nathan to do the same, and although he didn't want to follow in my footsteps, he did. You heard two weeks ago about how he defended the Hernandez brothers, who couldn't afford an attorney. And you learned that the defense now believes that what Nathan learned while defending the brothers led to his death."

Brian eyes teared up, and his voice became hoarse with emotion. He paused for a minute before he went on.

"The thing is, Your Honor, I've learned in the past few weeks that the defense is wrong. Ella Lawrence and Lucas Owens aren't responsible for Nate's death. And neither is the Menendez Cartel."

Brian paused, and Andy watched him deliberately make eye contact with Judge Carter and hold his gaze. Andy braced himself to hear just how guilty and despicable Brian thought he was. But finally, Brian said, "And neither is the defendant."

Axel was on his feet. "I object, Your Honor. This is not a proper victim impact statement."

But Andy could see that the judge was intrigued. "He has the right to speak, Mr. Saldana. Please continue, Mr. McClellan."

"Your Honor, Nathan believed with all his heart that innocent people should go free. I realize this is unorthodox, but I have the witness who can identify Nathan's killer. She came forward to me in my professional capacity but also because I'm Nathan's father. In memory of my son, I'm asking that the court reopen the defense motion for a new trial and listen to this witness."

"Sit down, Mr. Saldana," Judge Carter said. "I know you object. Fine. You can take your objection to the court of appeal. But I want to hear from Mr. McClellan's witness."

The judge signaled the bailiff to escort a tall, thin brunette into the courtroom. She was wearing a simple, but obviously expensive black dress. She had her hair pulled up into a graceful French twist, and she was wearing a pair of hammered gold earrings, also expensive. She settled into the witness chair and crossed her legs confidently, but Andy could see that she was nervous. He wondered what Jennifer Marie Kelly was going to say.

"Jen, why don't you start by telling us how you knew my son, Nate."

"We went to school together."

"And what about Andy Owens?"

"Same. Andy, Gavin, Kyle, Kinsley, and I were all classmates from first grade through high school."

"And Kinsley is Kinsley Wyatt, correct?"

"Right. Nate's fiancée. Or former fiancée."

"When did you contact me, Jen, with the information that you wanted share about my son's death?"

"On Monday of this week."

"And why did you contact me?"

"I had read about the new evidence in Andy's case, and the new trial motion. And I read that it went against him. And I knew that was wrong."

"Why did you know that?"

"Because I know who killed Nate, and it wasn't Andy."

"Objection!" Axel roared.

"Overruled," Judge Carter said. "This is technically still part of Mr. McClellan's victim impact statement. I'll give you some latitude to use leading questions, if you need them, Mr. McClellan."

"Thank you, Your Honor."

"Jen, let's talk about how you know that Andy didn't kill my son. Were you involved in Nate's planned wedding to Kinsley?"

"Yes. I was her maid of honor."

"And were you romantically involved with anyone in the wedding party?"

"Kyle Jamison. But that relationship has since ended."

"I see. So what were you doing on the night of June 9, 2018?"

"Kinsley and I worked late with a client at our studio in La Jolla. We owned an interior design business together. We knew that the guys had decided to meet for dinner in Coronado, so we decided to have dinner together that night."

"And what time was that?"

"Around eight, I think. Our client stayed for quite a while at our studio. Then we went for Chinese a couple of doors down, and then we went to a bar nearby and had a drink."

"And did you hear from my son during this time?"

"I didn't, but Kinsley did. I heard from Kyle, though. They were all in Coronado eating and hanging out at the Owens' villa."

"Where did you and Kinsley go from there?"

"We went to her parents' house in Mission Hills. Her mother wanted to talk to her about some of the arrangements for the wedding."

"And where did you go after that?"

"Nowhere. By then, Kyle had told me that the guys were partying at a strip club, so Kinsley and I decided to spend the night in her old bedroom at her parents' house. We'd had a fair amount to drink and were tired."

"So what happened next?"

"We went to bed. And then Kinsley got a phone call from Nate."

"What time did she receive the call?"

"It was around one or one-fifteen."

"What happened after Kinsley received the call?"

"She talked to Nate briefly and then hung up. I could see that she was angry with him."

"What happened next?"

"Almost as soon as she hung up, he called me. I could tell

he'd been drinking a lot, and he sounded really upset. He wanted me to persuade Kinsley to come to Coronado and talk to him about the wedding. He said he had doubts."

"Did you agree to do that?"

"Not at first. I told him everyone had doubts about a wedding, and he just needed a good night's sleep. I thought it would all blow over by morning. But he insisted. He said it was urgent. He had decided that he wanted to marry Tina Hernandez, and he was meeting her for breakfast to propose. And he wanted to end everything with Kinsley that night."

"So what did you do?"

"I thought maybe it would be better for the two of them to talk immediately. I was hoping Nate was just drunk and rambling about having feelings for Andy's ex."

"Did you know that my son had been seeing Tina?"

"Not romantically. All of us knew was that he was helping her brothers with their legal case."

"Did Andy know?"

"No. None of us told him that Tina's brothers were in trouble because Andy was still so hurt about the breakup."

"So Andy did not know about any relationship between Nate and Tina?"

"That's right."

"So what happened next?"

"I persuaded Kinsley to get up and get dressed and go talk to Nate. I drove us to Coronado because, of the two of us, I was the most sober."

"What happened when you arrived at the villa?"

"We texted Nate that we were there. And then we rang the

449

doorbell, and he came out. I could see there was quite a party going on inside."

"Did you get a glimpse of Andy at the party?"

"Briefly. When Nate opened the door to come outside, I could see him leaning on the shoulder of a blond woman. He was obviously very, very drunk."

"After Nate came out on the porch, the three of us sat down and talked. He'd had a lot to drink, and she'd had a lot to drink, so I tried to calm them both down and put off any real talk about their relationship until morning when they were sober."

"Did it work?"

"It seemed to. Kinsley started to talk about how happy the wedding was going to make their families. And Nate got sentimental about their past. Kinsley went inside to use the restroom, and Nate promised me that he wouldn't see Tina in the morning until he'd had time to sleep on everything. When Kinsley came back, she asked him if he'd spend the rest of the night with her on the yacht, and he agreed."

"So what did you?"

"I went home. I thought everything had blown over."

"And did you see Nate again after that?"

"No."

"What about Kinsley?"

"Yes."

"When did you see her?"

"Around four thirty the next morning, she woke me up banging on my front door."

"And where do you live?"

"I live in La Jolla Shores."

"About forty-five minutes from the Owens' villa?"

"That's right."

"So what did you do next?"

"I got up and let Kinsley in. She was white and shaking and very upset."

"And what did she say?"

"She said that she'd taken care of Nate for good because he wanted to call off the wedding."

"Did you believe her?"

"Not at first. I was in shock, and I didn't want it to be true. We all loved Nate. None of us wanted to lose him. And Kinsley could be difficult, but she didn't seem capable of what she said she'd done. But she kept talking and talking, and finally I realized it was true."

"What did she tell you?"

"She said that she'd retrieved Lucas' gun when she went into the villa to use the restroom."

"So she knew about the gun?"

"We all did. We'd all shot it off at one time or another at various parties that Lucas had."

"Why did she want the gun?"

"She'd decided to kill Nate if he said anything else about calling off the wedding. After they went to the yacht, she tried to make him promise to go through with it. The wedding was huge for Kinsley. She'd grown up believing that she'd marry Nate, and their families wanted it."

"Would he promise not to call if off?"

"No. They got into another fight, and she said she shot him. She said she panicked at first and thought of calling the police to say it was an accident. But she didn't think they'd believe her. She decided to take the yacht out to the Coronado Islands and used the swim platform to dispose of Nate's body."

"Had she ever driven the yacht before?"

"We all had at one time or another. Lucas especially liked to let the women passengers drive so he could sit next to them. But she obviously wasn't an expert because she had that accident on the way back."

"Did she tell you why she came to your place that morning to confess? Why didn't she keep quiet to you?"

"She came because she knew that Lucas and Ella had lots of surveillance at the villa. We'd be seen on the camera on the porch. She wanted me to say that I'd left with her."

"Did you agree to that?"

"I never agreed to lie for her."

"What did she say about who would be blamed for my son's death?"

"I don't really want to repeat what she said."

"Please tell us, Ms. Kelly," Judge Carter said. "I need to hear all of it in order to make my decision."

"She said that everyone would believe that Andy got drunk and did it, especially because the yacht had been wrecked. She said nothing bad would happen to any of us because Andy's parents would get him off, and he was too dumb to discover the truth."

"And why did you wait until Monday to come forward, Jen?"

Her eyes were teary again. "Because it's all been so awful. I realized later that no one knew I was there that night, so I didn't have to lie for Kinsley. And I did think somehow Lucas and Ella's money would keep Andy out of any serious trouble. But when I realized that he was going to prison for life and when I found out who Lucas and Ella really are, I had to come tell you that Andy is innocent."

"Thank you, Jen," Brian smiled gently at her. "Your Honor, I would like to conclude my victim impact statement by moving for Andy Owens' immediate release from custody."

"Thank you, Mr. McClellan," Judge Carter said. "Before I rule on your request, I have one final question for Ms. Kelly. Could you describe Ms. Wyatt's appearance that night?"

"She's about my height, very thin. Very short hair. We were both wearing jeans and a T-shirt. Only she was wearing a baseball cap."

"Could she have appeared to be male to someone who didn't know her?" the judge asked.

"Absolutely."

EPILOGUE

Tuesday, December 24, 2019, Christmas Eve, Pacific Beach

Andy left Crown Manor at midnight although Hugh's Christmas party was still going strong. Sean had been there. He had just come back from his long leave of absence from Goldstein, Miller. They'd become friends, and Andy was glad to see him looking better.

Erin had invited him to spend the night at the mansion, but he'd declined. He'd been away from home all day, and he was anxious to have some time alone in his cottage in Pacific Beach to reflect on the changes in his life and on the prospect of Christmas morning with the McClellans.

He smiled as he parked the faithful white Camry in his driveway and got out and opened his front door. This tiny, two-bedroom cottage in one of San Diego's sought-after beach communities had been the only extravagance he'd permitted himself amidst the collapse of his father and mother's financial empire. What had been left from their years of crooked dealings had been just enough to allow Andy to endow Tina's clinic-to-be in Chula Vista. The Nathan McClellan Neighborhood Clinic was a few years away because Tina and her husband had to finish medical school. But the money had been placed in a trust and conservatively invested so that it would be ready for them when the time came.

He hadn't allowed himself any alcohol at Hugh's because he'd wanted to drive himself home that night. And he'd had only a couple of glasses of champagne to toast the bride and groom at Tina's wedding that morning. Alcohol had never been his problem. It had always been loneliness and isolation. Now he took a beer out of his refrigerator and changed into a hoodie and sweatpants and went outside to turn on the electric firepit in his small backyard.

It was cold, but he was warm by his fire. The sky was clear and studded with bright stars. The remaining sliver of cold, Christmas moon was just about to set in the western sky. A year ago, it had looked as if he was on his way to prison for life. Now he was freer and happier than he'd ever dreamed he could be.

He smiled as he thought about Tina's wedding that morning. The wedding itself in the chapel of St. Michael's Catholic Church had been very small and intimate. He'd been touched to be one of the handful of guests outside of the family in attendance. But the reception afterward at the nearby Hilton had filled the hotel's largest ballroom because Tina and Paul Lopez, her new husband, had big families and many friends.

Hernandez Moving was prosperous again. As soon as Andy had passed the bar in July and had been sworn in, he'd seen to it that the trucks were returned with monetary damages for the wrongful taking. And he'd torn up the lease contracts and arranged for the certificates of ownership to go straight to Luis in the office.

Now as he sat under the stars, he felt a twinge of envy as he pictured Paul waiting at the altar for Tina that morning. He was a year ahead of her in medical school. He had grown up in Sacramento, and, like Tina, he was from an extended Latino family whose members worked together in a family business, a restaurant. He'd overcome the same kinds of hurdles that Tina had to make it into one of the country's top medical schools. Andy admired and liked him, but it made him sad to admit that Paul had far more in common with Tina than he did.

But he also had to admit that his life had now gone in a direction that probably wouldn't have been compatible with Tina's. She was going to be working long hours in her clinic. He was now working long hours with Brian McClellan. It would have been difficult to create a marriage under those circumstances.

Hugh and Erin had offered him a place at the Innocence Project. Sean had asked him to join the firm's white-collar practice and work with him. Andy had been tempted by both offers, but the firm of Wyatt and McClellan could be no more now that Kinsley was charged with Nate's murder. Brian McClellan had offered to train Andy to take over the reins of his entire practice in a couple of years. The offer to learn the ropes of criminal defense from Nate's father plus the prospect of running his own shop, was too good to pass up.

And then, too, Brian was his family now. Faced with the prospect of Rosemary Spencer's testimony against him for the murder of Matt Estes and Bert Campbell's testimony about his business activities, his father had taken plea deals that stacked state and federal sentences so long that he would never leave prison. And he hadn't deserved any leniency. He'd known who his victim was that night at the Four Seasons. He'd killed Charlotte's husband to clear a path for himself back into her life.

His mother was still fighting her charges, but Andy knew she was merely postponing the day when she, too, would enter prison for the rest of her life. Detective Merrill had found a confidential informant who would testify that the cartel's attempts on Charlotte's life that began when she was still living in D.C., had been ordered by Joey Menendez. But his mother, ever jealous of his father's feelings for Charlotte, was responsible for the final one.

But a new year was about to begin, and it was time to put the sadness of the past behind him. He smiled again as he thought of the reception. Tina and Esmeralda had conspired to keep him dancing with all the single women in the room, including Tina's bridesmaids and medical school classmates and all of the Hernandez and Lopez cousins over the age of eighteen. Andy had been touched by all of the attention.

One day, he told himself. One day it would all feel right with someone. For now, Brian had encouraged him to take on some projects with the Innocence Project in addition to working for their own clients. Andy's heart beat a little faster when he thought about his work with Erin.

But she was Hugh Mahoney's daughter. And although Hugh himself had had his legal problems and had been arrested once, Andy knew that he expected more for his beautiful and talented daughter than a reformed party boy who was the son of two convicted felons. He'd learned many things in the past year, including how to keep his emotions in check, so he wasn't going to let himself hope too much.

He finished his beer, turned off his electric fire, and went inside. He disposed of the can in the kitchen and switched off all the lights in his house except for the one by his bed. He took off his hoodie and put on a T-shirt and got into bed and turned out the light. He smiled as he thought about Christmas tomorrow with Brian and Louise and Nate's four sisters and their children. He'd bought presents for everyone and wrapped them carefully and stacked them in large shopping bags, ready for delivery in the morning. He looked forward to watching everyone open them.

He closed his eyes and savored the day one last time. And then, just as he dropped off to sleep, he thanked the Universe for his happiness, for Tina's happiness, and for the happiness of the years to come.

TO MY READERS

This comes to you on day 146 of COVID quarantine for me. I hope all of you and yours are well and safe. We are fine here. We have become used to being cozy at home now and enjoying small pleasures like good coffee ordered from far away and lots of time in the backyard with the Golden Retrievers.

When I started writing *Vengeance*, I didn't think it would take two years to finish. Something happened after the publication of *Keeping Secrets* that hurt me profoundly, and it was hard to get back to writing for quite a bit of time. I hadn't anticipated the hurt or my reaction to it. I love writing, and I don't want anything else to make me feel that discouraged again. I'm going to write a blog post about what happened after *Keeping Secrets* was published in the not-too-distant future. Stay tuned for the whole story.

I hope you enjoyed *Vengeance*. Please write to me at dhawkins8350@gmail.com and let me know your thoughts about Andy's transformation. He turned out to be a far more sympathetic character than I thought he would be when I first met him in my imagination.

Thanks to everyone who has taken time to leave a review on Amazon and Goodreads. Reviews help new readers find my books, and with more readers I can practice law less and write fiction faster.

I'll look forward to your emails. Tell me how you are doing in quarantine and what else you are reading to pass the time. If you haven't signed up for my newsletter, go to deborahhawkinsfiction.com and sign up. You'll get news of Book 6 of the Warrick, Thompson Files and news about my blog posts.

NOVELS BY DEBORAH HAWKINS

THE WARRICK THOMPSON FILES
Dark Moon, A Legal Thriller
Mirror, Mirror, A Legal Thriller
Keeping Secrets, A Legal Thriller
The Death of Distant Stars, A Legal Thriller
And
Ride Your Heart 'Til It Breaks
Winner Beverly Hills Book Award 2015

Dance for a Dead Princess
Finalist Foreword Reviews, 2013
Honorable Mention, Beverly Hills Book Award 2014

Made in the USA
Columbia, SC
20 December 2020

29228830R00281